"Hawley delights in her humorous and romantic paranormal debut. . . . Hawley ably navigates life and love among toxic family members, fantastical chaos, and small-town politics—with some steamy scenes and plenty of dad jokes along the way. This is a treat." —*Publishers Weekly*

"Hawley's delightful debut is a welcome addition to the witchy rom-com genre, with its ecological flavor, fresh take on the demon realm with a fascinating cosmology, and enticing secondary characters who deserve their own stories." —*Booklist*

"A delightful, smile-inducing romantic comedy between a witch and the demon she fake dates to save face in front of her demanding family, *A Witch's Guide to Fake Dating a Demon* is perfect for all fans of unlikely soulmates, banter galore, hilarious family dynamics, and April Asher's *Not the Witch You Wed*." —The Nerd Daily

"If you're craving some witchy vibes or want all the feelings of a cozy romance, then this is it." —Culturess

A
DEMON'S GUIDE
TO WOOING
A WITCH

SARAH HAWLEY

BERKLEY ROMANCE
NEW YORK

BERKLEY ROMANCE
Published by Berkley
An imprint of Penguin Random House LLC
penguinrandomhouse.com

Library of Congress Cataloging-in-Publication Data

Names: Hawley, Sarah, author.
Title: A demon's guide to wooing a witch / Sarah Hawley.
Description: First edition. | New York: Berkley Romance, 2023.
Identifiers: LCCN 2023025956 (print) | LCCN 2023025957 (ebook) |
ISBN 9780593547946 (trade paperback) | ISBN 9780593547953 (ebook)
Subjects: LCGFT: Paranormal fiction. | Romance fiction. | Novels.
Classification: LCC PS3608.A8937 D46 2023 (print) |
LCC PS3608.A8937 (ebook) | DDC 813/.6—dc23/eng/20230530
LC record available at https://lccn.loc.gov/2023025956
LC ebook record available at https://lccn.loc.gov/2023025957

First Edition: November 2023

Printed in the United States of America
1st Printing

Book design by Daniel Brount

For all the angry girls who were told they were too much.

A
DEMON'S GUIDE
TO WOOING
A WITCH

ONE

ASTAROTH OF THE NINE—DEMONIC HIGH COUNCIL MEMBER, legendary soul bargainer, and renowned liar—was having a very bad day.

He limped down a firelit stone corridor within the high council's grand temple on the demon plane, leaning heavily on his cane sword and cursing witches and traitor demons under his breath. His former protégé, Ozroth the Ruthless, had just handed him a neat and complete defeat, turning a soul bargain that ought to have been a coup for Astaroth into an embarrassment. And for what?

Love.

Astaroth scoffed at the absurdity. A demon soul bargainer falling in love with the witch whose soul he was supposed to take? Human-demon pairings were rare, but they did happen—Astaroth knew that all too well—but this was unprecedented.

It should have been a simple bargain. After Ozroth had shown signs of decreased performance as a soul bargainer, thanks to accidentally gaining a human soul during a bargain gone awry,

Astaroth had been determined to help his protégé recover his edge. When Mariel Spark, a powerhouse of a witch, had accidentally summoned Ozroth for a bargain, it had seemed the perfect opportunity to resurrect Ozroth's ruthlessness and gain a beautiful, bright human soul for the demon plane.

Ozroth hadn't claimed the witch's soul though. No, he'd dawdled and brooded and pined for the witch like bloody Lord Byron himself (and Astaroth ought to know, since he'd shagged that dramatic bastard for a few months in the early nineteenth century). Unlike old Georgie though, Ozroth lacked the charisma and sartorial panache to pull off romantic brooding, so Astaroth had quickly stepped in to make the deal himself and save both of them embarrassment.

Then it had all gone wrong.

A few impossible spells later, Ozroth and Mariel remained in a disgustingly happy relationship with both partners still in possession of their souls. And Astaroth had bargained away any leverage he might use to punish them.

He scowled at a torch sconce shaped like a hellhound's three gaping maws. The other members of the demonic high council would rip into him as viciously as a pack of hounds if they sensed an opportunity to reduce his influence and promote their allies. The scent of his blood was in the air, and there was no shortage of aspirants in the hunt for power.

The huge black doors leading to council chambers loomed ahead. Each was banded in silver and held half of the crest of the high council: a nonagon with nine spokes arrowing toward a stylized flame in the center.

Dread squeezed his insides with an iron fist. Astaroth rested with his back against the wall for a moment, closing his eyes and breathing through the surge of undemonlike fear. After six centuries, he knew how to force his secret weaknesses under control.

His aching leg welcomed the respite. It had been broken during his defeat thanks to one of Mariel's allies, a violent blond witch wearing *spandex*, of all things. Humiliating enough to be punched in the throat, kneed in the groin, and nearly launched into the stratosphere by the witch; her naff attire had added insult to injury. The same accelerated healing that kept demons immortal allowed him to walk on the damaged leg, but he hadn't had time to change out of his dirt-and-bloodstained white suit before being summoned to council quarters.

It's fine, he told himself, tapping his sword cane against one white, stack-heeled dress shoe, as if that could knock off the grime ground into the leather. *So you lost this bet. Make another one, then win that.*

The high council was fond of bets and wagers, which were an excellent way to test rivals, since it was dishonorable to refuse a bet. Frustrated after centuries of deadlock with his main rival on the council, an aggressive demon fundamentalist named Moloch, and with the council muttering about Ozroth's fitness to continue as a soul bargainer, Astaroth had rolled the dice. If Ozroth succeeded in his next bargain within the allotted time, Astaroth would win whatever prize or punishment he wanted from Moloch. If Ozroth failed, Moloch could decide the prize or punishment.

A wager with open-ended terms was a risky move, but Ozroth had never failed to complete a bargain, even if he had felt some guilt about it recently. Astaroth had been sure Ozroth would seize the witch's soul and win the bet.

Ah, to return to such an innocent time.

The door's silver sigil gleamed in the wavering glow of torchlight like a bright, flame-pupiled eye, judging Astaroth with its stare. Bets had been lost in the high council before. The results were never pretty.

But Astaroth had centuries of cunning and experience on his side, and he was determined not to go down without a fight. Besides, any legendary schemer had a backup plan. He'd been investigating Moloch for years, looking for a weak spot to target, and he'd finally discovered the evidence he needed to take out his greatest enemy on the council. Moloch might win this bet, but he would soon lose everything else.

Astaroth straightened, cracking his neck before shifting his weight onto both legs. Sharp pain shot through the injured leg, but he gritted his teeth and started walking without a limp.

The scent of his blood might be in the air, but Astaroth had fangs as sharp as any hellhound's.

Time to show them.

◆ ◆ ◆

THE EIGHT OTHER DEMONS OF THE HIGH COUNCIL SAT AROUND a table shaped like the council crest. The slab of basalt was carved with the sigil's design, and molten silver circulated through the grooves. Thanks to a spell commissioned from some long-ago warlock, the silver never cooled, nor did it damage the stone. It flowed endlessly, making the flame shape at the center seem to dance. Torches burned in sconces around the room, highlighting rich tapestries depicting famous demon victories, but the high ceiling was shrouded in shadow. Living stone gargoyles perched in the rafters, barely visible in the darkness.

Astaroth had always appreciated a bold aesthetic, and the council chambers delivered. Gothic drama practically dripped down the walls, and although most of the demons in this room, Astaroth included, had smartphones in their pockets, for the next hour they would all pretend they were suspended out of time.

The council members stared as Astaroth strolled toward his chair with an air of lazy arrogance. He lowered himself onto the emerald-green velvet seat, biting back a sigh of relief. Appearances mattered more than substance in his world. Reality was crafted from lies on top of lies, and Astaroth had long been the best liar of all.

Baphomet, the eldest demon on the high council, raised one disdainful eyebrow. "About time you joined us."

The demon was massive, with a braided red beard and thick ivory horns that curved along the sides of his head before ending in wicked points. Astaroth was fairly sure Baphomet filed his horns to make the tips that sharp, and he shuddered at the thought of doing the same to his own sleek black horns. Baphomet dressed like he was straight out of the Viking Age—which he was—in furs, metal, and leather. The attire smelled unpleasantly musty, but Astaroth couldn't deny the demon had cultivated a distinct brand.

Baphomet was the most important person in the room. He was the council's nominal head, having committed to a centrist position, and he served as tiebreaker whenever the four conservative and four liberal demons failed to come to an agreement. He also played dictator as needed.

It was his position both Moloch and Astaroth had their eyes on.

"I was held up," Astaroth said. Unlike the other demons, his accent was crisply British, thanks to centuries spent living mostly in London on the mortal plane, rather than here on the demon plane. *To better understand and manipulate mortals*, he'd told the council.

They didn't need to know his reason for spending time with humans was more complicated than that.

"You look wretched," Sandranella, the demoness to Baphomet's right, said. Her dark skin and black horns contrasted sharply with her cloud of white hair, and she was dressed in her typical elegant-but-don't-fuck-with-me attire: a sapphire brocade gown with a metal breastplate. She was as close to a friend as Astaroth would allow himself to claim.

"I'm trying out a new aesthetic," Astaroth said, examining his nails.

"What, looking like you got your ass kicked and then rolled around in mud?"

That was exactly what had happened, but Astaroth wasn't about to admit it. An image of his assailant flashed through his mind: brown eyes, blond ponytail, an oval face with a determined chin. The woman had been tall and leanly muscled, but she was merely human, and nothing about her had screamed *Your balls are in danger!* "It's called deliberately distressed clothing," he said, shoving thoughts of the witch away.

"It's certainly distressing me," Sandranella said, looking him up and down disapprovingly.

"Enough chatter," Baphomet boomed. Astaroth wondered if the demon practiced that voice alone in his den, calculating which volume level best qualified as "booming." "We are here to resolve the wager proposed by Moloch."

Astaroth maintained an indolent smile, despite the urge to grind his teeth and spit at Moloch. His longtime nemesis sat across from Astaroth, an oily smirk on his face. Moloch might look cherubic, with rosy cheeks, blue eyes, and curly brown hair, but he was the cruelest snake Astaroth had ever met. Admirable—except that his treachery was often aimed at Astaroth. They'd been born around the same time, and their fierce rivalry had intensified over the centuries as Moloch had become the preeminent demon warrior and Astaroth the preeminent soul bargainer.

When Astaroth had been named to the high council, he'd thought he'd finally surpassed Moloch in status . . . until Moloch had been raised to the council that same day. Now there was only one position left to fight over: Baphomet's.

Astaroth had been searching for dirt on Moloch for a long time. He would need to be careful how he revealed his recent discoveries, considering the situation.

Moloch stood, smoothing a curl over one dun-colored horn. He wore a gray tunic over a blue shirt—an echo of his origin in the late 1300s, though his gray trousers were more modern. "Before we learn how Astaroth has fared, let us recap the terms of the bet," he said. His eyes glittered in the torchlight, and the satisfaction in them said he knew exactly how Astaroth had fared. "One month ago, we discussed Ozroth the Ruthless during a high council meeting. His failure to deliver a warlock's soul to the demon realm, and the subsequent discovery that he accidentally absorbed that human soul, caused grave concern among the council. When it was recommended he be put down to avoid future failures, Astaroth interceded, promising that Ozroth would deliver a new soul within a month."

Astaroth's expression didn't change, though he was entertaining a fantasy of garotting Moloch. "Don't use such passive language, Moloch," he said lightly. "You were the sole member of the council to recommend my protégé be killed rather than given a chance to prove himself."

Moloch shrugged. "A faulty weapon is more likely to harm the wielder. With the demon plane dependent on souls, it made sense to eliminate the problem as quickly as possible."

Without the human souls that drifted like enormous fireflies in the perpetual twilight of the demon plane, all life within the plane would gradually die. It was why demons and witches had formed a symbiotic relationship. The witch or warlock provided a soul—their magic—to keep the demon plane alive, and in exchange, a soul bargainer granted them a wish.

Moloch didn't care about the demon plane so much as he cared about spiting Astaroth though. "One would think after all these years you'd have learned patience," Astaroth said, "but you've never seemed to enjoy the long game."

A dimple appeared on Moloch's cheek. "I'm enjoying it right now."

Not as much as I'll enjoy airing your dirty laundry at this table in a few minutes, Astaroth thought. Moloch had won the battle, but Astaroth would win the war.

"Enough posturing," Sandranella said. "Or at least whip your dicks out and measure them so we can get this over with. I have a happy hour on the elven plane to get to."

"No need," Astaroth said. "My dick is definitely bigger."

Moloch cleared his throat and puffed up his chest. "That's patently false, but let's move on. The wager dictated that if Ozroth succeeded in his next soul bargain before the end of the mortal month of October, Astaroth could decide the consequences dealt to me. If Ozroth failed, I would decide the consequences dealt to him."

Sandranella met Astaroth's eyes and shook her head. *Bad choice*, she mouthed.

Yes, he was well aware.

Moloch's grin was sharp. "So, Astaroth, did Ozroth succeed in claiming a soul within the allotted time frame?"

A muscle under Astaroth's eye started twitching. "No."

A murmur went around the table. The conservative demons looked chuffed—they were undoubtedly hoping for Astaroth's removal from the high council so one of their allies could take his place.

"Would you care to tell us what went wrong?" Moloch asked, clearly hoping for an opportunity to humiliate Astaroth further.

"No," Astaroth said.

"Will Ozroth be returning to his duties as a soul bargainer?" Moloch pressed.

"Also no. Are you done with the pointless questions?" Because as soon as Astaroth claimed the floor, he would let the rest of the council know what kind of snake they held to their bosom.

"Not quite." Moloch sauntered around the table, looking like the cat that got the canary. "You've always been overly fascinated with humans, haven't you?"

Foreboding prickled down Astaroth's spine. "I would hardly call it a fascination," he said, striving for a bored tone. "I spend time among them to better learn how to manipulate them into bargains."

"So you've always said. The flat in London, the many, many mortals you've had carnal relations with—yes, I know all about that—the ridiculous fashion shows you attend . . . all of it is to better manipulate humans, hmm?"

Moloch knowing that Astaroth had shagged mortals was not good. While many demons appreciated humans, seeing them as symbiotic counterparts, the conservative members of the high council disdained them as lesser beings, and Astaroth had always been careful to keep the, ah, *extent* of his interactions with humans a secret. "What's your point?" he asked.

"I've wondered about you for centuries." Moloch stopped just out of range of the sword hidden in Astaroth's cane. Pity. "Something's always seemed . . . different about you."

The smile vanished as cold sweat beaded on Astaroth's forehead. Moloch couldn't know . . . could he? "It's probably the long track record of success," Astaroth said. "You haven't had a decent war to fight in decades."

"I did some research," Moloch said, ignoring the barb. "The records around your birth are surprisingly sparse. With a mother like Lilith, one would think she'd trumpet the immediate arrival of an heir, rather than wait forty years to claim you as her son."

"Who can say why Lilith does anything?" Astaroth asked. "She's mad." Fear festered in his gut though, and his throat felt tight. There was a reason his wonderful, exasperating mother hadn't publicly claimed him right away, and if it was revealed, the high council would never see Astaroth the same way again. Which would be a death sentence for his ambitions.

Ambition—power—was everything. It was the *only* thing.

"I do agree she's insane," Moloch said. He reached into his pocket and pulled out a leather-bound book with gilt edges. "But Lilith's diary contains some very interesting information."

Bloody fucking fuck. Did his cursed mother have to document her entire life? She had a whole bookshelf of similar-looking diaries in her den, filled out over the centuries, but Astaroth had never dreamed she'd write down the secret the two of them alone shared.

"What part of *Lilith is insane* are you missing?" Astaroth snapped to cover up his unseemly fear. "Just because she wrote something down doesn't mean it's true. She writes explicit Wars of the Roses tentacle fan fiction, too." Way, way too much Wars of the Roses tentacle fan fiction, which she posted to AO3 like a horny human teenager rather than the millennia-old demoness she was.

"Wow," Sandranella drawled. "Are the tentacles aligned with Lancaster or York?"

"I wouldn't say *aligned with* so much as *inside of*," Astaroth said, "but that's not the point. If she can confidently write Henry VI taking it up the arse from a Yorkist squid, she very well might have invented all sorts of falsehoods about me."

Moloch bared his teeth. "You're very defensive for someone who doesn't even know what I'm accusing you of. Unless you do?"

Astaroth struggled to shove down his rising panic. Proper demons—powerful demons—didn't panic. Moloch was speaking in vagaries in hopes of prompting a confession. "Whatever it is, I know it's nonsense."

"Maybe," Moloch said with a shrug. "We'll find out soon enough."

Baphomet tapped on the table. "Enough of these cryptic clues," he said in that rumbling bass voice. "Let's move on with the session."

Right. Because after whatever devastating punishment Astaroth was about to receive, the council would carry on as always, discussing everything from community resources to the growing unrest among the hybrids who chose to live in the demon plane rather than the plane of origin of their nondemon parent.

Astaroth's stomach churned again. He was one of the few voices on the high council in favor of protecting the rights of the hybrids and nondemons who lived on-plane. It was a tricky balancing act, and without his input, more conservative voices would prevail. If Baphomet didn't intervene—and he wouldn't if the majority were in favor of Moloch's plans—the council would swerve in a fundamentalist direction it would take centuries to course-correct.

"Very well," Moloch said. "Let's discuss the terms of my victory. Obviously, Astaroth will be removed from the high council."

Astaroth's blood raged at the demotion, though he had planned to do the same to Moloch. Still, the punishment could have been worse, and there was always scheming to be done. Once Moloch was discredited, Astaroth would be back on top. "If you insist, I will gracefully resign for the moment," he said, preparing to stand. "But first, I have some information to share with the council—"

"I'm not finished," Moloch said sharply. He snapped his fingers, and a gargoyle leaped down from the rafters to open the council room doors. "The second part of your punishment will take place now."

Astaroth stared, confused and alarmed, as a woman with long black hair and pointed ears entered. She wore glitter-spangled velvet robes and a necklace with a dramatic, cage-like silver pendant. When he opened his demon senses, he saw the golden glow of a soul emanating from her chest. A human witch, then, one descended from some fae creature. "Who is this?"

Moloch smirked. "You'll find out."

Another snap, and more gargoyles jumped down. These ones gripped Astaroth's arms with granite fingers, keeping him in his chair.

"Get your hands off me," Astaroth said, struggling to break free. There was a reason the gargoyles were used as demonic security though, and their stony strength was more than enough to subdue him. "Everyone needs to know something about Moloch—"

Moloch talked over him again. "Astaroth, formerly of the Nine, I hereby banish you to Earth."

Astaroth's head spun. "What? No!" He liked Earth, but he couldn't shape demon politics if he was stuck there full-time.

Sandranella stood, looking alarmed. "Moloch, that's an excessive punishment."

Moloch shrugged. "He accepted the wager."

Sandranella turned to Baphomet. "You must put a stop to this. It sets a dangerous precedent."

"Moloch is right," Baphomet said. "Astaroth accepted the wager. He can take the punishment."

Astaroth's heels scraped over the flagstones as he tried to escape, but it was no use. The pain in his still-healing leg was nothing compared to the riot of agonized emotion in his chest. He'd always felt more than a demon ought to, and the surge of anger and fear threatened to drown him. "You can't do this," Astaroth said. His mask of control had disintegrated. "You can't!"

"Watch me." Moloch motioned to the witch, who raised her hands. She moved them in an intricate, roiling dance, inscribing symbols in the air.

"What is she doing?" Sandranella asked, looking between Astaroth and Moloch. "We don't need her to banish him."

"Oh, she's not here to banish him," Moloch said. "She's here to do something else . . . and once she does, I'll finally have proof that Astaroth has been lying to us for centuries."

Magic built in the air, prickling like electricity. The witch spoke a spell in the language of magic, and a concussive wave of power slammed into Astaroth's chest. He shouted as fire writhed through his veins, and his vision whited out. His mind seemed to split into kaleidoscopic fragments.

"What did she do?" Sandranella asked, the words garbled as if he was hearing them from underwater.

Moloch's voice echoed distantly. "Once the witch confirms it worked, I will reveal all."

Astaroth felt sick and sluggish. He couldn't let it end like this. He needed to let the council know about Moloch's crimes.

He forced his thick tongue into motion. "Once the others find out what you've been doing—" he slurred, "they'll—"

"What I'm doing is taking out the trash," Moloch interrupted.

"Baphomet," Astaroth said, turning blurred eyes in the direction of the council head. "You must listen to me."

"Enough," Baphomet said. "End this, Moloch."

Moloch snapped his sharp canines at Astaroth. "Ready to go?"

The haze cleared from Astaroth's vision in time for him to see Moloch open a portal. The fiery-edged oval hovered in midair; through it, he saw a darkened suburban street on the mortal plane. Iron lamps cast pools of gold over the pavement, and trees rustled in the wind.

The gargoyles muscled Astaroth out of the chair and shoved him toward the portal.

"No, wait—" Astaroth's head was spinning, his normally ordered thoughts a chaotic jumble. Terror wrapped around him like clinging vines.

Moloch was grinning like a fiend. "See you soon," he whispered.

Then Moloch kicked Astaroth in the backside, and Astaroth stumbled through the portal into the mortal realm. The pavement rushed toward him, and the world went black.

TWO

"CHEERS, BITCHES!"

Calladia raised the tequila shot, spilling some of the alcohol on her wrist. It was her fourth—or maybe fifth?—shot since arriving at Le Chapeau Magique to celebrate Mariel and Oz's victory over Astaroth of the Nine, demonic dickhead. The dive bar was full of their friends chatting, singing, and swaying to the music pouring from a battered jukebox. Christmas lights were strung around the ceiling, and the wood-paneled room had taken on a hazy, pleasant glow.

Calladia licked salt from the hand holding the glass, tossed the shot back, then sucked the quarter of lime she held in her other hand. Sharp citrus sang along her taste buds, and the alcohol burned just the right amount going down. She did a full body shudder. "Whew!"

Calladia wasn't normally a big drinker—she despised hangovers and tried to eat and drink relatively healthily—but her best friend defeating an agent of evil was a big fucking deal. Calladia getting to punch said agent of evil had been pretty cool, too.

Calladia closed her eyes, remembering Astaroth's shocked expression after she'd punched him. That snooty motherfucker hadn't known who he was messing with.

"I love everyone in this bar!"

Calladia opened her eyes at the slurred exclamation and smiled at Themmie. The Filipino American pixie was "in her cups," as some might say, her brown eyes half closed, her mouth tilted in a goofy smile. Themmie slammed her own shot of tequila, iridescent wings twitching as she gasped.

"I'm going to regret this in the morning," Calladia said, bracing herself against the bar as her head spun. She belched, then thumped her chest with her fist. "I haven't done a shot since college."

"Really?" Themmie wrinkled her nose. "The so-called 'real world' sounds terrible."

Five years younger than Calladia and Mariel, Themmie was a senior in college studying anthropology and business, with a goal of going to law school *to become an advocate for the disenfranchised*, as she said when sober or going to interviews. *To fuck the man!* was what she was more likely to say when drunk or in private.

"Which man?" Mariel had slurred once at happy hour, to which Themmie had wrinkled her nose, looked at the ceiling, and responded, "The one with a capital *M*."

Calladia agreed wholeheartedly. Every day, she felt worse and worse about . . . well, most things. Her dating prospects, her mother's reign of terror as the mayor of Glimmer Falls, and all the ways life had gradually ground her down until she was more sharp edges than anything else.

"The real world is terrible," Calladia said. "But there's no homework, so that's good."

Themmie shook her head. "Not for me. Practicing law is like weaponized homework." She blinked at Calladia. "You really don't do shots anymore?"

Calladia eyed the empty shot glass. The hazy contentment she'd been feeling all night was a welcome change from her normal agitated state. Why had she stopped doing shots, again?

Her temples started throbbing. Oh, right.

"My sweet summer child," Calladia said with what she imagined to be great dignity, "there's something you're going to get well acquainted with over the coming years. It's called a hangover. I hear that by the time we're thirty, we'll get one just from prolonged eye contact with alcohol."

"Boo." Themmie's eyes wandered over the selection of bottles behind the bar. "We're not thirty yet. Want another one?"

The tequila already consumed said yes, but the shred of rational thought remaining said absolutely not. Calladia made eye contact with the bartender, a nonbinary centaur named Hylo who had a buzz cut, a labrum piercing, and hooves adorned with neon nail polish. "Water?" she said hopefully.

Hylo trotted over with an enormous glass. "Want to add an anti-hangover supplement? We're trying out a new elven manufacturer."

"Absolutely." Calladia eyed Themmie, who had her phone out for a selfie and was making alarming faces at the camera. "One for her, too."

The roan-patterned centaur snorted as they pulled a bottle of glittering green powder out and began stirring it into the water. "Themmie, you better not be posting those."

Themmie hiccupped. "My followers love slices of real life."

"So do mine, but there's something to be said for a prudent amount of editing."

"You're a Pixtagram influencer, too?" Calladia asked. Themmie made a tidy profit from endorsements for her colorful photos and videos, and though Calladia itched at the thought of receiving that much attention from strangers, she had to admire the pixie's hustle.

"Not Pixtagram," Hylo said. "ClipClop."

Calladia's brow furrowed. "ClipClop?" Hecate, there were way too many apps to keep track of these days.

"It's where centaurs show off their original dances," Themmie slurred. "Hylo specializes in Irish step dancing."

Calladia's drink-fuzzed brain couldn't imagine a centaur performing *Riverdance*, but she'd bet it was noisy. "Sounds neat."

"Thanks." Hylo handed over the glass.

Calladia took a glug of the green-tinged water. "Ugh," she said, spitting it out. "Why does that taste like moss?"

"Elves," Hylo said succinctly. "Just chug it."

Calladia did, grimacing. Anti-hangover powders were always hit or miss. One species' hangover didn't translate to another's, and quacks loved selling knockoffs of elven potions or minotaur semen that had no actual health benefits. Calladia wasn't brave enough for the supposed cure-all elixir of minotaur cum, and she despised fake supplements, so she usually just suffered the occasional hangover in peace.

Tonight was a different case. Shots had been had, and her head would hopefully thank her tomorrow. Horrible remedy downed, Calladia wiped her mouth on her forearm and looked at the dance floor. It wasn't a slow song, but Mariel was wrapped around Oz, the two of them swaying to a beat all their own. The big, normally surly demon was beaming down at Mariel, looking utterly enraptured, and Mariel's pink cheeks and shining hazel eyes showed she felt the same in return.

Calladia's chest felt tight. She hadn't liked Oz at first, but there was no denying the couple were great together. She was delighted for her best friend and fully acknowledged she'd been wrong about Oz—or, at least, that he had vastly improved after spending more time in the mortal realm and embracing his new soul. Still, no matter how happy Calladia was for them, seeing their joy was bittersweet.

Could a perfect match ever happen for Calladia? She wasn't like Mariel, who was beautiful, sweet, and giving. Calladia was prickly, aggressive, and damaged. If Mariel represented the best of people, Calladia was, though not the worst, at least on the "uh oh" end of the spectrum.

Calladia shook her head and tipped her empty shot glass into her mouth, then grimaced when she realized there was no more tequila to be had.

A voice sounded from her right. "What are you drinking?"

Calladia stiffened. The voice wasn't familiar, but the tone was. She turned to see a smug-looking white man with styled brown hair, pointed ears, and a square jaw. He looked like a movie star, and Calladia already hated him. "What do you want?" she said, hoping he could hear the warning in her flat tone.

The man eyed her up and down, then licked his lips. "Whatever you're offering, baby."

Calladia's temper was rarely fully banked, especially these days. At those words, the embers flared to life, burning through the haze of alcohol. She straightened, only wobbling a bit, then pinned him with her meanest stare. "I'm no one's baby," she said, slow and exaggerated from the tequila. "In fact, I've been a grown woman for a while now."

The man scoffed. "Oh, come on, don't be like that. You wore those pants for a reason. Let's just have a drink, yeah? Get to know each other?"

"Oh, shit," Themmie said, backing away. She tripped but righted herself with a sharp flap of her wings.

Calladia didn't literally see red, but her vision narrowed in on this asshole like a James Bond credit sequence when the gun fired. Her "pants" were workout leggings, and whatever this dude thought, they were designed for ease of movement rather than enticing lovers.

She had a flashback to the way Astaroth had sneered at her

during their confrontation earlier that day. When she'd dissed his fedora, he'd said, *I don't take sartorial critiques from people wearing spandex.*

At least Astaroth had objected to the spandex rather than ogling her body. Calladia had had no problem ruining the hot demon's day; she would have no qualms about putting this pathetic bar slime in his place either.

"Do you know why I wear these leggings?" Calladia asked. Her pulse raced with familiar, addicting adrenaline. When the guy smiled, she bared her teeth. "It's easier to kick assholes."

To her fury, the man laughed. "You're a spicy one, aren't you?"

He reached out, lightly resting his hand on her arm, and Calladia snapped.

"Don't touch me," she said loudly, yanking her arm away. That had been one of her kickboxing instructor's biggest tips: people remembered what they heard, so if she needed to tussle, she should make it clear the other person had instigated it. As the pointy-eared man lurched off-balance, Calladia grabbed his upper arm and used his momentum to slam him ribs-first into the bar. Not hard enough for an assault charge—hopefully—but hard enough to knock the air out of his lungs. Then she fisted her hand in his hair and gently introduced his face to the bartop.

Okay, not that gently.

The commotion got the attention of everyone in the vicinity. "Not again," Hylo groaned. The centaur hurried over, black tail flicking agitatedly. "What happened?"

"He touched my arm," Calladia said, glaring at the man who was currently bent over, wheezing and clutching both his gut and his nose.

"Did you consider using your words before beating him up?"

"Not my fault he doesn't respect boundaries."

A dwarven bouncer hurried over, barrel chest straining his *Le Chapeau Magique* T-shirt. He picked up the harasser by the collar and dragged him out with no trouble, despite being half the man's height. Then the bouncer returned and pointed at Calladia, hitching a thumb over his shoulder.

"Wait, I have to leave, too?" Calladia asked incredulously.

Hylo sighed. "I get that he crossed a line, but so did you, Calladia. He was already incapacitated when you smashed his head into the bar."

"But he touched me," Calladia argued, swaying.

"And he'll be blacklisted for that, believe me, but the bouncers could have taken care of the issue without you starting a fistfight."

"Maybe I like fistfights," Calladia muttered.

"I get it," Hylo said, "I really do, but you're practically begging for criminal charges. I know you're on the blacklist at a few other bars in town because you keep brawling."

Themmie's brown eyes went wide, and she turned on Calladia. "You've been fighting that much?"

Calladia's cheeks felt hot. She'd always been a rough-and-tumble sort and had gotten in a variety of scrapes over the course of her life, but she couldn't deny things had gotten worse over the last few years. Anger simmered in her gut on a frequent basis, an ember that blazed into violence with the slightest encouragement. Yeah, this dude had had it coming, and she didn't feel bad about it, but could she say the same for last week, when she'd leaped into a shape-shifter brawl that hadn't remotely involved her, ultimately getting kicked out for smashing a stool over someone's head?

Dozens of humans and supernatural creatures were gaping at Calladia, which made her feel itchy. Mariel hurried over, Oz at her side. "What happened?" Mariel asked. "Are you okay?"

Fuck. This was Oz and Mariel's celebration, and Calladia had just messed it up, the way she messed up most things. "Sorry," Calladia said. "I'm fine. Just . . . yeah."

"The guy was harassing her," Themmie said, wings twitching.

"Calladia . . ." Hylo jerked their head at the door. "Out. At least for a few minutes. You need to cool down."

"Wait," Mariel said, looking between Hylo and Calladia. "She's my friend—"

"It's fine." Calladia pushed off the bar, managing not to sway. "I need to drink some water and go to sleep anyway." She mustered up a wink, but considering Oz and Mariel's expressions, it wasn't a very good one. "Bye. Happy for you and your domestic bliss and shit."

Before Mariel could say anything else, Calladia turned and strode out of Le Chapeau Magique, brushing off Themmie's attempt to follow. She hadn't paid her tab, but Hylo knew how to find her, and there was no way she was going to stay with all those eyes pinned on her. Her cheeks burned, and her stomach churned with anxiety along with the alcohol.

The autumn air felt crisp against her flushed skin. Calladia took a deep breath, welcoming the icy spear in her lungs. The bar harasser was nowhere to be seen, so she closed her eyes and leaned against the brick exterior of the building. Despite Hylo's instructions to cool down, the change of venue was doing no such thing for Calladia. Her pulse raced, and she still felt the hot surge of anger and shame.

A pained male cry sounded from nearby. Calladia looked around, trying to pinpoint the source. Another shout was followed by a voice. "Where am I? Who are you? Leave me alone!"

A sweep of déjà vu washed over Calladia at the man's posh British accent. Astaroth had had an accent just like that.

"Ow! Bloody hell."

Lots of people had British accents though, and Glimmer Falls was full of tourists who had come for the magical town's world-renowned Autumn Festival. Whoever the man was, he seemed to be in trouble, so Calladia pushed off the wall, determined to see what was happening and help if need be.

And fight if need be, right? her mind whispered, but she brushed it off. Sometimes violence was necessary. If it was in this case, she'd be doing a good deed, right?

She turned into an alleyway. A man with curly brown hair stood over a body on the ground, a knife in his hand. He kicked the body, eliciting a groan of pain. "I thought I'd kill you right away," he said in an accent eerily similar to Oz's, "but I like the idea of carving up that pretty face. Let you live with it for a while."

"Who are you?" the man on the ground repeated. He was curled up with his arms over his head, so Calladia couldn't see much of him, but there were bloodstains on his light-colored coat.

The other man tipped his head back and laughed, and Calladia stiffened as moonlight glanced off light brown horns. Another demon!

"What is this, an infestation?" she muttered as she strode forward. She'd lived her entire life in Glimmer Falls without seeing a demon, and now this was the third in a single month. She pulled a hank of thread from her pocket. Magic needed to be grounded in words and action, and while some witches preferred chalking runes or performing elaborate ritual dances, Calladia liked the intricacy and portability of thread for casting. "Get away from him," she said loudly.

The demon's head whipped around. He was weirdly sweet-looking, with brown hair, blue eyes, and dimpled cheeks. He looked her up and down, then returned his attention to his victim. "Shall I cut your nose off first?" the demon asked the man. "Maybe an ear?"

Calladia didn't like being ignored. She wound the thread around her fingers and began tying the elaborate knots that would ground her spell in physical action. "*Defienez el daemon,*" she said, tying the final knot.

The demon flew backward, hitting the brick wall. Calladia's spell kept him pinned there like an insect. She sauntered up to him, smirking at his outraged expression. "What, you don't like humans interrupting your demonic crimes?" she asked with only a slight slur.

He sneered at her. "Out of my way, witch."

"You're not going to offer me a bargain?" Astaroth had tried that earlier, offering her money, fame, love . . . whatever she wanted in exchange for her soul and her magic.

She knew better than to believe in such empty promises. Like anything else worth having, love was earned, not seized.

The demon scoffed. "You're dealing with Moloch of the Nine, witch." At Calladia's uncomprehending stare, he clarified. "I'm a warrior, not a bargainer." His muscles strained as he fought against the spell, and Calladia felt the magical bonds weakening. Hecate, he was strong.

"Not much of a warrior right now," she said, brazening it out as she started tying a new string of knots. "You aren't welcome here."

She wove a circle of protection around herself and the unfortunate man in the gutter, who she hadn't had a chance to look at yet. Better safe than sorry. It turned out to be an excellent impulse, as Moloch broke free of her original spell and lunged at her. He ricocheted off the shield, and Calladia laughed.

Moloch's face twisted in an expression of rage so potent it made Calladia retreat a step. "This isn't over," he said. Then he made a circular gesture with his fingers, and a flame-edged oval the size of a door appeared in the air. A portal. With a final glower at the man on the ground, Moloch stepped through, and the portal sealed behind him.

Calladia blew out a heavy breath. "Wow. What a dick."

A pained groan sounded from behind her. "You can say that again," the British man said. "Bloody hell."

Calladia dropped to her knees to examine the man for injuries. "Are you hurt—" She broke off as the man straightened from the fetal position and rolled to face her, revealing black horns and a familiar face. "Oh, hell no," she said, scrambling away.

Had she seriously just rescued her enemy?

Astaroth looked like shit, at least. His white suit was stained with dirt and blood, his chiseled face was wan, and the skin around his eye was rapidly purpling. "Thank you," he said weakly, pushing to a seated position.

"Nuh uh," Calladia said, standing and backing away. She started tying new knots, trying to decide if she should forcibly fling him to Oregon or turn him into a newt. "You aren't welcome here either."

Astaroth's forehead furrowed. "Sorry, have we met?"

Calladia laughed disbelievingly. "Forgotten me so quickly? Maybe my fist in your face will help you remember."

He winced and prodded the swelling skin around his eye. "Forgotten . . ." His eyes widened with what looked like panic. "Wait, where am I? And who are you?"

THREE

ASTAROTH'S FACE HURT, AND HIS BRAIN WAS FOGGY. HE
stared at the angry witch standing over him, trying to figure
out where he knew her from. She clearly knew him, after all, and
she didn't seem to like him much, despite having saved him from
whoever that Moloch fellow was.

He tried to remember anything prior to the past few minutes.
He had a jumbled impression of vaguely familiar faces, the flicker
of firelight . . . and nothing else. Just the residual emotional echo
of some horror.

Who was this woman? Who was the demon who had punched
Astaroth in the face before threatening to skewer him alive? Why
did his head feel like it was stuffed with cotton?

"What do you mean, where are you and who am I?" The witch
crossed her arms, displaying a pair of impressive biceps. She was
tall and lean, with sun-kissed white skin, long blond hair tied up
in a ponytail, and a thunderous expression. She was wearing a pair
of daisy-patterned leggings and a shirt that said *Sweat Like a Girl*.
The cheap fabric of her leggings made Astaroth shudder with

distaste, though he could admit it highlighted her arse in a compelling way.

"I can't remember anything," Astaroth said, rubbing his aching temples. His head pounded, and not just from being punched by Moloch. "I don't know how I got here or where I am."

"You've got to be kidding me," the woman said. "Can demons get amnesia?"

He reached up to touch one of his horns. He knew they were black, the way he knew his name was Astaroth and that spandex was repellent in most contexts. But although he had a general sense of self, he had no idea what that self had been up to before the preceding minutes. "I suppose they can," he said, rubbing his forehead with his palms. "Lucifer, my head hurts." Pain pulsed inside his skull, punctuated by sharp, fiery stabs.

The witch shifted from foot to foot, looking between him and the entrance to the alleyway. "You really don't recognize me?"

A thought emerged from the chaos in his head. "Are we lovers?" He had a vivid image of her crushing him between her muscular thighs, though he couldn't tell if that was a memory or wishful thinking.

"No!" She looked horrified.

Astaroth winced. All right, not lovers. His gaze dropped to her thighs again. "Pity."

She snapped her fingers. "Eyes up, asshole."

Astaroth returned his focus to her face, blinking when his vision wavered. "Are we enemies, then?"

Her laugh sounded wild. "Yes, you could say that."

"Ah." He was off to a terrific start. "And your name is . . . ?"

"Calladia." She dug her fingers into the top of her ponytail, messing it up, then groaned. "Hecate, what am I supposed to do?"

Astaroth forced himself to stand, biting down a whimper as he put weight on a sore leg. Clearly something terrible had happened to him before Moloch had decided to deliver a beating. "I suppose you have the advantage, since I've no idea what's happening," he said. "I've got to warn you, if you try to murder me, I won't cooperate."

Standing helped the pain somewhat, although the fresh surge of dizziness was unwelcome. Upright, he could recall that people had tried to murder him before. He had a flash of memory from one of the Jacobite uprisings or another, back when he'd dabbled in mortal warfare. A troll had swung a mace at him, knocking him down and leaving a dent in his favorite breastplate.

Why could he remember fighting in a Jacobite uprising but not arriving on this street in the here and now? What had he been up to since the 1700s? It was clearly a long time past then, but while he recognized various modern features—neon lights, the flicker of a television from a nearby window, the blink of aircraft lights far overhead—he wasn't sure of his place among them. It was like receiving a script for a play that contained nothing but descriptions of props and staging, and Astaroth had just been shoved onstage to perform an unknown part for a hostile audience.

Calladia was pacing in tight switchbacks. Step step step turn, step step step turn. "Damn it," she said, kicking a pebble into the brick wall of the alley. "I should leave you here."

That was better than the alternative of her murdering him, not that he could see where she might hide a weapon in that ensemble. She could perform a spell to smack him into the wall the way she had Moloch though. "Ah, where is here?" he asked.

"Glimmer Falls."

The name was vaguely familiar. He mouthed the words, begging them to spark a memory.

They did not.

Was Glimmer Falls where he resided? He'd bounced between various locations in Europe for centuries, though the details of where he'd lived grew hazy after the American Revolution. What a time that had been! Masquerading as a redcoat, he'd played all sides, manipulating countless souls out of magically gifted soldiers and commanders desperate for victory.

Given the accents surrounding him, including Calladia's, he was once again in America. He couldn't imagine having purchased a town house here, rather than in England or on the Continent, but perhaps his preferences had changed over the years.

He tried to think past the late 1700s, but it was like hitting an impenetrable wall in his mind. Even the centuries that came before that were foggy, available only in patchwork pieces. A country manor filled with blurry-faced people in formal clothes, a peaceful afternoon lying in a field while sheep ambled nearby, the glint of sunlight on bloody steel as he skewered the troll who had dented his armor. Even those images were hard to fit into a sequence, but at least something of his history had survived whatever trauma he'd endured. Hopefully more would return soon.

"Do I live in Glimmer Falls?" he asked, giving up on shaking the answer loose.

"Definitely not." Calladia's mouth twisted. "Moloch is going to come back, isn't he?"

"Stands to reason, given how vehemently he dislikes me." Astaroth's forehead furrowed. "I seem to have a lot of enemies."

The witch snorted. "Shocking." Then she shook her head. "This is a terrible idea," she muttered, "but I can't fight you when you're incapacitated. It wouldn't be fair."

The sentiment surprised Astaroth. "You care about fairness?" Moloch certainly hadn't. Astaroth suspected he didn't either.

Hang it, why could he remember the American War of Independence, but not the demon who wanted to kill him?

Calladia nibbled her lower lip and looked over her shoulder toward where Moloch had disappeared. "Look, whatever's going on, I don't want to wait for that dickhead to come back." She pointed a stern finger at him. "But if you try anything funny, I will explode your testicles."

Astaroth winced at the graphic threat. "Noted."

She nodded, then started walking away. "Well?" she called over her shoulder. "Are you coming or not?"

She was inviting him to join her? Astaroth considered her retreating form. She'd openly admitted to being his enemy, but she'd also admitted to valuing fairness, and it was possible he had other enemies lying in wait who didn't have such scruples.

His eyes dropped to her arse again. Maybe fair fights and spandex had some merit, after all.

"Lead the way," he said, limping after her.

✦ ✦ ✦

ASTAROTH FOLLOWED CALLADIA ONTO A STREET LINED WITH shops and restaurants. Iron lampposts marched down the pavement, and humans, centaurs, pixies, and other creatures ambled by in pairs and groups, laughing and chatting.

A newspaper box sat at the edge of the curb, displaying the day's headline. Astaroth checked the date.

He was missing over two centuries of memories.

Fear climbed his throat, and the nausea intensified. Panicking on a public street would only attract attention and convey weakness to any enemies who might be watching, so he shoved the fear down, straightened his shoulders, and resolved to playact this game of improvisation as well as he could until the memories returned.

A woman's voice slipped into his head, echoing the thought. *They cannot know what you are*, she murmured in an accent as familiar as it was unidentifiable. The syllables were sharp, with the echo of antiquity laid upon them.

Who did the voice belong to? When he tried to think of people he knew, there was little to grasp onto. Apparently personal relationships had been relegated to the same dark hole as the events of the last two hundred years.

Dithering about it wouldn't help matters, so Astaroth breathed deeply, aiming for calm. He caught a whiff of autumn leaves, cooking meat, and alcohol. Alcohol that was definitely wafting from his new companion. "Are you drunk?" he asked.

"So what if I am?" Calladia glared at him. "At least I'm not an amoral, insufferable piece of shit."

"Ouch," Astaroth said blandly. "Why are you drunk?"

"Why do you care?"

He shrugged. "It gives us something to talk about, since I don't remember the rest of our acquaintance."

"Not much of an acquaintance," Calladia muttered. She sidestepped a gnome who had stopped to photograph a pumpkin. It was carved to show a grinning face, and a candle flickered inside. A word surfaced in Astaroth's brain like a bubble popping to the surface of a glass of champagne: *Halloween*. An image came with it of small children in costumes begging for sweets, and the emotion that came with the flash of memory was warm and bright. Apparently he liked Halloween.

"Do you like Halloween?" he asked the witch.

Calladia's forehead furrowed. "What?"

"I just remembered giving candy to children. It was nice."

"What, to lure them into your van?" At Astaroth's uncomprehending stare, Calladia sighed. "Yes, I like Halloween. But why would you hand out candy? And why would you think it was *nice*?"

"Why wouldn't I?" He was fairly certain it was standard practice around the holiday, even if he didn't remember much else.

"Because you're an evil, despicable monster with no heart?"

"You have a tremendously poor opinion of me," he said. "How long have we been enemies?"

They had reached a park set in the midst of town. At its entrance was a red clock with multiple faces and so many erratically spinning hands that Astaroth had to turn away before he vomited.

Calladia studied the clock. "Approximately . . . twelve hours," she said.

Astaroth laughed. "You've got to be joking." When Calladia raised her eyebrows, he realized she was, in fact, serious. "That's a short time to have formed such a strong opinion," he said. "What did I do to you?"

Those blond brows remained elevated, conveying disdain and disbelief. "You tried to steal my friend's soul and murder her boyfriend."

"Oh." That didn't ring any bells, but he'd always had a responsibility to his species as a soul bargainer, so it stood to reason he was still up to it. He wasn't as sure about the murder, but as he consulted his lack of intense reaction to the news, it didn't feel out of the realm of possibility either. "What do you mean I *tried* to steal her soul?"

"You failed," she said smugly.

That made no sense. Once agreed upon, a soul bargain was inviolable. The trade—a soul for a favor accomplished through demonic magic—had to occur, or the demon would never be able to leave the witch's side. Maybe she meant he'd encouraged her friend to make a deal, but the friend had refused?

Pain spiked at his temple, and he decided to revisit that question later. "And the murder?" he asked. "Why did I try that?"

She threw her hands up. "Why would I know? I'm just the muscle of the gang."

He looked her up and down again—quickly this time—and concluded she was correct. She had muscular calves, strong thighs, and the general build of someone who could do real damage, despite her lean frame. A tingle of appreciation raced down his spine. Why had his past self chosen to make an enemy of her rather than seizing the opportunity to use those thighs as earmuffs?

"So you remember handing out candy at Halloween," Calladia

said, interrupting his musings, "but you don't remember trying to murder Oz or steal Mariel's soul?"

The names pinged around his brain, eliciting a surge of dissatisfaction. "The name Oz is vaguely familiar," he said, trying to pinpoint more of that elusive, unsettling feeling.

"Ozroth the Ruthless," Calladia said. "Your protégé in soul bargaining."

His headache intensified, and Astaroth rubbed his temples. "Lucifer, this is awful."

"Do you remember hitting your head?"

Astaroth squeezed his eyes shut, racking his brain for the earliest memory after . . . whatever had happened to him. "I remember being on the ground and looking up at that Moloch bloke while he gave a speech about ending my miserable existence. Before that it's just darkness, except for some snippets from centuries ago."

The gap—nay, chasm—in his existence made him feel ill. How could he know he was a demon yet not remember his enemies? How could he remember giving candy to children on Halloween but not whatever had landed him in this situation?

Demons healed quickly though, so perhaps his memory was resurrecting itself one piece at a time, like a quilt being patched together.

It was concerning he'd only encountered enemies so far. He seemed to make a lot of them, but that could be due to sample size. "Do I have friends?" he blurted.

Calladia huffed. "If you do, I don't want to meet them."

The past twelve hours had apparently been upsetting for her, but was the situation any less upsetting for him? "Look," he said, feeling a surge of irritation, "I understand you have some grievance against me, but considering my lack of memory, aren't I the victim here?"

She tossed her head back and laughed. The sound was as bright and bold as the rest of her and drew admiring stares from a nearby group of iridescent-winged pixies. Astaroth scowled at them, and their gazes darted away.

"You think you're the victim," Calladia said, turning to face him. They were blocking the path, but other late-night pedestrians wisely gave them a wide berth. "You, who tried to take Mariel's soul. Who threatened Oz with a sword. Who tried to ruin their lives to win a bet."

Astaroth perked up. "I have a sword?" Amnesia would feel a lot more comfortable if he was armed.

Calladia threw her hands up. "That's what you care about?"

"What kind of sword?" He'd gone through a variety in centuries past—broadsword, rapier, saber, cutlass—and it was a relief to know some things hadn't changed.

"Hopeless. You are absolutely hopeless." Calladia started walking away.

Astaroth followed, pondering the likelihood she would tell him where to find said sword. He gave it approximately a zero percent chance, but might as well make an attempt. "Any idea where it is?"

"Up your ass," she shot back.

"How unsafe." Apparently she wouldn't be much help in locating it, but something else she'd said caught his attention. "Wait, what bet did I try to win? What were the terms?"

"How should I know?" Calladia increased her pace, striding down the pavement like she could power walk him into the dust. "I'm not your nurse, your secretary, or your emotional support animal. Once I drop you off at the hospital, that's it."

He grimaced, trying to match her aggressive pace. Besides the splitting pain in his head, his leg still throbbed, and his ribs weren't feeling great after receiving Moloch's boot several times. "The hospital?" he asked.

"That's where injured people go."

Panic abruptly swamped him, and the same mysterious woman's

voice echoed in his head. *Don't trust doctors. They might figure it out.* He still couldn't place the voice with a face or an identity, nor did he know what doctors were at risk of finding out, but he knew— he *knew*—that bad things would happen if he went to a hospital.

"Wait," he said. When Calladia kept striding ahead, he halted, bracing himself against a lamppost. "Stop!"

She turned on him with an annoyed look that seemed to be her default expression. "What?"

"I can't go to hospital." He pressed a hand to his chest, feeling the race of his heart.

"Why not?"

"I don't know."

Calladia rolled her eyes. "Let's just get this over with." She started walking again but stopped when she realized he wasn't following. "Are you serious?"

Astaroth's breaths were coming too fast. Anxiety buzzed beneath his skin and coiled around his lungs and stomach, squeezing hard. Hot pain stabbed his temple, and all at once, it was too much to handle. His knees buckled, and he sagged against the pole.

"Whoa," Calladia said, hurrying over. She lifted her hands as if to steady him, then balled them into fists and dropped them to her sides. "What's going on?"

"I don't know!" Astaroth shouted, losing the grip on his temper. "Is it not obvious that I have no bloody idea what's happening or where I am or where to go?"

For once, she looked uneasy rather than simply pissed off. "If you go to the hospital . . ."

Astaroth smacked his fist against his thigh, instantly regretting it when the pain echoed in his bones. "Will you listen to me for a second? Or would you rather start speechifying about how horrible I am again, instead?"

Calladia planted her hands on her hips, not backing down. "Look, I'm being nice to you—"

Astaroth laughed. "This is nice? I'd love to see what you consider mean." He should stop talking, but damn it, his head hurt like the dickens and his body wasn't much better, and it was infuriating and terrifying to be faced with a black hole in the place of his memories. "Other than a few nonsensical snippets from centuries ago, the only things I remember are getting kicked in the ribs and you lecturing me about what a horrible demon I am. And Halloween candy, for some bloody reason. And now I've remembered one other thing, and it's that I should never see a doctor, yet you are determined to drag me to some mortal hospital where Lucifer knows what will happen, just because you're so eager to be rid of me." He paused to take a deep breath, as if that might help him wrestle his emotions into submission. It didn't, and shame fermented in his gut at his lack of control. "Look," he said, digging his knuckles into his closed eyes, "just leave me here. Go home and forget about my horrible, evil presence. Soon enough, Moloch or someone else will find me, and you can rest easy knowing I'm no longer your problem."

Calladia's eyes had widened over the course of his diatribe. They were a lovely shade of chestnut brown, he noticed for no reason whatsoever. Nice eyes for a very not-nice woman. "That was quite a speech," she said.

Astaroth bared his teeth at her.

Her eyes flicked to his mouth. "Point taken. But I can't just leave you here to die."

"Why not?" Astaroth asked. "Surely it would be a relief, considering how much you hate me. Why did you even help me to begin with?"

"I didn't know it was you. I thought it was a stranger in trouble." She tightened her ponytail aggressively, and Astaroth briefly imagined yanking on her hair instead. Maybe wrapping it around his fist so he could force her to stay still and *listen* to him. "And once I realized it was you . . ." She sighed. "Look, I'm not a bad person. Fair to middling, maybe, but not bad. I wouldn't feel right leaving you alone and hurt with Moloch nearby."

"But you do feel right belittling an injured amnesiac? Your morality seems to have a sliding scale."

She shrugged. "I said fair to middling, not good."

Well, at least she was honest. "My head hurts and I just want to sleep," Astaroth said. "Can you direct me to a hotel?"

"Do you have money for a room?"

Right. Demons bartered, bargained, and traded favors, but money was the main currency of the human plane. Astaroth patted his pockets and pulled out a smartphone but nothing else. When he pressed a button, a passcode entry screen popped up, but he had no idea what that code might be. "Apparently not."

"Right." Calladia looked up at the moon, then checked a band around her wrist that held a digital display. Astaroth racked his useless brain. It wasn't just a watch, but a . . . curses, what were those things called? The ones that tracked heart rate and whatnot, because humans loved to take any activity and suck the joy out of it.

Calladia made a face. "It's really late." She bit her lip, looking between the wrist thing, him, and the now-deserted street. "This is a dumb idea," she muttered before squaring her shoulders and taking a deep breath. "You can stay in my spare room. For one night only."

Astaroth perked up. She was taking him home? That was an improvement on *You're an evil, despicable monster with no heart.* "Oh, lovely, thank—"

Calladia talked over him. "But there will be no funny business or mischief or acts of evil while under my roof. I'm going to weave so many wards, your testicles will be obliterated if you so much as sneeze wrong."

So much for an improvement. "That seems excessive."

"Yeah, well, sue me for being paranoid when letting a demon

who *just tried to steal my friend's soul* crash at my place." Calladia started walking away. "Hurry up."

Hostile or not, she hadn't tried to murder him yet, and maybe she'd have more answers to help fill in the missing pieces of his identity. "I would never pass up the opportunity to bask in more of your radiant company," he said, following her.

She raised a hand, showing the string that dangled from her fingertips. "Testicles. Exploded."

He winced. "I shall be on my least abominable behavior."

FOUR

THIS WAS DUMB.

No, not just dumb. This was the single worst idea anyone had ever had.

Calladia lingered at the door to her spare bedroom, watching Astaroth poke around. He investigated the bookshelf, picked up a few trinkets, then fingered the lacy curtains. He was an odd sight in the cheery room: gorgeously disheveled above the neck, alarmingly blood-spattered below. His hand kept twitching at his side, and Calladia wondered if he was instinctively reaching for his cane.

A cane topped with a crystal skull, which she'd learned contained a sword, of all things. It was outrageously unnecessary, but the more time she spent with the demon, the more it seemed to suit him.

He tugged open a drawer and started digging through her scarves, and Calladia had had enough. "Stop snooping," she ordered.

He adopted an innocent expression that didn't fool her for a moment. "You can't expect me to spend the night in a strange place without assessing the territory."

She rolled her eyes. "Do you want to assess my front lawn? Because I'm tempted to make you sleep outside."

He shivered. "No, this will do." He was holding a lumpy knitted blue-and-purple scarf—a gift from Themmie during the pixie's intense but short-lived obsession with knitting. As he let it trail through his fingers, a tingle raced down Calladia's spine. Those hands had leveled a sword at Oz's throat earlier that day. They'd probably dealt more death over the centuries than she could imagine. And now they were touching her things.

It was like having a dangerous exotic animal prowling loose in her house. The bedroom was bright and comfortable, decorated in yellows and whites, and Calladia had assembled the simple furniture herself after buying it from the werewolf-run furniture and home accessory store LYKEA. It was a casual space suited for laughter and relaxation, not Astaroth's elegant brand of menace. His white suit, blood-spattered as it was, was clearly expensive, and his black horns were sharp against his white-blond hair. Even his face was sharp, with high cheekbones, an elegant nose, and a chiseled jaw that would have been at home on a magazine cover. When he flicked his ice-blue eyes in her direction, Calladia resisted the urge to flinch.

"Are you going to stare at me all night?" he asked in that posh British accent.

"Are you going to keep being nosy?"

He shrugged one shoulder. "I don't know anything about you except that you hate me. It makes sense to learn more about my enemies."

Hecate, why was she doing this again?

Oh yeah, because she was incapable of stepping away from a fight or a person in need. Also? Tequila.

Her buzz had worn off, but even with common sense back in action, Calladia didn't like the idea of kicking Astaroth out of her house. Sure, she'd made Oz sleep on the lawn when she'd first met him and he'd been a real dick, but Oz hadn't been hurt. Astaroth's right eye was starting to swell, and although he'd clearly tried to mask it, by the time they reached her house, he'd been limping. Not to mention the blood that had dried in the hair near his left temple, which she suspected hid a nasty cut.

What had happened to make him lose his memory? Had *she* been the one to hurt him that badly? Sure, her spell had launched him over the mountains, but demons were hardy and healed quickly. Oz had staggered into town a few hours after she'd done the same to him, barely the worse for wear. It had been over twelve hours since she'd punched Astaroth, and he still looked like shit.

Astaroth shrugged out of his suit coat and hung it on the back of the desk chair. His vest went next, and before Calladia could process what was happening, he was unbuttoning his bloodstained white shirt.

"What are you doing?" she yelped, turning around and shielding her eyes.

"Getting ready for bed." He sounded infuriatingly unbothered. "You seemed inclined to watch."

"No, I just—" Shoot, why was she still standing there? "I wanted to, um, set some wards."

Cheeks burning, Calladia pulled the hank of thread from her pocket, focusing on the outcome she wanted. Distracted thoughts were one reason a spell could go awry, and she'd trained hard over the years to be able to focus through emotional distress—a handy talent with a mother like Cynthia Cunnington, mayor of Glimmer Falls and the embodiment of parental disapproval. Calladia closed her eyes, imagining a golden cage shimmering into life at the boundaries of the room, then started weaving.

"I can feel your magic," Astaroth said. "You're strong."

Calladia ignored him, contemplating what mix of words and knots would be best for this spell. The language of magic was difficult, complex, and irrational. It was an amalgamation of many languages, with chaotic elements all its own. Speaking the words wasn't necessary for small spells—especially not for a spellcaster as accomplished as Calladia—but for a working like this, it was essential to ground the spell in both language and action. The string dug into her fingers, winding in tightening loops as she added varieties of knots. One knot for safety, one for captivity, one for violence should her mystical boundary be breached.

"Are you going to allow me access to the loo?" Astaroth asked.

"Demons don't eat, drink, or use the bathroom as often as humans do. You'll be fine."

"If you want to risk it. They're your sheets."

Damn. Calladia unraveled a few knots, then made new loops to extend the parameter, adjusting her mental picture to allow a narrow corridor between the spare bedroom and the bathroom. Hopefully she wouldn't run into him in the middle of the night.

"*Astaroth din indelammsen,*" she whispered. With a final tug, the spell settled into place, and Calladia shivered with the pleasant sensation of magic sparkling through her body. It felt like a banked forge in her chest had roared to life, filling her with heat and light.

She opened her eyes and turned around. "All set—*what the fuck?*" The last words came out way too high-pitched, because Astaroth hadn't stopped with the shirt.

No, the demon was standing by the foot of the bed, hands on his lean hips, completely nude.

Calladia's eyes darted down against her will, then immediately up again. Whoa. That was . . .

Yeah. No. Ew.

She shook her head as if that could dislodge the image, then covered her eyes with her hands for good measure. Nevertheless, his frame was imprinted in her brain: pale skin stretched over lean muscle, and between his legs . . .

"Nope," she said, refusing to contemplate it.

"Something not to your liking?" he asked.

"All of it, actually."

"Are you sure? You haven't even seen all of *it* yet." His voice practically dripped with wickedness.

"And I never will," Calladia vowed. "Now go to sleep, you menace."

She didn't move until she heard the rustle of sheets. When she peeked out from between her fingers, she saw him sitting upright in bed, arms crossed behind his head as if to better show off his cut torso. Thankfully, his legs and . . . yeah . . . were covered by the sheets.

"My wards will cause serious damage if you go anywhere but this room and the bathroom," she said, trying to ignore the warmth in her cheeks. "So don't fuck with me."

"I wouldn't dream of it." His lips curved up on one side in a devilish smirk that implied otherwise. His burgeoning black eye should have diminished his appeal, but Calladia had always been a sucker for a good fight.

She turned off the light. "Don't get too comfortable. I'm getting rid of you tomorrow, one way or another."

His voice trailed after her. "If you say so . . ."

◆   ◆   ◆

CALLADIA BANGED ON THE DEMON'S DOOR THE NEXT MORNING. "Up and at 'em!" she called. When the only answer she got was a groan, she opened the door. The demon was a lump under the covers, so she marched to the window and opened the curtains and blinds to let in the morning light.

"Bloody hell." Astaroth's voice was fuzzed with sleep. His head poked up from the covers, and Calladia stifled a laugh. His hair stuck up chaotically around his horns, his eyes were half closed, and he was giving her a surly scowl that aimed for "intimidating monster" but landed on "pathetic morning grump." His black eye had purpled but didn't seem too swollen.

"Do you remember everything yet?" Calladia asked.

Astaroth groaned. "It's too early for speech."

She checked her smartwatch. "It's nine a.m. and I've already been to the gym." Thank Hecate for that hangover tonic. Her freshly washed hair was pulled up in a loose bun, and she was buzzing with an endorphin glow.

Calladia wasn't naturally a morning person, but she'd gotten in the habit of going to the gym early. Working out had been her drug of choice for years. She'd always enjoyed sports, and exercise was a helpful coping tool to survive life's stresses—not least of which was the pressure exerted by her mother. The older Calladia got and the more she'd struggled with her place in the world and an identity outside of "Cynthia Cunnington's daughter," the more she'd hit the gym. Calladia's mother wouldn't be caught dead sweating or performing any kind of manual labor, and it felt good to have a hobby separate from her mom's polished, fake world.

She'd only fallen off her routine during those years with Sam . . . but no, she refused to think about that now. Would rather never think of her ex again, if only brains could be trained like one of Mariel's plants to bloom only in appropriate directions.

"Come on," she said when Astaroth showed no signs of getting up. "I have stuff to do."

"Like what?" he groused, pushing himself to a seated position. The sheet slipped down, revealing carved muscles, and Calladia was instantly reminded he was nude. Her gaze darted to where the sheet bunched at his hips.

Calladia forced her attention upward. It didn't matter that

Astaroth was objectively attractive in a way that catered to Calladia's precise tastes, nor that he was currently naked in her spare room. He was an evil, horrible, manipulative demon, and she would be a bad person and a worse friend to lust after him. "I work as a personal trainer," she said, answering his question. "I have three clients this afternoon." Her mother despised Calladia's job, but Calladia loved it. Helping other people feel strong and confident was a reward beyond the paycheck.

Astaroth stretched, arms high over his head. His skin was smooth and alabaster pale. According to Mariel, demons had less body hair than humans, but the movement revealed tufts of reddish-gold hair in his armpits. Seeing that detail felt oddly intimate, like sharing a secret.

"It's not afternoon yet," Astaroth said, dropping his hands to his lap. "You could have let me sleep."

"Oh, stop being a whiny baby," Calladia said.

Astaroth's eyebrows shot up. "A whiny baby?" His voice was full of outrage. "I'm six centuries old. I've seen more mortal lives come and go than you can comprehend."

"Bully for you. You're still being a baby."

"Do you even know who I am?" Astaroth asked pissily.

It was Calladia's turn to raise her brows. "Do you?"

"I—" His mouth opened and closed a few times, and then Astaroth rubbed his temples, grimacing. He cursed under his breath, then swung his legs over the side of the bed and stood.

Calladia instantly averted her eyes. "You'd better wear that sheet like a toga. I refuse to sully my eyes with the sight of your dick."

"How you wound me." Astaroth's mutter was followed by the rustling of sheets. "Joyless harpy."

"No, just a joyless witch, but there's a harpy a few blocks down who'd be interested in meeting you. I'm sure she'd love the chance to devour some demon liver." Ocypete was actually a vegetarian who used her wings and claws to paint abstract art pieces, not disembowel her enemies, but Astaroth didn't need to know that.

Calladia risked a glance and was gratified to see the demon had wrapped the sheet around his waist. It didn't solve the issue of his pecs or a truly remarkable eight-pack, but at least she didn't have to worry about getting another eyeful of his equipment. "So," she said. "How's your head? Any memories come back?"

"It hurts," Astaroth said, rubbing his temple with the hand not clutching the sheet at his waist. "And no, not particularly."

"You know your age," Calladia pointed out.

He grimaced. "It's complicated. Some things I'm certain of, and I get flashes of images or words, but when I try to remember anything that's happened recently, it's just . . . blank."

"So there's really no change this morning?"

"None."

"Shoot." Calladia nibbled her lip, looking between Astaroth and the bright day outside. She couldn't deal with a demonic houseguest indefinitely. "Look, I know you don't like the idea of a hospital, but memory loss is a serious thing. You should at least get checked out."

"No." The refusal was instantaneous.

"What if they can help? What if every moment you wait, you risk the memories never coming back?"

"They'll come back," he said, but although his tone was confident, his darting eyes suggested he had doubts.

"What will you do if they don't?" Calladia pressed. "You can't stay here. Are you going to wander the streets indefinitely, waiting for Moloch to finish you off?"

Astaroth made a face. "He does seem like a touchy wanker."

"And you're vulnerable." She could tell Astaroth didn't like that, so she kept pushing. "You're injured and alone, without any information about your enemies. If you don't take steps to get treatment, then frankly, you'll deserve whatever happens to you."

"Lovely bedside demeanor you have," he said. "Do you offer inspirational speeches as well?"

"I prefer inspirational butt-kickings," Calladia said. "So I'm setting the rules. Either you go to the hospital or end up on the street, but you're not staying here a moment longer."

Seconds ticked past while Astaroth glared at her. Calladia folded her arms and glared right back. He wanted a standoff? He could have one.

As the silence stretched out, the scene struck Calladia as absurd. Here she was in her cheerful spare bedroom, sunlight spilling through the window, while a six-hundred-ish-year-old demon wearing a bedsheet glowered at her. He'd need to try way harder than that to intimidate her, but then again, she hadn't found him intimidating the previous day either.

Their first meeting was preserved so vividly in her mind, it was a marvel it hadn't imprinted itself just as deeply in his brain. Astaroth hadn't glared at her in the woods when Calladia had come to help Mariel. No, he'd sneered, as if she were no better than a bug beneath his boot. With his suit, cane, and that absurd fedora, he'd looked like a Hollywood version of an over-the-top villain. Swaggering and threatening, puffed up on his own importance.

Calladia shouldn't have found him physically attractive then. And she hadn't—not really—just a passing thought when she'd first clapped eyes on his cheekbones and lean, elegant frame, an objective observation soon subsumed by pure rage. She definitely shouldn't find him attractive now.

He was still glowering. Calladia turned her lips down in an exaggerated frown and cocked her head, mocking him.

"Blast," he muttered.

Calladia kept waiting. He might have the patience of an immortal, but she had the kind of patience that came from pure spite. No way he was winning this standoff.

Astaroth threw up his free hand. "Fine," he spat. "I'll go to hospital."

Triumph swelled in Calladia's chest. "That's what I thought," she said. "Now get dressed."

FIVE

I LOOK AWFUL," ASTAROTH GROUSED, RUNNING HIS FINGERS through sleep-tangled, blood-caked hair as he peered at himself in the mirror.

Calladia was leaning against the doorframe, watching him "primp," as she'd called it. "Yep," she said cheerfully.

"You don't have to agree." Astaroth scratched his neck, feeling disgruntled and uncomfortable. He eyed the shower. "I don't suppose your hospitality extends to a shower?"

Calladia sniffed in his direction, then wrinkled her nose. "You do smell rank."

"Lovely," he muttered. He turned to the shower and dropped the sheet.

"Do you have any modesty?" Calladia asked.

"No." Astaroth bent to turn the shower knob, biting the inside of his cheek when Calladia gasped. If she didn't like it, she could stop looking.

Once the water was steaming hot, he stepped in and slid the

door closed. Through the clouded glass, he saw Calladia's silhouette still in the doorway.

"Supervising?" he asked.

"I don't trust you not to use my good conditioner."

He studied the options on display. "None of these look good." Was that a three-in-one conditioner, shampoo, and body wash? The horror!

"I could make you wash with steel wool."

The only options were cheap-looking shampoo and conditioner or the dreaded three-in-one. How did she manage to have such soft-looking hair when she was abusing it with subpar products? He had too much self-esteem to go with the worst option, so he grabbed the basic bottles of shampoo and conditioner.

Five minutes later, he felt much better. The water at the bottom of the tub was running clear again after the blood had washed away, and he smelled like kiwi fruit.

"I'm coming out," he warned Calladia.

A yellow towel was tossed over the top of the shower. He caught it and dried off before wrapping it around his waist.

When he stepped out, Calladia handed him his clothes, folded as well as they could be with blood stiffening the fabric. He grimaced at the thought of getting dressed in them again.

Calladia sniffed the air a few times, and her jaw dropped in outrage. "You used my good conditioner!"

"No, I used your slightly-less-objectionable conditioner."

"Ugh." Calladia shook her head. "Hurry up. I'll be waiting in the hall."

After swiping her deodorant over his pits, Astaroth dressed quickly. The fabric was scratchy against his damp skin and smelled of body odor and dried blood. He slicked his hair back, studying his reflection.

His black eye wasn't puffy, thankfully, and he told himself the bruising looked rakish. The scabbed-over cut behind his left temple was impressively ugly. When he prodded the skin near it, pain clanged around his skull. He winced.

It wasn't his best look, but this wasn't his best moment. He contemplated Calladia's toothbrush, then decided she would definitely draw the line at him borrowing that, so he put toothpaste on his finger and ran it over his teeth.

"Ready?" Calladia asked.

Astaroth spit, then rinsed out his mouth. "As I'll ever be," he replied.

That unknown voice was still cautioning him against seeing a doctor—*they can't know what you are, or you'll never be able to claim your legacy*—but Astaroth didn't have any other ideas, and he needed his memories back as soon as possible to figure out what was happening.

Calladia was tapping her toe in the hallway. She seemed full of restless energy in general, as if she was most comfortable in motion. She gave him a cursory look, then turned and jogged down the stairs.

He followed, eyeing the decor curiously. Even in the dark, there'd been no missing the daffodil-yellow exterior of her narrow, two-story house, and inside was just as bright. The walls were painted cream with yellow accents, and woven blue rugs dotted the floorboards. The overall aesthetic reminded him of a summer sky.

Framed photographs lined the staircase. Roughly half of them depicted Calladia in workout clothes at the gym, smiling next to people she had presumably trained, while the others showed her eating, laughing, or taking selfies with other young-looking humans. There was no sign of a partner or child, nor were there any photos of what might be her parents.

The front parlor was cozy and sunlit, with white lace curtains and simple furniture. A plush blue couch topped with mismatched pillows faced a wall-mounted television, and a small barrel cactus sat in a terra-cotta pot on the windowsill.

It was a cheerful setting for someone who had threatened to obliterate his testicles, but humans were odd like that. One thing on the outside, another within. They might not be able to alter their physical forms the way werewolves or shape-shifters could, but they were shifters of a different sort, adapting themselves to new environments with ease.

In the light of day, Calladia was even prettier than he remembered. The sunlight caught in her butter-blond hair and made her tanned skin glow, and her lips were pink and lush. She hadn't smiled at him yet, but he'd caught glimpses of straight white teeth, and he imagined her grin would light up a room.

She grabbed a red windbreaker off the chair and shrugged it on. Beneath it, she wore tight black exercise leggings, a blue T-shirt with a cartoon penguin on it, and black trainers with blue laces.

He looked more closely at her shirt. "Is that penguin holding a knife?"

"Yes," Calladia said. "Stop staring at my tits."

"Stop putting your tits behind interesting pictures." Now that she mentioned it, they did deserve some attention. Her breasts were on the small side, especially considering the constraints of what was clearly a sports bra, but that didn't signify. Big tits, little tits, no tits—Astaroth found all sorts of bodies attractive. Each person was unique, with their own topography to explore.

He contemplated what her breasts would feel like in his hands. Were her nipples sensitive?

Calladia grabbed a coaster from the side table next to the couch and flung it like a throwing star. The cardboard square bounced off Astaroth's forehead. "No ogling the enemy," she said.

There was her ferocious scowl again. Some people required armor to look intimidating, but Calladia managed it just fine in workout gear. He imagined her in armor and stifled an appreciative shiver.

There were few things as appealing as a woman who was comfortable in her power. In times past, with a sword in her hands, she could have ruled empires.

To avoid the temptation of further ogling, he crossed to the front window and looked out. Her lawn was brown for the cold season, and the apple and pear trees at the edge of the yard were bare, but he could imagine it in the heat of summer. Verdant grass, buzzing insects, and Calladia's yellow house rising from all that green like a flower.

An orange shimmer in the air above her driveway caught his eye. It expanded into a flaming oval, framing the demon who stepped out of thin air.

Thoughts of summer died as a chill raced down Astaroth's spine. "Moloch," he said. "He's here."

"What?" Calladia hurried over to stand next to him. "How did he find us?"

"He must be tracking me." But how?

Moloch strode toward the house. He wore brown leather pants and a matching jerkin over a long-sleeved blue shirt, and a sword was strapped to his back. "Fancy seeing you here," Moloch shouted, audible through the window glass.

Astaroth swore and jammed a hand into his hair between his horns. "We need to barricade."

Calladia was already tying knots in a string she'd fished out of a pocket. "Lock the door," she ordered.

He obeyed, dragging a small bookshelf in front of it for good measure. Not that it would do much good. Moloch could just smash through the glass of Calladia's wide front windows.

An eerie grin stretched Moloch's mouth. "You can't escape, Astaroth. Whatever leverage you think you have over me means nothing."

Adrenaline rocketed through Astaroth's veins. His head buzzed with conflicting thoughts and impulses. *Leverage . . .* Why was that word pinging around his brain? The world slid sideways, then righted itself as Astaroth braced himself against the wall.

Leverage, leverage . . .

He knew something about Moloch, something that would destroy the demon surer than any weapon. The certainty settled in his chest, merging with the storm of rage and fear. "I'm going to take you down, Moloch," Astaroth shouted, following that intuition. "I have everything I need." Somewhere. If he could only remember what that leverage was.

Moloch's grin faltered. Then he recovered his oily smile. "Not if you're dead."

The demon held his hands palm-up before him.

Dread seized Astaroth by the breastbone. "Run!" he shouted, lunging for Calladia.

Calladia stopped in the middle of tying knots, her brown eyes wide with alarm. "What?"

Two fireballs appeared in Moloch's upraised hands.

Moving on instinct, Astaroth grabbed Calladia by the waist and threw her over his shoulder. He sprinted toward the connected kitchen, where he'd spied a back door leading to the yard.

Calladia hammered his back, screeching protests, but there was no time to argue. Those fireballs were the trademark of the warrior class of demons, and they would do a tremendous amount of damage.

Astaroth reached the door and yanked it open. Her backyard was small, with a low fence separating it from what looked like a public park. "Cover your ears," Astaroth ordered as he ran for the fence. He hurdled over it, wincing when the landing jarred his sore leg. There was no time to waste . . .

The air erupted behind them.

SIX

A ROARING NOISE FILLED CALLADIA'S EARS, FOLLOWED BY A cacophony of explosions and shattering glass. A wave of hot air smacked into them like a train, sending them flying. She screamed as she tumbled across the grass, shielding her head with her arms. A bush stopped her forward momentum, and she lay dazed in a cradle of broken branches.

When she looked back at her house, she cried out in horror. A plume of fire reached toward the sky, and black smoke roiled around it like a many-limbed monster. Ashes rained down, and the wind blew an acrid scent into her nostrils.

Astaroth staggered into view through the smoke, looking as battered as Calladia felt. "Come on," he said. "We've got to hide before he realizes we're alive."

Calladia couldn't tear her eyes away from the destruction. "My house." Her beautiful yellow house. Grief tightened her throat and burned her eyes.

Astaroth grabbed her hand and tugged her to her feet. "Later," he said. "We need to get away *right now*."

Calladia was in too much shock to argue. She let him drag her down a slope toward a copse of trees. Astaroth was muttering as he patted himself all over with his free hand. When his fingers quested behind his ear, he snarled and tugged at something.

"Bespelled tracking device," he said, showing it to Calladia. It was a small gold disk with miniature spikes covering one side. "Hunters use it on the demon plane; he must have applied it when we first fought."

She couldn't make sense of the words. *My house, my house, my house.* The mantra beat like a hammer, sending nails of grief deep inside her brain. Her eyes stung, but she couldn't seem to blink.

Astaroth released Calladia once they were under the shadow of the trees. "Can you cast a spell to put the tracker back in the wreckage?" he asked. When she didn't reply, he gripped her shoulders. "Calladia," he said urgently. "The tracker. We've got to get rid of it."

Right. She needed to send the bug back to the *wreckage*, aka all that remained of Calladia's home. She'd dropped her string when Astaroth picked her up, so she yanked out a strand of hair. A few knots and a whispered spell later, and the tiny golden disk was flying toward the burning house.

The magic sapped the rest of her energy. Calladia sank to her knees, staring at the flames. She'd only moved in a few months ago. A lot of her stuff was still in storage, thankfully, but still . . . That house was her pride and joy, the evidence that she'd made a life for herself separate from her family. No need to ask her mother for a loan, no obligation to fulfill any expectations but her own. She'd renovated the neglected building carefully, then painted it yellow like a daffodil, her favorite flower, imagining she was helping it bloom.

In that house, Calladia had hoped to bloom, too.

Now it was gone . . . and she had demons to blame for it.

She turned on Astaroth, fury burning hot as the flames. "This is your fault!"

Astaroth's eyebrows soared. "How is it mine? I wasn't the one throwing fireballs."

"You brought him here," she said, poking him in the chest. "My house is gone because of *you*."

"How was I supposed to know he'd put a tracker on me?" Astaroth asked. "You're welcome for saving your life, by the way."

Sanctimonious, despicable demon. "Ugh!" She threw up her hands. "I should have left you in that alley."

"Well, you didn't," Astaroth said. "And now we're here, and it isn't either of our faults, but we need to get away. Moloch will probably start sifting through the ashes looking for bones."

Calladia rubbed her cheek, then winced as she encountered a scratch from the bush. Her hand came away dotted with soot and blood. "Where will we even go?" she asked, voice trembling.

"How should I bloody know?" Astaroth asked, shoving his hand into his soot-streaked hair. He looked rather wild-eyed. "I'm just saying that wasting time arguing is a terrible idea."

Calladia stiffened. "Excuse me for wasting your precious time," she spat. "It's not like my house just got blown up."

"You can shout at me to your heart's content," Astaroth said. "*Later*. In a location farther away from the demon who just tried to murder us."

Calladia opened her mouth, then closed it again. He had a point. "Fine," she said through gritted teeth. "There's a bridge in the park we can hide under until he's gone, and then I'll get my truck. Assuming I still have a truck."

Her truck—a battered red pickup she'd named Clifford the Little Red Truck—had been parked on the street, since she hadn't wanted to disrupt a chalk drawing the neighbor children had made in her driveway. Maybe that distance had been enough to spare it.

Calladia led Astaroth toward the stream that cut through the park. Sirens wailed in the distance, and the people they passed were so fixated on the fire, they thankfully didn't pay attention to two soot-covered strangers limping by.

The bridge was a low wooden arch over the stream, just tall enough to sit beneath. Calladia sat on the bank, wrapping her arms around her knees, and Astaroth took up position opposite. Thankfully, he stayed quiet, giving Calladia space to think.

What was she going to do? She was now without a house or most of her everyday possessions. Things could be replaced, and the furnishings had been relatively cheap, but that didn't help the ache of loss in her chest.

Be practical, she told herself. *Focus on logistics.*

Calladia wasn't without resources. Her friends had accused her of being a "paranoid prepper" due to the emergency supplies stashed in her truck. She'd stocked up on gear in case a camping trip went wrong, and assuming Clifford had survived the blast, there should be enough in there to last at least a week: a go-bag, camping gear, blankets, emergency rations, spare clothes, and more.

How did the demon figure into her plans though?

Across the stream, Astaroth looked miserable. His knees were drawn up in a mirror of her position, and he was shivering. Probably cold, since demons had higher body temperatures than humans.

She should leave him behind. Let him sort through his own mess and fight his own enemy.

He shivered again, then touched his face gingerly, exploring the bruised skin around his eye. Soot darkened his blond hair, and a gnarly, scabbed-over gash was visible on the left side of his head. The amnesia-causing wound, presumably.

Astaroth may have been the reason she'd nearly died, but he'd also saved her life. Calladia hadn't known what the fire in Moloch's hands meant. If she'd stayed in her living room a few seconds longer, she wouldn't be here right now.

Even if she abandoned Astaroth, would that be enough to keep her safe? Or would Moloch see her as Astaroth's ally and try to kill her anyway?

Calladia frowned, remembering something Astaroth had shouted during the confrontation. *I'm going to take you down, Moloch. I have everything I need.*

"What did you mean about taking Moloch down?" Calladia asked. "You said you have everything you need."

Astaroth looked up at her. "Did I?" he asked, sounding distracted. His eyes were reddened from the smoke.

"You did," she confirmed. "Did you remember something about him?"

Astaroth's brow furrowed. Calladia waited, letting him sift through his memories.

"I don't know what I meant by that," Astaroth finally said. "I just looked at him and knew with utter certainty that I could hurt him."

"So how do we do it?" she asked. "How do we take Moloch out?"

Astaroth looked surprised. "We?"

Calladia winced. Damn her altruistic impulses. She was way too deep into this mess to back out. "Well, now I'm on his radar, too. And since I don't want to die . . ."

"We've got to collaborate."

Astaroth sounded so unenthused that Calladia bristled. "You don't have to sound so disappointed. At least this way there will be one functional brain between the two of us."

Astaroth made an annoyed sound. He started to respond, then winced and rubbed his forehead. "Lucifer, this headache. Zero stars for amnesia."

"There are painkillers in my truck," Calladia said. "If it survived."

"It's fine. Demons heal quickly."

Calladia wasn't so sure. He was still sporting a shiner, and from what she knew from other hyper-regenerative species, that should have disappeared by now. Then again, as Mariel had learned with Oz, demons were very different from how they were portrayed in most literature. Maybe fast healing was conditional, or maybe the knock on the head had disrupted his abilities.

Well, if he didn't want painkillers, that was his issue. Calladia rested her chin on her knees and planned her next steps.

First: check on Clifford the Little Red Truck. If Clifford was intact, they could drive somewhere and get help. Mariel and Themmie would gladly help with anything she needed, but she didn't want to admit she'd helped Astaroth, so she'd need to come up with a version of the truth that wouldn't make them ask too many questions.

Her friends would undoubtedly offer her a place to stay, but Astaroth wasn't the only reason to avoid that. If Moloch was targeting Calladia, she'd be damned before she put her friends at risk. But if Clifford had survived, so had her tent and emergency supplies, which meant she could camp out in the woods while figuring out next steps.

Emergency supplies wouldn't help her fight Moloch though. She needed to be ready for future battles, which meant finding thread and possibly potion ingredients, since her yarn and herbs had gone up in smoke. She should also probably review her Combat Magic 101 textbook.

Calladia's stomach dropped as she realized there was only one option: she had to go to her parents' house to pick up the boxes she'd been storing in their basement since college. She'd meant to clear out her belongings a long time ago, but since she avoided seeing her mom as much as possible, she'd never finished the job.

Cynthia Cunnington was a terror on the best of days, but if Calladia had to choose between facing her mother or Moloch, she'd pick her mother. Weaponized disappointment was easier to survive than a fireball.

They stayed under the bridge until the sirens cut off and the flames had been extinguished. Calladia passed the time by texting various people: her boss and clients for the next few days to let them know she couldn't make their training sessions, her friends to let them know her house had blown up—*it's a long story*—but she was okay and would stop by Mariel's house that evening to update them. Thank goodness she'd still had her phone, wallet, and keys in her windbreaker pocket after hitting the gym, or this would have been even more of a disaster.

She kept an eye out for Moloch, but he never showed up, which hopefully meant Astaroth was right and the demon thought they were dead.

By midafternoon, Astaroth's teeth were chattering. Deciding they'd waited long enough, Calladia stood, groaning when her knees popped. "Come on," she said. "Let's see if my truck survived."

They took the long route around the park before circling toward Calladia's house. By the time they arrived, the police and firefighters were long gone, and Moloch was thankfully nowhere to be seen.

Calladia nearly started crying with relief when she saw her truck parked at the curb, coated in ash but otherwise intact. "Clifford!" she cried out. She unlocked the truck with trembling fingers, relieved to see it was still full of her possessions. She climbed in, then traced her hands over the dusty dashboard and cracked bench seat. "Hi, baby," she whispered.

She couldn't stand to look at the blackened ruins of her house. She had insurance for magical mishaps and extraplanar acts of malice—any property owner in a town this steeped in magic did—but it was hard to imagine rebuilding. That little yellow house had been an extension of herself, a piece of her heart plunked down on a plot of land.

Her entire life, she'd struggled to break free from her perfectionist mother's expectations. Too loud, too messy, too angry, too coarse, too unambitious . . . Calladia had been *too much* of all the things her mother despised and *not enough* of everything else. Cynthia Cunnington had wanted a politician for a daughter, polished and polite. Instead, she'd gotten the town's most incorrigible tomboy, and Calladia's rebellion against expectations had only worsened over time. Now relations between them were at an all-time low after Calladia had publicly opposed her mom's plans to build a luxury spa in the woods—a plan Mariel had just foiled.

In the midst of that never-ending family drama, finally being able to buy a house with her own money had been a bright spot. A way to set herself apart and start building something of her own, untouched by her mother's judgments.

Now her home and all its promise had been turned into smoking rubble, and Calladia needed to face the person she most dreaded seeing.

Delaying wouldn't help, so Calladia cracked her neck and started the ignition. "Let's go," she told Astaroth, who had settled onto the bench seat beside her. "Our revenge plot starts now."

SEVEN

HOURS AFTER THE ATTACK, ASTAROTH WAS STILL FURIOUS. It was an ugly emotion, hot and stinging. It coiled around his spinal cord, balled in his gut, seized his lungs in a stranglehold. He clenched his fists in his lap, staring at his whitened knuckles. How *dare* that Moloch bastard try to kill Calladia? Whatever Astaroth's history with Moloch, he was sure he'd earned the demon's hatred on his own merit. All Calladia had done was try to help someone she hadn't needed—or wanted—to.

Calladia drummed her fingers over the steering wheel. Her own temper was evident in her set jaw and the aggressiveness with which she accelerated after each traffic light. The fact she was still moving, still planning, was awe-inspiring. Where someone else might have curled up in a ball and given up, Calladia had decided to fight.

Astaroth rubbed the spot behind his ear where the gold tracker had been. The skin still stung where its tiny barbs had dug in, and he despised the reminder that he'd been hunted down like an animal.

A thread of guilt mixed with the anger. Despite what he'd said earlier, Calladia had every right to be furious with him. He should have been warier. Even with his amnesia, he'd known about demonic fireballs and trackers—he just hadn't put the pieces together until too late.

He closed his eyes and breathed, trying to center his thoughts. The conflict with Moloch had shaken a few things loose, but trying to bring his memories into focus was frustrating. It felt like piecing together a puzzle, except the pieces were blurry and slid sideways whenever he reached for them.

Still, there was apparently a key to defeating Moloch buried somewhere in his memory. He just had to dig it out.

"I'm going to ask Oz for advice," Calladia abruptly said. When Astaroth looked up in surprise, she clarified. "About Moloch, not you."

"Why not about me?" He didn't remember Ozroth—and the fact he couldn't remember his own protégé made him feel ill—but Ozroth undoubtedly remembered him.

Calladia turned a corner so aggressively that a wheel jumped onto the sidewalk and they nearly took out a rubbish bin. Astaroth braced himself against the door. "Oh, I don't know," Calladia said waspishly. "Maybe because you tried to murder him recently? And steal his girlfriend's soul? I hear you weren't a particularly affectionate mentor either."

She had every right to be mad at him, but not for that last part. Even if he didn't recall his time as a mentor, he knew how things worked. "Mentors aren't supposed to be affectionate," he said. "They're teachers, not therapists." Their duty was to craft the strongest bargainers—or warriors or healers—by whatever means necessary in order to ensure the future of the demon plane.

"Whatever," Calladia said. "I'm still not telling him we're hanging out."

"Is that what we're doing?" He wasn't sure fleeing from a

murderous demon with the witch who hated him qualified as a "hangout."

Calladia sighed and pinched the bridge of her nose. "Just . . . be quiet for a bit, okay?"

Astaroth obliged, though he didn't like it. He picked at his blood-and-dirt-smudged clothes and brooded as he stared out the window.

Glimmer Falls appeared to be a charming, colorful town full of eateries, boutiques, and lively public spaces. Despite the nip in the air, people of all species were everywhere, walking, talking, embracing, casting spells, or eating on restaurant patios. It was a beautiful place that Astaroth had inadvertently brought a great deal of ugliness to.

It was aggravating being so useless. He had a strong sense of self despite the amnesia, and perpetual victimhood wasn't a look he enjoyed. He ought to have dueled with Moloch, skewered the bastard with his own sword, then charmed Calladia with some brilliant witticism. Instead, he'd retreated, and he still couldn't come up with a single memory about the demon or how to defeat him.

"Maybe I'll find *his* house," Astaroth muttered. "Blow it up, see how he likes it."

A soft noise caught his attention, and he looked over in time to see Calladia discreetly wipe her eye. The sound repeated, and to Astaroth's horror, he realized it was a sniffle.

"Are you crying?" he demanded.

"No," came the aggressive, if muffled, response. Then, "Shut up and mind your own business."

He tried, but it was difficult. The sound of her soft weeping sent him into an agitated state. He needed to move around, fight something, kill something, anything to make the tears stop. "What would make you stop crying?" he blurted out when he couldn't take it anymore.

"Just leave it, all right?" She wiped her nose, steering one-handed. "I'm sad about my house."

"That bastard shouldn't get to make you cry. He should be wearing his own entrails."

Calladia gave a watery chuckle. "Agreed." She wiped her eyes and nose again. "Why do you care if I cry anyway?"

Astaroth wasn't sure how to answer. "It makes me uncomfortable," he finally said.

"And everything's about you, right?" The sharp edge had returned to her voice, but at least the anger seemed to have stalled the tears.

Pissing her off further might prevent future crying, but it also might tempt her to explode his testicles. "Not necessarily," Astaroth said. "It's just . . . upsetting, that's all. That Moloch can hurt you like that."

Calladia pulled a crumpled tissue out of her pocket and blew her nose. "I'll recover. And when I do, he's going to regret ever crossing me."

Astaroth's lips quirked at the bloodthirsty promise. "Now that, I believe."

With the crying over, he was able to relax again—as much as he could with Calladia weaving in and out of traffic. The witch approached driving as combatively as everything else she did.

"Are we going to see Ozroth?" he asked, a bit nervous at the prospect.

"I have to pick a few things up first."

Something in her tone caught his attention. He studied her as they stopped at a red light. Her face was tight with stress, and her fingers were still drumming on the steering wheel. Her tapping foot joined the percussion, and since the ancient truck's engine rattled while at rest, the noise swelled into an annoying symphony. He was tempted to ask if there was a tambourine for him to bang when he caught the look in her eyes.

"What's wrong?" he asked, whipping his head around to study their surroundings. "Is it Moloch?" All he saw were innocuous-looking vehicles, a gaggle of cheerful pedestrians, and a street performer juggling flaming bowling pins.

"Is what Moloch?" Calladia asked, obviously confused.

"You look afraid." He'd only known her a short time, but he didn't like seeing that haunted expression on her face.

"I'm not afraid," she rebutted instantly. "And no, it isn't about Moloch." The light turned green, and she slammed on the accelerator, nearly taking out a centaur on an enormous modified moped who'd taken a wide right turn into her lane.

The centaur veered away, then flicked Calladia off. "Watch it," the centaur shouted.

"You watch it!" she shrieked, showing him her middle finger in return.

Astaroth side-eyed the witch, then decided not to push further.

Thankfully, they soon entered a residential neighborhood with fewer drivers for Calladia to antagonize. The road climbed up a substantial hill, and the houses grew more extravagant as they went. Columned porticos replaced simple front porches, and the buildings glowed from within as lamplight bounced off gold, silver, and crystal. Most houses had elaborate Halloween displays out front.

"Where are we going?" Astaroth asked.

"My parents' place is up ahead." The words were brusque and accompanied by a squeeze of the steering wheel. "I need to stock up on supplies."

Astaroth tried to reconcile this posh neighborhood with the foul-mouthed harpy beside him. "You grew up here?"

"Unfortunately, yes." She pointed ahead and to the left. "In the gray house at the top of the hill."

He was too distracted by the house opposite it, which was an absurd amalgamation of architectural styles from neoclassical to

Gothic to Tudor. A purple flag snapped in the wind atop a turret. "What is that monstrosity?" he asked.

"The Spark family home," Calladia said. "Subtlety isn't their thing."

He shuddered. "I respect a bold aesthetic, but it ought to at least be tasteful."

"That's not a Spark thing either. Mariel aside." Calladia pulled into the driveway before her parents' house and parked. "I'll try to be in and out quickly, but my mother is . . . yeah." She pointed at Astaroth. "Stay here and don't let anyone see you. Especially not my mother." Her voice was firm, but her eyes were still haunted.

Astaroth nodded, though he was rabidly curious. She could deny it all she liked, but she was looking at that house with dread.

Astaroth's fingers twitched, longing for the hilt of a sword.

Ludicrous. Calladia didn't need him to defend her against her own mother. And even if she did, a violent gutting probably wouldn't be her defense of choice.

"Right," Calladia said with a nod, as if replying to her own internal debate. "Rip the Band-Aid off." She got out of the truck, brushed off her clothes, and shook out her hair, sending residual ash flakes swirling. Then she walked toward the house, looking like a martyr marching toward her doom.

The house was three stories, constructed of gray stone that sparkled in the waning afternoon light. The lawn was neatly manicured, and even the curtains hung in perfectly symmetrical arcs, as if nothing dared step out of place. Astaroth hunkered down in the seat, watching over the dashboard as Calladia rang the doorbell. The door opened, and Calladia disappeared inside.

Well, this wouldn't do.

When faced with a mystery, Astaroth couldn't resist the urge to seek answers, and this was quite a mystery. Why was Calladia afraid to speak with her own mother?

Through a window on the ground floor, he saw two female

shapes come into view, silhouetted by light from a crystal chandelier. The window was cracked open.

If it was that convenient, he was practically obligated to eavesdrop.

Astaroth slipped out of the truck. This was just a stratagem, he told himself as he hurried across the lawn, hunkering low. *Know thy enemy* and all that. If he knew what truly rattled Calladia, he could wield that weakness against her if need be.

This was definitely *not* a ridiculous urge to play the hero if Calladia needed saving.

He positioned himself in the bushes below the window, straining his ears for female voices within. A strategy, yes. Some good, old-fashioned demon plotting.

And if his fingers still itched to hack apart whatever had upset his unpredictable, cantankerous enemy/savior? Chalk that up to the brain damage.

EIGHT

WHAT HAPPENED WHEN AMBITIOUS LITTLE GIRLS WERE taught to contort themselves into whatever shape society deemed proper, feelings and individual preferences be damned?

Mayor Cynthia Cunnington happened.

Calladia squeezed her hands in her lap as she sat opposite her mother in the living room, trying not to fidget. Her father wasn't there, of course, off on his never-ending business trip. The high-backed chair was stiff and uncomfortable, despite being covered in beautiful blue brocade. That summed up her childhood home in a nutshell—expensive, tasteful, and painful as hell.

Cynthia didn't look uncomfortable in the slightest. As Mariel would say, cacti had evolved to thrive in harsh environments. Calladia's mother perched at the edge of her chair, knees pressed together and feet tucked to the side. Her sheath dress was made of gray-blue satin, smooth as a glassy lake. She was sixty but hardly looked it, considering the mix of magical and nonmagical procedures she'd undergone to maintain the sharp line of her jaw and that stiff expanse of forehead. Her blond hair was rolled into a chignon, her lips were painted pink, and her blue eyes skewered Calladia like daggers.

"What did you say happened to your house?" Cynthia asked in a voice like ice. She'd never liked Calladia's house—too small, too bright, not at all appropriate for the Cunnington family heir.

"A demon blew it up." Calladia wasn't going to mince words; that would only necessitate staying longer.

A long, slow blink while Cynthia processed this. "You seem unharmed."

"Are you inquiring or informing me? Yes, I'm mostly fine, thank you so much for your concern." Calladia didn't bother to strip the sarcasm from her tone. She knew better than to expect motherly fretting, but the tepid response still stung, and the only defense was to sting right back.

"Watch your tone." Cynthia touched the strand of pearls that perpetually adorned her neck. Not a threat, precisely, but a reminder of where the power in this room resided. Calladia wove spells with thread, but her mother's necklaces were her own talismans, and the spinning and twisting of beads could portend a nasty spell.

Ambition could twist easily into ruthlessness, and if her mother had ever struggled to fit the Cunnington family mold the way Calladia did, there was no sign of it now. Cunningtons had always been socialites and politicians, as judgmental as they were influential.

"My tone is fine," Calladia said. "Especially considering I'm nearly thirty years old and you no longer supervise my every action."

She despised the defensive edge to her words. No matter how much time passed, she still felt like a rebellious teenager, and with the stress of the day wearing at her, Calladia was slipping into old patterns.

Hecate, this house. It scratched at her like one of the poofy dresses she'd been forced to wear growing up. It was straight out of a magazine spread, all silk and brocade, silver and crystal, gray and blue and cream. The Spark family home across the street had also been oppressive for Mariel growing up, but at least that hodgepodge monstrosity had character. The Cunnington home felt like a frozen lake.

Calladia thought of sunshine yellow walls and golden wood, and the loss of her home stabbed her in the gut again.

"How did you antagonize this demon into exploding your house?" Cynthia asked.

"It wasn't my fault," Calladia protested. "He thought I was sheltering a rival demon. No idea where he got that from."

Telling the truth was out of the question. There was no way Cynthia would approve of harboring a demon, especially since a different demon—Oz—had accidentally nearly electrocuted her at the last town hall.

"If he heard that rumor, others may have as well. Is anyone else aware of the situation?" Cynthia grabbed her smartphone and started typing, no doubt some message to her beleaguered assistant, who was tasked with everything from procuring exotic potion ingredients to crafting social media responses to emergent crises. Crises such as family members pissing off demons, apparently.

"I mean, probably," Calladia said. "Considering all the smoke and fire." As explosions went, it hadn't been subtle.

"No, I mean, does anyone know it was an attack, not an accident?" Cynthia's thumbs stilled on her phone, and she looked up. If Calladia's announcement had temporarily stunned her, she was back in action, the crafty expression on her face indicating an upcoming bout of scheming. "Then again, that could be a compelling campaign trail narrative. An underhanded attack against my daughter, no doubt funded by a rival candidate—"

Calladia shot to her feet, outraged. "Do not twist the destruction of my house into propaganda. You aren't even up for reelection for two years."

"It's never too early to start planning." Cynthia typed more, then set the phone aside. She clasped her hands in her lap and widened her blue eyes in a sympathetic expression that made Calladia's teeth itch. That look was normally turned on unwitting constituents. "I understand this must have been upsetting, Calladia, but every setback carries an opportunity if you can control the message."

Calladia focused on regulating her breathing. Her mother sounded so earnest, like she was imparting essential wisdom to a beloved daughter. It was an act she'd gotten eerily good at since deciding to run for public office, and Calladia hated the mask even more than she hated her mother's overt disapproval. "I don't want to control a message," Calladia said. "I want to get some supplies from the basement and leave."

"Leave and go where?" Cynthia looked confused. "The guest room is available."

The guest room had once been Calladia's bedroom, not that there was any evidence of it now. The soccer posters and athletic trophies had vanished while she'd been away for her first semester at college, and the daisy-patterned bedspread had been replaced with a plain cream comforter. The carpet that had borne witness to a young witch's mishaps—burn marks, caked-on wax, spices ground into the fibers—had been ripped out and replaced with hardwood.

Calladia hadn't stayed in the guest room since college. The sanitized version of her childhood bedroom only reminded her that her mother would sanitize *her* if she could.

"Thank you, but no," Calladia said. "I just need some of my things from storage."

Cynthia sighed and rose to her feet, smoothing her already smooth skirt. "I don't understand why you insist on being spiteful. After all I've done—"

"What have you done?" Calladia demanded, the thin thread of her restraint snapping. "Other than constantly shame me for not turning out exactly like you."

"I don't need you to be exactly like me," Cynthia said. The two women were facing off now, shoulders set in the same confrontational angle. They'd always looked alike, eye color aside, with tempers to match. "But I do expect some amount of proper comportment. After all the etiquette lessons, the private schools, your father and I sparing no expense to give you a foundation for a prosperous life, this is how you repay me? With attitude and ingratitude?"

Her voice had risen, and Calladia felt a sick surge of malicious joy at having rattled her unflappable mother. "I don't need to repay you for anything," she said. "I just want the freedom to live my life the way I want."

Cynthia laughed scornfully. "And how is that? Lifting weights until you look like a man, wasting your talents on a menial job, living like you have no responsibilities to the family?"

Calladia flinched. She liked her bulky shoulders and muscled thighs, adored seeing the lines of strength in the mirror, but even if she knew her mother's idea of what a woman could be was outdated and reductive, the words stung. Sam had flung that accusation at her after a few months of dating, complaining he didn't like being seen with such a masculine woman. And Calladia, still young and desperate for the affection she'd been denied at home, had reshaped herself for him. Once she was weak enough to fit Sam's definition of beauty though, he'd found something else to harp on.

Her mother was still talking. "You make a fool of yourself in public. Getting in fights, dressing like a pauper, pulling stunts like mouthing off at the town hall. Now you're meddling with demons? You ought to be married and contributing to the family legacy, but you drove off your only high-value suitor, breaking off the engagement—"

Calladia's rage meter maxed out. "Don't you dare speak about Sam."

Cynthia made a frustrated noise and threw her hands up. "I want you to have a future!" she exclaimed. "But you fight me at every turn."

Calladia tugged at the neckline of her shirt as if that could ease the choking feeling. The house squeezed in around her; if she stayed, she would be crushed. "I'm getting my things," Calladia said through the tightness in her throat.

She turned, ignoring her mother's protests, and headed for the door leading to the basement. This dark, cluttered space was where the Cunningtons shoved everything not fit for public eyes. Storage boxes, files, abandoned exercise equipment, tacky family heirlooms . . . it was a wonder Calladia herself hadn't been locked up down here during her adolescence like some subterranean version of Rapunzel, left to rot in the dark.

She yanked the chain for the single bulb overhead, then jogged down the stairs, imagining Mariel at her side. *Mushrooms do quite well in the dark*, Mariel would say. *They clean up waste and toxins in the soil, and they build complex networks underground. They offer a lot more to the world than just looking pretty.*

Calladia could be a mushroom. Better that than a delicate flower slowly dying in a vase.

The few boxes of her belongings were crammed into a corner next to a box of old photo albums. The air smelled musty; some other fungus was probably eating the paper. She'd paged through those albums back in the day, marveling at the photos of her as a chubby-cheeked baby. Then she'd wondered why the photos had grown less frequent over the years, and why she had only ever been photographed fresh-scrubbed and wearing a dress, lips twisted in a forced smile.

There weren't any photos of her past age fifteen.

Calladia ignored the photos and started digging through the two boxes someone—probably Cynthia's assistant—had written *Calladia* on in cursive Sharpie. School textbooks, childhood books she hadn't been willing to get rid of, the ribbons and trophies she'd boxed up before the ones on display had been purged. She'd meant to retrieve them and move them into her house, but she'd always found a reason to postpone returning to her childhood home.

Her chest felt tight as she dug through the memories. There was no need to revisit report cards or the notebook she and Mariel had taken turns scribbling in during middle school, gushing about crushes and complaining about their mothers, but she did it anyway. These were artifacts, telling the story of the girl she'd been before hardening into the woman she was now.

As soon as she found somewhere new to live, she would take them with her.

The second box held college magic textbooks and spare equipment: a collapsible cauldron for potions on the go, a skein of rainbow-dyed yarn, chalk for marking inscriptions, and sachets of dried herbs. She picked up the whole box, not wanting to linger to pick and choose what would be most helpful.

Calladia's mother was waiting at the top of the stairs, mouth twisted in a frown. There were lines beside her eyes she either hadn't tried or hadn't been able to eliminate. "I know you don't believe me," Cynthia said, "but I've only ever wanted the best for you."

The worst part was, Calladia knew her mother was being, for once, entirely sincere. There was just one problem.

"Your idea of what's best and mine don't match, Mom." Calladia's voice sounded as tired as her mother looked. "I just wish you could understand that."

She left before her mother could say anything more.

NINE

ASTAROTH BARELY MADE IT BACK TO THE TRUCK BEFORE Calladia stormed out of the house. He hunkered down, heart racing and mind churning over what he'd overheard.

That conversation had been overflowing with toxicity. Did Calladia's mother truly not see her daughter's worth? Where Astaroth saw passion and fire, a willingness to fight for what was right, and an indomitable spirit and clever wit, Calladia's mother saw . . .

A disappointment.

The truck door was flung open, and Calladia shoved a cardboard box at him. "Take this," she ordered.

He did, propping it on his lap as he sat upright. "What's in here?"

"None of your business." Calladia backed out of the driveway like ghouls were chasing them, then sent the truck lurching forward. It stalled, and she cursed as she restarted the car, jammed the clutch in, and yanked on the shifter.

Astaroth's curiosity would make it his business, but he knew better than to start digging through the box while she was watching. "So," he said. "How'd it go?"

Calladia leveled him with a death glare. "I don't want to talk about it."

Astaroth chewed his lip, wondering what to say next. He couldn't admit he was listening in; that would just piss her off more. But how else was he going to get information out of her?

To be better able to manipulate her, of course. Blackmail and whatnot. Just in case.

Considering she was driving like she was actively seeking out adorable Disney animals to turn into roadkill, there wasn't much more pissing off to do before she hit her limit, so Astaroth went for it. "I was eavesdropping," he said. "Your mother seems like a treat."

Calladia slapped the steering wheel. "I told you to stay in the car!"

Astaroth shrugged. "I was curious. Were you really engaged to be married?"

It wasn't the question he'd planned to ask, but it was the one that popped out. Why that should be the thing he'd fixated on, who could say. It just seemed odd for someone so militantly independent to be engaged, that was all. Anyone would be curious.

The look Calladia threw him threatened to rearrange his insides. "None of your business," she repeated.

"Why'd you break it off?" he asked, undeterred. "Did you castrate and disembowel him and then have to make up a story to explain his absence?"

"I wish." Calladia grimaced. "He tried to make me small."

She didn't elaborate, but it was enough for Astaroth to start forming a picture. The kind of man Calladia's mother would have found "high-value" was probably some snooty fuck with strict expectations of female behavior. There were far too many men like that, on Earth and other planes, and Astaroth despised them. Not that he wasn't a snooty fuck—he was, and proudly—but he couldn't imagine trying or *wanting* to shape someone like Calladia into another form.

"Well." Astaroth cleared his throat. "As your sworn enemy, I can reliably inform you he did not succeed. It would take magic beyond the most powerful witch's abilities to turn you into anyone but exactly who you are."

Calladia's lips parted. As she coasted to a stop at an intersection, she stared at him. He couldn't identify the emotion in her eyes, but it made him feel awkward. He fidgeted and looked down at the box in his lap.

Calladia didn't say anything for a while. She drove on, eyes on the road and hands clasping the steering wheel, though her grip didn't seem as tight as it had before. "So," she eventually said. "We'll hit up Mariel's place next, and then we need to find a place to stay. I want to get out of town, just in case Moloch realizes we're alive. I have camping gear—"

Astaroth recoiled. "Camping? Like . . . in nature?" He may not remember much of the last few centuries, but his imperfect memory did contain strong opinions about having to bivouac when he'd tagged along with King George III's soldiers for a lark. Faced with mud, terrible rations, and a distinct lack of hygiene, he'd determined the camping lifestyle was (A) not a lark, and (B) not for him.

"Where else would you camp?" Calladia asked.

Astaroth shook his head. "Absolutely not. First off, there are bugs. And dirt. And probably bears and who knows what, and I'm not going to sleep on the *ground*."

Calladia looked at him askance. "Don't tell me you're one of those precious types who can't sleep unless they're in a proper bed."

"Is that precious?" Astaroth asked. "Or is it a reasonable expectation, considering the technology available? I was born in the late medieval period. Why would I choose to revisit it?"

"Well, for starters, camping isn't about comfort. It's about getting away and enjoying nature. Cooking over a fire and staring at the stars."

"I can enjoy nature through a window, thank you very much."

"Secondly," Calladia said, "we're on the lam. This isn't some five-star vacation getaway."

"That doesn't mean we need to lower all our standards—"

Calladia interrupted him. "Where's your wallet?"

Astaroth blinked, jolted out of his argument. "What?"

"Your wallet." She held out her hand, beckoning with quick flicks of her fingers. "Since you clearly have the cash to pay for a fancy hotel."

"I—" Astaroth closed his mouth, then opened it again. "I'm sure I have plenty of resources on the demon plane."

"The demon plane where Moloch lives? Sure, sounds good. Let's go there."

Curse her, she wasn't supposed to have a good point. "I'll pay you back. Eventually."

She scoffed. "Like I believe that."

"We could make a bargain," Astaroth offered. "Those are unbreakable."

Calladia slammed on the brakes so fast, Astaroth was thrown against the seat belt. "Don't ever offer me a bargain again," she said vehemently, jabbing a finger into his shoulder.

Astaroth rubbed the spot she'd poked. "Touchy, touchy."

Her scowl was even more ferocious than usual. "I know how bargains work. I ask for a favor, and you fulfill it, taking away all my magic and emotions while you do so, right?"

"Well . . . yes." Bargaining was woven into his being—even if he couldn't remember all the details, the instinct was there. Demonic bargainers devoted their lives to making deals that protected the species. Even the smallest demon child knew that without the light and magic provided by mortal souls, their plane would darken and die.

Calladia shook her head. "Absolutely not."

Astaroth felt a flicker of something he suspected might be guilt, but he suppressed the impulse to apologize. Bargaining was a noble calling; there was nothing to be ashamed of. "So that's a no on the bargaining. A shame. You have such a lovely soul."

She scoffed. "What does that even mean?"

"I can see your soul if I engage my demon senses. All souls glow, but yours is particularly bright." When he focused on it, it was like a miniature star centered behind her breastbone. If he'd been able to liberate that golden light from her body, he would have opened a portal to let it drift to the demon plane, where it would join countless others floating through the twilit sky. Hers would be one of the brightest, rejuvenating the demons who passed by and making flowers bloom in its wake.

It would be nice to see that soul floating about, but the Calladia left behind on Earth wouldn't be the one goggling at him now. Her combativeness and passion would fade, leaving an emotionless echo of the vibrant woman she'd been. She'd walk, talk, and act like a human being, but a crucial part would be missing.

That shouldn't bother Astaroth.

An ache started behind his sternum, and he rubbed his chest. Why did that bother him?

Calladia hit the gas. "Well, hands off my soul. I'm not a nice person like Mariel; I'm a total bitch, so you won't be able to find a soft spot to manipulate me with."

It struck Astaroth that Calladia had a rather poor opinion of herself. Sure, she was a bitch—and he meant that as a compliment of the highest order, just as he was a proud bastard—but it was obvious she had a strong sense of fairness, and the way she spoke of Mariel indicated a deep level of feeling for her loved ones. *Nice* was too tepid a word for her. But loyal, protective, and determined to do the right thing? Those were traits to admire.

If this was a bargaining mission, he would try to exploit her insecurities or her protectiveness toward her loved ones. Every human had something they were willing to give up their soul for. Love, money, power, revenge . . . all a clever demon had to do was pinpoint that weakness, stick the metaphorical knife in, and twist.

Astaroth was a clever demon, and Calladia had revealed several weak points, from her strained relationship with her mother to her broken engagement to her belief she wasn't a particularly good person. Throw in friends she adored and a destroyed house, and there was plenty he could offer in terms of demon magic.

Still, the idea bothered him.

He cleared his throat. "No bargaining. We shall maintain a semi-cordial partnership to accomplish our mutual goals."

He was surprised when Calladia laughed. "This is what you consider semi-cordial?"

"You haven't tried to gut me yet," he said. "That's something."

She chuckled again, and Astaroth's lips threatened to tug up at the corners in response. Proper demons didn't succumb to emotional impulses though, so he bit down on the smile and focused on the view out the window.

Glimmer Falls was a charming town in daytime, but it took on an ethereal glow at night. Hanging holiday lights decorated restaurant patios, candles flickered from windowsills, and magic displays sent cascades of vibrant color into the sky. A wide variety of species mingled freely everywhere he looked.

It was a far cry from the desperate times he remembered from Earth centuries ago. Then life had been hard for everyone, and people had generally gathered in groups to protect their mutual interests. The pixies stayed with the pixies, the witches with the warlocks, the nonmagical humans with each other. There was some cross-group pollination, but overall, the world had been cut into categories.

Now those boundaries were gone, and it was a marvel to see.

The advance of night had brought a drop in temperature though, and he shivered.

Calladia turned the heat on. "Are you cold?" she asked.

"A minor inconvenience, no more." He shivered again.

Calladia grumbled, then pulled into a strip mall, parking in front of a secondhand clothing store that was nestled between a ramen shop and a nail-and-talon salon. "What size do you wear?" she asked.

"Erm." Astaroth racked his brain. "I don't know. Whenever the Queen sent her tailor, they just measured me and delivered the clothing later." He'd been a particular pet of hers for a season, and she'd adored him in a gold waistcoat.

"The Queen?" Calladia's jaw dropped. "Like . . . the one in Buckingham Palace?"

"Probably not the same one," Astaroth said. "Unless Queen Charlotte has a life witch on call?" Witches who could expand life spans—both theirs and others—were extremely rare, and their methods were top secret.

Calladia rolled her eyes. "Stay here," she said. "I'll eyeball it."

He watched her enter the store with trepidation. There were some decent pieces in the window, but Calladia didn't display the best judgment when it came to her own clothing.

After ten minutes, she returned holding a bag. "You can change in the tent once I get it set up," she said, handing the clothes over. "No stripping in the truck."

He dug through the fabric as she started driving again. She'd picked up a pale blue shirt, an oversized hooded sweater, undershorts, socks and trainers, and black leather trousers. Or faux leather, as a check of the tag indicated it was made of various synthetics. Still, he raised a brow at the bold choice. "Do you enjoy a man in leather?" he asked. It matched his horns, and the blue shirt was close to the shade of his eyes. Simple garments, but functional, and she'd given at least some thought to aesthetics.

Was it his imagination or had her cheeks flushed? "It's the only thing I thought would fit. You're welcome, by the way."

Ah, yes. Manners. Important when buttering up one's enemies. "Thank you for buying me clothing," he said. And he meant it, truly. She'd used her own money to make him comfortable, and a warm, fuzzy feeling filled him at the gesture, growing warmer as he put the jumper on. "I'll pay you back, I promise."

"Don't bother. Secondhand stores are cheap." She slid him a glance. "Let me guess, you hate the idea of secondhand stores. That suit probably cost a fortune."

He couldn't say how much it had cost, but he resented the first bit of conjecture. "Excuse you. Shopping vintage and used is an excellent way to craft a unique style, as well as be more sustainable for the planet." He smirked and gestured at his torso. "As evidenced by myself, the best things are built to last."

Calladia let out a startled-sounding laugh. Her teeth dug into one side of her lower lip, and her eyes were bright. It was a real smile, surprised out of her, and it was just as stunning as he'd imagined.

She shook her head. "Ridiculous," she said, but for once, it didn't sound like an insult.

TEN

I T WAS FULL DARK BY THE TIME THEY ARRIVED AT MARIEL'S house. "Stay here," Calladia told Astaroth. "Head down."

"It's like you're embarrassed to be seen with me," he marveled. "How odd."

"That's exactly it." Ignoring Astaroth's huff, Calladia exited the truck. "I'll be back."

Mariel flung open the door a few seconds after Calladia knocked. The short, curvy brunette witch launched herself at Calladia, knocking her back a few steps. "I was so worried!" Mariel cried as she hugged Calladia fiercely. "I can't believe someone blew up your house."

"Me neither." Calladia squeezed Mariel tightly before releasing her. "Thanks for letting me stop by."

Mariel scoffed as she ushered Calladia in. "You know you can just walk into my house whenever you want."

Mariel's home was cozy and charming, full of colorful knick-knacks and woven rugs. They passed the den where Oz had spent days sleeping on the couch after Mariel had accidentally summoned him, then continued down the hall to the kitchen and adjacent dining nook. The air smelled like spices and cooking meat.

"Take a seat and tell us everything," Mariel said.

Calladia smiled at the people gathered in the kitchen. Themmie, of course, who was zooming toward her, but also the werewolf Ben Rosewood, a good friend and Mariel's boss at the garden shop he owned. Oz was chopping onions at the counter; he waved the knife in greeting, looking watery-eyed. "I would offer a hug," the demon said in his rumbling baritone, "but you might start crying from these cursed onions, too."

Themmie was so agitated she didn't land before hugging Calladia. The pixie's wings thrummed as she lifted Calladia off the ground. "I'm so glad you weren't barbecued," Themmie sobbed.

Despite everything, Calladia laughed. "Me, too. I hope you're ready to plot revenge."

Ben came to hug her next. The werewolf was tall and broad with shaggy brown hair and a neatly trimmed beard, but he eschewed the badass biker look a lot of werewolves enjoyed in favor of dressing like a math professor, a lumberjack, or a combination of both. Tonight was all math professor, complete with sweater vest and gold-rimmed glasses. "We'll pitch in to help you rebuild," he promised. "No detail's too small."

Calladia's eyes burned with unshed tears. "Thank you."

The group was completed by Alzapraz, Mariel's great-great-great-times-a-lot grandfather. When Mariel had heard there were demon issues afoot, she'd offered to invite the ancient warlock, who had more knowledge than the rest of them combined. No one knew what century he'd been born in, but he looked as old as he was, since he'd mastered enough life magic to extend his life span indefinitely, but not enough to preserve his health. He was more wrinkled than a pug, with a hunched back and a white beard that dangled to his waist. A pointy purple cap topped with a yarn pom-pom perched on his head.

Alzapraz waved a fork. "Glad you didn't die," he said in a creaky voice.

"Same!"

Oz was finally done with the onions, and after washing his hands, he came to give her a brief hug. "Sorry about the house."

Calladia smiled at Oz. "Thank you."

She'd mistrusted the big, serious demon at first, but she'd come to realize that behind his reserved exterior was a tender heart and a strong sense of loyalty. What he lacked in fancy words he made up for in actions, and his solid, protective presence was exactly the anchor flighty, dreamy Mariel needed.

They sat while Mariel resumed cooking coconut chicken curry. To Calladia's delight, Mariel had incorporated magic into her meal prep and was summoning ingredients with ease. A week ago, that had been nearly impossible due to Mariel's unpredictable spellcraft, but Mariel had finally realized her magic wasn't the issue—the pressure exerted by her overbearing family was. Set free to explore magic on her own terms, Mariel had begun to flourish.

"Tell us what happened," Themmie ordered. She'd clearly been crying; her cheeks were smudged with eyeliner, and her glitter eye shadow had migrated to seemingly every inch of her brown skin, from her forehead to the backs of her hands.

Calladia did, omitting the role Astaroth had played. Or rather, obfuscating. She'd concluded there was no way to leave the demon out of the story entirely, so she admitted accidentally interrupting Moloch's attack. "I guess Moloch must have fixated on me," she said. "He followed me home, convinced I was sheltering Astaroth."

Mariel snorted as she spooned curry onto plates. "Not in a million years."

Calladia forced a smile. "Obviously. But apparently he didn't believe me, because next thing I knew, he'd firebombed my house."

"With you inside?" Themmie asked. "How awful!" Her dark eyes were wide with distress.

Calladia squeezed Themmie's hand. "I'm okay. I was blown free and hid, but now I'm living out of my truck until I figure out how to get this Moloch asshole off my tail."

"You can stay with me!" multiple voices exclaimed at once—though Oz and Mariel both said *us*.

Calladia's heart warmed. "Thank you, but I'm not comfortable putting anyone else at risk until Moloch is taken care of." She faced Oz. "What can you tell me about Moloch and Astaroth and whatever that drama is?"

Oz picked at his curry—after directing praise and effusive thanks to a blushing Mariel—chewing slowly as he thought. "It's an odd situation. They're around the same age—Moloch was born in the late fourteenth century, Astaroth in the early fifteenth—and they've always been rivals. Astaroth has long been our most successful bargainer, and Moloch our most powerful warrior."

Calladia knew Astaroth was old, but it was startling to remember exactly *how* old, especially since he frequently acted like a petulant child.

Alzapraz snorted. "Amateurs," he croaked. "They should try being my age with my joints."

"How did Moloch manage fireballs?" Mariel asked. "I thought demons only had bargaining magic."

Oz shook his head. "There are other strains of magic, though they're just as rare as bargaining magic. For warriors, that's the ability to summon fire."

Thanks to Oz, the group had gotten a crash course in demonology, including the disturbing fact that children were separated from their parents and put into brutal, isolating training to develop whatever skills would benefit demon society. Oz and Astaroth had the power to harvest human souls—the combination of magic and emotion—and send them to the demon plane, and Oz would have continued in that career if he hadn't become an anomaly some months back. He'd accidentally *gained* a human soul during a bargain gone wrong, and it had given the previously stoic demon messy emotions, magic, and a human life span.

It was weird—Astaroth seemed way too emotional for what Oz had told them about most demons. Probably an effect of the head injury, which meant he'd return to his cold and calculating Vulcan-esque self eventually.

"If they've hated each other that long," Calladia said, "then why is Moloch only trying to kill him now?"

"I'm not sure." Oz's forehead furrowed. "Something must have happened on the demon plane. Astaroth said he'd made a wager with the high council. He obviously lost, so maybe this is the result."

"Hmm." Calladia considered as she took a forkful of curry. She moaned in appreciation of the rich flavor. "Mariel, you deserve a Michelin Star."

Mariel grinned. She was practically glowing, and although Cal-ladia was thrilled to see her friend so happy, there was an uncom-fortable tightness in her own chest. Oz leaned in to whisper something in Mariel's ear, and Mariel's freckled cheeks pinkened before she giggled and playfully slapped Oz away. *Naughty*, Mariel mouthed at the demon.

Calladia couldn't imagine what that kind of intimacy felt like. She hadn't dated seriously since Sam, and it had never been like that. No carefree, giddy joy, no mutual support, only an ever-escalating sense of unworthiness. The longer she'd spent with Sam, the smaller she'd felt, her life shaping itself around his judg-ments.

It was enough to make a witch reject the very idea of love, if only there weren't two such compelling examples of the phenom-enon sitting across the table.

"It sucks that Moloch's taking his issues out on Calladia," Themmie said. "He needs to buy her a new house, at least."

"Sure, that'll go well," Calladia said. "*Hey, Moloch, I know you tried to murder me with an enormous fireball, but would you mind sending some cash to cover the property damage?"* She shook her head and focused on Oz. "I don't know how to deal with this situation yet, but I need to learn everything you can tell me about Moloch. And Astaroth, for that matter. You know, just in case he turns up."

Just in case he's sitting in the passenger seat of my truck.

Oz obliged, painting character portraits of the two demons. Moloch was clever and charming, with a legendary knack for brutality that made him a figure out of nightmares for opponents. Most demons enjoyed scheming, but Moloch was especially conniving. He'd built a web of allies across demon society, and it was an open secret that the conservative half of the high council followed his lead. He sought to collect as much power as possible while eliminating his enemies along the way.

Cue Astaroth, Moloch's long-standing enemy. The two had brawled, dueled, and outwitted each other for centuries, with Astaroth one of the only challengers capable of limiting Moloch's manipulations in the high council. Oz spoke of his mentor in damning terms: scheming, conniving, manipulative, cynical, power-hungry. He'd raised Oz in a drafty stone castle, teaching him to wield a bargainer's magic while honing him into a perfect weapon. Demons weren't entirely emotionless—just less so compared to humans—but Astaroth had attempted to stamp out any weakness in his protégé. "He always spoke of the value of being cold," Oz said. "With coldness comes clarity, which means you can strike even the cruelest bargains without succumbing to guilt."

Mariel looked madder with every sentence. When Oz had finished detailing his experiences with Astaroth, she wrapped her arm around his neck and kissed his cheek. "I hope Moloch beats him up," she said.

Oz chuckled and kissed her back. "*Velina*, shocking as it may seem, I would still rather see Astaroth in power than Moloch.

Astaroth has an interest in human culture and supports protections for part-demon hybrids. Moloch despises anything other than pure demonkind and has long spoken of demonic supremacy over inferior life forms."

Calladia, Themmie, Ben, and Mariel made matching outraged sounds.

Oz raised his hands placatingly. "Not that humans are inferior. It's just how Moloch thinks. If he ever gains total control of the high council, I worry for anyone he doesn't deem a 'pure' enough demon."

"Does Moloch have weaknesses?" Calladia asked.

"Like any demon, a good beheading would take him out," Oz said, "but good luck getting anywhere near that point. He's an expert swordsman, better even than Astaroth."

Maybe they could ambush him. "Where does he usually hang out?"

"The demon plane, where he's heavily guarded. It's rare he'll make an appearance on Earth."

Not great. "So he's immortal, basically invincible, and won't show up unless he's actively trying to murder me?"

Oz winced.

"Cool," Calladia said, trying not to freak out. "Cool cool cool."

"It isn't fair you got sucked into this," Mariel said, distress filling her hazel eyes. "Alzapraz, do you have any idea what she should do?"

Alzapraz stroked his beard, leaving a streak of curry behind. "An immovable object can only be equaled by an unstoppable force," the ancient warlock said, beetle-black eyes barely visible beneath bristling white eyebrows. "When faced with a physically invincible being, you need the magical equivalent. Someone with power over life itself."

"Like you?" Calladia suggested.

Alzapraz's chuckle was like dry leaves skidding over autumn

grass. "Not me, child. You need one who's mastered the giving and, more importantly, the taking of life." He nodded and produced a smartphone from his voluminous sleeve. "I know just the person. Her name is Isobel, and she's a life witch with demon experience. She lives in the woods." He opened the map app and showed Calladia a swath of forest to the northeast. "Somewhere in there."

Calladia eyed the vast area. "That's as specific as you can get? Somewhere in there?"

"Her house moves." He held out a hand, his fingers as gnarled as the roots of an ancient oak. "Give me your phone and I'll jot down more detailed directions."

Calladia did, watching the warlock slowly tap at the screen. It would be nice if the old school of witches and warlocks would embrace things like street addresses and GPS coordinates, but alas, many of them treated even a simple social call as an epic quest. "You really think this Isobel can help us with Moloch?"

"Possibly," Alzapraz said. "She's vicious, and she'll do anything for enough money. She's well-rounded, too. Life curses, memory magic . . ."

"Memory magic?" Calladia asked, perking up.

"The giving and taking of memories. Restoring that which is lost." Alzapraz winked. "A very versatile talent, Isobel. She's older than even me."

"Does she look just as young and spry?" Calladia asked.

Alzapraz's laugh turned into a wracking cough. "Believe it or not," he wheezed once he'd recovered, "she looks no older than you do. When I said she'd mastered life magic, I meant it." He grimaced. "Wish the bitch would share some tips."

He handed the phone back, and Calladia slid it into the pocket of her windbreaker. "Thanks, Alzapraz."

"Don't mention it." He leaned in, voice dropping to a whisper. "A little bird told me you might like that tip about memory magic."

A prickle went down Calladia's spine. She looked around, but the others were talking among themselves. "What do you mean, a little bird?" she asked just as quietly.

Alzapraz tapped the side of his bulbous nose and smiled. "A starling. Cheeky little thing, loves sunflower seeds and gossip. My bird spies are one of the secrets to my seeming omniscience, so don't tell anyone."

Narced on by a literal bird. "And this bird saw . . ."

"More like heard," Alzapraz said. "That explosion drew a lot of interest, and she was perched on a bridge in the park while investigating." He patted her hand. "Don't worry, I won't tell. After the debacle with Oz, I'm learning to keep my mouth shut until I have all the facts of a situation."

Alzapraz had attacked Oz upon realizing he was a demon, suspecting him of nefarious intentions toward Mariel. It had been the same day Calladia had kicked Oz's ass, but Oz didn't seem to hold it against either of them. In fact, he'd said he liked that Mariel had people to protect her.

Calladia felt a rush of gratitude. "Thank you," she said. "I promise it's not as weird as it seems." She grimaced. "Or maybe it is as weird as it seems. It's complicated."

"All the good sex is," Alzapraz said, raising his glass.

Calladia choked. "Wait, that's not—"

"Just ask Isobel when you see her," Alzapraz continued. "Tell her I haven't forgotten that thing she had me do in 1286."

"So," Mariel said, interrupting the conversation just in time, "where are you going to go, since you won't stay here?"

"It's been a while since I've gone camping," Calladia said, "and if there's a life witch hiding in the woods who can help us defeat Moloch, that's where we'll go."

"We?" Ben asked, fork halfway to his mouth.

Damn, the werewolf didn't miss a thing. "It was a figurative sort of *we*," Calladia said, fidgeting. "Like me, but on behalf of us.

The community. At large." She pointedly looked at her smart-watch. "I hate to run, but I want to get on the road before it gets too late."

Mariel stood. "If you need anything, and I mean literally anything, give me a call."

"Give any of us a call," Themmie said. "Super squad to the rescue!"

A flurry of goodbyes followed another round of hugs, and the group trooped to the front door to wave Calladia off. She glanced nervously at her truck, but Astaroth was thankfully out of sight.

"Remember," Mariel said, pulling Calladia into yet another hug, "you're not alone."

Calladia blinked against the tears that threatened. She was lucky to have such wonderful friends. "Thank you. I'll defeat the demon and be back before you know it."

Then life would return to normal, Calladia could rebuild, and she'd never have to see Astaroth or Moloch ever again.

ELEVEN

ASTAROTH CROUCHED ON THE TRUCK FLOORBOARD, KEEP-ing his head down. The position was uncomfortable, but he didn't want to risk being seen.

After what felt like an eternity, footsteps approached. His pulse accelerated . . . then calmed when Calladia appeared at the driver's side door.

"Took you long enough," Astaroth groused, clambering onto the seat once he'd peeked out the window to confirm no one was watching. His knees popped, and his muscles ached from being in one position too long. A faint, delicious smell hit his nostrils, and he sniffed. Instantly, he was transported to another time and place. "You ate curry?" he asked, mouth watering. "There's an Indian restaurant down the street from my flat. Nothing quite like it."

"Yeah? Tell me more about your flat," Calladia said, starting the truck.

"My flat is . . ." Astaroth trailed off, realizing he'd spoken without thinking and produced something tangible. "Wait, I remembered something!"

Her lips curved. "You sure did."

Exhilaration rushed through him. It was as if the spiced scent of curry had roused the memory from its slumber. A scene played out vividly in his head: rain-slicked pavement, the whoosh of passing black cabs, the lights and chatter of a London night. "I have a flat in Islington," he said, thinking of black upholstery and Art Deco interior design. "I've lived all over England, but London's always been my favorite. There's so much of humanity to experience there."

"You like experiencing humanity?" Calladia asked as she drove out of the neighborhood. "That seems odd for a demon."

"Mortals live such colorful lives. It's fascinating." Humans were bright but fleeting, like flowers that opened at dawn and perished at dusk. He outlived them all, yet they still managed to surprise him.

No one was more surprising than this particular mortal. He studied Calladia, contemplating her contradictions. Her features were delicate, but her demeanor was ferocious. She might weep, then immediately vow revenge. She hated him but had rescued him anyway, and now she was taking him with her.

"What did you learn from Ozroth?" he asked.

"Apparently you and Moloch have hated each other for pretty much forever," Calladia said. "As for why he's trying to kill you, Oz thinks it has something to do with a wager you lost, but he doesn't know the specifics. Just that you placed a bet on his success in taking Mariel's soul."

Wagers were an essential method of conflict resolution in demonic society. What price had been named though? The uncertainty was maddening. "What else did he say? What weaknesses does Moloch have?"

"Beheading, I guess." Calladia flicked on the turn signal. "But he's apparently an incredible swordsman who will gut us before we get near, so we'll need to get creative."

The words *we* and *us* hung in the air between them like shining Christmas baubles, beautiful yet fragile. Astaroth didn't remark on it, lest she immediately revise the sentiment into something less collaborative, but a warm spark lit in his chest.

Calladia unlocked her phone and gave it to him. "Here, read these instructions."

Astaroth squinted at the notes on the screen. "What's this?"

"Alzapraz is Mariel's ancestor, and he referred us to a life witch who can hopefully help us kill Moloch or at least mess him up. She also does memory magic and can maybe help your amnesia."

"What?" Hope surged as Astaroth looked up. "Wait, did you tell them about me?"

She shook her head. "Alzapraz knows, but he'll keep it a secret. Anyway, this witch is named Isobel, and she's super old and lives in the woods." She jerked her chin at him. "Directions, please."

Astaroth cleared his throat, then started reading. "Head east and begin the fable. Stalk the red deer, and when you have found it, ask for advice. You shall be directed toward nature's bosom and the middle of the beginning of the end of your journey."

"Wait, what?" Calladia pulled over, then snatched the phone out of his hand. "Give me that." She reread the words, lips moving silently, then gaped at the screen. "What the actual fuck is this?"

"A quest, apparently," Astaroth said. "You didn't ask for more details?"

"I didn't think I'd need to." She poked the screen, then held the phone to her ear. Astaroth heard faint, tinny ringing. He leaned in, unabashedly eavesdropping, until Calladia rolled her eyes and put the phone on speaker.

"Hello, Calladia," an ancient-sounding man said.

"Hey, Alzapraz," Calladia said. "I just looked at the directions you gave. They make no sense."

"Sense can be surprisingly subjective."

Calladia looked like she was biting back a sharp retort. "What do they mean, then?"

Alzapraz coughed before replying. "I thought it was fairly obvious."

Calladia covered her eyes with her free hand. "Alzapraz, this is a bunch of nonsense about fables and a red deer and nature's bosom."

"It is!" He sounded delighted.

"Bloody warlocks," Astaroth muttered under his breath.

"You don't have an address or anything?" Calladia asked. "Or a phone number?"

"What would be the fun in that? This is the half of the puzzle I have, and the red deer will have the rest." Chatter sounded in the background. "Ooh, brownies. Happy questing!"

The call disconnected.

Calladia tossed the phone onto the seat, then thumped her forehead against the steering wheel. "Why?" she asked. Another thump. "Why can't anything be easy?"

Astaroth was inclined to agree. There was a time and place for witchy drama, but this was not it. "Did he say how long the trip would be?"

"No, but he showed me the general area on the map. I'd bet a day or two." She sat up straight, yanking on her disheveled ponytail. "There's nothing to be done for it tonight. Let's find a camping spot."

As they headed east, Calladia explained that the first part of the quest, at least, wouldn't be too bad. Because of the steep hills and mountains bordering Glimmer Falls to the east, there was only one road leading that way. It wound up a slope between the area's famed hot springs, then dipped into the next valley. Halfway down the hill was a pullout that led to a decent camping spot near a stream.

Astaroth liked the sound of that stream. They both smelled like smoke, and he wanted to wash the remaining soot out of his hair. Granted, it would be followed by sleeping on the ground like an animal, but at least he'd be a clean animal.

The forest surrounded them, trees interlacing overhead and blocking out the night sky. Calladia's headlights provided the only illumination, highlighting the twists of the road as they rose in elevation. Periodically, the beams caught something in the woods: a plume of steam rising from the ground, the scaled green loop of a snake dangling from a branch, a flash of movement that set the bushes rustling.

It was a beautiful area, vibrant with life and magic. He might have enjoyed exploring if it wasn't for the situation, but right now he only wanted three things: his memory, a bath, and a sword. Moloch's severed head would be a bonus, but as that was unlikely to fall in his lap, he focused on more attainable things.

"Do you know where to get a sword?" he asked Calladia.

"Yes."

Astaroth perked up. "Can we go there?"

"Nope." She gave him a sardonic look. "I may be helping you find Isobel, but I'm not going to arm you."

"How else will I behead Moloch?"

"Did you miss the *super successful and scary swordsman* part? Ozroth says he's better than you."

Astaroth scowled. "Don't underestimate my ability with a blade, I have at least one foggy memory of wreaking havoc on a battlefield."

"Cool story, bro," she said. "Let me know when you spot a battle-field."

The witch was *mean*. Oddly, Astaroth didn't find it upsetting. He eyed her profile, amused that someone with the bone structure of a storybook princess had the manners of a feral cat. She was full of contradictions, which made Astaroth want to learn everything about her. "You'd be fearsome on a battlefield, too," he said. "Eviscerating enemies right and left with that sharp tongue."

"I'm going to eviscerate you with more than my tongue if you don't shut up and let me drive." Her lips had quirked at his comment though.

Astaroth settled against the seat, satisfied at having provoked the smile from her. "Very well. My vow of silence begins now."

"How long will it last?" she asked.

He made a show of considering. "At least . . . two minutes."

Calladia made a stifled snorting sound. "Don't make me gag you."

"Kinky," he said, biting his lower lip. "Will you tie me up, too?"

"Yep, I'll tie you to a tree in the woods overnight. It's supposed to rain."

Astaroth shivered. Tent camping was bad enough. "I'm shutting up."

Calladia smirked. "Atta demon."

TWELVE

D ESPITE HIS GRUMBLING ABOUT SLEEPING OUTDOORS, Astaroth proved adept at helping set up the tent. Calladia hammered in a stake by the light of a glowing orb she'd conjured, sneaking glances at him. His brow was furrowed with concentration as he threaded a pole through the orange rain fly.

It felt odd to work together like this. Sure, they'd fought Moloch and fled together, but that hadn't been an organized effort. This was a smaller, more domestic task, and the way he took direction and anticipated what tools she needed was honestly kind of nice.

"I would kill for a bath," Astaroth said once the tent was assembled. He wiped his forehead. "There's soot caked in unmentionable areas."

Calladia retrieved her bugout bag from the back seat of the truck and dug through it until she found wet wipes and dry shampoo. "Here," she said, tossing them over. "Better than nothing. The stream's down the slope." Once he was done, she'd take a turn.

"I'll return shortly." Astaroth scooped up the bag of clothes she'd bought him and a battery-powered lantern and disappeared into the forest.

Calladia turned to scan the woods opposite. This wasn't an official campground, just a secret spot she and Mariel had discovered that was barely large enough for a tent. Calladia breathed in the scent of pine trees and sighed, shoulders relaxing for maybe the first time that day.

Astaroth returned dressed in the black pants and blue shirt she'd bought him. He bent to stash the bag in the tent, and Calladia couldn't help a quick ogle. The pants looked unreasonably good stretched over his muscular ass, and she cursed herself for not buying a pair of baggy sweatpants instead. It was just that in the store, her eyes had been drawn to the black sheen of faux leather, and she'd instantly known he would like them.

Why that should matter, she didn't know.

"How are the clothes?" she asked.

He turned to face her, holding out his arms in a *ta-da* pose. "What do you think?"

The shirt was a bit baggy, but the pale blue color echoed his eyes, and the pants looked indecently good from the front as well. Calladia swallowed. "Seems fine," she said, trying to sound indifferent. "Do the shoes fit?"

He looked down at the plain white tennis shoes. "A bit naff, but very comfortable."

Calladia wasn't going to ask what *naff* meant. "Good," she said. She grabbed a water bottle from the truck and tossed it to him. "I'm going to change and grab some kindling so we can get a fire going."

She conjured another magical light and took the wet wipes, travel toiletries, and a fresh change of clothes with her. "Who's paranoid now?" she muttered as she picked her way between trees, the glowing orb bobbing above her. Mariel and Themmie teased her for having so much survival gear in her truck, but this was exactly the sort of scenario she'd planned for.

Well, maybe not exactly. She'd envisioned an earthquake or getting stranded in the wilderness, not having her house blown up and running from a demon. Either way, she was glad she'd prepared.

At the stream, she stripped off her top and bra, then splashed water over her face and armpits, cursing at how cold it was. But that was November in the Pacific Northwest. It hadn't snowed yet, but this stream was fed from high in the Cascades, and mountain water was frigid. She hurried through wiping down her top half before changing into a new sports bra and a button-up flannel. She peed behind a bush, then cleaned her bottom half even more quickly, shivering as goosebumps erupted over her bare skin. Fresh underwear and jeans helped with the chill, as did woolen socks and hiking boots. Workout gear was comfortable, but not suited for the wilderness, especially not at this time of year.

Dry shampoo was followed by a thorough combing and braiding of her hair, and Calladia finally felt halfway decent. She gathered her things and headed to the campsite, collecting sticks as she went. When she looked up, the night sky looked like it was spattered with diamonds.

Back at the clearing, she found Astaroth arranging firewood inside a shallow, freshly dug pit. Calladia stopped, taken aback.

Having someone help set up camp was a novelty. She'd camped with her friends before, but Themmic's talents ran toward making the campsite aesthetically appealing for Pixtagram, and Mariel, bless her nature witch heart, usually got so distracted greeting and petting new plants that she forgot to gather wood. Calladia was happy to shoulder the practical burdens if it meant spending time with her adorably eccentric friends, but this felt . . . refreshing.

Not the sentiment she ought to be feeling around a demon. Calladia busied herself augmenting his base structure with her own kindling, reminding herself this situation was temporary. They'd find Isobel the life witch and figure out how Astaroth could recover his memory and defeat Moloch, and then Calladia would cheerfully send him off to face the demon alone. She'd return to Glimmer Falls, crash on Mariel's couch until she could figure out her housing situation, and move on with her life, hopefully never seeing Astaroth again.

This was only an interlude. A brief detour in the journey of her life, soon to be nothing but a story to tell.

Calladia adjusted Astaroth's logs here and there, and though he shot her a few dark looks, he let her meddle with his campfire structure. A few years in Girl Scouts had kick-started her love of camping, but she'd been pissed she couldn't do the rougher things Boy Scouts got up to, and the stupid uniform skirt was an affront to practicality as well as a depressing imposition of gender norms, so she'd dropped out and started reading survivalist books at the library instead.

Her mother had, naturally, disapproved. "Girl Scouting is very respectable," she'd said at the time. "And after a few years, you can switch to the Witch Scout corps. Don't you want that?"

Had young Calladia wanted to join the older girls in Witch Scouts, who at the time held the mysterious glamour of adolescence? Yes, but not enough to wear skirts.

"Do you have matches?" Astaroth asked.

She held up a fire starter. "Better." Then she slid a look at him, considering. "Unless you have some kind of demon trick?"

He shook his head, then crouched beside the logs. "I don't have that kind of magic."

She tore her gaze away from the stretch of fake leather over his thighs. "Too bad. Then you could literally fight Moloch's fire with fire." She scraped the fire starter, and sparks erupted, raining down on the kindling. A few more strikes, and the pine needles started smoldering.

She had a portable camp stove bundled away under the passenger seat, but Calladia preferred a campfire if possible. The warmth, the light, the smell . . . something about it relaxed her in a way she rarely felt.

When the smoke hit her nostrils though, she flinched.

"Everything all right?" Astaroth asked.

Calladia closed her eyes and breathed in deeply. This wasn't the acrid, horrible smell of her burning house. This was good and natural—a fire built for comfort and safety, not destruction. She kept breathing, letting go of her knee-jerk panic response. Moloch had ruined her house; she wouldn't let him ruin her enjoyment of a decent campfire.

"Yeah," she said, opening her eyes to find Astaroth studying her intently. "I'm just peachy."

His incisive gaze told Calladia he saw beneath her pretense, but he didn't say anything. Calladia was grateful for his restraint. She might be off-kilter and sensitive from a rough day, but she would fake it until she made it.

As the flames grew, Calladia settled back on her haunches. "I've got a can of chili we can crack open," she said. "Although I'm not sure how hungry you are, since demons only eat every few weeks."

"I am exceedingly hungry." Astaroth dragged over a log, then sat on one end and patted the bark. "You're welcome to share the log, if it isn't too close to my objectionable person."

Calladia didn't feel like getting close to him, but the ground was cold, and it wasn't like they'd be snuggling or anything. She got up to retrieve the chili before positioning the open can in the glowing embers at the edge of the fire. Then she grabbed two blankets and handed one to Astaroth before sitting next to him.

Astaroth looked surprised at the offering, but he accepted it without comment, wrapping the fabric around himself. "So," he said, "where do we go tomorrow?"

Calladia blew out a breath, shifting a ribbon of hair that had slid out of her braid. "I guess we start looking for a red deer in the woods."

He sighed. "Witches are so dramatic."

"Like you aren't?"

"I didn't say it was a bad thing." He grabbed a stick and poked at the fire, sending sparks shooting up. "I wonder if Isobel can enchant my flat to move around," he mused. "I could use more drama."

"What, the last few days haven't been dramatic enough?" Calladia asked incredulously.

"Not that sort of drama. I'm talking about branding. An aesthetic to help accomplish your goals." He nudged the fire again. "Proper presentation can set you at an advantage before you even engage with an opponent."

Calladia wasn't following. "And a moving flat is . . . ?"

"Unpredictable," he said. "And implies the existence of powerful allies."

"Huh." She cocked her head, remembering their first meeting. "Is that why you carried that stupid cane sword? Because it looks dramatic?"

He pointed the stick at her. "It isn't stupid. You're just jealous."

"I don't see why having a sword matters that much."

"Well, first off, it's sharp," he said. "But functionality aside, swords mesh well with a variety of aesthetics."

"Tell me more about these aesthetics," Calladia said, wanting to hear more of his weird opinions.

"Well, enemies base their actions on how they perceive you, so you can dress and accessorize to intimidate them or make them underestimate you. Or you can craft a persona that's wealthy or chaotic or violent." He shrugged. "Simple tactics, but so few people think of a personal brand as a weapon."

How had she ended up in the woods getting a marketing lecture from a six-hundred-year-old embodiment of evil? "So what's your brand?" she asked. "Or what would it be, if you could remember?"

"I remember enough of the early centuries," he said, prodding the logs again. The firelight flickered over the sharp planes of his face, casting shadows under his cheekbones. "Those were more violent times, so making a good first impression was crucial to avoid random beheadings." He raised his free hand, ticking off points on his fingers. "People have always respected wealth, so I made sure to portray myself as a society elite whenever possible. They also respect violence, so visible weaponry and a few displays of murderous temper made people not want to cross me. And they admire and are intimidated by beauty, so I've always maintained excellent hygiene and accessorized to accentuate my best features." He shrugged. "Shag a few society influencers and add in a good skincare routine, and you're already at an advantage."

Calladia was torn between the urge to laugh and a grudging respect for his tactics. She was familiar with the complicated game of crafting a persona for public consumption, thanks to Themmie and her massive Pixtagram following, but she'd never thought about how other people might leverage their looks to gain power. Themmie's brand was whimsical, energetic, and bright—the sunshiny parts of her personality dialed up to 11, with any flaws or negative emotions saved for offline spaces. Astaroth's brand was apparently "fashionable sexy murderer." "I don't think I have a brand," she said.

Astaroth scoffed. "Of course you do. No makeup, workout clothes that show off your muscles, a few well-placed conversational barbs, and a general combative air. You want everyone to know you're strong, don't care how they expect you to act or look, and won't suffer fools."

She blinked. That was . . . huh. He'd said it matter-of-factly, with no hint of judgment in his tone. "It's not like I sat down to create a strategy," she said, oddly pleased by his description. "I like comfortable clothing, and makeup is a waste of time and makes my face itch."

His lips tilted in a crooked smile that made Calladia's heart rate pick up. He had probably practiced that wickedly appealing look in a mirror. "I'm not saying it's a bad choice," he said. "You can choose comfort and practicality for yourself, not just to cater to the expectations of others. But humans are social animals, so how you present yourself is inherently part of a larger game."

The chili was bubbling, so Calladia took a break to grab spoons. After hesitating, she decided it wouldn't kill her to eat from the same can as Astaroth rather than dirtying her collapsible camping bowls. She handed him a spoon and set the can on the log between them, using the blanket to shield her fingers from the hot metal. "We'll want to let it cool—"

She broke off as Astaroth shoveled a spoonful of steaming chili into his mouth. Rather than screaming in pain, he closed his eyes, seeming to savor the mouthful. "Delectable," he said after he'd swallowed. "Rich and savory, with balanced flavors and spices."

Right. Demons liked hot things—she remembered Mariel telling her Oz hadn't needed to spend any time adjusting to the high temperatures of the hot springs near Glimmer Falls. "It's not fine dining," she said. "This can cost less than two bucks."

He ate another spoonful. "You don't realize how dismal food is on a lot of planes," he said. "There's a reason demons often order takeout from Earth. Even simple human meals have complex flavor profiles."

Calladia took her own spoonful, blowing on the chili before tentatively nibbling. It was hot, but manageable. As she chewed, she considered the flavors. That one mouthful contained beans, meat, tomato, onion, chili peppers, and a variety of spices she couldn't name. Mariel would know, but Calladia had never pretended to be a great cook. Her blender was the most-used tool in her kitchen.

If Astaroth hadn't commented on the flavors, she would have wolfed it down without a thought for anything but the protein. He was right; it was good.

"I'm curious," she said after a few minutes. "You mentioned only remembering things from the past, but modern life doesn't seem to faze you. Why do you think that is?"

He looked thoughtful as he chewed. "I'm not certain. It's not like I remember everything about the past—more like my memory is a patchwork quilt with squares missing. Sometimes I can recall things easily, and sometimes images or sounds come to me at random. And some things seem automatic, like my mind and body know how to exist in this time, even if I can't recall having done so."

It struck Calladia that he was very well-spoken. Not that she hadn't noticed how articulate he was before, but this was the first time the adrenaline rush had slowed down enough for her to really pay attention and give him room to speak at length. "You remembered your flat," she said. "And pumpkins, right? Anything else?"

Astaroth closed his eyes. His eyelids flickered like he was dreaming. "There's a woman," he said. "One with red hair, but I can't make out her face. I hear her voice sometimes, warning me about things." He huffed. "Like hospitals."

Calladia felt a weird surge of irritation. Why did it matter if he had some woman's voice in his head? "What else did she warn you about?"

"She said they can never find out what I am, or I won't be able to claim my legacy."

Calladia's brow furrowed as she considered the strange

warning. "What does she mean, *what you are*? It's not like you're hiding your horns or anything. And what kind of legacy?"

He made a frustrated sound, and his eyes popped open. "I don't know, curse it. It's something to do with me being the son of . . . someone." He shook his head and grabbed the stick to stab the fire again. The aggressive blows made a log collapse, and sparks leaped into the air. "Bloody ridiculous," he groused. "I can't even remember who my parents are. I'm sure we weren't close, but still."

Calladia's chest ached at the reminder that she wasn't particularly close with her parents either. Cynthia Cunnington was the household tyrant, and Calladia's father, Bertrand, had practically made "absentee father" a career. "Why do you assume you weren't close?" she asked.

"Bargainers are trained outside the home," he said. "You've got to learn to be cold, so nothing you do affects you. Demons might not feel emotions as strongly as humans do, but we still feel them, and the moment guilt or doubt creeps in, a bargainer becomes useless."

The words were an echo of what Oz had said. It was strange though—Astaroth seemed the opposite of cold. He was a snarky bastard, but she could begrudgingly admit he was a bit funny. He seemed vibrant, for lack of a better word. Fully alive, with an outsize presence, charisma, and the guts to march confidently through the world despite the tremendous blow of losing his memory.

Also? Total drama queen.

He probably wouldn't like being told he was a drama queen rather than the ice-cold badass he clearly thought he was. And who knew, maybe the head blow really had altered his personality. Calladia let that aspect drop, though she wanted to know more about the parent situation. "Why would growing up in a family make you more likely to feel guilt?" she asked.

"Emotional connections are weaknesses. If you show vulnerability, enemies can manipulate you, and that's not including the self-sabotage demons might get up to if they regret a deal." He shrugged. "Learning how to shed weaknesses as a child is a gift."

Calladia didn't like that one bit. "Emotional connections can be strengths, too," she said. "Mariel and Oz kicked your ass in the name of love."

He narrowed his eyes. "What exactly happened with them?"

She hesitated. What if reminding him of the particulars of his battle with Oz and Mariel resurrected his memories, and he shifted back into evil-asshole mode? He was downright pleasant now compared to their first interaction.

"I'm tired," she said instead. She stretched and yawned, then checked her watch. "Hecate, it's nearly midnight." Astaroth was still glowering, so she offered an olive branch. "I'll tell you another time."

He shook his head, then stood and started kicking dirt onto the embers of the smoldering fire. "Do you have extra bedding or are we sharing?"

"What?" Calladia stared at him in horror. "What do you mean, are we sharing?"

He pointed at the tent. "I assume we will be sharing that flimsy excuse for shelter tonight. Do you have enough blankets and pillows for both of us, or will we be combining body heat?"

Calladia nearly swallowed her tongue. "No," she choked out. "Absolutely zero body heat sharing. Ew." He would probably be way too warm, making her sweat, and what if he was a cuddler? He could end up snoring on top of her, pinning her down with all those muscles and—"Ew," she repeated. "Horrible. Terrible. The worst."

He looked affronted. "People don't generally respond so poorly to the thought of sharing my bed."

"It's not a bed," she said. "It's a tent. One you will be sleeping in with a few blankets, while I will be occupying the sole sleeping bag." Her forehead furrowed as she considered something. "Wait, demons don't sleep as often as humans, do they? Or eat or pee. I mean, not that I've seen you pee—"

"I did," he confirmed, pointing into the woods. "Took a piss on that tree."

She winced. "The point is, why do you need to sleep when you slept last night? Can't you go on a hike or something?"

He looked as confused as she felt. "You want me to hike around the freezing cold woods alone at night rather than resting? What if it aids my memory?"

Okay, that was a decent point. Demons typically slept once or twice a week, but maybe he needed extra sleep because of the injury? Or maybe she'd caught him at some weird part of the demon cycle where they needed to eat, sleep, and go to the bathroom for a few days in a row. Demonic ovulation of the metaphorical type. It was possible; the only things she knew about demons came from Oz and an Interplanal Relationships course she'd taken in college that had been light on details.

"Fine," she said, eyeing the tent with a burgeoning sense of dread. "You can sleep with me." At his smirk, she hurried to clarify. "Next to me, that is. Not with me. Preferably as far from me as the tent will allow."

He sighed. "If you insist you don't want to share warmth . . ."

"I do." She wasn't even going to think about having his hot skin pressed against her or his breath puffing against her ear or his . . . "I'm going to sleep now," she announced, cheeks flaming.

As she hurried toward the small orange tent, she swore she heard his chuckle behind her.

THIRTEEN

CALLADIA WAS NOT A GRACEFUL SLEEPER.

Astaroth watched the rise and fall of her chest beneath the sleeping bag. Her forehead was furrowed, and periodically she thrashed around, kicking or flailing as she changed position. She'd rotated more than a rotisserie chicken over the last hour, and it was tremendously fun to watch.

"Baggins," she muttered, wrinkling her nose. "Shhh."

She was also a sleep talker, much to his delight. Her soft breaths had been interspersed with nonsensical words and snuffles, and it made him want to know what she was dreaming about.

She shifted again and flung out an arm, smacking his cheek where he lay on his side facing her.

"Ow," he said blandly.

"Pastrami," she replied before flipping to face away from him. "Gimme."

Astaroth yawned, and his jaw cracked. He'd slept briefly before Calladia's latest dream had woken him up, and then he'd been too entertained to close his eyes again. It was also deucedly uncomfortable in the tent. Calladia had her sleeping bag, a pillow, and a narrow roll-up mat to provide some cushion from the hard ground, but Astaroth was left trying to fashion a cocoon out of three blankets she'd provided, one of which was an annoyingly crinkly emergency blanket. The flannel beneath him at least helped with the chill creeping up from the ground, but it was bloody cold regardless, and his neck had a crick after trying to use his dirty, balled-up suit jacket as a pillow.

After chugging a few bottles of water, he also needed to relieve himself again. He groaned at the idea of having to go outside. A light rain had started, pattering against the tent fabric. The sound was soothing, and it conjured up a sense memory of lying in bed in his London flat, listening to rain smacking the glass. Pleasant, so long as the damp remained outside and he remained inside.

His bladder would not be denied though, so he eased out of the cocoon and shoved his feet into his discarded trainers. He unzipped the tent gently so as not to disrupt Calladia, although if hitting him in the face hadn't woken her up, it stood to reason a little noise wouldn't either.

The night was frigid and damp. Rain tapped against his horns and sank into his hair as he made his way to the tree line. The sky was overcast, but as a cloud shifted, a sliver of moon appeared.

Astaroth exhaled as he relieved himself. Calladia had been right about demons having less frequent bodily urges than humans, so it was odd that he was sleeping, eating, and using the loo two days in a row, but maybe it was a symptom of the accident. His scrambled brain must be sending mixed messages to his body.

He tipped his head back, looking at the scudding clouds overhead. The moon peeped out again, then hid its face coyly. When another patch of sky was revealed, he saw stars shining brilliant and pure against the blackness.

There were no stars in the demon plane, only a perpetual twilight that ranged from gray to purple to deepest black. Mist wound through the city streets, and the golden orbs of human souls drifted like fireflies.

Those souls harvested from witches and warlocks were the key to the realm's existence. Many ages past, the demon Lucifer had been banished from the mortal realm by an evil warlock. He'd opened a portal onto a world of dark, primordial chaos, but he'd brought the soul of a human he'd aided with him, and the light had pushed the darkness back. As other demons sought refuge from persecution, the lights had multiplied, and soon the plane was thriving. That essence—that pure, magical *life*—had been the seed to grow everything from red-blossomed fire lilies to three-headed hellhounds to the shimmering golden fish that leaped above rivers of lava. Without human souls, the plane would return to darkness, and its occupants would grow frail and eventually die—demons included.

Making bargains was a sacred responsibility, and he'd never hesitated to do whatever it took to gain those souls. Blackmail, threats, violence, manipulation . . . a human had to initiate the bargain, but some could be pushed into doing so, and others required a nudge to complete one after the initial summoning. If Astaroth could twist the words of a bargain to deliver less than what a mortal expected, so much the better. There was pride to be had in subverting the absurd deals some megalomaniacal witches and warlocks requested. One didn't want to initiate an apocalypse while performing one's duty, after all. As a tool wielded for the good of the species, trickery was considered a form of honor for demons, and no one had built a reputation for trickery better than his.

When Astaroth thought back though, he couldn't remember many of his deals. A love bargain here, a revenge bargain there . . . The endless cycle of coups and fortunes and passion and violence blurred together. He'd meddled in the affairs of humans for centuries, but even revisiting a few impressive bargains, such as the kingdom he'd single-handedly toppled in the 1600s, elicited little enthusiasm. It was like flipping through the pages of a history book and reading the dry details of someone else's accomplishments.

He sighed as he tore his gaze from the stars and headed to the tent. Maybe the last century or so had held more interesting deals, but of all the things he wanted to remember, those bargains didn't seem that pressing.

"I'm too old," he muttered, shivering as the night chill sank into him. Old and bored enough that bargains had lost their luster, and amnesia, while a devastating setback, was also refreshingly interesting. How else to explain the dullness he felt when thinking back on his exploits, versus the spark of excitement when he wondered what Calladia was muttering in her sleep now or what they would bicker about tomorrow?

Time wore everything down like water over stone. Astaroth's body would never age—although it was certainly taking its time to heal from his recent injuries—but inside he recognized the dulling contours of his past self. He'd burned in those early centuries, consumed by ambition, drunk on the power of shaping worlds and lives. But life had lost its ability to surprise sometime in the murky past.

Calladia, at least, was always surprising. Mortals tended to be, with their brief lives and oversized hungers. Maybe that was why he'd started spending more time on Earth over the centuries, even if he'd sworn it was from a dedication to duty that allowed no respite.

He slipped into the tent and zipped it behind him. When he turned, he saw Calladia looking at him beneath heavy lids. "'S raining?" she mumbled.

"It is," he confirmed as he toed off his shoes. He clambered into the blankets.

Calladia's head dropped to the pillow. "Good," she said, closing her eyes. "The sandwich is safe."

He stifled a laugh at the nonsensical words. Still asleep, then, or sliding back into it so quickly that dreams and reality blurred. Soon she was breathing deeply, one hand curled next to her face. Her blond braid was a mess after all that thrashing, and a section of loose hair curved over her cheek, the ends tickling her lips with every exhale.

Astaroth reached out and gently tucked the strands behind her ear.

Then he turned over with a curse, putting his back to her.

As the rain and her soft breathing mingled, he wondered: Why, when he had been shivering a few seconds ago, did his chest now feel oddly warm?

✦ ✦ ✦

"HEAD EAST AND BEGIN THE FABLE. STALK THE RED DEER." Astaroth scoffed. "Bloody nonsense. You'd think the witch would at least have a postcode."

They were winding down a mountain road the next morning, passing in and out of patches of mist. There hadn't been many turnoffs, and Calladia swore this road was the one that old warlock had instructed her to take, but with every kilometer farther into the forest, Astaroth doubted this plan more.

Calladia's fingers drummed against the steering wheel. "I thought you liked drama."

"As a concept, yes. When it's impeding my goals? Less so."

He was feeling decidedly cranky this morning after a night tossing and turning. Calladia had provided him with a granola bar for breakfast, but his stomach still felt hollow. This frequent eating and sleeping business was obnoxious. Astaroth scratched his neck and glared out the window, as if the pine trees might answer for the wrongs he was suffering. At that moment, his stomach gave a loud grumble.

Calladia looked askance at him. "You're hungry again? Already?"

"Another symptom of my brain damage, apparently." A thought spun up from the hazy recesses of his mind: *Bing might have information about amnesia.* He racked his brain, trying to remember who Bing was, but came up blank. "Do you know of an oracle named Bing?" he asked. "I just had a random thought that I might be able to ask them about this."

Calladia burst into loud laughter. Astaroth jumped at the noise, then found himself unable to tear his gaze away from Calladia as she cackled and slapped the steering wheel. "An oracle," she wheezed. "You think Bing is an oracle. Even more remarkably, you use *Bing*!"

"No need to mock me," he said, torn between embarrassment and a fascination with her amusement. She laughed as boldly as she did everything else, and as soon as the sound tapered off, he found himself wanting to hear it again.

"Sorry," she said, wiping her eyes. "It's just . . . gosh. I love that. Every time I Google something, I'm going to call it 'consulting the oracle.'" She was still grinning as she glanced at him. "Bing and Google are internet search engines. You type things on your computer or your phone, and it shows results from across the web."

"Ah. The internet." That did sound familiar. He pulled the phone out of his pocket, tapping the screen and scowling when it requested a passcode. "If only I could remember how to get into this blasted thing."

"You don't have biometrics set up?" Calladia asked. "Like unlocking it with your fingerprint?"

The words felt familiar, but with little to anchor them in his head, the idea struck him as absurd. It was astounding how much had changed over the course of his long life. At the moment, his most vivid memories involved swinging a sword on European bat-tlefields or entertaining queens by firelight. Now it was possible for a device the size of his palm to be unlocked with a fingerprint so the user could search the internet for information.

He slid his finger over the case, pressing it to various promising-looking spots. "It doesn't seem like I do."

Calladia swerved to avoid an oversized chipmunk sitting in the middle of the road—one with purple fur, wings, and fangs. "Prob-ably for the best," she said. "I heard it's easy to hack those things with the right tools. Someone lifts a fingerprint, prints it on special paper, and bam, they can unlock your shit."

Interesting. He'd need to look into that in case the technique could be helpful for soul bargaining.

Calladia switched on the radio and scanned through stations. Static, laughter, static, opera, static . . . then a familiar female voice danced over a rhythmic guitar line. Astaroth nodded along.

He didn't realize he was quietly singing until Calladia gasped. "Wait," she said. "No way."

She was probably surprised by his recall of the lyrics—as was Astaroth, now that he thought of it. "I don't know how I know the song," he said. "It's just familiar. Maybe there's an amnesia excep-tion for music?"

"Not that," she said, flapping her hand. "You're a *Swiftie?*"

He squinted, confused. "Is that a species? We've already estab-lished I'm a demon."

Calladia cackled again, flashing her spellbinding grin. "So Bing's an oracle and Swifties are a species. This is perfect."

"Come on," he said, once again annoyed and entranced. His lips tugged at the corners like he might join her hilarity, but fear-some demons didn't laugh at themselves.

"Swifties are fans of Taylor Swift," Calladia said once she'd stopped chuckling. "She's a pop singer. Well, she started in country, but she's branched out since then."

Taylor Swift. He turned the name over in his head, but no images appeared. He shrugged. "Apparently I'm a Swiftie."

This seemed to delight Calladia even more. "Me, too!" she exclaimed. She turned the song up, then alternated between singing—loudly and with a questionable understanding of pitch—and explaining the inspiration for the song. "She writes about her exes a lot," she practically yelled over the music. "In this one, she's singing about a guy she dated when she was younger. He was older and more experienced, so it was kind of a problematic age gap."

"How much older?" Astaroth asked, intrigued by what she considered problematic. Three centuries? Five?

She made a face. "Thirteen years."

Astaroth choked on his own spit. He coughed, pounding his chest. "You think *thirteen years* is problematic?" he wheezed when he was finally able to speak.

"She was only nineteen!" Calladia said defensively. "That's a big maturity gap."

"Huh." Astaroth felt an odd tightness in his chest. It was worry, he realized, though why he should worry about Calladia's age preferences was a mystery. "So you wouldn't date someone thirteen years older than you?"

"I would," Calladia said, "but I'm not nineteen. I'm twenty-eight. A lot of growth happens during your twenties."

Twenty-eight. Lucifer, that was young. Yes, he knew she was human and thus subject to a short life span, but he hadn't really *thought* about it specifically. When Astaroth had been twenty-eight, he'd been . . .

He frowned. What had he been up to at twenty-eight? He'd struck his first bargain around forty, but before then . . .

Fog.

Hang it, why couldn't he remember?

"I guess that seems silly to you," Calladia said.

Astaroth snapped back to the conversation. "What?"

"A thirteen-year age gap being problematic." She slid him a glance. "Since you're older than dirt."

"I object," Astaroth said. "Dirt is substantially older than me."

"Still, you must have had, ah, *relations* with plenty of people younger than you."

"I have," he said. "Though it all blurs together after a while." Nameless faces, nameless bodies, the dances of attraction or manipulation or boredom or some mix of the three. There had been princes and priestesses, demons and elves and humans. None of them stood out as being particularly remarkable.

"Hmm."

He couldn't tell what sentiment lay behind that syllable, but her jaw looked tighter than it had before. "You disapprove?"

"Not at all. If I was six hundred years old or whatever, I'd probably have a massive body count, too." Her fingers flexed on the steering wheel. "I guess you get good at it after that long."

"Oh, I was good at it from the start." He smirked at her eye roll. "Why, looking for tips?"

He'd gladly give her some. Or literally *the* tip, should she express interest. The spandex had been packed away, but her well-worn jeans were just as much of a problem, as he suspected anything would be that had the fortune of cupping that remarkable arse. He eyed the fall of her messy blond braid over her shoulder, imagining wrapping the bright length around his hand while he thrust into her from behind.

His trousers grew tighter.

"No, thank you," she said vehemently.

It wasn't the enthusiastic response a demon might hope for, but it was the response he'd expected. Still, he deflated a bit. Metaphorically. The trouser situation remained an issue.

Calladia braked, and Astaroth was distracted from her rebuttal and his erection by the sight of a stop sign. The road terminated in an intersection, where a green sign with white arrows indicated what lay ahead: SCENIC LOOKOUT, 5 MILES to the left, and FABLE FARMS, 15 MILES to the right.

Calladia pointed to the sign. "Maybe Alzapraz's instructions weren't so bad, after all. 'Head east and begin the fable.'"

"It's a bit of a reach," Astaroth said. "Shouldn't he have said 'begin *at* the Fable' if he meant it as a literal place? Or, I don't know, 'drive to Fable Farms,' if he really wanted to be helpful?" A certain type of warlock adored riddle shite like this, and though it was a solid branding move, it was deeply obnoxious for the people forced to solve those riddles.

Calladia flicked on her blinker. "It's the best clue we've gotten, and I'm driving, so you can shut up and go along for the ride." Her lips curved. "Or you can sing more pop songs. Silence or singing—those are your options."

The radio had moved on to something jangly and unpleasant. He sighed. "Silence it is."

FOURTEEN

CALLADIA STOOD WITH HANDS ON HER HIPS AND TOE TAP-
ping, gazing down the main drag of Fable Farms. And by
main drag, she meant the only drag.

"Bit underwhelming," Astaroth commented. He stood beside
her on the sidewalk next to Clifford the Little Red Truck.

Calladia grunted in agreement. She was used to life in a rea-
sonably small town, but this was something else. Unpaved roads
wound into the trees, where a few buildings were visible, but the
one paved street housed a general store, a gas station, a few unidentifiable structures, what looked like some kind of hunting lodge,
and an antiques market/clothing boutique/ice-cream parlor/sports
equipment store with a sign declaring KAI'S KORNER. Other than
the gas station, the buildings were built from timber, giving the
impression of an Oregon Trail settlement that had survived to
modern times.

"Presumably the red deer is in the forest somewhere," Calladia
said. "I guess we start hiking?"

Astaroth's stomach chose that moment to grumble.

"After we eat something," Calladia said. She was peckish herself, and lunch with a demon wasn't the worst idea she'd ever had.

No, rescuing the demon in the first place had definitely been the worst idea.

A blue convertible was parked outside the general store, and a large man in a green shirt stood by it, guzzling a sports drink. Maybe he could direct them where to eat.

Calladia waved and jogged over. "Hello," she called out.

The man wiped his mouth on his sleeve, and she realized he was wearing a rugby kit. *Fable Farms Furies* was emblazoned in an arc across his chest. His reddish-brown skin had a damp post-workout glow. "Well, hello to you," he said in a New Zealand accent. "We don't get many tourists here. Where are you coming from?"

He was handsome, with dark eyes, a roguish smile, and a bold nose that had clearly been broken several times. His massively muscled build, combined with the shaggy quality of his black hair, led Calladia to suspect he was a werewolf. Once she was close enough to feel the animalistic energy radiating off him, she was sure of it.

"Glimmer Falls," Calladia said.

"Sweet as." He shook her hand, and Calladia noticed an intricate tattoo extending from the sleeve of his jersey to his right elbow. "My name's Kai. Auckland by origin, but I've made my home in these woods for a decade. What brings you to Fable Farms?"

"I'm Calladia," she said, "and I'm on a quest."

"A quest to Fable Farms, population 203?" Kai laughed. "What an exciting life you lead."

Calladia huffed in shared amusement. "I'm trying to find a red deer. Any idea where it might be?"

"Who sent you on this quest? Welp?" Kai asked, referencing the mobile app that posted crowd-sourced reviews of budget food options. The app's tagline was *Good enough, I guess*, and Calladia had found some great dive bars using it. Kai grinned and pointed down the street. "The best food in miles is at the Red Deer, end of the road."

Calladia looked at the building he'd pointed out—the one resembling a hunting lodge. "Oh! I hadn't considered it might be a place, not an actual animal. We'll check it out."

"We?" Kai asked, cocking a brow. He looked over her shoulder, and his eyes widened. "Sweet Remus and Romulus, that fucker has horns."

Calladia bit her cheek. "He does indeed."

Kai returned his startled gaze to her. "What is he?"

"Demon."

Kai whistled. "Never seen one of those before. Are you, you know, with him?" He gave the last two words heavy emphasis.

"We're traveling together, yes."

Kai clicked his tongue. "No, I meant like . . . *with him*, with him."

It took Calladia a moment to understand the implication. "Oh!" She frantically slashed her hands in a *no* gesture. "Absolutely not. We hate each other. Two sworn enemies on a quest, that's all." Totally normal. Everyone ended up on a road trip with their disgustingly attractive nemesis at some point, right?

"Ah." Kai relaxed and gave her another charming grin. "Well, in that case, may I offer my phone number to a very lovely tourist in case she needs directions, assistance, or a nice dinner sometime?"

Was he hitting on her? The few advances she'd received were more along the lines of that lout whose face she'd slammed into the bartop. But here was a charming werewolf offering to take her to dinner, and he'd nailed Asking a Woman Out 101 by offering her his number, rather than requesting hers, allowing her to choose whether or not to contact him.

"I, uh, sure?" Calladia said, feeling flustered. Themmie would have known exactly how to proceed, but this was not a situation rough-and-tumble Calladia was equipped to handle. Was she supposed to flirt back? Did she even want to? Men were more trouble than they were worth, as she'd learned the hard way.

Kai reached out. "Can I put my number in your phone?" Apparently noting her hesitation, he held his hands up. "No pressure. It was just a thought."

Calladia was still tongue-tied, but she had to do something, and he was being awfully polite about the whole thing. She fished the phone out of her windbreaker and handed it over, and Kai started typing.

"What's this?" Astaroth's voice came from very close by.

Calladia turned to find the demon scowling beside her, hands on his hips. "This is Kai," she said, cheeks heating. "He's been very helpful."

"I'm sure he has." Astaroth narrowed his eyes at the werewolf. Kai met his gaze, smirked, then kept typing, and Astaroth's fists clenched.

Wait. Surely he hadn't just sounded . . . jealous?

There was no way. Astaroth hated her, like she hated him. He probably just wanted to make sure no one distracted his quest-helper.

The tension growing in the air set Calladia's teeth on edge. Even glowering, Astaroth looked gorgeous, albeit in a different way from the werewolf. Where Kai was bulky, Astaroth was leanly muscular; where Kai's features were rugged, Astaroth's seemed to have been carved from marble. Astaroth wasn't a massive man, certainly nowhere near the size of the werewolf, but when he looked like this, territorial and pissed off, he seemed . . .

Dangerous.

And damn if Calladia didn't like that.

She felt the urge to beat her head into a wall. Curse her miserable luck to get stuck with a demon who looked like her every fantasy come to life. On paper, a jacked werewolf ought to be exactly

Calladia's type, but her tastes had always run counter to expectation. She liked that she and Astaroth were the same height. She liked his snide comments and aura of elegant menace. She even liked how polished he was, despite how aggravating all that perfection could be, because it made her want to muss him up. Tackle him into a pit of mud, maybe, and watch his sneer turn into sputtering outrage.

Calladia didn't want to date some burly bruiser.

She wanted to *be* the burly bruiser.

Kai handed the phone back, breaking her reverie. "I'm glad I met you, fair Calladia." He winked. "I'm sure our paths will cross again soon."

Astaroth looked about to say something withering, so Calladia grabbed the demon's elbow and steered him around. "Thanks for the directions, Kai," she called over her shoulder.

Kai grinned and waved.

"What was that?" Calladia demanded once they were out of earshot. "You looked ready to strangle him."

"What was *that*?" Astaroth retorted. "He was practically drooling over you."

His appalled tone seemed over-the-top. Sure, Calladia wasn't the peak of femininity, but it wasn't out of the realm of possibility that a man might like her. "Turns out some men have taste," she said. "Just because you think I'm a violent harridan with no fashion sense doesn't mean other people agree."

"But you are a violent harridan with no fashion sense."

Stung, Calladia stopped in her tracks, yanking her hand away from his arm. "Screw you."

Astaroth looked startled. "What?"

Her cheeks were still hot, but this time it was shame causing the flush. "You may not find me attractive," she said, "but other people do. You don't need to be cruel about it."

He squinted like she'd said something ludicrous. "When did I say you aren't attractive?"

"Oh, maybe the unfashionable harridan insult?"

"It wasn't an insult, just a bit of banter." At Calladia's disbelieving look, Astaroth winced. "All right, I can see how my comments on fashion could be controversial, but you've made it clear you don't care about that. Why should it bother you?"

Did he even hear half the things that came out of his stupidly pretty mouth? Calladia started marching down the street again, not checking to see if he followed. "I don't care about fashion," she said. "But in what world is calling me a harridan a compliment?"

"This world," he said, catching up to her. "Didn't we talk about the importance of building a personal brand? You've done an excellent job."

Her glare threatened to flay him on the spot.

Astaroth held up his hands. "Perhaps I also worded that poorly."

"You think? Apparently that knock on the head took away your social skills—if you had any to begin with." Her gut churned with humiliation, and anger burned red-hot in her veins. By Hecate, she wanted to grab him by the horns, slam him into the nearest wall, and—

"I'm sorry."

The soft apology accomplished what nothing else could have. Calladia stopped, her anger warping into confusion. "What?"

Astaroth ran a hand through his hair, ruffling it so the pale gold layers feathered over his black horns. "I forgot that what demons take as compliments, others might not."

Calladia didn't understand. "Calling someone a violent harridan would be a compliment for demons?" She could only imagine what Dear Sphinxie—the *Glimmer Falls Gazette* advice columnist— would say.

"I've been called a diabolical, ruthless, remorseless monster," he said. "And many other things, of course." He shrugged. "That means I've cultivated a reputation that makes people fear me. If they say it to my face, it means they respect me enough to admit that fear."

Calladia blinked. "That's—wow." *Fucked up* was what came to mind. "So by insulting me, you meant to tell me you fear me?"

"It's not fear," he said. "I just have a healthy respect for your anger and your right hook. Would you rather I pretend you're some delicate flower?"

Calladia had never been a delicate flower, and she never would be. She stared at him, recalculating their hostile encounters through this upside-down demon lens. He engaged in their arguments eagerly, which she'd considered a mark of dislike. Everything she gave, he dished right back.

Had he actually been telling her he respected her and saw her as an equal in their sparring matches?

She shook her head. If Sam had taught her anything, it was that men twisted words to keep themselves in the right and their partners at a perpetual disadvantage. *You need to lose weight* could be explained away as *I'm only looking out for your health. You're too loud and argumentative* twisted into *You're embarrassing yourself, and I want to make sure my friends respect you the way I do.*

Astaroth's expression held no trace of Sam's trademark disappointment though. And while Sam had tried to reshape Calladia into his ideal woman—a delicate flower, indeed—Astaroth seemed to want her to be herself, no matter how rude or aggressive that was.

This was too much to process at the moment. Her head was spinning, and she was still on edge from being asked out, nice as Kai had seemed. "Well, here's a tip," she said. "In the human plane, we don't insult people we like." She paused, recalling how she twitted Mariel for her flights of fancy and how Themmie sometimes called Calladia "Rocky Balboa." "Or at least, we say it like a joke."

She replayed her words, then hurried to clarify. "Not that you like me, of course. But there are better ways to express respect for your enemies. Or whatever."

"Noted." Astaroth fell in beside her. A few awkward moments passed before he spoke again. "So, my warrior queen, where are we going?"

Calladia nearly tripped over her feet. A laugh burst from her. "What did you just call me?"

Astaroth gave her a crooked smile. "I was aiming for a new spin on *violent harridan* that would express the respect element more."

Oh, dear. She liked that far better than she ought to. "We'll keep workshopping it," she said lightly, despite the racing of her pulse. "And we're going to the Red Deer, which is that building at the end. Apparently they serve the best lunch in town, in addition to dispensing clues." Foolish or not, she couldn't resist poking at him again. "I told you Kai was helpful."

"Hmm." Astaroth's jaw worked. "We'll see how helpful. I dread to learn what a werewolf considers fine dining."

Such a snob. With the immediate conflict past and their conversation back in banter mode, Calladia felt better. "I hope whatever you order is vile," she said.

He gasped. "Your hostility wounds me."

Calladia bit her lip, fighting the urge to laugh. "Good. You could use some wounding."

"Is brain damage not enough for you?"

"You're still speaking, so clearly not."

Astaroth slapped a hand against his chest. "The warrior queen delivers a mortal blow."

This time Calladia hid her smile in her hand, pretending to scratch her nose.

The Red Deer turned out to be a hotel/restaurant, with a sign advertising free Wi-Fi and a continental breakfast. A neon red VACANCY sign shone in the window. The two-story building had log walls and a pitched roof, and the front door was framed by racks of antlers.

The rustic look continued inside. The lobby was filled with heavy, hand-carved wooden furniture, and tapestries mingled with more antlers on the walls. The stuffed head of a wolf was mounted over the fireplace.

"Are you kidding me?" Calladia asked, staring at the head in outrage. "Themmie would go apeshit if she were here." Calladia might, too. She'd met Themmie in the Glimmer Falls Environmental Club, and they shared a passion for protecting the local ecosystem. "Maybe wolf poachers would think twice if someone poached their asses," she grumbled.

A voice sounded from the front desk. "It's not real, I promise. The antlers are fake, too."

Calladia didn't see anyone at first. Then a woman's figure emerged from the wall, a process like melting in reverse. Her skin was nearly the same shade as the logs, and bark lined her hairline. A dryad—a tree nymph who could merge with wood. She wore a black uniform shirt, and her dark green eyes were wide and extravagantly lashed.

"That's good to hear," Calladia said, approaching the desk. "I was about to post something salty on Welp."

The dryad laughed. "I would be the first to raze this place to the ground if that was real. The local werewolf pack just has an odd sense of humor." She cocked her head, and a hank of thick black hair slid over her shoulder, brushing the name tag that said BRONWYN. "Looking for a room?"

"Lunch, actually." Calladia tapped her fingers against her thigh, already feeling restless to continue the quest. "And we're following directions to get to Isobel the life witch. Do you know where she is?"

Bronwyn groaned. "She's still refusing to give out her address?" She stepped out from behind the desk, gesturing for

Calladia and Astaroth to follow. "Let's get you settled, and I'll check our notes to see what your next step is supposed to be."

Another stuffed wolf head presided over the dining room. This one's glass eyes were crossed, giving it a comedic air, and a red felt tongue stuck out one side of its mouth. A trestle table sat beneath it, and there was a pool table in the corner near a fireplace. A roaring fire cast a cheery glow over the scratched wooden floorboards.

Bronwyn led them to a table and handed them menus. Calladia ordered a panini, while Astaroth settled on the salmon, which was what she should have expected from his pretentious ass.

After Bronwyn left, Calladia propped her elbows on the table and leaned in. "Salmon, huh? On my dime?"

"I promised I'd pay you back." Astaroth looked utterly unruffled—and utterly gorgeous—and Calladia despised him for both, almost as much as she'd hated letting him share her toothbrush that morning. While she was a scruffy, smelly mess with tangled hair, Astaroth looked like he'd stepped off the cover of a magazine. Being a demon, he had no stubble, and his blond hair came across as stylishly tousled. Worse, he still managed to smell good, the tang of sweat merging with his apparently natural scent of pine trees and exotic spices. Calladia had wiped her pits down at the stream and was still worried about raising her arms too high.

She really should find a mud pit to toss him in.

She wasn't actually concerned about him paying her back. Insurance would cover the loss of the house, and as a Cunnington, she had a trust fund. A trust fund she'd adamantly refused to dip into, not wanting to become more like her entitled mother, but it was a hell of a safety net, and she knew she was privileged to have it.

It was an uncomfortable balance, hating what she'd been raised to be while still profiting off her family's wealth. Was she a hypocrite? Probably. But as she'd told Astaroth, she wasn't a good person, just a fair-to-middling one.

A loud ringing split the air, and they both jumped. Astaroth fished in his pocket and pulled out his phone. "What in all the planes?" he asked, squinting at it. "Why is it making that infernal noise?"

Calladia snatched the phone and looked at the screen, then promptly gasped. "It says *Mum*!"

She wasn't sure what was more startling: that Astaroth had a mother, versus having emerged fully formed from a lava pit, or that he had her listed as *Mum* in his contacts. Calladia had switched her mom's contact info to *Cynthia Cunnington* a decade ago.

Astaroth looked freaked out. "I don't remember."

Calladia wasn't going to let this opportunity slide. She tapped the screen to answer, hit the speaker button, then handed it to Astaroth. "Roll with it," she whispered. "We might get some answers."

Astaroth took the phone gingerly. "Um, yes, hello?" he said, holding the phone to his ear.

"ASTAROTH!"

Astaroth recoiled at the loud exclamation, and Calladia stifled a laugh. "It's on speaker," she murmured. "Put it on the table."

He did, shooting her a chiding look. "This is he," he said.

"Obviously it's you," Astaroth's mother said in an unidentifiable accent. "What's this I'm hearing about you getting ejected from the council? I don't know who they think they are—well, scratch that, I know exactly who they think they are, pretentious little worms—but you're worth a thousand of them. Why did they banish you?"

Astaroth eyed the phone like it might leap off the table and bite him. "Erm . . . the demon high council?" he said tentatively.

"I heard Moloch is to blame," the woman continued. "I will wear his intestines like a feather boa, I swear to you. They didn't find out, did they?"

Astaroth looked thoroughly freaked out, and Calladia didn't blame him. "Find out what?"

His mother scoffed. "Playing dumb? Really?"

Astaroth rubbed his temples, and Calladia wondered if his headache was troubling him again. "I'm sorry," he said. "It's been an eventful few days. Humor me?"

"You know how Moloch feels about hybrids," she said. "He didn't find out you're half human, did he?"

Calladia's jaw dropped. Astaroth was *what*?

FIFTEEN

I'M—EXCUSE ME?" ASTAROTH ASKED, STARING DAZEDLY AT the phone.

Demon-human hybrids were rare. Some took after their mortal parent and lived on Earth, but others lived on the demon plane. They weren't respected by fundamentalist demons though, and none had ever gained political power.

If Astaroth knew anything about himself, it was that he'd always sought power. There was no way he was anything other than a full-blooded demon.

Right?

"Are you even listening?" The woman who was apparently his mother sounded annoyed. And Lucifer, how could he not remember his mother? Sure, his memory was spotty even for events long past, but a parent was a fairly pivotal part of one's life. "You know your power rests on your reputation," she said. "You didn't have an emotional outburst, did you? You were doing so well at masking your human traits."

Human traits. Emotional outbursts.

Astaroth started to sweat. He wanted to shout that he was a pure-blooded demon, with horns and the immortal life span to prove it, but that meant little. While many hybrids had small horns or none at all, others had normal horns. And though some had finite life spans, immortal hybrids existed as well. The quirks of genetics had created an array of possibilities should a demon procreate outside the species.

His temples throbbed. He wanted to scream denials, maybe throw something. Tear the whole bloody room apart if that would somehow prove his full-blooded status.

But that would be an emotional outburst, wouldn't it?

He met Calladia's wide brown eyes. She looked as shocked as he felt. That was comforting, at least—but then again, a proper demon wouldn't crave comfort, would they?

Half human.

Maybe the knock on the head wasn't to blame for his volatility, after all. But if he was a hybrid . . . Lucifer, what a nightmare.

The most traditional demons considered humans a prey species, essential for maintaining the demon ecosystem but not worthy of respect. Astaroth had always supported hybrid rights on the demon plane, but that didn't mean anything, did it? It was practical to encourage genetic diversification. And if mortals were interesting enough to convince him to live mostly on Earth, that had been a tactic to better learn how to manipulate them, right?

Or had it been a lie to cover up the real reason: that Astaroth felt a kinship with humans?

The trouble with truth was that once it got bold enough to punch you in the face, it was impossible to ignore. He could throw out countless arguments, but when Astaroth took stock of his tumultuous inner landscape, this revelation *felt* true. And although he gleefully lied to others, he didn't want to lie to himself.

His reality shifted on its axis.

"So?" His mother's voice burst from the speakers. "Did the high council find out what you are?"

Fresh revelations aside, there was still a conversation to navigate, and Astaroth didn't want to admit his amnesia yet. "I don't think so," he said. Technically true, since it was impossible to speculate without any evidence. He cleared his throat. "What have you heard?"

"That they removed you from the high council and banished you to Earth, the soon-to-be-eviscerated wretches, but that's a minor setback, so long as they don't know the rest of it. We'll get you back in power in no time. No one treats me and mine like this, and if Moloch has forgotten the name Lilith, I will happily remind him." She cackled. "I'll carve it into his skin over and over again until my name echoes in his bones."

Lilith.

The name unlocked a memory of a woman's face bent over him while sunshine cascaded through her red hair. Astaroth had been small then, seated in her lap and looking in awe at her black horns while she regaled him with stories of her conquests. *Someday,* she'd said, stroking his hair, *your horns will grow bigger even than mine and you'll have enemies of your own to destroy.*

He'd wanted nothing more.

The memories spilled out from there, like tiles tumbling into an artist's hand, bright pieces that, once assembled in the correct order, would form the mosaic of his past. He envisioned Lilith bundled in furs with a sword strapped to her back, hair gleaming like fire against a snow-capped peak. Lilith playing cards and stabbing a knife through her opponent's hand, then telling Astaroth— over the man's screams—that if cheating failed to prosper, violence was always an option. Lilith scribbling in a leather-bound book, her hair in wild tangles as she giggled to herself about tentacle jousting and something called AO3.

Lilith cupping his cheeks, pale blue eyes glinting with love and an edge of madness. *They must never find out what you are, or you won't be able to seize your legacy as my son.*

"You've got to be shitting me," Calladia whispered across the table. "Lilith, like super-duper old and scary demon Lilith?"

Lilith was famous, he now recalled. Feared and respected across the planes, notorious for her great age, insanity, and unpredictable, often violent behavior. To be her son was a legacy, indeed.

"Who was that?" Lilith asked. "Are you with someone?"

Calladia widened her eyes and shook her head.

Astaroth was still reeling from the bombshells Lilith had dropped. "No, just me," he said, wincing at how unconvincing he sounded.

A squeal and clapping of hands came over the line. "You are! Who is it? Tell me the species, at least. Man, woman, or other? What's their name? Or their names, if it's a group situation."

There would be no wiggling out of this one. Astaroth looked to Calladia and raised a brow, silently asking permission. She winced, then nodded.

"Human," he said. "A witch named Calladia." The most aggravating, perfectly vicious harridan of a witch, whose blond hair and brown eyes haunted his dreams. In centuries past, she would have been the literal warrior queen he'd termed her, leading armies into battle.

Now he just wanted her to battle him.

"Calladia." Lilith repeated the syllables, which sounded heavier in her accent—an accent he could now identify as a unique amalgamation of hundreds of languages learned and abandoned over time. "You've always liked fornicating with humans. Obviously you get that from me." She sighed dreamily. "That traveling minstrel who contributed his sperm had skills, even if he didn't stick around to see the results."

Calladia nearly choked on her water. *Fornicating?* she mouthed.

Yes, please, he thought, head spinning from the influx of information and emotion.

"I hope this witch is as beautiful, conniving, and deadly as you deserve," Lilith said. She clicked her tongue. "Like that human a few centuries back. Who was she, the one I liked? The poisoner?"

"Lucrezia Borgia," Astaroth said dazedly, pulling the name from the ether.

Calladia clapped a hand to her mouth and made a muted squealing sound.

Lilith chuckled. "Such a vicious woman. Very feisty. Her brother, too. What was his name?"

"Cesare," Astaroth said, recalling dim memories of carnal entertainments with corrupt, red-robed cardinals.

"Unbelievable," Calladia muttered through her fingers. "Your life should be a TV show."

"I wouldn't have minded being the meat in the middle of that sandwich myself," Lilith said. "It's lovely they didn't mind sharing you."

Calladia smacked the table hard enough to rattle the napkin holder. "You hooked up with both Cesare and Lucrezia Borgia?" she whisper-shrieked. "Separately, or . . ."

Astaroth winced. "Now's not a good time," he told his mother. "We're eating lunch."

Lilith cooed. "A date! Lovely. It's nice to see you socializing again. Ever since you took in that pup . . . when was it? Eight centuries ago? Twelve? Lucifer knows the years run together."

Astaroth had no idea what she was talking about. "I'm only six centuries old."

"You took your duty as a mentor so seriously," she said. "I always told you even purebred demons are allowed to enjoy themselves sometimes. Especially if you embrace insanity!" Lilith paused. "Or did I only say that to myself?"

Astaroth's head pulsed with pain. The world spun, and he gripped the edges of the table.

"Astaroth?" Lilith asked. "Are you still there?"

"Astaroth?" Calladia repeated in a gentler tone, looking concerned. She rested her hand on the table near his.

Cold sweat beaded at his brow. It was abruptly too much. The influx of memories, a surprise phone call from his mother, learning he had finally attained a position on the demon high council only to lose it, not to mention that *half human* revelation . . .

He stifled a whimper and looked at Calladia, silently begging for help.

Calladia grabbed the phone. "Sorry, food is here," she told Lilith. "Got to go!"

"Oh, all right," Lilith said. "Enjoy your meal, lovebirds. But don't worry, I'm going to find out more about Moloch's aims. We'll work on a strategy together. You'll be back at the high table before you know it, and I'll be drinking Moloch's blood out of a decorative chalice made from his skull." She made kissy noises into the phone. "Talk soon!"

The line went dead.

Astaroth stared at the phone. He was breathing too fast, so he pressed a hand to his diaphragm, took a deep breath in, and let it out slowly.

"Here." Calladia nudged the water toward him. "You look like you're going to pass out."

"I would never," he grumbled before chugging the entire glass. The frantic throb of his headache began to fade, but he still felt dizzy.

Astaroth of the Nine. Astaroth the *half human*. The two ideas were so opposed, it was difficult to hold them in his mind at the same time.

And Lilith, the ancient and famously unhinged demoness—his mother!

Calladia cleared her throat. "Food's coming."

Astaroth sat up straight, determined not to show his inner tur-moil. The dryad, Bronwyn, appeared with plates of steaming food, and he murmured thanks.

After Bronwyn had left, Calladia speared her side salad with a fork. She chewed, eyeing Astaroth with a clinical eye that indi-cated an interrogation was imminent. Astaroth braced himself, poking half-heartedly at the salmon.

"So," Calladia finally said. "Your mom is Lilith. Like . . . *the* Lilith."

"It would seem so." He took a bite of salmon and made an ap-preciative noise. "This is quite good. I wonder if they'd be willing to share the recipe for this marinade?"

Calladia ignored his attempt at deflection. "In college we spent an entire class period talking about Lilith. It was a gen ed class, Interplanar History 101: Sex, Violence, and Batshittery. They called her the Mother of All Demons."

The nickname was familiar, and it provoked a surge of corre-sponding disdain. He'd heard that *a lot*, he realized. "She would have needed to be very busy to accomplish that. And she's old, but not *that* old." Lilith had been wreaking havoc for thousands of years, but no one even had an estimate for when Lucifer had founded the demon plane.

"Apparently she's the mother of at least one demon though," Calladia said.

Astaroth squeezed the fork tightly enough to hurt. "I re-member a bit of her now," he said. "Her voice . . . she was the one warning me away from hospitals. She said they couldn't learn what I was." His throat bobbed. "A *hybrid*, apparently." The word was sour on his tongue.

How had every meaningful memory been knocked out of his head, and only random snippets remained? What good did it do him to remember dining, fighting, and fornicating across Europe if he had no clue what he actually was?

"Maybe that's why you eat and sleep so much," Calladia said around a mouthful of food. "It's the human half."

He didn't want to talk about his genetics, especially not with the human who vexed and fascinated him in equal measure, so Astaroth decided to pick a fight instead. "Your table manners are atrocious."

Calladia narrowed her eyes, then reached across the table and dipped her finger in the ramekin holding the sauce for Astaroth's salmon. She loudly sucked the sauce off her finger while making unblinking eye contact.

Astaroth gaped, horrified and aroused. As an expression of dominance, it was unorthodox but effective. He'd thrown the gauntlet, and she'd picked it up. "Appalling behavior," he said, eyes dropping to where her pink lips were wrapped around her finger. "Truly distressing."

Calladia popped her finger out of her mouth. "Enough about my table manners," she said. "Let's talk about the fact that your mom is Lilith, you're half human, and you had a thing with the Borgias, which you apparently remember clearly."

"When she mentioned them, I remembered." His appetite had vanished, but he started cutting his salmon into small pieces for lack of anything better to do. "I was young then, less than a century old, and I was studying human behavior across the Papal States." More hazy memories unfurled, and he closed his eyes to focus on them past the residual echoes of his headache. "Mum sent me there. She said I needed to see what humans were capable of, and the Church was the best place to see the absolute worst behavior."

"That's very interesting," Calladia said, "but I can't get past the Borgia bit. Did you really date both of them?" She leaned in, practically salivating.

"I don't know if I would classify it as dating . . ." He envisioned red satin sheets and bare skin, but when he tried to focus on the person beneath him in that memory, he only saw Calladia's face.

Lucifer, this wasn't good. Carnal thirst was a slippery slope. Soon, he might find himself—horror of horrors—*pining* for the witch.

Astaroth shifted in his chair, trying to push the image of a nude Calladia out of his mind. "We had a bit of fun, that's all."

She scoffed. "That's what you call hooking up with two of history's most notorious schemers and murderers? Come on, drama queen. Give me the dirty details. Was it separately? Or like . . . at the same time?"

Astaroth might not know much these days, but he had a suspicion Calladia's moral scruples wouldn't stretch far enough to condone incestuous threesomes. "A gentleman doesn't shag and tell," he said in a dignified tone.

Calladia clapped a hand to her mouth. She was making a stuttering, high-pitched sound it took Astaroth a moment to identify as laughter. Her shoulders shook, and her eyes were bright with hilarity.

Astaroth was torn between fascination and annoyance. She laughed so infrequently, and never in these bubbly giggles, as light and intoxicating as champagne. But what was there to laugh about? His life was in shambles, and he'd just been clobbered upside the head—metaphorically this time—with details of his existence he didn't know how to process.

"This isn't funny," he snapped.

"Oh, come on," she said through her fingers. "You had a threesome with the Borgias!"

All right, maybe her morals did stretch that far. A good thing if she was going to spend more time around him, since more memories of hedonism would certainly follow.

Not that she was going to spend more time with him. This was a brief quest she had reluctantly embarked on due to some foolish notion of responsibility. Once her duty was carried out, she'd return to her life and leave him behind.

His chest ached at the thought. He rubbed his sternum, wondering if he'd cracked a rib somehow.

"Sorry," Calladia said when Astaroth didn't reply. She took a deep breath and blew it out slowly. "I shouldn't have laughed. I just can't believe I'm hanging out with the sixteenth century's most gutsy lothario."

He scowled. "How did I not remember being a hybrid?" he blurted out. "Or being a member of the high council? I craved that bloody position for centuries, and now I can't remember getting it?" His temple throbbed again, and he stabbed his plate with the fork, eliciting a loud metallic screech. "Lucifer, this is a disaster."

"How is it a disaster? You're remembering more and more every day."

Astaroth made a frustrated sound and jabbed the plate again. "There aren't many demon hybrids, and feelings about them have always been . . . complicated. Some of the most influential demons don't consider them true demons at all, and there's never been one in power before."

"Until you," Calladia said. "That has to be gratifying."

It should be, but it wasn't. "How, when I can't remember gaining power? When I have no idea how or why I lost it? When I know if my secret gets out, I'll never hold a position of influence again?" A thought seized him, accompanied by tendrils of icy dread that wrapped around his ribs. "What if they did find out, and that's why I'm here?"

Saying half demons were controversial was just the start. While there were those who lived and thrived in the demon plane, albeit without much institutional support, others had been sent to live off-plane or disowned entirely. The ones who did remain tended to have more demonic traits, such as horns and immortality.

Hybrid minds are weak, someone had once told him, the sneering words echoing through history. *How can we allow human frailty to shape demon society? Only the strong can lead the strong.*

Who had said that? Moloch? Another demon?

Astaroth scraped his fork over the plate again, then jabbed the tines into the salmon repeatedly, wishing he had a sword and could murder something for real. Curse his rumbling stomach and his aching head. Curse his feeble brain, curse his human heritage and whatever weakness it had imparted to him, curse Moloch and the demon high council and the great, yawning expanse of the past that no doubt hid countless other nasty surprises. Curse the whole bloody universe!

"If they booted you out for that," Calladia said, "then the high council needs to get with the times. They're begging for a wrongful termination lawsuit on the basis of discrimination."

"Americans and your lawsuits," Astaroth groused. "Swords are more effective at conflict resolution."

"Oh, yes, let's promote a new era of tolerance by skewering people. Excellent choice."

Astaroth stabbed the salmon extra hard, eliciting a horrendous screech of metal.

Calladia grabbed his wrist, stilling his agitated motions. "Eat the food. Don't poke at it."

Astaroth stilled, looking at where her finger covered his pulse. She hadn't touched him like this before. There had been incidental brushes from being trapped in close proximity, but it had all been practical and impersonal.

This though.

This was new.

Her skin was cool against his demon heat, a balm that soothed his agitation. Her nails were filed short, and the rasp of calluses against his skin spoke of her strength.

There was a softness to her, too, echoed in the gentle slope of her jawline and the curve of her parted lips. He shivered, imagined those lips trailing kisses over his torso, each one an autumn raindrop to cool the angry fire burning in his chest. He would drink that sweet relief down like a dying man, but he suspected it would never be enough.

Calladia snatched her hand back and cleared her throat. "Plotting is better done on a full stomach, right?" she asked as she grabbed her sandwich. Her cheeks were pinker than they had been a minute before. "Overhauling demon society can wait until we've found Isobel and recovered your memories."

Astaroth nodded dumbly as she took a hearty bite of the panini. He'd never been envious of bread before. "Plotting," he repeated. "Right." When she licked her lips, he mirrored the action reflexively.

Calladia paused midchew. Her eyes dropped to his mouth.

The main door swung open, and a chorus of male voices echoed through the main lobby, shattering the moment. Astaroth looked over to see who had intruded, then scowled.

A group of very tall, very muscular men in sweat-darkened green rugby uniforms were laughing and slapping one another on the back. Given how hirsute they were, they must be werewolves, a notion borne out by the appearance of that Kai fellow in the midst of them. Astaroth narrowed his eyes, full of abrupt loathing.

Curse werewolves, along with everything else. Did they need to be so bloody big?

"Guess it's the local pack," Calladia said.

Astaroth made a disgruntled sound as someone whooped. "Noisy, aren't they?"

Calladia snickered. "This just in: old curmudgeon finds the youths too noisy. Story at six."

Astaroth switched his glare to her. "I'm not a curmudgeon. And they are making an indecent amount of noise." As if to prove

his point, the werewolves gathered in a circle and started chant-
ing, swaying back and forth with their arms around one another.

"Sure, Father Time," Calladia said. "It's not that you're a six-
hundred-year-old grump who wants the kids to get off your lawn."

"I don't have a lawn. London flat, remember?"

The werewolves culminated with a shout and began making
their noisy way toward the dining room, following Bronwyn.

"This round's on me," Kai said. He stopped in his tracks when
he spotted Calladia. "A vision!" he proclaimed, clapping a hand to
his chest. "Fair Calladia, I knew our paths would cross again."

"Because you told her to eat lunch here, you git," Astaroth muttered under his breath. He gripped his fork, envisioning how it
would look embedded in Kai's neck.

If Kai heard him—and he certainly did, with heightened werewolf senses—he gave no sign. He swept an extravagant bow toward
Calladia while his teammates snickered. "I apologize for these
hoodlums. They're not used to polite company."

"Oh, shut up," a werewolf with brown hair said. "This clown
scores two tries and thinks he's Lycaon's gift to womankind."

Kai scoffed. "Oh, please, Avram. I'm the best number eight this
side of the international date line."

The other werewolf slapped Kai upside the head. "The best?
Maybe in the peewee league."

"Exactly." Kai winked at Calladia, which nearly earned him a
fork through the eye. "Those little fuckers don't stand a chance."

"Stop flirting with customers," Bronwyn said, bumping him
with her hip. The dryad only came up to Kai's shoulder, but she
carried herself with the confidence of someone who knew she
could snap her fingers and the whole pack would come running.
"These two are looking for Isobel."

"Two?" Kai asked. "I only have eyes for the lovely lady."

Astaroth scoffed. "Oh, please."

Calladia looked like she was biting back a smile. "Nice to meet you all," she said to the team at large. "I'm Calladia."

Why was Calladia entertaining the crude advances of this oaf? Anyone could see she was out of his league.

Kai scooped up her hand, bent over, and kissed it. "The pleasure is all ours." He glanced up with his lips still pressed against her skin and winked again. "Especially mine."

Astaroth's hold on his temper snapped. He shot to his feet, sending silverware flying. "Get your hands off her."

Calladia jolted in her chair, pulling her hand back. She blinked at Astaroth owlishly. "Astaroth, it's fine."

"Is it, though?" It had been a piss-poor few days, and after everything that had happened with his mother, he wasn't in the mood to watch a bloody werewolf flirt with *his* witch.

"Easy, mate," Kai said. His eyes were fixed on Astaroth's horns, and his jovial expression had vanished, replaced with the calculating look of a man sizing up an opponent. "Don't you think that's a bit possessive for someone not dating her?"

Astaroth crossed his arms, scowling.

"You aren't dating, right?" Kai's tone said he wasn't asking. "Just two sworn enemies on a quest, she said."

"And she's *my* sworn enemy, not yours," Astaroth snapped.

The other werewolves muttered and shifted as Kai looked Astaroth up and down. The air thrummed with tension. Werewolves were notorious for fighting at the slightest provocation, and although Astaroth wasn't keen to collect another head injury, he wished the werewolf would start something. Astaroth might be smaller, but he had speed, a pissy mood, and centuries of experience on his side, not to mention a fork that would look very festive in a werewolf's eyeball.

Calladia's chest rose and fell rapidly, and she licked her lips as she looked between the two males. Her hand curled into a fist.

After an interminable moment, Kai threw back his head and

let out a hearty laugh. "Good luck with that, mate. I'd rather make an ally of a pretty woman than an enemy, but you do you." His smile sharpened, and he snapped his teeth. A werewolf threat. "I suggest you operate carefully though. We take care of our own out here, and if you try to steal any souls or hurt the locals, there's going to be trouble." He turned to Calladia, his demeanor melting back into cocky flirtatiousness. "Should you crave better company, our table's by the window."

The werewolves trooped to a long trestle table, resuming their shouts and banter. Bronwyn looked at Astaroth and shook her head. "Pissing off a pack of werewolves never ends the way you think it will." She headed toward the bar and started pulling pints.

Calladia blew out a shuddering breath. "Damn. That would have been a good one."

"A good what?" Astaroth asked, distracted by the sight of Kai regaling his team with some story that involved copious hand-waving.

"A good fight." She tipped her head to each shoulder, cracking her neck. "I have to limit my brawling in Glimmer Falls so I don't get banned from my favorite spots, and a woman has needs."

Astaroth forgot all about the werewolves. The rest of the sentence faded away, too, irrelevant compared to those last four words: *a woman has needs.*

He plunked into his seat and leaned in, lacing his hands together on the table. "Needs, is it? Care to elaborate?"

Her needs would be extensive, he guessed. All that temper and fire needed an outlet. In bed, she'd be rough and demanding, expecting her partner to match her energy. It would be a fight for supremacy, no easy conquest, and she'd want the upper hand more often than not.

His pulse accelerated at the thought. He'd happily cede the upper hand if she wanted. Being pinned down and ridden until he couldn't see straight would be as much a victory as doing the pinning.

Calladia sighed and traced the rim of her glass with her finger. "I miss punching people."

Astaroth's fantasies smacked into the harsh wall of reality. She'd mentioned brawling, not shagging. Right. Except—

"Wait, you *want* to fight a pack of werewolves?" he asked incredulously.

"Wouldn't be the first time." Calladia looked at the wolves as if sizing them up.

No, Astaroth thought. *Look at me, not them.* "They're twice your size."

"Exactly." Calladia turned back to him. "It's a challenge, and they're very egalitarian. Lots of guys refuse to fight a woman, but werewolves respect anyone who steps up. It's actually safer than a lot of brawling, since they do it so much. No killing or maiming when it's recreational. They'll go from punching to buying each other drinks in a matter of minutes."

Astaroth couldn't believe this. "You've fought werewolves before," he said slowly. "And you think it's admirable they're willing to punch you?"

She shrugged. "Think of it like sparring in martial arts. If your opponent is capable, why not treat them that way?"

And yes, all right, Astaroth understood that line of thinking and had dueled a few lady pirates back in the day, but this was different. This was *Calladia*, and no matter how strong she was, all mortals were breakable. "They could hurt you."

"A little pain spices things up, don't you think?" As if that sentence wasn't enough to play havoc with the pleasure centers of Astaroth's brain, Calladia followed it up with a wink.

"Guh," was all he managed to say.

Fresh cacophony sounded from the entrance to the Red Deer.

"What now?" Astaroth asked, resenting this interruption even more than the first. To his horror, a second rugby team was jumping and shouting and smacking one another's bums in the lobby, these ones dressed in blue jerseys proclaiming *Soundview Shifters*. "*More* werewolves?"

Bronwyn passed by the table, menus in hand. "They're a mix of shifters, not werewolves." She pointed at the tallest man, who had a bushy brown beard and a bun. "The captain is Ranulf, a bear-shifter, and his second, Cooper, is a corgi-shifter."

Astaroth eyed the shorter man next to Ranulf. He looked buff, but still. "A corgi-shifter?" he asked skeptically.

"Have you ever seen a corgi at the dog park?" Bronwyn asked. "They give zero fucks." She smiled, then hurried away to greet the newcomers.

"This is exciting," Calladia said. "A rival team?"

He did not like the way she was ogling those shifters. "So, about the quest," he said in an attempt to distract her. "Should we—"

"Ranulf!" Kai shouted the name and launched out of his chair. "I'm amazed you have the courage to show up here after the beating we just delivered on the pitch. Eager for more?"

"Yes," Calladia hissed, doing a fist pump. "Rivals!"

Astaroth had no idea what she was excited about. All he knew was that there were thirty very large and very attractive wolves and shifters in the dining room, which was about thirty too many. In normal times he would have welcomed an overabundance of attractive people, but his thoughts had become obsessively fixed on one specific attractive person, and he urgently needed to hustle her out of here before any of the overgrown furballs propositioned her again.

"Come on," he said, standing up. "Let's retrieve Bronwyn and discuss next steps."

The dryad was nowhere to be seen though, and a rolling metal door had been pulled down to block the space above the bar. The door to the kitchen was barricaded with a table.

Ranulf sauntered into the middle of the room. "You might have won this match," the bear-shifter said, "but we still have the most wins in the league."

All the rugby players were standing now. Some were stretching, others punching their palms. One grabbed a pool cue and snapped it over his knee.

"Calladia," Astaroth said, gripping her elbow to help her out of her chair, "it isn't safe."

"Season isn't over," Kai said. "Next match, we're going to wipe the field with you again."

"How?" Ranulf shot back. "You incompetent degenerates can barely wipe your own asses."

The insult elicited a burst of outraged grumbling. "Calladia," Astaroth repeated more urgently, tugging at her arm. She didn't move, her attention fixed on the rapidly devolving scene.

"You're a hoity-toity jackass with an overinflated ego," Kai said.

"And you're a bum with mommy issues whose closest relationship is with your right hand," Ranulf snapped.

Kai's eyes looked about to bug out. "Your man bun is tasteless, and your beard smells like stale chips and defeat," he nearly screamed.

With a roar, Ranulf rushed forward and tackled Kai into a table, which broke under their weight. Instantly, the rest of the men sprang into action, pummeling one another with fists, pool cues, even chairs. Cooper the corgi-shifter headbutted a green-kitted wolf, and blood sprayed.

Definitely time to leave. Astaroth reached for Calladia again—

Only to realize she was no longer at his side.

He looked around frantically and caught a glimpse of a swinging blond braid. Then a swinging fist.

A blue-kitted shifter's head snapped back at Calladia's hit. "Damn," he said, rubbing his jaw. "A new player has joined the game."

He picked up a chair and swung it at Calladia.

Astaroth was already halfway across the room, but he wouldn't be fast enough. His heart hammered, and terror rose in his throat.

Calladia ducked and spun, jabbing her elbow into the shifter's ribs. The chair went flying.

Then Astaroth was in the thick of it, dodging fists and elbows as he tried to make it to her side.

"Well, well." Kai was abruptly in front of him, grinning with blood-slicked teeth. "The demon wants to play!"

Astaroth risked a glance at Calladia and was relieved to see her still on her feet. She cast him a feral grin before picking up a napkin holder and chucking it at someone's head.

Apparently they were doing this.

Astaroth cracked his neck. His leg had been a bit sore earlier, but the adrenaline pumping through him was enough to make him feel invincible.

"Come on, pretty boy," Kai taunted. "Show me what you've got."

This werewolf wanted a fight?

He was going to get one.

SIXTEEN

CALLADIA LAUGHED WILDLY AS SHE DODGED A PUNCH, THEN hammered her opponent's side. The wolf grunted. "Nice hook," he said before surprising her with a front kick to the gut.

The air rushed out of her as she crashed into a table. Silverware and condiment bottles went flying, and Calladia grabbed a ketchup bottle from midair before winging it back at the wolf who'd kicked her. This one was named Avram, she remembered. With his thick brown hair and big nose, he reminded her of Ben, her friend and Mariel's boss. She'd started targeting the blue-kitted shifters, but as all werewolf brawls went, it was a free-for-all now, with teammates fighting both their opponents and one another.

Avram caught the bottle and crowed in delight. "Kai, we have a new recruit!"

This was what she adored about werewolves and shifters. They were the only other people she'd met who seemed to understand fighting was *fun*.

A familiar shout caught her attention, and she whipped her

head around to see Astaroth take a punch to the cheek from Kai's massive fist. His head snapped to the side, but he embraced the momentum, completing an elegant spin that culminated in a roundhouse kick to Kai's ribs.

Ooh, nice move. Maybe Astaroth could run her through it later.

The werewolf wheezed and clutched his ribs. "Damn, demon. Didn't think you had it in you."

"You have no idea who you're dealing with." Astaroth grabbed a chair and swung at Kai's torso again. The wood exploded on impact, and one leg flew off and brained Ranulf, who had just been clambering to his feet from under the remnants of a table.

"Two for one!" Calladia hooted.

Astaroth looked at her and shook his head, grinning. "Witch, you're a menace."

She'd distracted him though, and Kai was already moving. "Watch out!" Calladia called. The werewolf was airborne and about to full-body tackle her demon.

Astaroth moved with liquid grace, dodging the tackle, and Kai crashed into the wall. Ranulf swung for Astaroth's head, and Astaroth performed some complicated maneuver that resulted in him suplexing the bear into the ground. As more opponents converged on him, Astaroth snapped a leg off an overturned table and held it in front of him like a sword. "Come and get it," he taunted. "Humiliation is free."

Calladia gaped as Astaroth handily defeated wolf after wolf with his fists, feet, and makeshift sword. He was smaller than his opponents, but he made tossing them around look easy.

A pulse started between her thighs.

Then a saltshaker brained her, and she staggered.

"Sorry!" Avram popped up in front of her. "I threw it before realizing you weren't looking."

Calladia laughed. "I'm looking now," she said, grabbing a floral centerpiece and flinging it at him. Avram grinned as he dodged. He reached for a decorative vase.

"Not that one!" A brown hand reached out from the wall. "It's my favorite."

Avram immediately set it down. "Sorry, Bronwyn. I'll put it somewhere safe."

The dryad's face emerged from the wooden planks. She looked at the chaos, then sighed. "I should have remembered it was match day and put away the breakables."

"You know we're good for it," Avram said. "Send the invoice to Kai."

Bronwyn rolled her eyes. "You werewolves will be the death of me." She winked before receding into the wall. "Give those blue shirts hell."

"What do you say?" Avram asked, looking at Calladia. "Teaming up could be fun."

Calladia grinned. "Let's do it."

◆　◆　◆

TEN MINUTES LATER, MOST OF THE FURNITURE HAD BEEN turned into matchsticks and over half the fighters were groaning on the floor. Calladia's cheek throbbed from a stray punch she'd caught, and her arm was lightly bleeding from a fork projectile, but she was giddy with delight. She never felt better than when larger, stronger beings treated her like an equal and, most importantly, a threat. When she spun, broken chair leg in hand, a blue-kitted shifter cringed away from her. "Mercy," he rasped, so she turned to look for another opponent.

Astaroth stood on the trestle table, which miraculously remained intact. He swung a table leg in vicious arcs, beating away enemies right and left. Apparently the remaining combatants had decided to gang up on him.

Calladia would have been worried, but she'd seen enough of

his fighting technique to know he had this on lock. He was precise and deadly, with preternatural reflexes and balance, and if Calladia had been a little turned on earlier, she was fully wet now. Fighting sometimes had that effect, since she had a lady boner for danger, but in this case, she knew exactly what had caused her state of arousal.

That damn demon.

He looked good and fought like hell, and if anything riled Calladia up, it was a display of competence. And oh, how competent he was.

She noticed a figure creeping around the back of the trestle table: Kai, carrying a jagged piece of wood. Astaroth was engaged with the werewolves in front and hadn't noticed.

Calladia hurried toward him, stepping over downed assailants. "Astaroth, behind you," she called, but the shouting was too loud, and she was too far away. Kai raised the stick, ready to strike.

Calladia gripped the chair leg like a javelin and launched it full force at the werewolf.

Too late, she realized she'd thrown it pointy end first. She watched in horror as the wood pierced Kai's shoulder. He toppled back, shattering the window.

The fighting abruptly stopped. Everyone in the room looked at Kai, then Calladia.

"Uh oh," she said. She'd violated the first rule of friendly brawl club: no maiming. She waved and smiled awkwardly. "Sorry, didn't mean to impale him."

Kai sat up from the pile of glass shards and tugged the wood out of his shoulder. It hadn't penetrated too deeply, thankfully. "Get her!" he called.

Calladia was reckless, but even she could recognize when it was time to cut her losses and retreat. She met Astaroth's wide eyes and jerked her thumb over her shoulder toward the exit. He nodded, then took a running leap over the heads of the werewolves surrounding the table. He landed with a cat's grace. "Time to go," he said, grabbing her hand.

They burst into the afternoon sunlight with a pack of were-wolves hot on their heels. It was an outright sprint down the street, and Calladia's heart raced as giddy laughter climbed in her throat. She only let go of Astaroth's hand once they'd reached the truck.

"Prepare for blastoff," she said as she started the engine and depressed the clutch. She put the truck in gear and hit the gas, upshifting quickly. Clifford the Little Red Truck might not look like much, but she had power where it counted. They careened down the street, steering around shouting werewolves. Soon the tiny town of Fable Farms was left in the dust.

Once she was certain they had escaped, Calladia let out a wild laugh. "That was incredible!"

Astaroth was white-knuckling the bench. "You," he said, "are the most reckless, ridiculous person I have ever met."

But he was grinning as he said it, and his eyes were bright, and below the bruise darkening his temple, his cheeks were flushed. When he burst into laughter, Calladia thought she'd never seen anything so beautiful.

Oh, Hecate. She was in trouble.

✦   ✦   ✦

"WE SEEM TO HAVE MADE A CRITICAL ERROR," ASTAROTH SAID thirty minutes later as they crested a hill. The terrain was growing rockier and more rugged as they climbed into the mountains. Douglas firs, western red cedars, pines, and other coniferous trees loomed over the narrow road, and snow-capped peaks stood stark against the slate-gray sky.

"Hmm?" Calladia said. The adrenaline from the fight was wearing off, and aches had started to set in. She rolled her neck, wondering if there was a hot spring nearby they could soak in.

"We forgot to ask Bronwyn about Isobel."

Calladia's eyes widened, and she hit the brakes. "Oh, shit." The truck lurched to a stop at the side of the road. Calladia tapped the steering wheel, pondering the best course of action. "We can't go back. Those werewolves were mad."

"I can't imagine why," Astaroth said dryly. "It's not like you skewered their leader like a shish kebab during a so-called 'recreational' brawl."

She glared at him. "I was saving you, thank you very much. And I didn't mean to skewer him. I threw the stick pointy-end first by accident." She shook her head and sighed dramatically. "Guess that dinner date with Kai is off."

Astaroth stiffened. "You were going to go to dinner with him?"

"Not sure." She shrugged. "I don't get asked out much, and he was more polite than the usual creeps who try to feel me up at bars."

Astaroth's jaw flexed like he was grinding his teeth. "First off," he said in a pissy tone, "that werewolf was a lout and not worthy of your attention. Secondly, who has been feeling you up in bars, and are their hands still attached?"

"Curious if I removed them?"

The furious look he shot her made her breath hitch. "If you didn't, I will."

Whoa. That was intense. And confusing. First he'd been upset about Kai hitting on her, and now he wanted to chop off the hands of anyone who sexually harassed her? She laughed awkwardly. "Why would you care about defending me? I'm your enemy, remember?"

"Why would you stab a werewolf to protect me?" he parroted. "I'm your enemy, remember?"

He had a point. Calladia's cheeks heated as she remembered how turned on she'd been watching Astaroth fight and how instinctively she'd acted to save him. Whatever they were doing was nowhere near traditional enemy behavior.

"I'll call the Red Deer," Calladia said, changing the subject to avoid having to answer his question. "I need to give Bronwyn my card information to pay for our meal anyway, since we dined, decked, and dashed." She pulled out her phone, relieved to see a few bars of service. She searched for the restaurant's contact info, then dialed.

"The Red Deer, Bronwyn speaking."

"Hey!" Calladia's greeting was a tad too enthusiastic. "This is Calladia Cunnington. Um, this is awkward, but I forgot to close my tab—"

"You!" The dryad let out a stream of creative curses. "Do you know how much babying I had to do after you left? The way Kai was carrying on, you practically stabbed him in the heart. He was inconsolable until I dosed him with enough whiskey to sedate an elephant."

Calladia cringed. "Is he okay? I really didn't mean to stab him."

"Oh, he's fine." Bronwyn snorted. "The wolves heal quickly, and I got paramedic training once I realized how often they were going to kick off in the restaurant. Thankfully, they pay for renovations, and Ranulf has a woodworking shop, so we never run out of furniture."

"I'm glad Kai is all right," Calladia said. Astaroth mumbled something that sounded like "I'm not," but Calladia ignored him. "Let me give you my card info to pay for lunch."

Once payment was sorted, Calladia asked Bronwyn about the next step to find Isobel.

"I looked up our notes, and it says go northeast until you see two mountains that look like boobs. The town of Griffin's Nest is at the top of a hill, and after that, the road forks. You'll take the right fork down into a valley. Cross the river, and when the road ends, hike due north at the bat sign and look for a red door."

Calladia blinked. "That was way less cryptic than I thought it would be."

Bronwyn's exhale was loud. "Yeah, well, after the thirtieth time telling a confused tourist, 'Seek nature's motherly embrace, and where one might take flight, instead venture low,' you get kinda sick of it."

Before she hung up, the dryad gave a final warning.

"You really made an impression," Bronwyn said. "I'm not sure if Kai wants to murder you or marry you on the spot, but keep an eye out, because the wolves are on the hunt."

"Thanks, Bronwyn," Calladia said. "I owe you one."

After Calladia hung up, she looked at Astaroth. "Mountains that look like boobs," she said. "Sounds easy enough."

"Kai wants to marry you?" Astaroth sounded appalled. "For stabbing him?"

"You aren't more worried about the murder bit?" Calladia asked, though she was pretty sure the dryad had been exaggerating.

Astaroth made a scornful noise. "As if he were capable of it. You'd kick his arse halfway to the moon."

Warmth filled Calladia's chest at his assessment. "Anyway," she said, pulling onto the road again, "he's not going to get the chance to murder or marry me. I like living, and I'm far too busy for romance."

Astaroth picked at the fabric of his faux-leather pants, brushing away invisible specks of dust. "You don't seem that busy to me."

She scowled. "Because I'm babysitting you, rather than following my normal routine."

"And your normal routine is so full of meaningful activity you have no room for romance?"

Calladia's stomach twisted uncomfortably, because no, her life wasn't full of much meaningful activity. She had her friends, her clients at the gym, and her hobbies, but there was a fundamental hollowness behind that. The kind of ache that swelled when she ate dinner alone or when she lay awake at night, wondering what the point of all of it was. The ache that turned into sharp pain when she thought of her absent father and perpetually disappointed mother, and how she would never be good enough for them.

"I have more important things to focus on, that's all," she said. "And men are more trouble than they're worth."

"Men are definitely trouble," he agreed. "But trouble can be fun."

She snorted as she took a hairpin curve. Past the railing, the ground dropped away sharply, tumbling toward a river far below. "Are you advocating for me to date Kai?"

"No!" Astaroth exclaimed. "Absolutely not. I'm just curious about your anti-romance stance."

She shot him a glance. He sounded more than just curious. She was reminded of how possessive he'd been over her and how jealous he'd seemed of Kai.

But that couldn't be right, could it? Maybe he was feeling some kind of involuntary physical attraction, one as inconvenient for him as it was for her. Or maybe he didn't want anyone stealing her away before she helped him recover his memories.

Calladia didn't like talking about her past heartache, but in the close air of the cab, with the engine rumbling and the landscape spreading below like a green-and-gray tapestry, it felt right to let the words spill out.

"I haven't had the best experience dating," she said past a lump in her throat. "Life is easier if I don't do it at all."

She braced herself for some snarky comment, but he seemed to be considering her words carefully.

"Bad experiences with multiple men?" he finally asked.

Calladia shook her head. "Just one."

"Is he still alive?"

She tried to laugh, but it was a broken thing. "Yes, and still in possession of both hands." Sam was probably thriving in his hoity-toity professor job, teaching students about ethics in the clinical, abstract manner that ought to have been a red flag that he saw ethics as no more than an intellectual exercise. Undergrads would worship him; hadn't she, after all? He would bask in their adulation and, if the opportunity presented itself, one of those starry-eyed worshippers would end up in his bed, convinced she was sophisticated beyond her years. Convinced a happily-ever-after was just down the line.

She was squeezing the steering wheel tightly enough to hurt, so she forced herself to relax her fingers.

"Calladia," Astaroth said in a low voice. "Pull over."

There was a scenic lookout ahead, and Calladia's eyes were getting watery, so she pulled into a parking spot at the edge of the cliff. She shut off the engine, then blinked hard to suppress any incipient tears before facing Astaroth.

Without the distraction of driving, she was forced to acknowledge how close they were sitting. Clifford was mighty but small, and there were no cupholders dividing the old-fashioned bench seat. Astaroth could shift a foot or two over and be pressed up against her.

She'd never seen him look quite like this. The usual ironic slant of his features was gone, replaced by deadly seriousness. His crystal-blue eyes bored into her, and she shifted, feeling like he was looking under her skin.

"Do you want to tell me about him?" Astaroth asked.

She still couldn't laugh right. After a pathetic sort of wheeze, she asked, "What is this, demonic psychotherapy?"

He didn't blink. "I mean it."

Tell the sexy demon she hated—or ought to hate—all the sordid details of her embarrassing failed relationship? The story made her look like a fool, but it was alarming how tempting the prospect was. The two of them were alone in the wilderness, with no shared past and no shared future. They were stuck together in the suspended moments between the end of one story and the beginning of another.

Her next story wouldn't include him, which meant her confessions wouldn't follow her like vengeful ghosts, but vulnerability wasn't something she knew how to do anymore. Fighting thirty werewolves? Easy. Stripping back her armor to reveal the soft, wounded creature beneath?

Impossible.

She shook her head. "No," she said. "I can't." And then, because she didn't like the unsettling feeling that she was slamming the door on a possibility, she clarified. "Not now, at least."

Astaroth nodded. "If you ever want to, I'll listen. And Calladia . . ." He set his hand on the bench, his pinkie finger a scant inch from her own, so close she felt the heat radiating from his skin. "You're a good person, even if you don't always believe it, but I'm not. Say the word, and I'll punish him in the vilest ways you can imagine."

Calladia's breath hitched at the deadly promise. Her fingers twitched, and she almost hooked her pinkie finger over his.

She came to her senses just before she made contact. "Thank you," she said, pulling her hand back into her lap and wondering if this was the beginning stage of madness. The words came out breathy, so she cleared her throat and tried again. "That's a very generous offer. I won't lie and say I haven't imagined castrating him, but I think the police would frown on it."

"You think human police would be able to stop me?" His smile was grim. "I've been around a long time, Calladia. Just because these are less violent times doesn't mean I've forgotten how to be a monster."

Shit. She shouldn't like that as much as she did. What kind of person threatened to destroy someone's sucky ex? And what kind of person found the idea not just intriguing, but titillating? Her lower belly felt tight, and the throb of arousal between her legs grew heavier with every moment their eyes stayed locked.

Calladia licked her lips, and Astaroth's eyes tracked the movement. He shifted closer, and she canted toward him in response, as if drawn by a magnet.

Alarm bells shrieked in Calladia's head. This was a demon, not some harmless date she'd swiped right on using Bumbelina or one of the other supernatural dating apps. He had *horns*, and that model-gorgeous face hid a cunning and ruthless mind.

Still, she wondered. *What would he taste like?*

"A mistake," she blurted.

Astaroth shook his head and blinked rapidly as if emerging from a spell. "What?"

Calladia fumbled with the keys, looking anywhere but at him. Dear Hecate, had she really been about six inches and one very bad decision away from kissing her nemesis? The demon who had tried to hurt her friend mere days ago? "Castrating my ex would be a mistake," she said, voice higher-pitched than normal. "Or any other maiming."

"What about light torture?" Astaroth asked, clearly aiming for levity but failing. The strain was as evident in his voice as it was in hers.

"No torture." Her heart raced, and the dizziness she felt as she reversed away from the cliff had nothing to do with the height. "The best revenge is to forget him and live a happy life."

"How odd," Astaroth said. "I always heard the best revenge was flaying a bloke alive, forcing him to eat his own liver, and lighting him on fire." He'd recovered the edge of snark that hinted he was *probably* kidding.

Calladia played along. "We really need to work on your conflict resolution skills."

Astaroth might be joking about flaying people alive, but he

hadn't been kidding about taking vengeance on her ex. He'd let his smiling mask slip, and for maybe the first time in their brief acquaintance, she'd seen the true monster beneath, the one that had spent six centuries in the hunt for power.

Whatever Astaroth said, Calladia wasn't a good person. How could she be, when seeing the monster inside . . . just made her want him more?

SEVENTEEN

ASTAROTH WANTED TO BANG HIS HORNS AGAINST THE
truck window.

Stupid, stupid, stupid.

How was it possible one witch had thrown him so off-kilter in
so short a time? Sure, the amnesia wasn't helping, but he wasn't
delusional enough to ascribe all his odd behavior to that. Amnesia
wasn't the reason he had leaped into a violent pack of werewolves,
then offered to hunt down Calladia's ex-partner and make him
suffer.

Historically, Astaroth didn't do things out of the goodness of
his heart. He did whatever it took to maintain his image and consolidate power, and while collecting souls benefitted the demon
plane, his motivations weren't exactly pure.

So why had he risked his safety for Calladia, when it was clear
she loved getting in fights? When she had, indeed, jumped straight
into one without hesitation? Had it been anyone else, he would
have left her to it and found something more productive to do with
his time.

"Griffin's Nest, five miles," Calladia said, pointing at a sign. It was the first either of them had spoken since the awkward leaning incident over an hour ago, when he'd been a heartbeat away from pressing his lips to hers.

He grunted in acknowledgment, then snuck a glance at her. Her profile was elegant for such an aggressive force of chaos, with a high forehead, classically straight nose, and pouty bottom lip. The fight had mussed her braid until gold hair escaped in haphazard clumps, and her tan skin practically glowed. She was so lovely it made his fingertips tingle with the urge to touch her.

Her skin would always be cool compared to his, and he'd bet anything the curve of her cheek would feel like satin under his fingertips. Naked, she would be exquisite, all firm muscle under smooth skin, the perfect mix of hard and soft.

Speaking of hard . . . Astaroth shifted on the bench seat, turning his hips away to disguise his growing erection. This was also abnormal. Astaroth had been shagging for centuries in every combination and permutation one could imagine. Sex could be a tool or a bit of fun, but he'd never been ruled by his desires.

Now? Just imagining the witch naked was enough to make him hard.

Trees flashed by, a mix of coniferous green and bare or autumn-clad branches. An osprey circled overhead, wings stabbing black against the gray sky. The demon plane was beautiful in its own way, but the brilliant shades of Earth were more to his taste. Rather than relying on outside magic to thrive, the human world produced its own, and he hadn't found anywhere else in the universe quite so vibrant.

Calladia switched the radio on and scanned through channels of static until she found a station she liked. It was a pop song similar to the one by Taylor Swift, though this one didn't trigger any memories. Calladia hummed along, voice wobbling above and below the melody.

Why was the witch so compelling? Astaroth stewed on the question as he snuck more surreptitious glances at her. He'd known courtesans and famed society beauties in centuries past and was familiar with the tools of attraction. Cosmetics, costume, and a puff of scent took care of the physical lure; polite conversation, flirtatious witticisms, and dazzling displays of talent accomplished the rest. Beauty was crafted like any other work of art, and its perfection took effort.

Calladia didn't try at all. She wore no makeup and didn't care about fashion. She sang off-key and was more likely to punch someone than engage in polite conversation with them.

And she was the most beautiful person Astaroth had ever seen.

"Tits!" Calladia exclaimed.

Astaroth was startled out of his reverie. "Tits?" he repeated dumbly. His eyes dipped to where her breasts were hidden by soft-looking flannel. Did she have tan lines? Or did she sunbathe nude? The thought wasn't helping the situation in his trousers, so he told himself not to imagine her bare breasts or speculate on the color of her nipples.

Shell pink, maybe. Or dusky rose, the hints of brown echoing her tan.

"Mother Nature's bosom or whatever." Calladia pointed ahead. "They just came into view."

Right, the quest. He followed the direction of her finger and saw two rounded hills rising in the distance past a deep valley, the slopes visible now that they'd topped this latest ridge. Jagged snowcapped peaks towered behind the "tits" as the mountains claimed the horizon.

A town sprawled along the top of the ridge, the buildings lining the road and extending into the trees. Unlike Fable Farms, these were far from uniform. There were wooden cabins, adobe buildings with flat tops, and spiraling towers with pieces of colored glass pressed into the stucco. A mounded hill with a door built into it indicated more housing underground, and a wooden platform ringing the top of a tree had rope bridges extending from it.

"Griffin's Nest, I presume." Astaroth rolled down his window, inhaling the crisp autumn air.

"It's cute." Calladia pulled to a stop outside a black-walled restaurant labeled NecroNomNomNoms. The menu posted outside was written in runes, and the acrid spices wafting from the building were enough to make Astaroth's eyes water. Calladia sniffed, then made a face. "Whew, someone's getting adventurous with valerian." She sniffed again. "Mandrake, wormwood, and horehound, too. And definitely some blood."

"You have a keen sense of smell," he said.

"My mom made me take a potions course in college." Calladia grimaced. "Not my favorite aspect of magic, but the scents stick with you after you've been sweating over a cauldron for a semester." She unbuckled her seat belt and opened the door. "I need to stretch my legs." Once outside the truck, she raised her brows. "Well? Are you coming?"

Astaroth's chest warmed at the thought that she wanted his company. He got out of the truck and shook out his legs before reaching overhead, groaning at the delicious ache in his muscles. "Lucifer, I'm stiff." He twisted his torso a few times, then noticed Calladia staring at him. Or rather, at his waist. He glanced down and realized the stretch had lifted his shirt to expose a strip of skin. Astaroth reached even higher, arching his back to show off more of his abs.

Calladia quickly looked away. "I was thinking we should stop here for the night," she said. "We only have another hour or two of sunlight, and I'd rather reach Isobel's place during the daytime. Visiting strange witches after dark is a good way to get hexed."

Relief washed over Astaroth at the realization that his time with Calladia would be extended. It was followed by swift self-condemnation, because that was the opposite of the scenario he should be hoping for. He needed to reach Isobel as soon as possible to learn how to restore his memories and kill Moloch; every minute spent delaying that goal was a minute he risked himself— and Calladia—encountering further danger. "Are you sure?" he asked. "The tent isn't exactly comfortable. We could push through and see if Isobel has a spare room."

She shot him a knowing look. "I find the tent perfectly comfortable, but I'm willing to take pity on your delicate constitution. We'll book a hotel."

"I'm not delicate," he objected, despite the relief he felt. "I'm discerning."

"Definitely delicate," she tossed over her shoulder as she walked away, hips swinging. "And a frightful snob, to boot."

He stifled a chuckle. "Do you know how many people dare disrespect me?" he asked in a mock-stern tone as he caught up to her.

"Not nearly enough, I bet."

Astaroth couldn't help it. He laughed, a full, hearty guffaw. "You're so bloody mean!"

She smirked. "You can take it."

"And so I shall, gladly," he said, placing a hand over his heart.

Calladia shook her head. "It's like you want me to insult you. Are you a masochist or something?"

"Just a demon who likes a challenge. A mortal constantly trying to take the piss out of me is unusual."

"So you like being called a delicate little purse dog because it's a novelty?" she asked.

They were passing a bakery with an array of large, colorfully shelled eggs in the window next to the pastries—a sure sign of griffin occupancy, since the creatures used their talons to puncture eggs before slurping up the yolks. On impulse, Astaroth cut Calladia off and backed her toward the window. She went without resistance, and her breath hitched when her shoulder blades met the glass.

Very interesting.

Astaroth planted his hands on either side of her head and leaned in until his mouth was inches from hers. Her eyelashes fluttered. "It is a novelty," he murmured, reveling in the pleasurable tension strung between them. "But part of the enjoyment comes from imagining all the ways I can prove you wrong."

"Oh, yeah?" Calladia asked. "How would you prove me wrong?"

She was trying to play tough, but the breathy quality to her voice sent triumph spinning through him. Every sense felt sharpened as he took her in. The unsteady waft of her breath, the pink tinge to her cheeks, her dilated pupils . . . she was far from unaffected by his nearness.

Did she want him as badly as he wanted her?

Astaroth brought his mouth even closer to hers, watching her eyelids sink to half-mast . . . then shifted until his lips brushed her ear. "You wouldn't call me delicate if you'd seen me in action," he murmured.

She shivered. "I saw you fight."

"Not the kind of action I meant."

Calladia made a shocked noise, then planted her hands on his chest and pushed. He stepped back, grinning at how flustered she looked. "You are incorrigible," she said, shaking her head.

Not a victory yet, but a tactical advantage. Astaroth slid his hands into his pockets and shrugged. "I think you like it."

"And I think you have delusions of grandeur." But as she turned to face the bakery window, Astaroth spied the points of her nipples pressing through her shirt.

Oh, yes, she liked it. Humans were a passionate species, and despite everything he'd done to antagonize her, she still wanted him.

Around her, he felt passionate, too. Had he been younger, he might have made his move right then and there, pressing her to the window and capturing her lips in a hungry kiss. But his witch was complicated. If seduction wasn't equally her idea, she'd never go along with it. Calladia wasn't a prize to be won—she was an equal competitor in this battle of wills and wants, and the only way to woo a woman like that was to leave her wanting until she got impatient and seized the prize herself.

Astaroth reached out to tuck back a loose strand of her hair, letting his fingers linger on the rim of her ear. She tipped her head to the side as if inviting him to trail his fingers down her jawline, then quickly straightened, narrowing her eyes.

Patience, he told himself as he withdrew the touch. *Play the long game.*

It was difficult when everything in him was screaming to seize her, kiss her, *pleasure* her.

Calladia shook her arms out and cracked her neck like she was shrugging off the carnally charged energy. "Come on," she said. "Let's find a place to stay."

Astaroth followed, his pulse tapping a giddy beat. As they headed down the street, he realized something startling. Despite centuries of being a master planner and manipulator who knew all the right buttons to push to influence people . . . Astaroth truly had no idea what Calladia would do next.

And fuck if he didn't like that.

❖   ❖   ❖

GRIFFIN'S NEST PROVED TO BE A QUIRKY, ECLECTIC TOWN DE-signed for ease of access. The pavements were wide, and all public buildings had landing pads for winged creatures and ramps for wheelchair users, centaurs, and others who couldn't navigate stairs with ease. Pride flags fluttered next to flags from around the world, and the windows were filled with signs advertising community events and cross-species sporting leagues and art classes.

Although Astaroth horns garnered a few curious looks, the people here didn't seem alarmed by his presence. Everyone they passed had a smile and a wave. There was one tense moment when they passed a sweet shop and a gnome in a pointed blue cap came barreling out, but although Astaroth instinctively braced himself for an attack, he ended up confronted by a tray of free caramel apple samples instead.

"Are you a minotaur like Dr. Shepard?" the gnome asked, looking curiously up at Astaroth. He was a teenager, with acne-spotted cheeks and a diminutive letter jacket bearing a gold Honor Roll star. "Or part minotaur? You have the horns, but you don't have a bull head like him."

Well, that question explained the community's general comfort with horned creatures. "I'm a demon," he said, accepting a toothpick bearing a green apple slice drizzled in caramel.

The gnome's jaw dropped. "No way? That's so cool. Dr. Shepard teaches history and interplanar cultures. I'll have to tell him I met you!"

Minotaurs had a fearsome reputation in most places, due to their penchant for lurking in caves and absconding with attractive people, but Astaroth was canny enough to recognize a marketing choice, and everyone he'd met who had been abducted by a minotaur had found the experience thrilling.

He sank his teeth into the apple and made an approving noise. "Lucifer, that's good."

"Right?" The gnome grinned. "The Wicked Witch provides the apples."

Calladia and Astaroth shared an alarmed glance. "Are these apples . . . doctored in any way?" Calladia asked as she tossed her own toothpick in the bin.

The gnome laughed. "Sorry, I forgot you're tourists. The Wicked Witch is a shop selling locally grown produce. It's owned by two of the sweetest witches you'll ever meet, and all they do with their magic is extend the growing season."

"Mariel would love that," Calladia said. "One of my best friends," she clarified at the gnome's curious look. "She's a nature witch."

The gnome launched into an excited spiel about garden magic, the quality of local produce, and various plant-related festivals Calladia's friend ought to visit for. Astaroth half listened while surreptitiously watching Calladia. Her face lit up whenever she mentioned Mariel, and it was clear she loved the witch very much.

And Astaroth had apparently tried—and failed—to collect Mariel's soul. He closed his eyes, begging his brain to produce anything related to the failed bargain that had turned Calladia into his enemy rather than something sweeter.

He had a flash of a wall of brambles and a furious-looking witch with curly brown hair. That image lurched abruptly into another: the same witch standing with a blank expression on her face while a demon with black horns and hair cried out, sounding agonized.

Was the brunette Mariel or some other witch he'd met during the centuries missing from his memory? Considering the presence of a heartbroken-looking demon, he suspected it was Mariel and he'd gotten a brief glimpse of the bargain gone awry. Which meant that large, very upset-looking demon was Ozroth, Astaroth's so-called protégé. Former protégé now, after choosing love for a human over his duty to the demon plane.

Astaroth's chest felt tight. He focused, trying to identify the emotion. It was . . . loss of some sort. A subtle yet bitter grief.

He chose them, Astaroth thought nonsensically.

"Earth to Astaroth," Calladia said.

Astaroth opened his eyes to find her snapping her fingers under his nose. The gnome was nowhere to be seen. The world spun, and he braced his feet farther apart to center himself. Curse these dizzy spells.

Calladia looked concerned. "Is everything all right? Where'd you go just now?"

He hesitated, wondering if mentioning Ozroth and Mariel would anger her. Then again, it wasn't like she'd forgotten what he'd done to them, even if he had. "I think I remembered Ozroth and Mariel."

Calladia stiffened. "What did you remember?"

"Not much." Astaroth weighed his words carefully. "I saw a woman with curly brown hair casting magic on a wall of plants. Then I saw a demon with black hair next to her."

"That does sound like Mariel and Oz." Wariness lurked in Calladia's brown eyes, and her posture was tense. "Anything else?"

He wasn't sure how to explain it, or even if he should. Calladia had made it clear he was the villain in her story; she wouldn't care about his feelings of loss.

But who else could he talk to about this? The people he'd known over his long life had been sorted into neat categories: ally, enemy, entertainment, prey. No one knew better than a bargainer how easy it was to manipulate feelings of intimacy and love, which was why effective bargainers eschewed close friendships or other emotional entanglements.

Calladia might not be his friend, but she'd seen him in a vulnerable place and helped him. And fundamentally, he *wanted* to talk to her.

"I felt an emotion," he said, pushing the words past his tight throat. "But I don't know why."

Calladia cocked her head, studying him. Then she reached out and touched his elbow. "Let's walk while you tell me more."

Astaroth had been bracing himself for her anger at the mention of what had transpired with Mariel. A relieved breath puffed out of him, and his shoulders relaxed. "It's odd," he said as they started walking. Her touch had been brief, but he still felt the echo of it against his skin. "It feels like I've lost something. There's this hollowness inside."

"What do you think you lost?"

Astaroth grimaced. "I don't know. It's just a sense of something missing." Or someone, he realized. Ozroth had chosen humanity over everything Astaroth had taught him, and he wasn't sure how to feel about that. He made a frustrated sound. "Never mind. Talking about feelings is obnoxious."

"If you think this is obnoxious, you should try therapy sometime," Calladia said with a lopsided smile. "It's great but also terrible."

He scoffed. "No therapist has the time to unpack six centuries of baggage, and proper demons don't need therapy anyway."

Except he wasn't a proper demon, was he? He was an anomaly. A hybrid who had somehow risen high in demon society before being brought very low.

Calladia dug into the sore spot mercilessly. "What do you think counts as a proper demon?"

"A strong, full-blooded one." Shame spiked at the reminder he was *less than*. "Feelings are a waste of time. All they do is complicate things or ruin a decent stratagem."

Calladia blew a raspberry. "Spare me the high council propaganda. Emotions are important."

"Not when the rest of your species doesn't feel them half so intensely," he said. "What kind of aberration am I, focusing on pointless emotions that won't help me accomplish my goals?"

Calladia was fussing with her braid, mussing up the strands further, and he wanted to smack her hand away, brush her hair out, and re-braid it properly. "You say *aberration* like it's a bad thing," she said, forehead furrowed in a contemplative expression.

He scoffed. "How can an aberration ever be considered a good thing?"

"Being different is just that: being different. It isn't a crime." Her voice rose as she continued. "My mother would say I'm an aberration, too, but do I give a shit? Absolutely not. And you shouldn't either."

By the way she was nearly shouting, Astaroth suspected she might, in fact, give a shit. He remembered the tense conversation he'd overheard at her childhood home. "You think your mother expects you to be exactly like her?"

Calladia kicked a rubbish bin at the edge of the curb. "She expects more than that. She wants a daughter, heiress, campaign manager, and hype woman all in one. Pearls and pantsuits and lipstick and all that bloody nonsense." She apparently realized what she'd said the moment Astaroth did, because she barreled on. "And now your Britishisms are rubbing off on me—great. The point is, I'm not *bloody* polite or scheming or diplomatic or whatever-the-fuck-else she expects. I'm rude and loud and too masculine for her standards, and I'm a disappointment to the family who will never make anything of myself if I don't fall in line and become the perfect little Cunnington *cunt*."

Apparently he'd hit a nerve. He liked it though. He wanted to hear her rant about anything and everything, especially if it meant she was opening up to him.

Opening up to him? Lucifer, had he really just thought that? In practical terms he'd experienced less than a day of being half human, and already he was growing mawkish.

Calladia cleared her throat and yanked on her braid again. "Anyway, that's not important. Back to your situation."

Astaroth wasn't going to let her get away with that misdirection. He fumbled for a response to make her feel better. "I think you're perfect just the way you are."

Calladia stopped walking. Her head snapped around. "What did you say?"

That had been too close to a confession of his growing infatuation. "Well, ah . . ." How to salvage this so she didn't sense his glaring, Calladia-sized vulnerability? "Obviously not *perfect*, perfect," he clarified. "You aren't some goddess, even if you'd be an excellent model for a statue of Athena." Wait, not better. He rushed onward. "What I mean to say is, you may be rude and loud, but some people find that interesting, and any talk of being too masculine is nonsense springing from a strict sense of the gender binary most species have moved beyond. You are wholly yourself, and that in itself is perfect, because anything else would be a lie."

He lapsed into awkward silence. That had been way too much. Any moment now she was going to smack him upside the head and tell him he was the worst.

Calladia looked shell-shocked. "Wow," she said. "That was actually really sweet."

"It's not sweet," Astaroth hurried to say. "You have many less-admirable qualities." He tried to come up with one. "You talk in your sleep, for instance. Horrific."

Calladia laughed and punched him in the shoulder. "Shut up."

"Gladly." He'd started to sweat from nerves, so he wiped his forehead as nonchalantly as he could.

"And hey," Calladia said, shifting from foot to foot. Her eyes darted before meeting his. "Thank you. For being sweet."

"Yeah, well, don't count on it. I'm still a horrible, irredeemable monster."

"Of course," she said, looping her arm through his. "I wouldn't expect anything less." When Astaroth stared at where she was touching him, Calladia rolled her eyes. "Come on, you secret softie. Let's find a place to stay."

Astaroth let himself be towed along, marveling that somehow, despite having little practice with honesty, he'd managed to say the exact right thing.

◆　◆　◆

"THIS IS IT?" ASTAROTH LOOKED SKEPTICALLY TOWARD THE canopy of a very thick, very tall tree. Rungs were hammered into the wood, and a structure was perched halfway up, mostly obscured by branches.

Calladia looked far too chipper for someone about to spend the night in a tree. "Best views in town, they said."

The eponymous proprietor of Tansy's Treehouse was a griffin, so it made sense they'd offer accommodation many meters off the ground. Tansy had spoken English with remarkable clarity for someone with an eagle beak, but some garbled screeching was to be expected with griffins, and Astaroth had failed to understand that *a cozy room with good views* translated to *you'll be sleeping in a flimsy wood shack in the fucking sky.*

"There has to be another option," Astaroth said. "How is this an improvement on camping? You're just sleeping in a tree rather than on the ground."

"You haven't even seen the room yet," Calladia said. "Tansy said it's very sturdy and comfortable. And besides, it's the only one available."

When Calladia and Astaroth had asked a naiad swimming in a fountain for directions to the nearest hotel, they'd been informed the Annual Griffin's Nest Mariachi Festival was about to begin, which meant accommodations would be difficult to find. The naiad had directed them to a small shop called Tansy's Trinkets to ask for a room, since Tansy oversaw a variety of properties in the area.

The griffin who had greeted them at the door had been a cheerful sort, with a glittery name badge saying TANSY, THEY/THEM, an impressive wingspan, and beads woven into their feathers. They'd shaved curving designs into their leonine fur, and a silver stud gleamed from their tongue every time they cawed.

Tansy had been thrilled to have more visitors and announced that Calladia and Astaroth had arrived just in time, because there was one room left for the night. Or maybe the griffin's mix of speech and screech had said *Sorry to suck* rather than *You're in luck*, and it had actually been a threat.

"Come on," Calladia said, tossing the ragged remnants of her braid over her shoulder and hitching her backpack higher. "Let's climb before it gets dark."

Astaroth prided himself on being a master tactician. He considered the elements at play and a variety of possible outcomes, then settled on a strategy. "You go first," he said, gesturing at the trunk.

Calladia shrugged and started climbing. Astaroth followed, gripping each rung tightly before shifting his weight. The climb was harrowing, but the wisdom of his strategy was proven whenever he looked up, because he'd never gotten to see her arse from this angle before.

Eventually, they reached a wide platform built around the trunk. Astaroth hauled himself up and collapsed on his back. "Tansy is begging for a wrongful death lawsuit," he said. "How is this safe?"

Calladia abruptly started laughing.

Astaroth turned his head to see what had amused her. A building had been erected around the trunk at the center of the platform, and Calladia was returning from the far side, where she'd evidently been exploring. Her grin was huge as she hiked a thumb over her shoulder. "We should have walked around the tree before trying to get up here."

Astaroth pushed to his feet and headed toward her. On the other side of the building, he stopped at the sight of an ornate metal cage. The cage was hooked to a pulley system drilled into a thick branch. "Wait," he said. "Is that—"

"An elevator!" Calladia leaned against the wall of their hotel room, clutching her ribs as she laughed. "We didn't need to climb."

Astaroth glared at the elevator, his new nemesis. "Very well, we should have looked more closely, but how were we supposed to call it down in the first place?"

Calladia was still chuckling. She reached into the pocket of her jeans and pulled out the key Tansy had given them. "I have a suspicion."

Astaroth eyed the key, which he hadn't paid much mind to, assuming it would electronically open the door. It was oval-shaped and carved out of soapstone, and at the base was a simple etching: ^ v.

Calladia brushed her thumb over the v. Instantly, the cage began to sink through a hole in the platform cut to its exact dimensions. It moved seamlessly, with no mechanical humming. Calladia hit the v again, which stopped the elevator. She tapped ^, and the cage rose.

"Magic," Astaroth said, impressed despite himself. "How did they manage that?"

"Binding objects is difficult," Calladia said as the cage returned to its position. "You have to layer spells to accomplish it, but basically, you infuse magic into two separate things and then force them to share the same resonance. It's like tricking them into thinking they're the same object."

"Like quantum entanglement," Astaroth said, having a flash of a science documentary he'd watched once while drunk. "Particles linked across a distance."

As had happened before, one memory unlocked another, and he recalled watching that documentary with a demoness who had dark skin, wild white hair, and black horns. He couldn't remember anything else about her, but it seemed like a good memory. Did he have a friend?

"Yes!" Calladia beamed. "So you charm multiple objects into acting like one. When I touch this stone, the pulley system responds."

Astaroth held out his hand, and Calladia dropped the stone into his palm. He turned it over, running his fingers over the waxy gray surface and toying with the runes so the cage bounced. "You're quite knowledgeable about magic," he said. "I can see your raw power, of course, but it takes more than that to be an accomplished witch."

Calladia's smile turned wistful. "My parents enrolled me in magic classes from a young age, hired private tutors, the works. I didn't like the expectations that came with it, but I loved learning."

She was looking out at the trees, but Astaroth had a feeling she wasn't seeing them. He wondered what road her thoughts were leading her down.

"It's a hard thing," she continued, "being good at magic. That sounds ridiculous, and it is, but you learn quickly that magic isn't just yours, and it isn't just a skill set. It's a legacy, passed down through generations. It doesn't come free." Then she scoffed and shook her head. "Listen to me, being maudlin for no reason." She looked around. "Where's my backpack?"

Astaroth retrieved it and handed it over.

"Thanks." She pulled her water bottle out of the side pocket and drank, then passed it to him so he could do the same. "Anyway, that doesn't matter," she said, wiping her mouth on her sleeve. "Let's check out the room."

Astaroth wanted to demand she stay there and share all her secrets with him, but that would make her snap and raise her defenses further. He pushed down his burning curiosity and bowed, sweeping his hand toward the door. "Then lead the way, oh fair nemesis."

EIGHTEEN

O H, FAIR NEMESIS.
       Ridiculous.

Astaroth was still bent over in a dramatic bow, eyes gleaming with mischief as he gazed up at her. He looked too damn good for someone who had spent two days on the road without a shower after sustaining a traumatic brain injury.

She needed to get him a new shirt though. And herself, for that matter. While she had another ratty flannel in the truck somewhere, it would be nice to wear something that wasn't wrinkled or sweat stained.

Calladia stepped around Astaroth to get to the door. The treehouse was shaped like an octagon around the wide trunk, with floor-to-ceiling windows shielded by moss-green curtains. The front door was large enough to accommodate even a griffin or centaur and had been carved to depict griffins in flight. Brass doorknobs stood at various heights, from the base to the top. Calladia slipped the key fob into a hollow above one knob, and the lock clicked.

Inside was just as charming as Tansy had cawed. The ceiling was angled, with exposed wooden beams, and the live trunk of the tree formed a rough central pillar. Calladia walked clockwise around the trunk, admiring the space as she opened curtains to let the late afternoon light in. A stove sat near the front—magically powered, presumably—along with a mini fridge, a sink, and an adjustable dining table and chairs built to accommodate beings of multiple sizes. Past the kitchen area was a Japanese folding screen painted with a forest scene. When Calladia pulled the screen back, she found a toilet and sink, a full-length mirror, and a massive porcelain bathtub/shower that caused her to let out an involuntary moan. She hadn't had a good soak in a long time, and boy, could she use one.

She pulled back the folding screen on the other side of the tub to continue her exploration. This seemed like a sitting area, with rustic furniture scattered around. There was a dresser and more eclectically constructed chairs, as well as shelves holding board games. Past that was a plush-looking four-poster bed and a small couch in front of a fireplace in which blue flames flickered. Calladia recognized the spell powering them: the fire would emanate warmth but no smoke, and it was limited to one spot, so there was no danger of burning the tree down.

The room was definitely cute. She'd have to compliment Tansy—

Calladia's thoughts ground to a halt.

Hang on.

She turned to face the bed.

The *only* bed.

"This can't be right," Calladia said. "I asked Tansy for two twins."

"Did they confirm there were two beds?" Astaroth asked. "I got lost with all that screeching."

Calladia thought back to her conversation with Tansy, which, now that she considered it, had seemed odd. When Calladia had requested two twins, the griffin had nodded sagely and said the request seemed redundant, but there were indeed two frames.

Or had the griffin actually said *consult the flames?*

Calladia hurried to inspect the fireplace. An engraved metal plate was screwed into the front:

> *For Love or Money*
> *For Family or Fame*
> *Your Heart Has a Want*
> *So Wish on the Flames*
> *This Wish Granter* Bespelled by Britannia the Benevolent, 1956.*

Below it were more lines in minuscule type:

*Results may vary. Do not make a wish on an empty stomach. If your wish is followed by acrid green smoke or disembodied cackling, evacuate immediately. If a wished-for erection lasts more than four hours, seek medical attention. No returns on babies or pets. Do not wish for the apocalypse; it won't work, and you'll look like a jerk. This statement has not been evaluated by the FDA.

"Oh, Hecate," Calladia said, slumping onto the couch before the fire. "Tansy thought I was making a wish."

"For what?" Astaroth asked, bending to peer at the engraving.

Calladia stifled a hysterical shriek, because it was the absolute last thing she would have wished for. "They thought I wanted to be a parent to twins. Two of them." She groaned. "No wonder Tansy thought my wish was redundant."

Astaroth straightened. "They thought you wanted to be in possession of *infants?*"

He sounded so horrified by the prospect that Calladia cracked and started laughing. "Right? And why would I ask for that at a hotel, of all places?" She mimed making a phone call. "Hello, I would like to book a room and also to be mystically impregnated. Do you provide room service?"

Astaroth gave a full-body shudder. "Imagine being responsible for two tiny, fragile, squalling organisms who need constant supervision to prevent them from accidental death."

"Exactly!" Calladia sat up straight and slapped her thigh. "My friends don't get it. They all want kids someday. Not that there's anything wrong with that; it just isn't for me."

Calladia had been waiting for some kind of biological clock to kick in and make the thought of being a parent more palatable. Sure, she had plenty of childbearing years left, but by their late twenties, most of her friends had already started speculating about when they'd have kids. They'd all seemed excited about it, too.

Calladia was thrilled for them and would be delighted to be an aunt figure in their children's lives, but whenever she considered having kids of her own, she had three immediate thoughts. One: expensive! Two: time-consuming! Three: don't wanna!

She'd started to wonder if something was wrong with her, given how enthusiastic everyone else seemed. *You'll want them with the right person*, Mariel had told her once, even before she'd met Oz and gotten all disgustingly cute and gooey. Mariel was undoubtedly dreaming about babies with freckles and adorable little horns, but Calladia's vision of a rosy future had always involved just her and someone she loved, the community they built around themselves, and a lifetime of adventure.

She wondered how Astaroth felt about the topic. He might be a pain in her ass, but he was an interesting one, and she wanted to know how his brain worked. "Do you want kids?" she asked. "I don't know how most demons feel about it, and you're—" She cut herself off, but not quickly enough.

"And I'm not a real demon, right?" Astaroth glowered at her, then switched his ire to the fireplace. "No," he said in the direction of the blue flames, "I've never wanted kids. Or at least, I don't think so." He grimaced and rapped the knuckles of his clenched fist against the mantel. "But who knows what I think about anything, since I didn't even know I was a hybrid until this afternoon."

"I guess you have to trust your instincts."

Astaroth ran his hand through his hair, making the strands stick up haphazardly. In a sexily disheveled way, of course, since he was incapable of looking bad. Calladia was single-handedly holding down the dirty gremlin role for the team.

"Amnesia is a dashed inconvenience," Astaroth grumbled.

He sounded like an aggrieved duke in a Jane Austen adaptation, and Calladia bit her lip on a smile. "What strong language," she said. "I'm scandalized."

Astaroth huffed. "If I haven't managed to scandalize you yet, I doubt anything could."

"Have you been trying to?" Calladia asked, genuinely curious.

"No, but it tends to happen anyway." He walked to the bed and stared at it with hands on his hips. "So we only have one bed. That shouldn't be a problem. The couch is big enough for you to curl up on, and we can add pillows."

"Sounds like a plan," Calladia said distractedly. Her gaze had slipped to his butt, which filled out those ridiculous pants nicely. Then she replayed what he'd said and felt a flare of outrage. "Wait, why am I curling up on the couch and not you?"

"You're smaller, so you'll be more comfortable."

Calladia guffawed. She pushed to her feet and went toe-to-toe with Astaroth. He didn't retreat, despite her standing uncomfortably close, but did he ever? "I'm not that much smaller than you," she said.

His eyes dipped to her mouth. "Small enough." The rough edge to his voice sent a shiver down her spine.

Calladia licked her lips, feeling the electric thrill of a challenge. "What about chivalry?"

"Fuck chivalry," Astaroth rebutted instantly. "I have amnesia."

"Oh, I'm so sorry," Calladia said with exaggerated concern. "I didn't realize you'd forgotten how to sleep on a couch."

"Well, I have." Astaroth sighed heavily. "It's a tragedy, but alas, there's nothing to be done for it. I shall make do with the bed."

Calladia tried not to laugh. "A gentleman would offer the bed to the lady."

"Do you see a gentleman here? Or a lady, for that matter?"

Calladia gasped. "Rude!"

Astaroth slid his hands into his pockets and shrugged one shoulder, eyes gleaming with mischief. "If you want me to treat you like a lady, I will, but I've got to warn you, proper ladies don't get in fistfights."

Good point. "Then I'll fistfight you for the bed," she said, switching tactics.

"You'd try to take advantage of a wounded man?" he asked, clapping a hand to his chest.

She was torn between laughing and rolling her eyes at the dramatics. "I don't know why you chose to be a bargainer when you clearly had a bright future on the stage."

"What makes you think I don't have time for both? I could have just finished a starring run on the West End for all we know." His grin was sharp and wicked. He was enjoying this banter.

Calladia was, too. Her breath came fast, and excitement buzzed under her skin. Sparring with the demon held the same out-of-control thrill as dancing at the edge of a cliff or standing outside in a thunderstorm, and Calladia was enough of an adrenaline junkie to crave more. She'd always been drawn to danger.

Tension thrummed between them like a plucked string. What would happen if she seized that thread and made something out of it, the way she wove magic from twine?

The cliff edge—and madness—beckoned.

Calladia dropped her gaze to the demon's lips and leaned in.

A shrill, jaunty melody started blaring from Calladia's backpack. She jumped, heart jolting into overdrive. "Guess I left my ringer on," she said with an awkward laugh, not sure whether she should curse or thank the phone for interrupting her ill-considered impulse.

Astaroth also looked startled. "What is that?" He listened for a moment, then started humming along. "Taylor Swift?"

Calladia hurried to her backpack and dug through it until she found her cell phone. The screen showed an incoming call from Cynthia Cunnington.

Calladia's stomach soured, and the playful energy drained out of her. She hesitated with her thumb over the screen, then rejected the call.

Silence fell over the room.

Calladia didn't look up right away, nervous about what she might see on Astaroth's face. Now that the phone had jolted her back to reality, she couldn't fathom what she'd been thinking.

Had she really almost kissed the demon? Again?

A mixture of arousal and guilt heated her skin and made her stomach clench. An almost-kiss was close to an almost-headbutt, right? She'd just gotten her wires crossed.

Sure, an inner voice mocked. *Tell yourself that if it makes you feel better.*

"Who was that?" Astaroth asked.

The phone buzzed with a text message.

Cynthia Cunnington: Rude not to answer the phone. Diantha says there's a rumor you left town to join the circus. I told her you're on a mindfulness retreat. Circus not good for optics. Be back for dinner tomorrow. Cocktail attire. Donors for reelection will be there.

A second text came swiftly after.

Cynthia Cunnington: Don't disappoint me again.

Calladia silenced the phone and shoved it in her bag. "Just my mother," she said. Her mother, the mayor of Glimmer Falls, scion of the community, whose expectations for Calladia were so high not even King Kong could climb them. How was she already thinking about reelection?

The excitement had been sucked out of Calladia so quickly, she felt dizzy and exhausted. She stood and stretched. "I need a bath."

She grabbed her backpack and brushed past Astaroth, hoping he wouldn't follow. She needed a good, long soak to wash off the dust of the road and regain her composure.

Behind the folding screen, Calladia pulled toiletries and pajamas out of the backpack. The blue onesie covered with a rubber duck pattern had been a gift from Themmie, and since it was warm but too ridiculous to wear in normal life, Calladia had put it in her camping supplies. The previous night she'd fallen asleep in her clothes, but it would be nice to wear something clean and comfortable after her bath.

Astaroth would probably give her shit for it, but whatever. She could put him in his place even in baby pajamas with a butt flap.

Calladia stripped and undid her braid, wincing as her fingers met tangles. She did a set of push-ups, crunches, squats, and lunges before rinsing the sweat off in a quick shower. She missed her morning workout routine at the gym. Her brain was restless even at the best of times, and tiring herself out first thing in the morning was the best way to maintain an even keel the rest of the day. Not that her version of an even keel was particularly balanced, but at least the exercise took the edge off her temper and anxieties.

Once the top layer of dirt was washed off, Calladia plugged the tub and let it fill. She dipped her feet in, hissing at the hot sting. Her feet and ankles turned cherry red, and she whimpered when she plunked the rest of her body down in the water. Pain was fleeting though, and besides, she deserved it after nearly hooking up with the demon who had tried to hurt her best friend, so she sat and endured the burn, waiting for her skin to acclimate.

"Everything all right?" Astaroth asked.

"Stop lurking," she called back.

"Where am I supposed to go? We're practically in the stratosphere."

She shook her head at his absurdity and started slopping water over her arms and shoulders. Then she ducked underwater, holding her breath while the heat sank into her scalp. Her hair drifted like seaweed, and her racing thoughts began to slow.

Calladia unfortunately didn't have gills to stay under indefinitely, so she surfaced and set about shampooing and soaping. Once her hair was slick with conditioner, she grabbed a combat magic textbook from her backpack and settled in to refresh her memory on spells that could be useful in the days ahead.

She read for a while, but the excitement of the last few days was catching up with her, and as warmth relaxed her muscles, Calladia's eyelids drooped. When she nearly dunked the book in the water, she gave up on reading and tossed it aside.

She'd just rest for a few moments. Astaroth and her mother and the stresses of the outside world could wait.

Calladia must have drifted off, because the next thing she knew, she was sneezing and coughing up soapy bathwater. Her eyes watered as she shoved herself upright, and water slopped onto the floor. She swiped the hair out of her eyes, cursing up a storm. So much for a relaxing bath.

A cleared throat came from the other side of the bathing screen. "Battling the Spanish Armada in there?" Astaroth asked.

Calladia glared at the screen. "Are you still eavesdropping?"

"It's hardly eavesdropping when you're that loud."

"Ugh. Go take a long walk off a short branch." She started untangling her conditioner-slick hair with her fingers, grimacing at the pull on her scalp.

"As delightful as plummeting to grievous injury sounds, I prefer to stay here." There was a long pause, during which Calladia scrubbed and stewed over her ruined bath. "Do you need anything?" Astaroth asked.

"Sure," Calladia said sarcastically. "A stiff drink, a quesadilla, and a new set of lungs." She coughed again, spitting out the last of the water.

Astaroth didn't respond, so Calladia dedicated herself to finishing off the bath. Near-drowning or not, exhaustion or not, aggravating text from her mother or not, she was going to squeeze whatever small amount of relaxation she could from this situation. She grabbed a loofah and scrubbed militantly until her skin stung.

All right, maybe she wasn't the best at relaxing. But by the time she was done, her skin was squeaky clean, her hair was wound in a wet bun on top of her head, and she smelled like sweet orange and lavender essential oils. Her self-care techniques might be aggressive, but the results were what mattered.

Calladia drained the tub and toweled off thoroughly. Through the window, the ruddy light of a dying afternoon had melted into the purple hues of twilight, and Calladia felt the urge to curl up under a blanket and let the lingering heat of the bath lull her to sleep. She put on clean underwear and shimmied into the onesie, buttoning up the front and that ridiculous butt flap.

When she looked at herself in the mirror, she hardly recognized the woman looking back at her. The duck pajamas were part of the effect, sure, but there was something else she couldn't put her finger on. An extra rosiness to her cheeks, maybe, or a luminosity to her eyes. It was as if some invisible tension had been lifted from her skin by the hot water. She looked . . . soft.

Calladia had never been soft. Yet she kept staring, enraptured by this vision of a woman who might have existed, had she not had to erect so many walls to protect herself.

Calladia shook her head and shoved the nonsensical thought

aside. It was probably heatstroke combined with the text from her mother making her emotional. Thinking about her mother punctured that hazy bubble of contentment, which proved it hadn't been meant to last. "Your turn," she said as she stepped into the main room. "Unless you like reveling in filth."

"Depends on the filth," Astaroth said. He turned from where he'd been leaning over the table, then recoiled. "Dear Lucifer, what are you wearing?"

Calladia was distracted by what he'd been leaning over: two take-out containers, a bowl of limes, and bottles of tequila, triple sec, and simple syrup. She rushed over. "Where did you get this?" she demanded. She inhaled deeply, then moaned at the spicy scent of Mexican food.

Astaroth crossed his arms, looking as smug as if he'd single-handedly taken down a mammoth with a spear and dragged it to his cave. "I found a take-out menu in the kitchen, and Tansy provides delivery service." He gestured to the spread. "Voila, quesadillas."

The fight had cut lunch short, and Calladia hadn't realized how hungry she was. She wanted to cry looking at the crisp tortillas overflowing with melted cheese. "Thank you."

"It's being charged to your card," Astaroth said.

Calladia laughed and swiped at her eye. Trust the demon to spike his own guns with a sardonic comment. She was getting to know his tells though, and she recognized he used snark to deflect attention whenever he did something heroic. And yes, the retrieval of Mexican food did count as heroism.

She dug in with a fork and knife from the kitchen, groaning when she realized the cheese was still hot and gooey. Peppers and rich chunks of pulled pork were dotted throughout.

When the sharp edge of her hunger had been dulled, she thought of something. "How did you order takeout if you can't unlock your phone?"

"I tried a few combinations of numbers," he said. He'd been eating slowly and neatly, cutting the quesadilla into small bites. "*1 2 3 4 5 6* worked."

"Seriously?" She chuckled. "That's, like, the least secure passcode in history. So much for being a master strategist."

He gave her a dark look. "It got you quesadillas, didn't it?"

She lifted her fork. "Touché. I rescind my mockery."

Astaroth picked up the tequila bottle and peered at the label. "How does one make a margarita anyway?"

Calladia was more than happy to teach him. She found a cocktail shaker and glasses in the kitchen and shook up two margaritas.

When Astaroth sipped, his face relaxed into a smile. "That's delicious."

Calladia felt a swell of pride, which was ridiculous. Making a margarita for a demon she despised wasn't exactly a life accomplishment.

Looking at his clever, compelling face though, she was forced to admit a truth that had been building for some time. She didn't despise him, no matter what she said. No matter how much she should.

She hadn't spent much time with him before he'd lost his memory, but this version of him was far more appealing than the sneering villain who'd insulted her after trying to hurt her friends. Sure, he was a snarky ass, but he was also generous and willing to back her up in a fight or order takeout if she was hungry.

Was this the true Astaroth? Or was the villain the real version?

As Calladia watched the skin beside Astaroth's eyes crinkle with a smile, she found herself wishing he'd never gain back his memories if it meant he'd stay like this.

◆ ◆ ◆

"I DO THIS SPELL AT HOME," CALLADIA SLURRED, POINTING AT the fireplace. The third margarita had been a mistake, but she was so full and relaxed she couldn't regret it. The sky was dark outside, and wind whistled through the treetops.

"Yeah?" Astaroth sounded buzzed, too. He reclined at the other end of the couch, a half-empty glass dangling from his fingertips. "How do you do it?"

Calladia fumbled in her pocket for a piece of yarn. She tried to knot it a few times, ultimately giving up when she realized she was tying a knot for *explosion* rather than *ignition*. This was why doing magic while drinking was a bad idea.

"There's more than one way to do it," she said, "but ultimately, it's a mix of action and words. You tie a few knots or scribble some runes to define what you want." She stared into the fire, thinking about what spells she might do if she weren't intoxicated. "I could tie one knot for fire, one for safety, one to contain it to the fireplace." She waved a hand. "Some other stuff to be thorough. And then you have to pick which spell words to speak."

"The language of magic is far too complicated," Astaroth said. "I don't know how witches and warlocks manage."

"You get used to it eventually." With a lot of memorization, since the rules of conjugation and grammar were haphazard. It was impossible to know every word of the language of magic, since people were always inventing new ones or jamming words together, so witches learned what was most helpful for the kind of magic they wanted to do and discarded the rest.

"Are your fires blue, too?" Astaroth asked.

"Yeah. You can pick what color you want, but I think blue looks nice with all the white and yellow in my house."

Except her house didn't exist anymore. Calladia rubbed her chest against the ache that swelled at the reminder.

Her beautiful house was gone, burned to ashes. In all the chaos of the last two days, it had been easier to ignore what she was leaving behind and focus on the next steps of the quest, but the loss still throbbed beneath, an unacknowledged wound.

That house hadn't gotten the opportunity to hold many memories, but damn it, the memories it did hold had been *hers*. She didn't care about the clothes that had gone up in smoke or the flimsy LYKEA furniture that had been blasted to smithereens. A structure could be rebuilt, and the things inside it were replaceable.

No, Calladia didn't mourn *stuff*. She missed cooking breakfast for Mariel after a night out or seeing Themmie curled up on a beanbag watching TV. She missed dinner parties and nights reading alone on her couch and the warm feeling of having a place that welcomed her exactly as she was.

"You look maudlin," Astaroth said. His head lolled on the sofa as he looked at her.

It wasn't a question, but Calladia answered anyway. "Just remembering that my house isn't there anymore."

"Ah." Astaroth lifted the glass to his lips. "Losing things gets easier with time."

He sounded a shade melancholy, but Calladia didn't want to be preached at. "Like your memory?" she asked waspishly.

Astaroth winced. "Touché."

Calladia sighed. She didn't need to jump down his throat because she was a grumpy woman with mommy issues and nowhere to live. "Sorry," she said. "I guess I'm still on edge from my mother calling."

"Yeah?" Astaroth shifted to face her, bracing his head on his hand. He looked drowsy and flushed, and his hair was still damp from his own bath. He'd donned a white robe they'd found in the dresser, and it was odd to see the demon looking so cuddly and domestic.

She'd thought of him as a wild animal when she'd first let him stay with her. Dangerous and unpredictable, an exotic intrusion into Calladia's boring life. His deadly edges seemed dulled, but how much of that was real, and how much a product of his amnesia?

And were they really dulled? Or had he blunted his edges for her alone?

Calladia liked that idea a bit too much, so she shrugged it off. What had they been talking about?

Oh. Right. Her mother.

Not great, but if she couldn't talk about her mom with the enemy-turned-road-trip-buddy she'd never see again after this trip, who could she talk to about the situation? At least if Calladia was truly in the wrong, he wouldn't pull his punches to tell her so.

"My mom's demanding," Calladia said. The word was woefully inadequate, so she tried again. "More than that. She knows exactly how the world should be, and if anything or anyone around her doesn't fit that vision, she either changes them or destroys them."

"Metaphorical destruction?" Astaroth asked. "Or is she as murderous as my own dear mother?"

There were books dedicated to Lilith's exploits over the centuries: the good, the bad, and the chaotic. Cynthia Cunnington would undoubtedly love to be memorialized to that extent, but so far she was only small-town famous, her printed legacy limited to op-eds and gossip pieces in the *Glimmer Falls Gazette*.

"She doesn't murder people," Calladia said. Although who could say what would happen should society devolve and public execution come into vogue again? "She does get people who disagree with her fired though. And she's good at gossip. Misinformation and all that."

Not that her mom would call it misinformation. She'd term it a *strategic communication choice*.

"Do you know why she called you?" Astaroth asked.

Blue reflections from the fire danced over his glossy black horns. Calladia watched the flickers, wondering if the aurora borealis looked something like that on a grander scale. "She wants me to come to dinner tomorrow."

Astaroth sat up straight, sending the margarita splashing over the rim of his glass. "You can't. We've got to see Isobel, and even if it only takes a few hours, there's the drive back to consider—"

"Don't work yourself into a tizzy," Calladia said. "I'm not going."

"Oh." Astaroth sagged back into the couch. "Good."

"She's going to be pissed though. More pissed than she already was anyway. I guess she's dealing with the rumor mill about me skipping town. But yeah, this will be bad." Calladia made a face. "She's meeting donors for her reelection campaign."

"Reelection for what?" Astaroth asked.

Calladia was taken aback. Everyone in her life knew Cynthia Cunnington, so she'd taken her mom's notoriety as fact. But Astaroth wasn't from Glimmer Falls and didn't care who was small-town famous. Even pre-amnesia, he likely wouldn't have known a thing about her mother.

The thought was oddly comforting. Calladia's life might have been shaped by one powerful, destructive force, like a sandstone cliff at the mercy of a raging river, but there were oodles of beings out there who didn't give a damn about Cynthia Cunnington and her machinations. The world—the universe—was far bigger than the petty politics of Glimmer Falls.

"She's the mayor," Calladia said. "Two years now, and years of campaigning before that."

If she had to pinpoint when her mother's expectations had grown toxic, versus simply overbearing, it had been the moment Cynthia had decided to run for office. Suddenly, Calladia's existence had become part of a political narrative—one that didn't allow for foul-mouthed daughters who didn't fit high society's expectations.

"Is she any good at it?" Astaroth asked.

Calladia was startled into a laugh. No one had ever asked her that. "I mean . . . no? Not in my opinion, at least. She doesn't think highly of nonwitches or working-class people, and she definitely takes bribes." Calladia had been disgusted when she'd realized how quickly her mother, the so-called "pillar of the community," had embraced being a crooked politician. "Did you know she supported bulldozing some of the forest to build a resort and spa for rich people? Like, she fully didn't care if the forest died or the fire salamanders went extinct, so long as her bank account stayed healthy."

Suddenly, Calladia remembered who she was talking to. Astaroth had been poisoning the woods, too—not to make way for a resort, but in an effort to force nature-loving Mariel into a soul bargain. He had been as devious as Cynthia in pursuit of his goals, with little care about who was hurt in the process.

Astaroth had also been the reason the resort was scrapped though. Mariel had eventually made a bargain, and in return, Astaroth had cured the woods and made it so no one could build on that protected land again. Even after Oz's magical UNO Reverse play to return Mariel's soul to her, nothing could cancel Astaroth's magic.

He'd saved the forest, but did that matter when his intentions were rotten?

"Why are you glowering at me all of a sudden?" Astaroth asked. He blinked slowly, his long, pale lashes sweeping his cheekbones. "Makes you look very fearsome. Duck onesie aside."

He'd made a few sly digs at her attire, but it wasn't like he could talk, since he was wearing a fluffy bathrobe. And after discussing her mother, Calladia was no longer in the mood to be twitted. "I was thinking about when we met," she said. "You were trying to kill the forest, too."

"So you've said." He drained his glass, then held it in his lap, turning it over. "Was I in cahoots with your mother, or did you decide it was easier to be pissed at me again, rather than her?"

Calladia set her own glass down on the floor. "I can be mad at two people at once."

"I am well aware." He stared into the empty glass like it held the answer to an unspoken question. "It does feel a bit like being punished for someone else's crimes though."

Oh, please. "I said I could be mad at both of you—"

"I'm not talking about your mother," Astaroth interrupted. "I'm talking about whatever version of me you met in the woods. You hate him, and for all I know you're right to, but since I can't remember a bloody thing, it seems unfair to keep being punished for it."

Calladia stood and retrieved both glasses, taking them to the kitchen. "Just because you can't remember doesn't mean you didn't do it," she tossed over her shoulder.

Astaroth made a frustrated sound. "And is my entire worth and identity boiled down to one incident? Will you always look at me and see the demon who hurt your friends, no matter what else I do or say?"

She was taken aback by the bitterness in his voice. Maybe the alcohol had broken his composure, the way being contacted by her mother had broken hers. Maybe both of them had learned too well how to shield themselves from the world.

Calladia wasn't sure how to respond, or even if she should. Was this an argument? It had an edge to it their usual banter didn't, like the uneven sharpness of broken glass. She didn't like it.

Was Astaroth looking to be comforted, absolved of his crimes? He didn't deserve such softness, any more than Calladia did.

Their eyes remained locked for long moments. Then Astaroth stood. "I'm going to sleep," he announced. He looked between her and the bed, then plopped back down on the couch. He lay on his side facing the fire, legs tucked up and head pillowed on his bicep.

Calladia stared at him. What happened to *fuck chivalry*?

He had been right though; the couch was too small for him to sleep on. His knees hung over the edge, his legs were jammed toward his chest, and if he shifted more than a few inches, he'd topple off.

Calladia sighed. Maybe it was the tequila speaking, but she didn't like seeing him uncomfortable. She didn't like fighting with him either—at least not like this.

She moved around the space, dousing lights before casting a quick spell to bank the flames to a subtle glow. Then she grabbed all the spare pillows she could find and made her way to the bed.

"What're you doing?" Astaroth's sullen voice came from behind her, and when she looked over her shoulder, she saw him peering over the back of the couch.

"Making a pillow wall, obviously." She'd constructed a soft barricade down the center of the bed. "I get the left side."

He blinked. "What?"

"I said I get the left side. You get the right." He seemed befuddled, so she shrugged. "If you want to sleep on the couch, I won't stop you, but the bed would be more comfortable."

Calladia went to brush her teeth, then left the brush and toothpaste on the counter for Astaroth to use if he wanted. She took her bun down and shook it out, finger-combing the damp strands. She'd brush it in the morning once it was dry.

When she returned to the bed, there was a demon-shaped lump under the covers on the right side. Calladia felt a twinge of something alarmingly close to fondness when she noticed the tips of his horns peeking out. Mariel had told her Oz slept bundled up like a burrito, his demon physiology demanding heat. Astaroth was apparently the same.

Calladia slid into the side of the bed closest to the window, where the air was cooler. Even with the pillow wall between them, she was far too aware of the demon's presence. His soft breathing was audible in the stillness, and the mattress dipped slightly in favor of his weight.

Rain began tapping against the roof and windows, and Calladia yawned. "Good night, dramatic demon," she mumbled as she curled up on her side.

Sleep reached for her with soft, dark fingers. She had nearly succumbed when Astaroth murmured a reply.

"Good night, grumpy witch."

Calladia smiled.

NINETEEN

A STAROTH WOKE UP WITH A MOUTHFUL OF HAIR.
He mumbled and spit it out, only to realize the hair had encroached elsewhere. Strands were wrapped around his neck, something brushed his ear, and when he breathed in, hair tickled his nostril. He nuzzled into the pillow to scratch his nose, then opened bleary eyes.

Dawn light spilled through the window, casting a bright rectangle across the bed. Astaroth was lying on his left side, and directly in front of him was a large quantity of the hair in question. It was long, straight, and buttery-blond, the texture silky where it wasn't tangled from sleep. The head to which the hair belonged rested on a pillow next to him, facing away in a mirror of his pose.

He inhaled the scent of Calladia's soap. She smelled like oranges and sun-warmed linen.

His sleep-fuddled mind didn't understand why she was so close to him. Hadn't she erected a pillow fortress? His right hand was resting on something soft; maybe the barrier hadn't been fully breached overnight.

When he raised his head, he realized he wasn't touching the pillow barricade. His hand was resting on the curve of Calladia's waist. Her chest rose and fell softly under blue, rubber duck–patterned fabric.

He slowly placed his head back on the pillow, not wanting to make any sudden movements and wake her. Resting with her, *touching* her, felt surreal. Lucifer, even seeing her relaxed and quiet was bizarre. She'd had a few lively conversations with herself during the night, but now her breathing was deep and even.

It could be like this between us, he thought. Days spent fighting the world and each other, nights and lazy mornings dedicated to peace. His witch was a powerhouse, a warrior queen, but even warriors had to rest between battles.

It was who they let themselves rest around that mattered.

Calladia shifted. "Freaking bulldozer," she muttered.

Astaroth bit back a laugh. His fingers gently flexed on her waist. The onesie was soft, but he felt the firm line of her body beneath it.

Had rubber ducks ever been so arousing?

Calladia made a grumpy noise. "Where'd you get the fedora?"

Astaroth froze. The words echoed in his head, ringing like a bell. *Where'd you get the fedora? Where'd you get the fedora?*

Where'd you get the fedora, a pickup artist convention?

His temple throbbed, and his head spun. Astaroth closed his eyes, swallowing against nausea.

A memory played out, one bracketed with green pines and sprawling brambles. The background was hazy, but one thing was clear and sharp: Calladia, standing with her fists clenched, a furious expression on her face. Her hair hung loose to her lower back, and she was wearing the same outfit from the first day: leggings patterned with daisies and a blue tank top that said *Sweat Like a Girl*.

In the memory, Astaroth stood opposite her, his white suit

clean of blood and a black fedora covering his horns. His hand rested on the crystal skull topper of his cane sword.

This motherfucker is Astaroth of the Nine? the Calladia of memory asked. *Where'd you get the fedora, a pickup artist convention?*

Memory Astaroth and current Astaroth were united in their outrage. *I don't take sartorial critiques from people wearing spandex,* he'd sneered.

Nearby, a short pixie with pink-and-green hair expressed alarm. Another of Calladia's friends, presumably. Whatever she said was lost, because Calladia was walking toward Astaroth, cracking her knuckles, and she was all he had focus for.

The last few days had taught Astaroth to be wary when she looked like that. The emotions captured in the memory didn't match what he felt now though. At the time, Astaroth had been full of disdain. He'd considered her annoying and irrelevant. Beneath him.

So you're the demon who's been destroying the forest? Calladia began tying her hair up, and Astaroth instantly knew this memory was about to devolve into a fight. *The demon who destroyed my best friend's greenhouse? The one trying to force Oz and Mariel to make a bargain?*

He'd looked at her soul then, opening his demon senses. It was brilliant, pure in its power. And Astaroth, greedy demon that he was, had wanted to claim it for himself. Seize a new victory out of the bitterness of recent defeat. Maybe with her soul as an offering, the high council would allow him to amend the terms of the wager. He could still come out on top.

Astaroth's sweat had felt cold in the forest air. Moloch couldn't win. Not before Astaroth revealed . . .

But the particulars of what Astaroth needed to reveal drifted away like mist.

Do you want to become a princess? he'd asked, determined to find the price that would convince her to hand over her soul. *Own a diamond mine? Say it, and it's yours.*

I do want something, she'd said, stopping just out of reach, *but I can't get it through a deal.*

What had she wanted? He desperately wanted to know. He'd wanted to know back then, too, but for a different reason. Until he knew her vulnerabilities, he wouldn't be able to use them for his own ends.

It was strange, feeling this split in himself. It seemed impossible he'd ever viewed her with sneering disdain, yet the memory was definitely his.

I can give you anything.

No thanks. I take what I want.

He'd noticed her beauty even then. The mix of classically delicate features and visible musculature had been interesting. His mind had traveled down speculative paths, considering what the angry, pretty witch would take if she could.

Then she'd punched him in the throat.

In the present day, Astaroth yelped and twitched. Calladia instantly sat upright, shoving hair out of her face to reveal flushed cheeks and heavy-lidded eyes. "What is it?" she asked, voice still blurred by sleep. "Who's there?"

He sat up, too, powered by a burst of outrage. "You punched me in the throat!"

"I did?" Calladia looked down at her hand, then back at him, blinking slowly. "Sorry, I'm an active sleeper. You look fine."

"Not in your sleep," he said through gritted teeth.

She squinted at him, and he saw when her mind finally caught up with the conversation. "Oh," she said. And then, "Oh! Wait, did your memory return?"

"Some of it," he said, crossing his arms. "I remember you hitting me."

"Well, at least it's a start," she said with a cocky grin. "I'm sure you'll remember the rest of the beatdown soon."

The casual way she spoke about it set his teeth on edge. "You sound awfully cheerful about it."

"And you seem upset, though I'm not sure why. We're enemies, remember?"

"Because . . . because . . ." Dash it, he wasn't sure why he was angry either. It was just that after all they'd been through together, being attacked by her stung. That the attack had happened before their recent adventures didn't seem to figure in to his addled brain. With memories popping up willy-nilly, it felt like she'd punched him moments ago.

And why did she have to say it like that? *We're enemies*, as if that neatly summed everything up. As if she still saw nothing more in him than a foe to be vanquished.

"You had it coming, if that helps," Calladia said, oblivious to how her words had skewered him through the heart. She looked around the bed, and her brow furrowed. "Where did the pillows go?"

"Hang the pillows." Astaroth rubbed his temples, struggling for calm. "Why didn't you tell me?"

Calladia grabbed a pillow from the floor and tossed it in his direction. "That I beat you up? I thought I had."

Pain stabbed through his head, and his eye twitched. "It was completely unprovoked."

"Mmmm, was it though?" she asked skeptically, chucking another pillow and narrowly missing his face.

She wasn't taking this seriously enough. He batted the next pillow aside. "I didn't do anything to you," he argued, "and then you hit me and insulted my hat—"

"It was a terrible hat," she said.

Astaroth gasped, because now he recalled it wasn't just a good hat; it was his favorite. "That fedora cost more than four hundred quid and came custom from my favorite London haberdasher!"

Calladia scoffed and shifted to kneel facing him, apparently giving up on the pillow wall. "I don't know why you're buying hats using sea creatures as currency—"

"I said *quid*, not *squid*."

"Either way, you overpaid." She looked him up and down condescendingly. "You looked like the flag bearer for the incel cause."

Astaroth made a face. "The what?"

"Incels," she said. "Does the word ring a bell?" When Astaroth shook his head, she continued. "If you forget anything you might have learned about them, it'll be the best thing amnesia does for you. *Incel* stands for 'involuntary celibate,' and they're misogynistic fuckwads who think women owe them sex."

Astaroth's fingers dug into his pillow as he contemplated ripping it apart. "You think I'm a misogynistic fuckwad?"

She blew a hank of hair out of her face, then gave him a mean smile. "They like fedoras is all I'm saying."

She was likely kidding, but Astaroth's irritation was spiraling out of control, heading in too many illogical directions. What was he really angry about? The hat? The dismissive way she spoke about beating him up?

Or was it because he'd come to trust, admire, and—curse it— *like* her, and that memory had been the emotional equivalent of getting punted in the crotch? Which she had done after the throat punch, he now recalled.

Was his anger even directed entirely at her? When he remembered the cynicism he'd felt facing her in those woods, his stomach churned.

Rather than performing a more in-depth interrogation of that uncomfortable feeling, Astaroth barreled on with the argument. "So you do think I'm a misogynistic fuckwad. Even more laughably, you think I'm a *celibate* one." The gall. He'd been bedding men, women, and nonbinary folks of multiple species for centuries and doing a grand job of it. Nothing but rave reviews.

Calladia's cheeks turned pinker, and a combative light shone in her eyes. "That's what you're upset about?" The humorous edge to her voice was gone; she wasn't teasing any longer, but picking up the gauntlet he'd thrown down. "Not that you might be a misogynist, but that I might think you're not getting laid on the regular?"

"No—"

"I must have missed your travel concubines," she continued, voice rising. "Or did you leave your Fleshlight in your other pants?"

"I don't even know what a Fleshlight is." And he'd never employed *travel concubines*, of all things.

Calladia poked him in the chest, a jab he felt through the fabric of his robe. "Well, let me tell you something, Casanova. I don't think you're a misogynist, for the record, but you clearly woke up on the wrong side of the bed and are determined to make it my problem. I have zero interest in that bullshit, especially when I haven't had coffee yet, so you and your attitude can go meet your hand in the bathroom and work it out."

Lucifer, she was mean. Agitated emotions churned inside Astaroth's chest like leaves in a cyclone. His skin tingled where she'd poked him, and the fury in her expression was sending mixed signals to his body. He wanted her to yell at him some more, pull his hair, maybe even slap him, and then he wanted to shut her up with his mouth and taste the full force of her passion.

Succumbing to instinct, Astaroth grabbed her hand and pulled until her finger hit his pectoral again. "Harder," he said.

Calladia's eyes widened. "What?"

"You heard me. Do it harder." He licked his lips. "Make me feel it."

Calladia's breath hitched. Complicated emotions flitted across her face. This wasn't just anger; whatever madness had gripped him had her in its claws as well.

He had a premonition: *This could destroy me.*

She *could destroy me.*

Astaroth didn't care. "Come on," he said, low and challenging. "Hurt me."

Calladia hesitated, but not for long. She was a creature of passion, after all, and she never retreated from a fight. "You," she said, jabbing him in the chest, "are obnoxious."

"More," he said, leaning in. He grabbed a handful of her golden hair, winding it around his wrist, and Calladia's eyelids grew heavy as her lips parted.

She drilled her finger into his chest again, harder this time. Not hard enough to bruise, though he wished it would. "You're an arrogant, volatile prick, and you drive me insane."

"Same," he gritted.

Another poke. "You're a conceited know-it-all."

"Takes one to know one," he shot back.

She glared as she delivered the coup de grâce. "Your cane sword is tacky, and you have horrible taste in hats."

Astaroth bared his teeth. "Take that back."

"Make me," she said, a challenging light in her eyes.

He would enjoy trying, but that wasn't what he wanted now. Watching her blown pupils and flushed cheeks, the rapid heaving of her breaths, he wanted to push her. See what would happen if she snapped. "Why would I do that," he asked, tightening his grip on her hair, "when you can just take what you want?"

Her eyes flared. The shared memory hung suspended between them, his words an echo of another time, another place. That time, she'd declared herself his enemy. This time . . .

Calladia made an incoherent screeching sound, fisted the lapels of his robe, and hauled him in for a searing kiss.

TWENTY

ASTAROTH'S MOUTH WAS HOT AGAINST CALLADIA'S. HE kissed her furiously, and she matched his aggression with her own. They licked and ate at each other in a mutual devouring. When Astaroth's tongue sank into her mouth, Calladia sucked on it, then bit his lower lip.

Astaroth groaned, then bit her back just as hard. There would be no quarter given on either side.

Calladia didn't want mercy. She wanted to make him feel the same churning, burning need eating her up. Anger and aggression had melted into a lust so powerful, it scalded her skin and sent need pulsing through her.

She wanted to hit him, bite him, leave her marks on his pale skin. She wanted to hear him moan and know it was for her.

Calladia was half in his lap already. She straddled him fully, wrapping her arms around his neck. His hands landed on her ass and squeezed, encouraging her to rock against him. Even through her pajamas and his robe, she could feel the hard length of his cock, and she ground against him, gasping as sensation jolted through her. Her clit was sensitive and swollen, begging for a direct touch.

There was too much fabric between them. Calladia tore at his robe, struggling to get it off, but she only managed to get the fabric over one shoulder before giving up and hauling him close again, too greedy for his mouth.

He tasted like smoke and spice. Like pure, distilled sin.

"You drive me mad," he said against her lips.

"Same, jackass." She yanked on the short strands of his hair—careful to avoid the healing cut near his left temple—and was rewarded by the surge of his hips, nearly lifting her off the bed.

Arousal pooled between her legs, soaking her underwear. This was madness, but she couldn't bear for it to stop. Not now that she finally had her hands and mouth on him.

He surged beneath her, flipping her to her back on the bed. Calladia gasped and squeezed his hips with her thighs.

"Got you," he whispered against her lips before kissing her hard and deep.

Calladia's competitive streak flared. She rocked her hips, grinding against him, then inserted her hand between their bodies and gripped his cock through the fluffy white fabric of his robe.

He gasped and tipped his head back. "Lucifer, I want you so badly."

Calladia took advantage of his moment of distraction, snapping her hips up and shoving his shoulder to topple him off her. She tried to pin him down, but he didn't cede the upper hand. They rolled once, twice . . .

Then toppled off the bed.

Astaroth landed beneath her with a grunt. He kept kissing her though, and then his long, clever fingers were sliding down her backside to press between her legs. He stroked her through the pajamas, and Calladia forgot about their power struggle. She needed his fingers and his tongue on her, then the hot, thick length of his cock splitting her open.

"More," she gasped.

Astaroth dumped her onto her back on the floorboards, then knelt between her legs and started unbuttoning her onesie. He fumbled with a button, and she realized his fingers were trembling.

"I've fantasized about this so much," he said once he'd bared a slice of skin. He shoved the halves apart and stared at her exposed breasts with an expression of awe that quickly turned to greed. His head dipped, and he took her nipple into his mouth.

Calladia jolted as he sucked hard. This wasn't a slow, gentle exploration; it was an explosion of lust, as rough as it was essential. "Touch me," she begged.

Astaroth lifted off her nipple, then tore at the rest of her buttons. He planted a hand between her breasts, then dragged his fingers down her sternum to her stomach, where he circled her navel.

Calladia's belly quivered. She arched her back, silently ordering his fingers to explore further. He obliged, trailing them over her bare stomach before pushing the unbuttoned fabric of her onesie aside. Then Astaroth was toying with the edge of her underwear, tracing the hem with maddening slowness.

Calladia bucked her hips up.

Astaroth chuckled. "Impatient?"

Yes, she was. Now that she'd crossed that line, Calladia didn't want to stop. She wanted to ride this impulse as far and as fast as she could before reality caught up with them.

To speed things up, Calladia ripped off the tie of Astaroth's robe, then reached beneath the fabric and wrapped her hand around his erection.

"Ah!" He collapsed forward, planting his free hand next to her head. He dropped his forehead against hers. "Witch, you feel so good."

He kissed her swiftly, and Calladia smiled against his mouth. She moved her hand up and down, learning the feel of him. The skin over that stiff column was velvety soft and hot as flame, and she wildly thought that the feel of him might be burned into her palm forever.

Astaroth's fingers finally slid under the edge of her panties. Calladia shivered as he brushed over her pubic hair, then delved lower. He slid one finger between her labia, and they groaned in unison.

"So wet," he said. He stroked her, gathering the moisture on his fingertips, then began rubbing her clit.

It was Calladia's turn to cry out. Her heels scraped the ground as she writhed, and her hand sped up on his cock. He matched her speed, and soon the air was filled with animalistic panting and grunting as they chased their mutual release.

Of course it would be like this between them, she thought hazily. A mutual unraveling, half fight and half collaboration. Neither was the type to lie back and take pleasure without giving it as well.

Astaroth slipped two fingers inside her while his thumb worked her clit. Heavy, liquid pleasure gathered between Calladia's legs, and tension built in her lower belly as the orgasm approached. Just a little more . . .

A loud thump came from the deck outside. Calladia and Astaroth froze, hands still positioned intimately.

"Maybe it's a raccoon?" Calladia said.

The thump was followed by a sound of wings being shaken out. Big wings. "Cawwwwwd moooorning!" came the distinctive, rasping voice of Tansy.

"Damn it," Calladia whispered, horniness shifting into frustration. "Not a raccoon."

"Bloody hell." Astaroth groaned as he slipped his fingers out of her, and Calladia wanted to scream at being denied her orgasm. "Cockblocked by a griffin."

Calladia didn't like being clitblocked either. She reluctantly released Astaroth's cock and glared at the door. Why was Tansy interrupting them when checkout time wasn't until eleven? Given the light, it didn't seem much past dawn, and if Calladia's vagina had led her into making this terrible choice, then by Hecate she wanted to enjoy it before the cascade of regret sure to come.

"Your frieeeeeeends are here!" Tansy screeched.

Calladia sat bolt upright and shot Astaroth an alarmed look. They weren't expecting anyone, which meant whoever had come to visit was likely not a friend at all.

Astaroth scrambled to his feet and reached for the dresser drawer he'd stashed his clothes in. Calladia dove for her own clothes, which were heaped untidily next to her backpack. Onesies were cozy but not good in a fight, so she dressed in jeans, a flannel shirt, and boots in record time. She pulled a length of yarn from her backpack and started weaving it between her fingers, setting the framework for a defensive spell.

Astaroth was now fully dressed and holding the fireplace poker like a sword. He motioned to the door, indicating he'd take the left side. Calladia nodded and positioned herself to the right, out of the line of fire should someone come barreling through.

"Lovebiiiiiirds?" Tansy called. "Are you caaaawwaake?"

Calladia cleared her throat. "Yes," she said.

"Awake, armed, and dangerous," Astaroth said.

The griffin let out a series of screeches. It took Calladia a moment to realize they were laughing. "Frieeeeeeeends," Tansy repeated, then burst into a rapid-fire explanation Calladia only caught half of. Something about hugging? And . . . a scare? She shared a baffled look with Astaroth.

"Did you say they're lovebirds?" a man asked, loud and clear. A man with a New Zealand accent.

Oh, shit. Calladia reran the griffin's words through her head. Tansy had said *rugby*, not *hugging*, and *were* instead of *scare*.

The werewolf pack had found them.

"Do we try diplomacy or shock and awe?" Astaroth whispered.

Calladia considered. They were trapped high above the ground in a room with one exit, outside of which stood at least one werewolf. Astaroth, with his demon immortality, would survive a jump to the forest floor, but Calladia would break a lot of bones at best.

"I hate to say it," she whispered back, "but I think we should attempt diplomacy."

Astaroth made a face. "Can't you cast a spell and turn his organs inside out or something?"

"Did you know werewolves have excellent hearing?" came Kai's response from outside.

Calladia winced. "We need to workshop your definition of justified violence," she told Astaroth. Then she took a deep breath and squared her shoulders. "I'm going out there."

"I reserve the right to bludgeon him to death with this poker," Astaroth said, waving the implement in question.

"I can still hear you," Kai said.

Waiting wouldn't accomplish anything, so Calladia unlocked the door and flung it open to reveal Tansy, Kai, and Avram, the brown-haired wolf she'd teamed up with during the brawl. She lifted her chin and marched out like a queen whose territory had been invaded. "What do you want?" she demanded.

Kai was dressed in charcoal slacks and a white button-up shirt with the sleeves rolled up to display muscular forearms. His left arm was in a sling, and the outline of a bandage was visible through the thin fabric of his dress shirt.

His right hand was behind his back. When he moved, Calladia braced herself for an attack, but instead, Kai produced a bouquet of red roses. "For you," the werewolf said.

Next to Calladia, Astaroth made an outraged noise. He swung

the fireplace poker at the bouquet, knocking the flowers to the floor.

"Oi!" Kai glared at the demon. "Mind your business."

Tansy cocked their head. Intelligent black eyes darted between Kai, Astaroth, Calladia, and the bouquet, and then the griffin squawked and raked one leonine paw against the floorboards. "Not friiieeeeeends." Their wings flapped in short, agitated bursts, and they snapped their beak at Kai. "Liiies. Bad customer seeeervice."

"Why are you here?" Calladia asked Kai. "And why do you have flowers?"

Kai sank to his knees and clapped his right hand to his chest, then winced. Apparently he'd jostled his injury. "I had to see you," he said. "It's not every day a beautiful woman stabs me through the heart."

Avram rolled his eyes. "She barely nicked your shoulder, bro."

"It's a metaphor, bro," Kai replied. "But a woman who can fuck me up is the absolute dream."

"Surprisingly," Astaroth muttered, "we're in agreement on that. But she's fucking *me* up, not you."

The two men eyed each other, visibly bristling. Calladia sighed. "So you came all this way to give me flowers?" she asked Kai. "At dawn?"

Kai's eyes darted away. "Well, not entirely."

Avram stepped forward. "Enough bullshit," he said. "This is a job. You can flirt later."

"What job?" Calladia asked suspiciously, looping more yarn around her fist.

Kai stood up. "Nothing terrible. Just a friendly bit of—"

"Bounty hunting," the other werewolf interjected.

Calladia started tying knots.

Astaroth settled into a combat stance, holding the poker like a sword. "Has that Moloch bastard come to try to finish me off?" he asked.

Calladia whispered a spell.

Kai made a high-pitched sound and cupped himself. "Calladia?" he asked, eyes so wide she saw the whites around his brown irises. "That has to be you, right?"

Astaroth's head whipped around. "What did you do to him?"

"Applied some judicious pressure to his testicles," Calladia said. "Don't get jealous."

"You should be applying pressure to *my* testicles," Astaroth muttered.

He didn't need to remind her. Calladia was grumpy, tired, and sexually frustrated, and she had zero patience for weird werewolf bullshit. "Who sent you?" she asked. "Was it Moloch?"

"Don't know who this Moloch bloke is," Kai wheezed, still gripping his crotch. "Can you let up a bit?"

In response, Calladia tied another knot to increase the pressure.

"Hnngh." Kai's eyes rolled back in his head. "I might like that."

"Oh, for Lycaon's sake." Avram turned toward Astaroth. "Word got around about the fight," the werewolf said, "and a demoness commissioned us to find you. She says she's your mother?"

TWENTY-ONE

ASTAROTH'S EMOTIONS RIOTED LIKE BEES WHOSE HIVE had been kicked. He was angry, randy, angry about the interruption to his randiness, confused, alarmed . . . It didn't help that, despite facing a hostile werewolf trying to nick his witch, his cock was still half hard.

Curse everyone on this platform who wasn't Calladia. Curse the entire universe for interrupting him when he'd been knuckle-deep in her luscious cunt.

Lucifer, the feel of her. The *sounds* she'd made. It had been everything he'd imagined and somehow, impossibly, more.

And now he was supposed to think about his mother?

Despite remembering very little about Lilith, Astaroth cringed at the juxtaposition of his mother and the grand time he'd been having fingering Calladia. It was enough to deflate his erection, which was probably good for his critical thinking skills.

Lilith had commissioned werewolf bounty hunters to find them? "What does she want?" he asked.

Kai cast him a scornful look. "I don't know, maybe you stayed out past curfew. Why don't you hurry home to mummy and let a real man take care of your girl?"

"Hey!" Calladia did something with the yarn wrapped around her knuckles, and Kai's knees buckled. "First off, I'm a woman, not a girl, and I don't belong to anyone."

Astaroth felt a fierce burst of pride. He might think of her as "his" witch, but that was a private, relational expression, not a claim of ownership. He was her demon as much as she was his witch. "Quite right," he said. "And, that *real man* nonsense is an artifact from less progressive times. Most species have moved beyond that."

Not demons though, he realized with an uncomfortable jolt. Gender relations had nothing to do with the power struggles on his home plane, but the concept of a "real" demon still held sway.

Astaroth didn't care if this werewolf deemed him less than a "real" man. So why did he care so much that he wasn't a "real" demon?

It was a disquieting thought he didn't have the time or focus to delve into, so he focused on practicalities. "Did Lilith seem hostile?" he asked Kai, wanting to get a sense of what he and Calladia might be walking into. His mother had sounded friendly on the phone, but she was famously (and proudly) insane.

Kai gasped. "Her name is Lilith? Like . . . *the* Lilith?"

"I'm sure there are others with that name," Astaroth said, "but none with her notoriety."

Kai whistled. "Damn. *And* she's a MILF. You'd better get down there and talk to her before she rips out someone's spine."

"She's here?" Calladia asked.

Kai pointed over the edge. "And she brought a friend."

Astaroth looked to Calladia, because she was his partner in this quest and he wasn't willing to go anywhere without her. "Shall we?"

She straightened, regal as an empress. "Lead the way."

✦ ✦ ✦

THE ELEVATOR WAS UNCOMFORTABLY SLOW. THE WINCH MECH-anism ran on magic, so there was nothing to do but stand and wait during the descent.

Despite the November chill and his lack of a coat, Astaroth was sweating. It was one thing to talk on the phone with the mother he barely remembered. Meeting her was another thing entirely. It would be nearly impossible to hide his amnesiac condition, and he had no idea how she would take it. Probably not well, considering all her talk of power and vengeance and drinking blood out of the skulls of her enemies.

Calladia laid her hand over his. "Hey," she said. "How are you feeling?"

Her consideration took him aback. Not just because he thought he'd been doing an admirable job of hiding his trepidation, but because she sounded downright *sweet*. He liked all her itera-tions up to and including "vengeful harpy," but this gentle consideration . . .

Well. It rearranged something inside him.

"A bit nervous, to be honest," he said.

"Same. I wish we knew what she wanted."

The werewolves hadn't been much help, especially since Tansy had promptly picked the two up with their talons and flown them away, squawking about poor customer service and Tansy's good reputation. Or at least that's what Astaroth assumed the griffin had been upset about.

"Maybe she just wants to talk in person," Astaroth said.

Calladia looked skeptical. "So she hired bounty hunters rather than calling you and setting up a time to meet?"

He grimaced. "Good point."

"If she causes trouble, I'll take care of it." Calladia held up the yarn she'd already tied a few knots in.

Her confidence was marvelous. Calladia hadn't even survived three decades on Earth, and she was ready and willing to challenge one of the oldest demons in existence.

"Let's hope it doesn't come to that," Astaroth said.

The elevator finally hit the ground. Calladia slid the door open and tried to walk out first, but Astaroth stepped in front of her. If they were heading into danger, he wanted to face it first.

Two black-horned demonesses stood at the base of the tree. One was tall, with deep brown skin and a shock of white curls, and he instantly recognized her from his memory of drunkenly watching a science documentary. The other was shorter, with pale skin and waist-length red hair dotted with braids.

A wave of emotion nearly knocked the breath from him. He *knew* them.

"There you are, Astaroth!" Lilith said, striding toward him. She wore buckskin trousers, tall boots, and a ruffled white blouse with a red sash. A dagger was sheathed at her waist. For a moment he wondered if she was going to stab him, but she stopped within arms' reach, looked him up and down, then made a tsking sound. "What are you wearing? This isn't on brand at all."

He looked down at his black faux-leather trousers and rumpled blue shirt. "It looks better when it's clean," he said, for lack of anything else. Whatever reception he'd been expecting, it hadn't been so mundane.

Then again, Lilith didn't know he was an amnesiac. Maybe only a week or two had passed since she'd seen him last, and this wasn't as momentous an occasion for her as it was for him.

Lilith's eyes were the same pale blue shade as his own. They traveled from his horns to his shoes, and she gasped and clapped her hands when she spotted the fireplace poker he was carrying.

"I'm not familiar with that weapon," she said, bending down to peer at it. "What is it? Something for disemboweling? The hook doesn't seem sharp enough, but sometimes a blunt tool is more fun, right?" Her smile was bright as she straightened. "Makes the suffering last longer."

"Ah." Astaroth awkwardly lifted the implement. "It's a fireplace poker. For tending the fire."

"Ooh, do you brand people with it?"

"Not recently," Astaroth said.

The other demoness approached with an elegant, gliding walk. She wore a wine-red gown with a golden breastplate, and rings adorned her fingers. "Astaroth," she said in a rich alto voice. "Glad to see Moloch didn't put you out of commission for good."

"Quite." Astaroth gave her a tight-lipped smile, wishing he could remember her name and what the nature of their relationship was.

Calladia stepped forward with her hand out. "I'm Calladia," she announced, and Astaroth felt a surge of gratitude. Clever Calladia had taken the initiative to gain the information he lacked.

"Sandranella," the white-haired demoness said, and the name pinged through Astaroth's head, nudging at buried memories. She nodded at Calladia but didn't shake her hand.

Calladia twined her fingers through the yarn again. A subtle threat, should Sandranella be familiar enough with the knots some witches used to cast spells. "So, why'd you send bounty hunters after us?" she asked, blunt as ever.

"It's one of my love languages, obviously," Lilith said.

"That and abductions," Sandranella pointed out with a smirk.

"He has a phone," Calladia said. "You could have called."

Lilith waved her hand. "What's the fun in that?"

Sandranella turned her attention to Astaroth. "Is this human a . . . ?" She trailed off, jerking her head in Calladia's direction.

Astaroth wasn't sure what she was asking. "A what?"

"You may have been banished," she said, "but knowing you, you haven't stopped working."

"Oh!" Now Astaroth understood her meaning. "No, we haven't made a bargain. In fact, we're . . ." It was his turn to trail off as he debated how to describe Calladia. His ally? His enemy? Some odd combination of the two?

The woman whom he couldn't seem to keep his eyes, thoughts, or hands off?

"They're banging," Lilith announced. "Astaroth has been dipping his quill in mortal ink again. Isn't that right, dear?"

Calladia and Astaroth winced in unison.

Sandranella looked taken aback. "Have you?" she asked Astaroth. "One would think you'd have better things to focus on, such as plotting Moloch's downfall and regaining your position."

Astaroth shrugged. "I can multitask."

Calladia shot him a withering glance before turning her attention to the two women. "We aren't banging. I'm accompanying him on a quest."

"Ooh, a quest." Lilith's eyes gleamed with excitement. "Love a good quest. What are you hunting?"

"The secret to taking down Moloch," Calladia said. "And—" She snapped her mouth shut, apparently realizing she'd nearly given away his amnesia.

Bollocks, Astaroth thought. His mum wasn't likely to skim over that juicy clue.

Sure enough, Lilith pounced on the information. "And what?" she asked. "A legendary weapon? A dragon's heart? Those are tasty," she informed Sandranella in an aside, "and they can be a potent aphrodisiac. Just ask Henry VI. After he rode one into battle, he carved out its heart and ate it, praying for victory."

"Uh, what?" Calladia asked. "Dragons stopped being used as war weapons in the 1400s because they were becoming endangered."

"Lilith," the other demoness said gently, "was that perhaps something you read in a fanfic?"

Lilith's brow furrowed. "The dragon heart? I'm sure that was canon. Right before that tentacle monster stumbled upon him." She cackled. "Or oozed onto him, rather. Slurped up to him? Smacked sucker-marks into his ass?"

Sandranella winced. "Definitely fanfic. I don't think I'll ever recover after reading that link you sent me." She gave Astaroth a sympathetic look. "I heard she forced you to beta read her latest explicit fic on AO3. My condolences."

Astaroth wasn't sure what in Lucifer's name they were talking about, so he grunted.

"Anyway," Sandranella continued, "what's this about searching for the secret to take down Moloch? You told me you were working on a scheme."

"Did I?" he asked, then quickly revised the sentiment. "Ah, yes. I did." A long pause. "Remind me which details I shared with you?"

Sandranella pursed her lips, looking disapproving. "You wouldn't tell me. You said you wanted an airtight case before confronting him at the high council."

Astaroth mentally kicked his past self for being so secretive. "Quite right," he said, forcing a laugh. "I was just testing you."

Sandranella gave him an odd look. "What did that spell do to you?"

"Erm . . ." Astaroth met Calladia's gaze. He widened his eyes, silently begging her to jump in.

"What spell?" Calladia asked, thankfully drawing Sandranella's attention away from him. "I'm not up to speed on the particulars of his banishment."

"Why do you need to know?" Sandranella's tone wasn't mean, just matter-of-fact. "This is demon business."

Astaroth jumped in before Calladia could argue. "She's an ally. I trust her."

Beside him, Calladia inhaled sharply.

"So much of an ally you didn't bother to tell her about the spell?" Sandranella folded her arms over her breastplate. "Some trust."

"He's probably embarrassed," Lilith said. "Performance anxiety and all that."

"What?" Astaroth looked down his body, horrified at the idea a spell might affect his prowess. "I can perform just fine," he hurriedly assured Calladia.

Lilith patted his forearm. "Don't worry, dear. Aging must be mortifying, but we'll find a way to fix this."

An icy chill swept over Astaroth's skin. Not a product of the wind, but a premonition. "Sorry," he said, rubbing his temples and wondering if he'd misheard. "It's been a busy few days. What do you mean, aging?"

Lilith frowned and pressed the back of her hand against his forehead. "Are you feeling all right? I always say you'll catch a chill spending so much time on Earth." She shuddered. "At least move to the Bahamas, rather than that dismal, rainy country."

How was he supposed to talk his way out of this? Did he even need to? His mother seemed odd but caring, and Sandranella didn't come across as hostile either. But trusting another demon with the truth of his amnesia would leave him open to attack should his gut instinct be wrong.

Sandranella narrowed her dark brown eyes. "There's something he's not telling us."

"Ooh," Lilith said. "I forgot to ask. Astaroth, what is the pedigree of the mortal you're fornicating with?"

Astaroth nearly choked.

Calladia gasped. "Excuse me, did you just ask about my pedigree? Like I'm a show poodle?"

Lilith's brow furrowed as she looked Calladia over. "Oh, are you a shifter? Please say you're house-trained, at least."

Calladia made an outraged sound.

Sandranella sighed loudly. "Lilith, I know you're thousands of years old and afflicted by madness, but can we please focus for a moment?"

"I'm not afflicted by madness." Lilith winked. "Madness is afflicted by me."

Sandranella pointedly turned away from Lilith and focused solely on Astaroth. "Astaroth, how long have we known each other?"

Bollocks. "A while?" he guessed.

She nodded as if he'd confirmed a theory. "What's the last thing we did together before that high council meeting?"

"It's . . . ah . . ." He racked his brain, but nothing emerged. "Went to brunch?" he guessed.

Sandranella snapped her fingers. "I knew it! You don't remember, do you?"

Apparently the charade was over. Risky or not, he needed to come clean. "I may have a mild bout of amnesia."

"Tell us everything," Sandranella ordered.

Astaroth gave the condensed summary: a blinding headache, patchwork memories, and no recollection of whatever had happened to him before Moloch had portaled to Earth and attempted to kill him. After a recommendation from a warlock, they were currently on their way to a witch who could help restore Astaroth's damaged brain and recover his memories so they could defeat Moloch, or, barring that, who might hold the key to ending the demon's life.

Lilith did not take the news well.

"That wretched, smiling weasel had the gall to try to murder *my* son? I'm going to rip his entrails out, knit them into a scarf, and wear it while I cut him into pieces!" She unsheathed the dagger at her waist and flung it, skewering a birch tree with so much force the trunk split in half. "I'm going to use his shattered bones for toothpicks!"

"So you don't even remember the spell." Sandranella winced. "You may want to sit down for this."

"Just tell me," Astaroth said. "It's not like things can get worse."

A breeze sighed through the clearing, ruffling Sandranella's white curls. "Moloch brought a witch to your banishment. He said she would cast a spell to prove you'd been lying to the council. You seized up when she cast it, and then Moloch booted you through a portal to Earth. After you were gone, he told us the witch could alter human life spans, and since she had just altered yours, it was proof of your half-human heritage." She gave Astaroth a scathing look. "You should have told me about that centuries ago. You know I support hybrid rights."

"In his defense," Lilith said, "I told him if anyone found out he would be stripped of power and publicly humiliated. Oh, and possibly tortured for lying to the high council." She shrugged. "I wish society wasn't so regressive, but it is what it is."

Astaroth was stuck on one thing. "What did the witch do to my life span?" he asked, feeling a heavy swell of dread.

Sandranella grimaced. "I'm sorry to tell you, but the witch . . . made you mortal."

✦   ✦   ✦

MORTAL.

Astaroth stared at the demoness, head spinning. "She can do that?" he asked, dumbfounded.

The word kept echoing in his head like a bell calling the dwindling hours of his life. *Mortal. Mortal. Mortal.*

Mortal meant slower healing of injuries. It meant wrinkles and white hair and droopy bollocks, and he wanted nothing to do with it.

Calladia looked shocked. "That must be why you're sleeping and eating so much," she said.

Astaroth had never felt such a nauseating mix of terror and helplessness. "Can it be magically reversed?"

"I don't know." Calladia's forehead furrowed. "I've never even heard of a spell like that."

"I'll find that bitch of a witch and make her reverse it," Lilith vowed. "It's amazing what a good vivisection can accomplish."

Mortal, mortal, mortal.

Lucifer, what was he supposed to do? His cells were already degrading. Soon he would be afflicted with age spots and impotence, unless they could reverse it. Which meant finding the witch who had done this to him . . . or one similarly gifted in life magic.

"That warlock who advised you," he told Calladia in a surge of desperation. "The one whose name sounds like a prescription drug."

"Alzapraz," Calladia said. "Mariel's ancestor."

"He's immortal, right? Can he reverse this?"

Her mouth twisted. "I'll call him and see, but he's not a complete expert. He's not going to die, but his body is still aging."

Oh, fiery Lucifer. Mortal didn't just mean droopy balls. It meant *death*.

Astaroth's breaths came faster and faster. How did humans bear this sense of inevitability? How could they carelessly enjoy life, knowing it would one day be ripped from them? The forest spun around him, and he swayed.

Calladia was instantly at his elbow, helping him sit on a log. "Easy," she said. "Deep breaths."

"I don't want to die," Astaroth said in a small voice.

"Me neither, but you're nowhere near that yet. We have time."

"Do we?" His laugh was hysterical. "I could trip over a tree root in five minutes, hit my head, and that's it."

"You're not going to trip on a tree root." Calladia grabbed her phone out of her pocket and started dialing. "I'm calling Alzapraz."

Lilith and Sandranella hovered nearby, blatantly listening in.

"Hello?" The wheezy voice was barely audible.

Calladia put the phone on speaker. "Hey, Alzapraz. Is now a good time?"

"Is it ever a good time?" the warlock asked. "Objectively, I don't think time can be assigned a value."

Lilith nodded, looking thoughtful. "That's a good point."

"Who's that?" Alzapraz asked. "Are you with friends?"

"Not really," Calladia said. "Or, kind of? It's a long story, but basically, a few demons."

Astaroth expected the warlock to express panic. Instead, Alzapraz mildly said, "Oh, have you added more to the party?"

"Who are you?" Lilith asked loudly.

"A gentleman never tells," Alzapraz said. "To whom am I speaking?"

Calladia was shaking her head, but Lilith launched straight into it. "This is Lilith, first of her name."

"The Mother of All Demons?" Alzapraz gasped.

Lilith looked pleased. "Oh, you know my AO3 username! What's your favorite fic?"

"He doesn't mean that," Astaroth said distractedly. His head still hurt, full of the clanging of *mortal, mortal, mortal.* "He means that old religious rumor."

"Oh." Lilith laughed merrily. "That silly stuff again. No, I may be a massive slut, and proud of it, but I'm only the mother of one demon." She waggled her fingers at Astaroth. "Isn't that right, dear?"

"The point is," Calladia said, "we're having an issue. Do you know how to cut someone's life short?"

There was a pause. "I mean, there are lots of methods," Alzapraz said, "but you can probably Witchipedia *murder* and pick a favorite."

"Magically, I mean."

The silence this time was longer. "Calladia," he finally said, "what have you gotten yourself mixed up in?"

"Long story. Think an immortal human-demon hybrid cursed with a mortal life span by a witch. Can it be reversed?"

Alzapraz whistled. "Not a lot of life witches will mess with that. Nasty stuff, and very advanced. I don't know how it's done, unfortunately."

Astaroth's stomach fell. There went that hope.

"Do you know how to restore immortality, then?" Calladia asked.

Alzapraz coughed. "The problem with life magic is that there's always a price. I managed to extend my life, but it came at the expense of my health. It's possible we could look into something similar for your hybrid, but I have to warn you, the extreme geriatric lifestyle isn't for everyone."

Horror filled Astaroth at the possibility. "I'll pass." He didn't want to be hauling his brittle old bones around the demon plane in a few centuries, complaining about his joints.

"So that's it?" Calladia asked. "He just has to live with it?"

Or die with it, Astaroth thought bitterly.

"I'd ask Isobel, if you haven't already seen her," Alzapraz said. "She's been around for a long time. She's never cared about any life span but her own, but she's knowledgeable about rare magic, especially life magic."

Calladia thanked the warlock before hanging up. "So," she said, looking at Astaroth, "looks like Isobel is still our best play."

Astaroth stood. "Then let's get going."

"Wait," Sandranella said, sharing a look with Lilith. "There's something we still need to tell you."

TWENTY-TWO

CALLADIA COULDN'T BELIEVE HOW SURREAL THE MORNING had gotten. A surprise werewolf ambush, the appearance of demons, and now the revelation that Astaroth was no longer immortal . . . It was a lot to process when the sun had been up for less than two hours. Not to mention what had happened before the werewolves, but Calladia was good at compartmentalizing, so she shoved that interlude into a box in her brain. There would be time to panic about it later.

She felt out of place among the demons. She'd gotten used to Astaroth's otherworldly beauty, but now she was faced with two more stunning people. Lilith's face held the same sharp angles as Astaroth's, and her hair looked like molten fire. Her swashbuckling outfit was beyond cool. Sandranella's face was perfectly heart-shaped, her eyes were dark and intense, and she resembled a warrior goddess in her wine-and-gold dress.

Were demons universally sexy? A question for a later time.

"Go on," Astaroth said, sounding defeated. "What other disaster awaits?"

Sandranella looked grave. "Moloch is moving quickly to consolidate power. He's suggested Tirana as your successor."

"Tirana, Tirana . . ." Astaroth wore a look of concentration, and then his eyes widened. "No, you can't choose her. She's a powder keg, and she's even more vocal than Moloch about hating hybrids."

"You remember her?" Calladia asked.

He grimaced. "A particularly unpleasant memory from the Spanish Inquisition just popped up."

"Trust me, I don't want her on the council either," Sandranella said. "But without you, the progressives are outnumbered, and Baphomet is showing signs of being receptive to Tirana and Moloch's arguments. I fear without your return to strengthen our alliance, the council will regress further into the Middle Ages."

Lilith made a face. "The Middle Ages were so dull. Everyone stank."

"Who's Baphomet?" Calladia asked, looking between them.

"The lead demon on the high council," Astaroth said. "At least he was when I was young. He must still be."

It was promising that he was recovering memories of the demon plane—well, sort of, since she didn't want him to turn into a villain again—but learning there were more demonic enemies to face wasn't exactly reassuring.

"We need you, Astaroth," Sandranella said, "but not like this. We need the old Astaroth, the one with a master plan to take Moloch down. If you can eliminate him, Baphomet can be persuaded to undo the banishment."

Astaroth grimaced and ran his hands through his hair. "I wish I could bloody remember that master plan. Can the decision on a replacement be postponed?"

"Maybe, but Moloch is pushing hard."

Lilith made a rude noise. "I don't care what that pathetic worm wants. He can wait." She grabbed one of her braids and started chewing on it. "I'll create a distraction," she said around a mouthful of hair. "There's a fyre drake who owes me a favor. If she torches a few key buildings, the council will have to investigate."

Calladia was starting to like Lilith.

"Let's fight on multiple fronts," Sandranella said. "I'll start a word-of-mouth campaign that Astaroth will be returning, more powerful than ever."

Calladia could think of one major flaw in that plan. She raised her hand. "Um, slight problem. Moloch thinks Astaroth is dead. If he finds out otherwise, he'll come after us again."

"Not if we keep him busy enough." Sandranella looked at Astaroth. "You know returning will be easier if the public is primed for it. The hybrid community would also welcome the news. Morale has been low since your banishment."

"Wait, I thought no one knew he was a hybrid," Calladia said. She knew next to nothing about demon politics, and it was rapidly growing confusing.

"They don't," Sandranella confirmed. "But Astaroth and I have been vocal about protecting the rights of hybrids."

"What if the news gets out?" Astaroth asked. His face was tight, stress carving lines in it she hadn't seen before. "I'll be a laughingstock."

Calladia bristled. "Hey, being part human isn't that bad."

The demons ignored her. "Baphomet will make sure the information doesn't leak," Sandranella said. "It makes him look negligent to allow a half demon to hold power for so long."

Lilith abruptly clapped her hands, and Calladia jumped. "So we're decided," Astaroth's mother said. "Sandranella and I will wreak havoc on the demon plane while Astaroth seeks out this witch who may be able to restore his memories and immortality. I'll also do some digging through Astaroth's den to see if I can uncover whatever information he was compiling on Moloch."

"My den?" Astaroth asked, sounding surprised. "It's mystically locked, since I'm rarely there. How do you plan to get in?"

Lilith smiled indulgently. "Oh, sweetie, I dug a tunnel into your bedroom centuries ago." Everyone turned appalled looks on her, and she shrugged. "What? Sometimes a mother likes to watch her baby sleep."

"Well, that's unsettling," Astaroth said, "but convenient, I suppose, since I can't return to the demon plane like this."

"What about your flat?" Calladia asked. "Would you have stored information there?"

"I portal into his closet in London frequently," Lilith said. "I'll check there, too."

"Seriously?" Astaroth asked incredulously. "You've been spying on me all this time?"

Lilith blew him a kiss. "Stalking is my love language."

"I thought commissioning bounty hunters was her love language," Calladia muttered. "And kidnapping."

Lilith turned her icy blue eyes on Calladia. "Love can be expressed in any number of ways," she said solemnly.

The woman was mad as a hatter, but Calladia felt a twinge of jealousy. How was it possible the legendarily deadly Lilith was a better mother than Cynthia Cunnington? Lilith might stalk Astaroth, but she clearly loved and supported him, up to and including drinking blood from the skulls of his enemies.

Would Calladia's mom do the same? No, she would not. Skull chalices would be deemed bad for campaign optics, just like Calladia herself was.

Sandranella motioned, and a portal appeared in the air. "We'll head out. Do hurry on your quest, Astaroth. The demon plane needs you."

Lilith made kissing sounds. "Bye-bye, dear, can't wait to vanquish Moloch with you." The demonesses stepped through the portal, which vanished as if it had never been.

"Well," Calladia said. Her legs felt weak, so she sat on the log. "That was a lot." She ground the toe of her boot into the mulch. "I don't understand why everyone talks about being part human like it's some terrible thing. What's so wrong about us?"

Astaroth raised his hand and started ticking items off. "Humans are fragile. They live short, cosmically meaningless lives. They're overly emotional. They—"

"All right, all right," Calladia said. "I get the picture, even if I disagree with it. But you are—or you were—immortal, and you're hardly fragile. What does it matter if you get emotional?"

"To give in to sentiment is to embrace weakness."

Calladia was going to call bullshit and brainwashing on that one. "Lilith loves you. Is she weak?"

He scowled. "No. But she was already insane by the time I was born. Everyone accepts that's the way she is."

Calladia shrugged. "Maybe if you came out as a hybrid, everyone would accept you, too."

"I would say I appreciate the optimism, but it would be a lie. With demons like Moloch shaping policy, there's no way hybrids will be granted equal rights."

Calladia disliked Moloch more and more as time went on, which was really saying something, since her second encounter with him had involved him blowing up her house. "Then pull a French Revolution. Overthrow his snooty, purebred ass and create a new political system."

Astaroth let out a pained laugh. "Calladia, you are far too naive."

She bristled. "I am not."

"You're thinking like a human. Your political dynasties rise and fall in the blink of an eye compared to the demonic power structure. Our course can't be changed so easily."

Calladia rolled her eyes. Definitely calling bullshit on that one. "You know what I think the problem is? You're falling into the same trap people like Moloch do. You think of humans as inferior."

"I do not," he said, outrage suffusing his face. "I've always been fond of humans."

"But you hate the part of you that is human, don't you?"

Astaroth didn't reply.

Just as she thought. Calladia was tempted to smack Astaroth across the horns and tell him to expand his worldview. "Maybe you think human politics are too brief to pay attention to," she said. "But the demon plane sounds stagnant, in my opinion."

Now he looked offended. "It's a beautiful realm with a long and storied history. Just because we live longer doesn't mean we're stagnant."

"And yet hybrid rights haven't advanced much since you were born *six hundred years ago*."

Astaroth opened his mouth, then closed it again. He looked down at his lap and started fussing with the hem of his T-shirt.

Gotcha. Calladia might prefer solving problems with her fists, but not every problem was a nail in need of a hammer. Some required a more delicate touch. "I think," she said, "that being half human can be an asset when confronting Moloch. Everyone expects you to behave and think like a purebred demon. So what if you don't? What if you forget everything about long, storied traditions of discrimination and take drastic action to change things?"

Astaroth picked at a loose thread. "It won't work. Who would want to listen to me after they learn the truth? They'll call me emotional and weak, my logical mind clouded by my heritage."

"Who would want to listen to you? The entire hybrid community, for starters."

Astaroth looked up quizzically. "The hybrids? What could they possibly do?"

"Maybe they aren't just victims in need of protection. Maybe they're warriors waiting for a chance to fight for their cause." Sensing his hesitation, Calladia went in for the kill. "Maybe they're strong, disciplined, and cunning . . . like you."

She shifted, insecure and a bit embarrassed at having delivered the compliment. The two of them didn't say nice things about each other. They bickered and joked, and, yes, sometimes felt each other up, but their dynamic had little room for softness. But with the way Astaroth was staring at her like she'd blown his mind and hung the moon all at once, she couldn't regret it.

While she waited for his response, Calladia closed her eyes and lifted her face to the sun. The woods were wild and awake, full of buzzes, chirps, and rustles. The wind that tugged at her hair also ruffled the treetops and raced over the hills and valleys, like the exhalations of some great beast of the earth.

Being in nature made her feel small, but in a good way. Maybe that was part of being human. In the long stretch of time, she was just a blip. And when you were a blip, you didn't have to worry about the weight of eons. You could live as loudly as you wanted in the space allotted to you.

Calladia's life had been lacking in joy for a while. Had she let her fear of being hurt stop her from living boldly?

Could she make a different choice, as she was asking Astaroth to do now?

Astaroth's hand covered hers on the log. Calladia opened her eyes to find him still staring at her with that wonderstruck expression. "Calladia Cunnington," he said, "you are a marvel."

Her smile probably looked goofy, but who cared? She tossed her hair over her shoulder and lifted her chin. "It's because I'm human," she said in a teasing tone. "Small life, big dreams, zero fucks to give." Like a corgi in the universe's dog park.

He lifted her hand to his mouth. "Your life is many things," he said, lips pressed to her skin, "but it's far from small."

◆   ◆   ◆

IT WAS AFTERNOON BY THE TIME THEY REACHED THE SPOT where the road terminated at a parking lot overlooking the river. Narrow trailheads branched out from there, winding through the woods like roots.

Calladia eyed the forest. "I don't love the idea of leaving Clifford." Her beloved truck was the closest thing she had to a home at the moment.

"This means camping again, doesn't it?" Astaroth sounded dismal. But when she glanced at him, he gave her a crooked smile. "Somehow, my delicate constitution and I will endure."

She shouldn't find him so entertaining. But over the course of the trip, the evil demon had transformed into a snarky yet supportive rascal. She liked this version of Astaroth, with his clever wit and absurdities. It was worrisome how much she liked him.

Would he remain the same once his memories were recovered though?

Calladia felt uneasy at the thought. Realistically, he needed to be whole again to confront Moloch and enact change on the demon plane, but would he still be willing to publicly fight for the hybrid cause once his memories returned? Or would he fall back into stagnation, cynicism, and easy, glib lies? He'd spent his long life in the pursuit of power, not justice, after all.

In aiding him, was Calladia inadvertently creating one more corrupt politician who could break her heart?

Stop it, she told herself. She wasn't in love with him or anything. Would it be depressing to see Astaroth become the merciless demon of legend once more, rather than the flawed but fascinating man he was now? Yes. Would it break her? No.

Calladia didn't break. Even at her lowest, she'd clawed her way back up.

"Let's go." She shrugged on the pack that held her sleeping bag and other necessary supplies. They'd stopped at a grocery store and clothing outlet in Griffin's Nest, so they were fully provisioned. Astaroth had insisted on his own backpack to carry the tent and the other half of their supplies (which he still swore he'd pay her back for). When she'd teased him about chivalry, he'd gotten annoyed and said it was called teamwork and that the chivalric code had been left in medieval times for a reason, and he'd thank her not to reintroduce that church-and-state-focused propaganda to the modern world.

Each trailhead had a carved rock at its base depicting various animals. They chose the one with a bat etched into it—thanks, Bronwyn!—and started hiking. The trail quickly grew steep, the trees closing in overhead and blocking out the sky. Roots jutted out of the ground like gnarled knuckles. Soon the path dwindled to a mere track, and forward progress required shoving branches aside.

"Are you sure this is the right path?" Astaroth asked after a thin branch whacked him in the face. He spat out a dead leaf.

"I didn't see any other bat signs," Calladia said.

"Why go to the trouble of setting up a whole bloody quest leading to her house when she clearly doesn't want to be found?"

"Drama," Calladia said. "Alzapraz once spent a year crafting a hedge maze to his front door. It was only when he tried to order delivery that he realized what a bad idea that was." According to Mariel, her great-great-etcetera-grandfather had pitched a fit when the delivery person had given up and thrown the pizza over the hedge in the general direction of the house. The next day, the maze was gone.

The air was cool, but the exertion warmed Calladia up, and sweat began to collect between her breasts and at the small of her back. She took off her pack, then stripped off her flannel and tied it around her waist, revealing her sports bra.

A choking sound was followed by crashing and the snapping of twigs. Calladia turned to see Astaroth half inside a large bush he'd apparently walked into. He staggered back, tripped over a root, and landed on his ass.

She burst out laughing.

"Rude," Astaroth said. "I could have been injured." He scrambled to his feet and brushed off his backside, then picked leaves out of his hair.

Calladia was still chuckling. "The mighty Astaroth, brought low by a bush."

"Brought low by your strip show," he said, flicking his eyes up from where he was inspecting his shirt. The desire reflected in his pale blue irises made Calladia's cheeks heat.

"I'm sure you've seen plenty of people in their bras." This bra wasn't what one might term seductive either—it was black, with a sturdy band and a scooped front that barely hinted at cleavage.

"Yes," Astaroth said, "but none of them were you."

Calladia, who had so far managed the hike with no trouble, was suddenly breathing hard, and a hot throbbing started between her legs. It was the way he was looking at her from beneath his brows, all smoldering intensity and barely restrained lust.

She shouldn't have let him finger her this morning. Now she was desperate for him to do it again.

He would oblige if she asked, she was sure. He could have her up against a tree in seconds, his hand diving between her legs as his lips fastened on her nipple through the sports bra.

Calladia felt the lure of the cliff edge again. A wicked impulse seized her. "If I asked you to make me orgasm right now, would you?" she asked.

"Yes." Astaroth shrugged off his backpack and strode toward her, face set in determined lines.

Calladia was addicted to the push and pull of power between them. When he was close enough to touch, she stopped him with a hand planted on his chest. His pectoral was firm beneath her fingers. "Tell me," she said.

"Tell you what?" His hands settled on her hips, a light touch that burned with promise.

She leaned in until her lips brushed his ear. "What you would do."

He made a low, rough sound. "Wicked witch. You want to hear the dirty details? Wouldn't you rather I show you?"

She definitely wanted him to show her, but the tease was too delicious. "Tell me," she repeated.

He was so close she could have closed the gap between them in the span of a heartbeat. "I would start with kissing you," he said. "Slow at first, but not for long. I wouldn't be able to resist tasting you deeper, kissing you harder."

"Mmm." She liked the sound of that. "And then?"

His smile was slow and sensuous, and Calladia's eyes dropped to his lips. They were nicely shaped, and she knew from experience that though they were soft, he could wield them like a weapon. "You need to learn patience," he said. "The best things are worth waiting for."

She cocked a brow. "Are they? I think the best things are worth seizing when you want them."

"Which is why you're making me talk dirty rather than using my mouth on you, right?" His chuckle wafted over the corner of her lips. "You like these games, Calladia."

"Maybe," she answered breathlessly.

"I think you'd like other games, too. We can play them, if you like. The game where I tie you to a bed and tease you for hours until you're begging me to fuck you would be a fun one."

"Maybe I'll tease *you* for hours," she rebutted, though she'd gotten wetter imagining him tightening knots around her wrists.

"Also a good game," he agreed. "How about the one where we fight to see who ends up on top? Or the game where you've got to stay quiet, no matter what I do?"

She shuddered. "Could be fun." She aimed for nonchalance, but the raggedness of her voice gave away how aroused she was.

"I have so many games we could play." Astaroth nuzzled her ear with his lips, and the ghost of his laugh brushed over her skin when she shivered. "But let me tell you how this one would play out."

One hand traveled slowly up her bare side, stopping with his thumb under the curve of her breast. The fingers of his other hand stretched over her ass, squeezing lightly. Calladia brought her other hand to his chest as well, bracing herself against him.

"I would take off this bra," Astaroth said, "and then I would kiss your gorgeous tits all over. Suck on your nipples, bite them if you like the pain." His teeth lightly pinched her earlobe. "Do you?"

She nodded, incapable of speech.

"I'd suck and pinch your nipples until they're sensitive and swollen, and when you beg me to stop, I'll kiss my way down your stomach."

"I never beg," Calladia said.

"Not yet anyway." He pulled back enough to give her a wicked smile. "If you were wearing leggings, I'd pull them down with my teeth, but for these I'll use my hands." He ran his fingers along the waistband of her jeans, and the touch made her belly quiver. She wanted his fingers to creep lower, but he kept them tucked into the waistband—a hint of what he would give her, should she let him. "I'll strip you naked, then go to my knees."

"Oh." Calladia felt dizzy at the thought. It had been a long time since she'd received oral, and it had always been clear her partners were doing it out of obligation. "You don't have to," she said. "I'm fine without it."

"But do you enjoy it?"

With him looking her directly in the eye, it was impossible to lie, so she nodded wordlessly.

His smile widened. "I do, too. And I *will*, the moment you give me permission. I'll kiss and lick your beautiful cunt until you're screaming, and then I'll do it some more. You'll need to push me away to stop me."

Sweet. Fucking. Hecate. He was so vehement, she had no choice but to believe him. It made her want to whimper and strip off her jeans.

He whispered the next part in her ear. "Unlike you, impatient witch, I know how to take my time. I'll make you wait. Just for the first orgasm, you understand. Once you're begging for it—and you will beg—I'll give it to you, and after the first I'll make you come over and over again, even when you claim you can't take it anymore. Because you can, and I'll show you how."

Calladia whimpered, and her knees wobbled. She nearly stumbled, but the hand still anchoring her ass held her steady.

"Oh, my warrior queen," Astaroth said softly. "Has anyone ever worshipped you the way you deserve?"

Calladia wasn't sure what she deserved. She wasn't particularly pure of heart or noble of spirit, and her life had been spent spitting in the faces of people who called her loud, aggressive, unfeminine, embarrassing, *not good for optics*. She faced the world with teeth and claws bared.

When she didn't answer, Astaroth growled and shifted his grip from her butt to her hair. "Listen to me," he said, fisting the strands at their roots. "You deserve everything you want. You should *take* everything you want, the way you once promised me you would. And if you can't do that yet, say the word and I'll do it for you."

Calladia wasn't sure if she wanted to leap on top of him or cry. One would be a loss of horny composure, the other a lack of emotional composure, and she wasn't ready to relinquish either yet, so she grabbed his hand, removing it from her hair. "What would you do after all these hypothetical orgasms?" she asked. When he looked like he wanted to keep giving her a sexy pep talk, she sucked one of his fingers into her mouth and cocked a brow as if to say, *Well?*

He tipped his head back and groaned. The light shifted over his horns with the movement, and Calladia wondered what they would feel like. They were glossy as obsidian; would they be silky smooth? Cool, or hot like the rest of him?

He gave her the frankest, dirtiest look she'd ever received. "Then," he told her, "I'd fuck you."

He didn't provide details, but he didn't need to. Calladia's imagination took over, envisioning all the ways he could take her. Up against a tree, her leg hooked around his ass, or bent over a nearby fallen log. Maybe on her back in the mulch, the two of them too caught up in animal urges to care about comfort or dirt. She'd flip him over before long, riding him hard and fast, and then it would be a battle, like he'd said. A game to find out who would end up on top.

This game had reached the tipping point. They stared into each other's eyes, breathing heavily, bodies close but barely touching. With the slightest movement, she could turn words into reality.

The look on his face was too delicious though. He looked *desperate*. And Calladia liked playing games, but she liked winning them even more.

She pulled his finger to her mouth again, sucked it, then bit the tip. Then she dropped his hand and stepped back. "Interesting," she said. "Let's keep hiking."

His exhale was half groan. "Witch, you're going to kill me." His erection tented the fabric of his pants. He was going to have a hell of a time hiking like that, and Calladia had enough of the devil in her to like that. It was only fair, since her underwear was soaked and the inseam of her jeans pressed against her clit with every movement.

She winked and turned away. "Try to keep up, demon," she called over her shoulder as she grabbed her pack and set out again.

TWENTY-THREE

THE WITCH HAD A CRUEL STREAK.

And Astaroth liked it.

He'd spent the afternoon torn between laughing, screaming, and resisting the urge to jerk off into a nearby bush. Whenever he thought he'd wrestled his arousal under control, she'd done something to set it off again. A long, graceful stretch with her arms over her head, followed by touching her toes. A wicked wink over her shoulder as she'd slid her hand over a wrist-sized branch to duck under it. In one particularly cruel moment, she'd uncapped her water bottle, taken a drink, then let some slop over her chest, the water glistening against her tan skin.

Even when she hadn't been deliberately trying to wind him up, she'd managed. Her jeans weren't the tightest, but every step highlighted the taut curve of her bum, and without her shirt, he could see the flex of her biceps and the toned stretch of her abdomen.

The things he would do to get his mouth on her.

He didn't care that the trail had all but disappeared or that a stray branch had scratched his cheek. He didn't care that he was sweaty and gross. He didn't even care that Isobel's cabin was no-where to be found.

This was *exciting*.

The feeling was a novelty for an immortal like him. Former immortal, that was. Soon-to-be-immortal-again, once he figured out how to manage it. After centuries of the same dramas played out over and over, people blurred together, and even wars became routine.

Calladia though . . .

He'd never met anyone like her.

Ahead of him, she stopped with a sigh. "Maybe we're on the wrong path."

"Generous to call it a path."

Calladia narrowed her eyes at him. "Not helpful."

"Maybe we should stop for the night," he said. "The light's fad-ing." The snippets of sky visible through the branches held sunset hues, and beneath the canopy it was growing dark. Soon it would be risky to keep clambering over roots and rocks.

"More helpful." Calladia rubbed her neck. "We'll need to find a clearing to set the tent up in."

"True." Astaroth eyed the tangle of bushes and trunks on ei-ther side of the track. "Easier said than done."

Calladia set her pack down, shrugged her flannel back on—alas—then pulled out the yarn she'd tied knots in earlier. She undid them, then wove a design between her fingers, whisper-ing to herself. Astraroth watched, intrigued by the intricate movements. Not many witches preferred thread work to ground their spells, as it was a notoriously difficult discipline. There were countless types and combinations of knots to remember, and even the tightness of a particular knot could change the desired effect.

He took a moment to look at her soul using his demon senses. It glowed in her chest like a small sun, golden and radiant. In olden days he would have considered the potential of removing it from her, but he liked seeing it there, where it belonged.

As a bargainer, he should feel ashamed for a thought like that. But as a bargainer, there was a lot he was doing that he should feel ashamed about. He'd gone from a stone-cold manipulator with a fearsome reputation to . . .

Well, a demon who was currently smiling giddily at the witch he was feeling an alarming amount of emotion toward.

A stick rose from the ground and hovered in front of Calladia at waist height. It was Y-shaped, like a dowsing rod. The stick quivered, rotated in a circle, then snapped to the right, pointing off the path.

"What spell was that?" Astaroth asked.

Calladia began shoving through the bushes in the direction the rod had indicated. "A spell to find fresh running water. That's a good start for a decent campsite."

Astaroth followed, ducking under branches and pushing foliage aside. He noticed Calladia was doing her best not to damage the undergrowth, so he followed suit, contorting himself into odd positions rather than snapping twigs off.

The sound of trickling water grew louder. They reached a small stream tumbling down the slope. The terrain was still uneven, but Calladia made a triumphant sound and pointed. "There we go."

Downstream, the water curved around a boulder. On the opposite bank was a shelf of rock, and beyond that a narrow patch of earth before the trees crowded in. Calladia led the way, picking over rocks and fallen wood, and Astaroth followed. Curious about the potential for a bath, he dipped a finger in the water, then shuddered. He would *not* be washing in that.

"Do you know any bathing spells?" he asked. "The water's bloody freezing."

She laughed. "Not really, but I do know spells to make you smell better. Do you want to smell like roses or lilies?"

Astaroth considered. "Lilies, if I must."

"Wow, I was sure you were going to ask me to make you smell like sandalwood and leather or something." She wrinkled her nose. "I'm not really sure what sandalwood smells like, to be honest."

"It's a nice scent, if cliché." Somewhere along the line, romantic literature had informed men they could smell like a few oddly specific things: sandalwood, pine, leather, and musk. What kind of musk? Who could say. Since some perfumers expressed beaver anal glands to produce castoreum as a tincture, he suspected most people would rather not know the particulars.

"Someday I will find a subject you don't have a hoity-toity opinion on," Calladia said, shaking her head.

They reached the curve in the stream where the water shallowed by the rock ledge. The stone was cool, though it held a modicum of heat from the setting sun. Not enough to please a demon, but true heat was hard to come by this time of year.

They set up the tent in the strip of earth beside the ledge. It was a decent spot, and the overhanging branches provided a barrier in case of rain.

Once everything was set up and their packs tucked away, Calladia stretched. "I'm hoping we can find a hot spring nearby." She undid the knots in the yarn and tied more. "*Tarqui en pinnisen.*" Moments later, the dowsing rod zoomed into view, coming to a quivering stop in front of her. Calladia wound the cord around her wrist and palm. "*Pinnisibsen a chauvodasi.*"

The stick started gliding into the woods.

Calladia grabbed towels from her pack. "Come on," she said. "Let's get warm."

◆   ◆   ◆

THE HOT SPRING WAS SMALL, TUCKED AWAY AT THE BASE OF A hill formed from an old rockslide. Wafts of steam rose toward the sky, which had darkened to a dusky purple spattered with stars.

Calladia cast another spell, and two floating yellow orbs sparked to life, casting a gentle glow over the scene. The pool was cloudy turquoise ringed by orange mineral buildup, and flowers bloomed around it in a riot of color. The blossom-tinged air had a faintly sulfurous edge, though Astaroth's nose acclimated within a few breaths.

"Isn't it late in the season for flowers?" he asked, leaning down to touch the purple petals of a night-blooming orchid. Its stamen gleamed as silvery white as the stars above.

"There's magic in these mountains," Calladia said. "It's most concentrated in Glimmer Falls and the area immediately around it, but the ley lines extend all over the place. Hot springs tend to pop up over those ley lines, and the magic and heat keep the foliage blooming year-round." She gave him a crooked smile. "Mariel explained that to me. She can feel the magic in the earth in a way I can't."

Mariel's name hovered in the air between them, an invisible reminder of the conflict holding them apart. Astaroth didn't feel like reliving whatever he'd done to Mariel, but instinctively, he knew she was the key to breaking down the remaining antipathy between him and Calladia. "Tell me about her," he said.

Calladia looked surprised. "What do you want to know?"

Astaroth bent to unlace his shoes. "What's she like? How did you become friends?" He toed off his shoes and socks, then stripped off his jacket and shirt.

Calladia was staring at his chest. When he cleared his throat, she shook her head and turned away. "She's funny," Calladia said as she started unbuttoning her own top. "Her brain jumps all over the place, and she asks the weirdest questions. And she's kind. Like, freakishly so. She bakes muffins for the neighbors, goes out of her way to rescue lost people or animals, and will drop everything to help a friend out."

Great. Astaroth had not only harmed Calladia's friend; he'd

harmed a muffin-baking philanthropist. "You said she can feel the magic in the earth," he said, shoving his trousers down. He considered stripping off his undergarments, then decided against it for the moment. "She must be very powerful."

"You still can't have her soul," Calladia snapped.

Hurt arrowed through Astaroth's chest. "That's not why I'm asking."

"Then why are you asking?" Calladia asked, planting her hands on her hips. She looked suspicious, which was the exact opposite of what he'd hoped to accomplish.

Astaroth scrambled to defuse her temper. "Because she matters to you, and I want to know everything about you."

Calladia's lips parted, and suspicion turned to surprise.

Astaroth shifted, feeling awkward. That had been too much to reveal. If she suspected the depth of his obsession with her, she'd probably be disgusted.

"Well," Calladia said. "That's . . ."

"So," he blurted. "Tell me more. If you want, of course." He hurried to the edge of the hot spring and sat on the edge, dunking his feet in the water. Oh, that was nice. He slid into the pool, gripping the edge until his feet found purchase. The water came up to midchest, and it was rapidly warming him up to a decent temperature. He'd been chilled for days, his physiology struggling in the colder human realm.

Calladia continued stripping, a process Astaroth watched avidly. Unfortunately, she stopped with bra and underwear still on, but the view was still divine. Her thighs were thick with muscle, her calves sharply defined, and the curves of her hips and breasts were subtle but elegant. Her body was a finely honed weapon, and Astaroth would gladly be her victim.

"You're ogling me," she said as she approached the pool.

"I am," he readily agreed. Her underwear looked to be plain gray cotton, and he wanted to get his mouth on her until the fabric darkened with her arousal. Then he'd pull them aside, licking all over her slick skin before sucking her clit.

Below the water, his cock began to stiffen.

She shook her head as she lowered herself to the edge of the pool. "Shameless." She dipped her toes in and hissed.

Astaroth ducked under and came back up, then made a show of shaking out his hair, sending drops flying.

Calladia shrieked, shielding her face, then started laughing. "Bad demon! We aren't all blessed with your tolerance for heat."

He watched as she slowly submerged her feet. "So," he said, returning to the earlier conversation. "Tell me more about Mariel."

Calladia did, painting a brief yet vivid sketch of a sweet, beautiful woman with a good heart and unpredictable magic. Witches tended to be specialists or generalists; while Calladia was a generalist, good at most things, Mariel was clearly a specialist with an incredible affinity for plants. The two women had been friends since childhood, forming a strong bond based partly on having control-freak mothers.

Calladia's deep love for her friend was obvious, and Astaroth felt a mix of guilt and envy. Guilt that he'd targeted someone Calladia valued this much, even if he couldn't remember it, and envy that someone else got to experience the gift of her unshakable loyalty. She might deny being a good person, but Calladia loved deeply and fought hard for the people she valued, and if that wasn't goodness, what was?

A buzzing came from Calladia's backpack, and she stiffened. "Oh, no," she said, dread creeping into her tone. "I forgot about my mom's event."

"You wouldn't have been able to make it anyway," Astaroth said.

"Yeah, but that's not going to stop her from being pissed at me." She sighed and got up, then walked to her pack.

"Why answer?" Astaroth asked as she pulled out the phone.

She put her finger to her lips. "Hey, Mom." When a muffled but clearly angry voice responded, Calladia pulled the phone from her ear, made a face, then put it on speaker.

"—told you it was important! Josiah Jenkins is a high-value possible donor, and he's big on family values. What am I supposed to tell him about your absence?"

"Tell him I'm out of town at that fake wellness retreat," Calladia said. "Or tell him a demon recently blew up my house and I don't have time for political dinners."

"I've already spread the word it was a gas leak, so make sure you stick to that story. Bad enough to have one demon in town; if people suspect you're involved with more demon business, it's going to ruin your reputation."

"You mean your reputation?" Calladia shot back. "I don't have a reputation to protect." She sat, setting the phone on the rock next to her, then plunked her feet and lower legs in the water all at once, wincing at what must be a sting of sudden heat.

Over the phone, Calladia's mother sighed. "I know you don't value it now, but someday you will, and you'll be grateful I went to these lengths to keep you respectable."

"I don't want to be respectable. I want to be me."

"You mean reckless, violent, rude, and unmotivated?" Cynthia's laugh sounded bitter. "Sometimes I wonder what I've done to deserve such an ungrateful daughter."

Calladia flinched. Astaroth waded toward her, tempted to grab the phone and drop it in the hot spring.

How could Cynthia treat her own child like this?

It took a lot to truly appall Astaroth, but after only this short conversation, he was horrified. "Has she always been like this?" he asked softly.

Calladia's eyes were wet, but she wiped the drops away with the back of her hand and held up her finger, signaling him to wait.

"I'm not ungrateful," she said. "You kept me fed and a roof over my head when I was a kid. You paid for school and magic tutoring."

"A substantial amount, too!"

"A substantial amount," Calladia echoed. "But that doesn't mean I'm going to end up exactly like you. I have my own dreams, my own goals."

Cynthia scoffed. "And what are those? Besides embarrassing me every time your name ends up in the gossip column for fighting."

"Maybe I wouldn't fight all the time if I wasn't so bloody mad all the time!" Calladia shouted. "Maybe I'm reacting to an atmosphere of constant disapproval. You ever think of that?"

Astaroth gripped her calf beneath the water as if he could anchor her and keep her safe as this storm swept through.

"Why are you swearing like a British person?" Cynthia asked. "And really, what do you have to be angry about? You've lived a charmed life. You've had anything and everything you wanted, whenever you wanted it."

"Everything except your approval."

"Approval has to be earned," Cynthia snapped. "So far, you've only tried to spite me."

"Bullshit," Astaroth said softly, holding Calladia's gaze. Her eyes were glassy with unshed tears. He stepped in front of her, grabbing her other calf as well. There was nothing sexual in the touch; he just wanted to be there for her.

Calladia closed her eyes and took a deep breath, blowing it out through pursed lips. He saw her pulling herself together as her expression smoothed into a calm mask. Then she nodded. "I won't be at dinner tonight," she said into the phone, mirroring her mother's icy tone. "I'm your daughter, not a prop for the campaign trail. And until you can see me as that again, I won't be attending any other dinners either."

She hung up. The phone immediately began vibrating again,

but she switched it off and threw it overhand into the forest. "Good riddance," she muttered.

Her legs had relaxed enough for Astaroth to step between them. He moved his grip from her calves to her face, directing her to look at him. "That was appalling," he said.

"Which part?"

He looked at her incredulously. Did she have to ask? "Every word out of your mother's mouth. I'm a demon, and even I think that was downright cruel."

"Yeah, well, welcome to my life." Her shoulders sagged. "Maybe she's right. I do go out of my way to piss her off."

"No." His denial was loud. "Don't let her diminish you. You're a warrior, Calladia, and you don't need to apologize for being who you are."

Her lips trembled as she smiled, and a tear slid down her cheek. "When did you get so nice?"

He scoffed. "I'm not nice. I'm honest."

"I thought you were a famed liar." She swiped at her eyes.

"To the rest of the world, maybe. Not with you." He held her gaze, willing her to see his sincerity. "Like calls to like, Calladia. You're a force to be reckoned with, no matter what your mother says. I'm six hundred years old, and you still put me in my place."

Her mouth twisted. "That doesn't sound like a compliment."

"It is. You're just not used to people who admire strength." He considered the hunch in her shoulders and the tragedy still written across her features, wanting to erase them and bring back his proud, fierce queen. "You're more than strong though. You're funny and loyal and witty. You're adventurous. You *burn*, Calladia, and it's not your failing if other people can't handle your light."

The glow from the floating torches cast stars across her watery eyes, and her hair gleamed gold. She was luminous without even trying.

To Astaroth's shock, she wrapped her arms around him and

leaned down, pressing her face into his shoulder. It couldn't have been a comfortable position, perched above him on the ledge as she was, but she settled into him with a sigh. "Thank you," she whispered.

He nodded and placed his hands at her waist, heart pumping madly.

Once her breathing had slowed, Calladia spoke again. "You asked if she's always been like this. Yes and no. She was always strict when I was growing up, and she wanted me to be polite and tidy and all that, and she would have preferred I take up piano instead of rugby, but it was never this bad."

"What changed?" Astaroth asked, rubbing her lower back.

"Running for office." Calladia nosed at his neck. "It was wild how fast the shift happened. One minute she was my disapproving, perfectionist mom, and the next it was like all her toxic traits had hardened into her whole identity. Like the power suits and back-alley deals became her personality."

"And your father?" he asked. Calladia hadn't spoken of him.

Her laugh was bitter. "We've never really had a relationship. To be honest, I think he's hiding from her. He traveled for business a lot when I was little—I had a nanny—but now he's gone all the time. I'm pretty sure he's renting a house in Thailand." She shrugged. "I haven't seen him in two years, and Mom tells everyone he's away on business or likes to keep his life private."

Astaroth's throat felt thick. At least his mother, unpredictable as she seemed, clearly cared for him. Calladia had grown up with an absent father and a disapproving mother. What she described was a cold, lonely sort of isolation, a prison of neglect and impossible expectations.

"They're both wrong," he said softly. "Wrong to abandon you, wrong to make you feel small."

She sat up again, and he reluctantly released his grip on her waist, but she kept her hands on his shoulders. "Thank you," she said. "You know, you're the only person besides Mariel and Themmie who knows how bad it is. Mom plays up the whole 'happy-but-busy family' impression, and everyone assumes things are fine."

"They're not fine."

"No, they're not." She sighed. "I thought Mariel had it worse for a long time, since she's had all this prophecy and magical legacy shit hanging over her head since childhood. And her mom's over-bearing, too, but I think it comes from a place of love, twisted as it is. She wanted Mariel to be the most powerful version of herself, and yeah, it was to fit the family legacy, but it was also because her mom wanted her to be successful. They just didn't define success the same way." Her fingers flexed over his skin. She was cold; Astaroth wanted to tug her into the pool and warm her up, but he didn't dare do anything to disrupt the moment. Having her willingly touch him felt a bit like having a butterfly land on his finger, and he didn't want her to fly away. "But you know what happened when Mariel said she'd cut contact until her mom started treating her with more respect?" Calladia asked.

"What?"

"Her mom apologized." Calladia's mouth tipped in a crooked smile. "We'll see if it lasts, but she's apparently trying. And if her mom acts the way she did before, Mariel isn't going to tolerate that behavior."

Human relationships were tricky. No one knew that better than a demon who had spent his career finding new ways to sink his hooks into their vulnerabilities. Astaroth was aware that what he was about to ask might backfire, but it needed to be said. "Have you thought about cutting contact with your mother?"

Calladia's gaze focused somewhere over his shoulder, but he could tell she wasn't looking at anything in particular. She was thinking.

"I have," she finally said. "But it makes me sad."

"You would be far from the first human to make that choice to protect themselves." Astaroth had seen it before, had even helped facilitate it. Sometimes family could be so toxic, there was no other option. Of course, the witches and warlocks desperate to cut contact with cruel or downright evil relatives had stopped caring after their soul bargains, since the "soul" in question included emotion, but they'd been better off after.

Or had they? An uneasy doubt crept in. He wouldn't want Calladia to become an emotionless echo of her vibrant self. She was also the first human he'd really, truly let himself grow close to. Oh, he'd enjoyed sex and war and politicking with humans, but none of them had touched him on a deeper level.

Calladia, with her prickliness and courage, had.

For the first time, Astaroth wondered if what he'd done as a bargainer was wrong on some level. The demon plane required souls to survive, but was that enough of a reason to manipulate mortals into giving up their very essence?

What if there was another way to bring life to the plane, but demon society was so steeped in tradition they hadn't considered making a change?

Stagnant, Calladia had called it. Closed borders, closed minds.

"I hope she loses the next election," Calladia said. "Maybe she'll return to normal once she's not so power-hungry." She made a face. "Not that normal was great, but there's a difference between an overbearing mother and a dictator."

"She might," Astaroth said cautiously, "but she also might not. Not everyone is capable of change."

"I know." Calladia took a deep breath, then shook out her arms and cracked her neck in a way he recognized meant she was shrugging off heavy feelings so she could move on. "Anyway," she said, "that conversation is done for now. She can leave all the voicemails she wants, but I'm not turning the phone back on until tomorrow." She frowned toward the woods. "Assuming I can find it."

Astaroth wasn't going to push the issue. It was already remarkable she'd shared what she had. "The water's warm," he said, sinking neck-deep.

"Is it?" she asked, expression turning sly. This storm was passing, and Calladia, ever resilient, was coming out on the other side with a smile. She kicked her feet, splashing him. "I couldn't tell."

He wiped water off his face. "You look cold," he said. "If you come in here I can warm you up."

"An interesting proposition. And a totally selfless one, I'm sure."

Wanting to tease more of her bad mood away, Astaroth looked around, then leaned in conspiratorially. "And—" He broke off, plunging beneath the surface with a shout and a splash. He flailed his arms wildly. "Help!" he shouted as he burst from the surface again. "The kraken!"

Calladia was already halfway in the pool and looked ready to strangle whatever was attacking him. When she realized he was joking, she laughed, then shoved a wave of water at him. "You jackass! I thought you were drowning."

He coughed out the water that had splashed into his mouth. "Not yet. But you're welcome to finish the job."

She slid the rest of the way in and headed toward him. "You know what? I think I will."

Well, there were worse ways to go.

TWENTY-FOUR

CALLADIA COULDN'T BELIEVE THE DEMON HAD PRETENDED to be attacked by a kraken, of all things. Not a fire salamander, not the tiny hot spring fish that liked nibbling toes. A *kraken*.

He was grinning now, looking wicked and not at all repentant. His hair was plastered to his skull, and water droplets gleamed on his alabaster skin. It was so far from the icy Astaroth she'd first met that it was hard to believe this was the same person.

The fear rose again: What if, once he regained his memories, he changed?

Her chest still ached with residual hurt after speaking with her mother, but the water was hot, the demon was hotter, and Calladia wasn't the type to fall victim to long bouts of introspection. She would seize what she could from the day and deal with any repercussions later.

Right now, Astaroth was here, he was smiling, and he was hers.

She leaped on top of him and shoved his head underwater.

The demon broke the surface a few moments later, gasping and sputtering. "Bloody hell!"

"I thought hell didn't exist," she teased. "Unless you really are Satan's spawn?"

The hell question had been a point of confusion when Oz had first shown up, but he'd quickly clarified that demons were a separate species who lived on a plane adjacent to Earth, not evil diabolical creatures of the underworld.

Astaroth swiped water from his brow. "Mortal cursing is catchy," he said. "And Lilith would resent that comparison."

"Too evil?" Calladia guessed.

He shook his head. "Too cliché. Satan's been done to death, don't you think?"

His dry humor was too much. She splashed him again.

"Careful," he said. "When attacked, I retaliate." He glided toward her through the hot water, and Calladia slipped away, circling around the edge of the pool. She couldn't move quickly in the chest-deep water, but neither could he. An even battleground.

The rock basin of the pool was smooth underfoot. Calladia pushed off, half swimming toward the edge of the pool closest to the rockfall. When she turned to see if Astaroth had followed, he was nowhere to be seen.

A hand curled around her ankle and yanked. Calladia's shriek was swallowed by the water as it closed over her head. She kicked at Astaroth, then shot to the surface. "Cheater!" she said, spitting out a mouthful of water. Her braid had wrapped around her throat, so she pulled the tie out and started unwinding the sections.

Astaroth had popped up laughing next to her. The skin next to his eyes crinkled adorably, and he looked more carefree than she'd ever seen him. "You had it coming."

"Yeah, I guess I did." She brought her loose hair over her shoulder, finger-combing it, and grimaced when she encountered a snag.

"Here," Astaroth said, moving behind her. "Let me."

The breath caught in Calladia's throat. He fanned her hair out, running his fingers through the strands gently. She held still, very aware that they were mostly nude. With a slight shift, he could wrap his arms around her. His hands could wander past her hair, disappearing below the surface to explore other territory.

Astaroth massaged her scalp, and Calladia moaned. His motions stuttered before resuming.

"Your hair is beautiful," he said.

"It's plain blond."

"Nothing plain about it." He draped the length of it over her left shoulder, and his right hand settled on her waist. "It's like liquid sunlight."

No one had ever said anything like that before. Objectively, Calladia knew she was pretty, but she'd built up such a don't-mess-with-me attitude that the rare approaches she'd received were mostly from creeps who didn't know any better. And this was Astaroth complimenting her—the single most attractive man she'd ever seen.

His hand slid to her stomach, and he pulled her against his chest. His erection prodded her ass, and warm lips brushed the sensitive spot below her ear. Calladia sighed and leaned her head to the side, and Astaroth nibbled his way down her neck.

Should she feel guilty? Calladia didn't know anymore. If he was the old Astaroth, yes. But this one . . .

This one she liked very much.

Calladia turned her head to look over her shoulder. His eyes were heavy-lidded, his face flushed with a combination of heat and arousal. He licked his lower lip. "Calladia . . ." he murmured, naked longing in his voice. His hands slid to her hips, anchoring her against him.

Maybe this had always been inevitable. Calladia let go of any doubts, craned her neck, and kissed him.

He kissed her back, slow and sensual. This wasn't the hot, furious passion of the morning; it was a thorough, mutual exploration. His lips were damp from the water, but she licked the mineral-tinged drops away until all she could taste was him.

Astaroth's tongue delved lightly into her open mouth, then traced the edges of her teeth. Calladia laced her hands behind his neck, arching her back as she pressed her behind into his crotch.

Astaroth met her movement and elaborated on it, setting a slow, sensual grind below the water. One of his hands dragged up her waist to her breast, cupping her through the wet sports bra. The other crept lower, fingers brushing over the fabric covering her mound.

Calladia felt like she was on fire, and he'd barely begun touching her. She wanted more: his lips around her nipple, the pump of his fingers inside her, the powerful wave of his body surging over hers. She turned in his arms to face him, pulling him close and kissing him more deeply.

Astaroth groaned softly as his palms landed on her ass. "You drive me wild," he said between kisses. "You're beautiful, you know that?"

Calladia didn't want to waste breath on words when she could be devouring him instead. She stroked her tongue against his, then nipped his lower lip. Her hands slid up his neck to toy with his wet, silky hair, and she gave in to an urge she'd felt for a while and gripped his horns.

Astaroth made a stunned sound, and his hips jerked. Encouraged by the response, Calladia stroked up and down his horns with the same eagerness she'd given to jerking him off that morning. They were hard and smooth, the ends slightly blunted rather than razor sharp.

What a marvel his body was. Lean and cut and utterly responsive to her touch. The horn job was apparently really doing it for him, because he was grinding against her aggressively, and his kisses grew frantic.

"Lucifer," he gasped. "I need more."

"More of what?" she asked playfully. Then she went up on her toes and dragged her tongue over one horn. It tasted faintly smoky and wholly delicious.

The noise Astaroth made was feral. He fisted a hand in her hair and pulled her head back. "More of you," he growled. Then he hefted her into his arms and carried her to the side of the pool. He deposited her on the edge, then wasted no time tugging her sports bra off. The position put his head at the height of her breasts. He stared for a moment, then lunged forward and wrapped his lips around a nipple.

Calladia gasped and clutched his horns. Her nipples were sensitive, and the searing heat of his mouth intensified the pleasure. Astaroth massaged her other breast, then lightly pinched one nipple while his teeth nipped at the other, and an electric thrill shot through her.

He switched between her breasts, giving them the same thorough treatment until her nipples were rosy and swollen. When he blew air over the peaks, she twitched.

"So sensitive," he said, smiling wickedly up at her. "I wonder what else is?"

Calladia widened her legs in invitation. "Let's find out."

Astaroth looked thrilled by the prospect. He kissed his way down her stomach, then hooked his fingers in her panties and dragged them off. The fabric made a wet slap against the stones as he tossed it aside, and she was fully nude.

She expected him to dive right in, but Astaroth took his time exploring her. His hands coasted over her body, mapping her shoulders and arms, the bumps of her ribs, and the curve of her waist and hips. He followed the touches with hungry, open-mouthed kisses, like he wanted to taste every inch of her.

Then he pushed her thighs wide and sank lower in the water. She felt his gaze like a physical touch, and his pale blue irises, once reminiscent of ice, now reminded her of the hot core of a flame. Together, they were burning out of control.

He dragged his finger over her pubic hair and lower, parting her labia. "Exquisite," he said. Then he buried his face between her legs, kissing her ravenously.

"Oh!" Calladia jerked against him. Hecate, he was good at this. He tasted her with long, strong swipes of his tongue, mapping out every contour, even sinking his tongue inside her. His horns rubbed against her sensitive inner thighs, and Calladia leaned back, bracing herself on her hands to get a better view.

Astaroth of the Nine wasn't precisely on his knees, but he kissed her with the ardent fervor of a zealot praying to his god. He used his entire face, rubbing his cheeks and chin against her labia and wet inner thighs. His clever tongue traced designs over her clit as if he were inscribing a secret poem. He was merciless, not letting up for a single moment, gripping her hips to hold her in place. When he sucked hard on her clit, Calladia's arms gave out. She flopped onto her back, staring dazedly at the night sky as Astaroth built and built her pleasure. The stars had vanished behind clouds, and a drop of rain struck her cheek.

Her existence narrowed to this small slice of space, seemingly suspended out of time. It was a world of sharp contrasts: the heat of Astaroth's mouth and hands versus the cool raindrops beginning to patter down, the hard rock beneath her back versus the soft press of skin. She was coming undone, hands scrabbling at the ground while her thighs twitched. The pleasure was building quickly, so intense it was almost frightening. As tension seized her lower belly and her clit grew so sensitive each lick nearly hurt, she instinctively tried to snap her legs shut, but Astaroth kept them pinned wide. He didn't let up as she moaned and bucked, her cries growing desperate.

The climax rushed toward her. For a moment, Calladia couldn't breathe, and she opened her mouth on a silent scream as her body grew taut as a bow. Then the pressure released all at once, a series of rolling waves that racked her. Her inner muscles clenched rhythmically, and heat flooded her skin.

Astaroth kept going, never varying the rhythm or pressure that had tipped her over the edge, and the pleasure stretched out for long moments. When the last tremor had shaken through her, Calladia went limp, gasping for air.

Astaroth straightened. He rubbed his hands over her waist, hips, and thighs, looking extremely smug. She couldn't begrudge him that; he could be as smug as he pleased after delivering that steamroller of an orgasm.

He licked his lips, which still gleamed with her arousal. "Delicious. My witch tastes sweet."

Was she *his* witch? Her body certainly thought so. Her head was airy light, and her muscles felt like they'd melted. At that moment, he could have asked her for anything, and she would have done it.

The sky opened up and fat raindrops came pounding down, stinging her skin. Calladia sat upright with a laugh, and when she wobbled and would have collapsed again, Astaroth steadied her.

"Rain," was all she managed to say, and she giggled at the absurdity. Of course he knew it was raining. She laughed again, high on endorphins, and Astaroth grinned back.

The rain beat a tattoo against the rock, and where it struck the pond, small jets of water exploded up from the displacement. "Should we make a run for it?" Astaroth asked, wiping drops off his face.

Calladia staggered to her feet, then reached down to help him out of the pool. He accepted the gesture, though he didn't let her bear much of his weight. She ran her eyes up and down his nearly naked body admiringly. His cock jutted out against the fabric of his underwear, thick and long, and she couldn't wait to get her mouth on it.

Astaroth shivered.

Right. Demon. If she thought the night was chilly, he was probably freezing now that he was out of the hot water. She hurried to grab her backpack and phone—which had landed in a nearby bush—though the bra and underwear she left behind, figuring they'd get musty if she packed them up while still wet. She'd get them in the morning.

"Come on," she said, casting him her version of a rakish grin. "I'll race you to the tent."

TWENTY-FIVE

Astaroth was soaking wet and clammy with cold by the time they made it back to the tent, but he couldn't care less. His heart raced with excitement, and his cheeks hurt from how wide he was smiling. It turned out losing a footrace wasn't so bad if the consolation prize was getting to watch Calladia's bare arse and strong legs leave him in the dust.

Dear Lucifer, her *taste*. It lingered on his tongue, an addictive mix of musky, tangy, and sweet. He would feast on her every chance she gave him.

The glow orbs she'd summoned had followed, casting golden light over her curves as she bent to unzip the tent. Every centimeter of her was perfect, from her plump pussy lips to the tangle of light brown hair covering her mound. He palmed his cock through his underwear, wondering if she'd let him go down on her again straight away or if she was sensitive enough to need a break.

She didn't straighten immediately, instead looking over her shoulder with a wink and a waggle of her hips. "Leering, old man?"

"Yes," he said with no shame.

She chuckled and ducked into the tent, and the summoned lights followed. Her silhouette danced across the tent fabric as she dropped to her knees, then crawled onto her sleeping bag. "Come on, then," she called from inside.

Astaroth didn't need to be told twice. He followed her in, pausing to wipe his feet on the towel she'd set at the entrance. His feet were cold and tender from running over bare ground, but he would have chased her for hours.

Calladia sat cross-legged on her sleeping bag, twisting her hair into a wet bun. Then she pulled a piece of yarn out of her pack and started weaving. "*Ayorva en aerquí*," she said. The air inside the tent instantly warmed.

Astaroth sighed in relief as he finished zipping the tent shut. "Thanks."

"Can't let the delicate demon freeze to death." She handed him a towel to pat himself dry, then leaned back, bracing herself on her arms. The maneuver had the happy effect of pushing her breasts up and out. They were perky, with puffy pink nipples, and a faint constellation of moles dotted the side of her right breast. He wanted to map every mark on her body with his tongue.

"You look like you've never seen boobs before," Calladia said.

"Correction," he said, hunching to avoid stabbing holes in the canvas with his horns. The lights swirled around him before settling into place at the peaked top of the tent. "I've never seen *your* boobs before."

Amusement glimmered in her eyes. "Surely after six centuries they all look the same."

"Absolutely not." Astaroth loved breasts—and bodies—of all sizes and shapes, but he had to admit this pair had a stunning feature that set them leagues beyond any others. They belonged to Calladia. "I can confidently say this is the best pair of breasts in the universe. And if they were smaller or bigger or you only had one or none at all, it would be just as perfect."

She wrinkled her nose. "How's that?"

"Because you, Calladia, are perfect. Is your body a certified wonder that drives me wild with lust? Absolutely." He lightly tapped the side of her head. "But what's in here matters most."

Her eyes softened, and she shifted, unthreading her crossed legs. She drew her knees up and spread her thighs, revealing her glistening pink center. "And what's up in my head that's so arousing?" she asked. "Is it the pigheaded obstinacy or the inclination to violence?"

"Both."

"Hey!" She slapped his shoulder, though she was laughing. "You're not supposed to agree."

"I like obstinate, pigheaded brawlers," he said. "I think you like being one, too."

She grinned. "Maybe."

"Isn't that fortunate for us?" Astaroth returned her smile, enjoying how her breath hitched. His gaze dropped to her pussy. "Are you ready for me to go down on you again?"

"Again?" Her eyebrows soared. "Don't you want me to give you a blow job instead?"

The thought of her smart mouth wrapping around his cock made it twitch in anticipation, but no self-respecting hedonist would skip indulging in her body as many times as she let him. "If that's something you want to do, then I'm all for it, but I've been fantasizing about making you come for days. You really think one orgasm is all I want from you?"

"I was hoping for two," she said. "The appetizer and the main course."

He scoffed. Two? Two was for amateurs. She deserved so many orgasms she lost the ability to move. "Calladia, that first orgasm was just the aperitif."

"I don't know what that word means." She sounded breathless. Her cheeks still held the pink glow of her pleasure, and he wanted to see that color deepen and spread across her entire body.

"An aperitif is an alcoholic beverage drunk before a meal to whet the appetite." He grinned and snapped his teeth at her. "We haven't even gotten to the appetizers."

She shook her head. "Only you could turn dirty talk into a lesson on fine dining."

"Speaking of dining . . ." He licked his lips. "I think it's time for the next course."

She scrambled back like a crab, laughing. "Astaroth!"

"Calladia!" he said, mocking her shocked tone.

"You can't go down on me forever and not let me reciprocate." Insecurity tinged her voice, the worry of someone who wasn't used to receiving more than she gave.

"Forever might be a stretch," he agreed, "considering my newly mortal state, but I'll give it a go anyway."

Before she could argue, because Lucifer knew the woman would find a reason to argue about anything and everything, Astaroth lowered himself between her legs. His shoulders pressed her thighs wide, and he hooked his arms around them to keep her in place.

Calladia let out a shocked noise when he licked her in a long stripe from back to front. She wriggled, but he held her down, then dipped even lower, circling her puckered hole with his tongue.

"Demons eat ass," she said faintly. "Who knew?"

If she was able to commentate, he wasn't working hard enough. Astaroth bent himself to the task with the thoroughness and patience of an immortal, tasting every centimeter of accessible skin. By the time he'd worked his way up to her clit, she was squirming.

He slid a finger inside her as he sucked her clit, and Calladia half sat up with a loud cry. She grabbed his horns and ground against his face, and Astaroth nearly came. Demon horns were practically another sex organ in the right circumstance, and shivers raced down his spine as her cool hands gripped him. He snarled and shook his head, rubbing his nose and chin over her.

"Get on your back," Calladia ordered.

He made a noise of disagreement and slipped a second finger inside her. He crooked his fingers and dragged them out slowly, massaging her inner wall.

"Get on your back *right now*."

Was she upset? Astaroth stopped instantly and knelt upright. "Are you all right?" he asked, swiping his forearm over his mouth.

Sweat beaded Calladia's hairline, and she looked like she wanted to eat him alive. "About to be even better." She planted a hand in the center of his chest and pushed.

Not upset, then. Good. Astaroth went to his back without a fight, curious what she wanted to do.

Calladia straddled his face, then swung her leg around to face backward. She tugged his underwear down, and then her mouth closed around the tip of his cock.

Astaroth let out a long, low groan. Calladia bobbed up and down, gradually taking more of him, then sucked her way up until the tip popped out from between her lips. That maneuver was followed by the swirl of her tongue around the sensitive crown of his shaft.

Battle lines had been drawn.

Astaroth tugged her down against his face, determined to make her orgasm fast and hard. He licked and ate at her ravenously, clutching her so close he could barely breathe.

Calladia moaned around his dick, then bobbed her head more aggressively, matching his energy. She wrapped her hand around the base of his cock and pumped in time with her movements, and Astaroth had to grit his teeth and focus on his technique to avoid coming down her throat.

Of course oral sex would be a competition between them. It was how they did things. And Calladia might be a fearsome competitor, but Astaroth was still going to win.

He rubbed her clit with his fingers, using the firm circles he'd found she liked best, while his mouth covered the rest of her with wet, sloppy kisses.

Calladia's rhythm faltered, and she gasped for air. "Damn you," she wheezed. "You're going to make me come."

"Mm-hmm," he murmured against her, rubbing even harder. He tilted his head to nip her inner thigh, and Calladia exploded.

"Oh!" she cried. He could feel the orgasm rolling through her as her hips frantically jerked, and fresh, delectable wetness drenched his tongue. He lapped at her as triumph swelled in his chest.

When she finally sagged, pressing her forehead to his hip, he announced, "I win."

Her laugh was half wheeze. "Ridiculous." She shifted off his face, then turned and straddled him. Her face, neck, and upper chest were red, and her bun sagged to one side of her head. She looked messy and giddy with pleasure, and Astaroth felt the urge to beat his chest like a gorilla. Maybe point at her and grunt. *My mouth did that.*

Calladia stretched her arms high overhead, showing off the lean, muscled lines of her torso. Her powerful thighs flexed, squeezing his hips. Astaroth loved her strength and how comfortably she wielded it.

"Ready for another yet?" he asked, tapping his lips.

She laughed and leaned forward, planting her hands on his chest. "Are you trying to set a world record?"

"If you think three orgasms is a record, I need to educate you. Let me tie you to a bed for a few days and we'll see what we can accomplish."

She scooted forward until his erection pressed against her lower belly. "Maybe I'll tie you up," she said, gripping his wrists where they rested beside his head. She pinned them down as she leaned in for a long, deep kiss.

He tasted the two of them on her tongue, the combination simultaneously crude and sublime. This was what he'd craved badly enough to spend untold years on Earth: raw, animalistic passion, impolite and uninhibited. He wanted to drown in her.

"So," Calladia said against his mouth. "Want to fuck?"

"Absolutely." He could hardly believe this was happening. Their relationship—if it could be called that—had escalated quickly.

Then again, considering the two of them, was there another way for it to play out? Escalation was the name of their game, since neither of them backed down from a challenge.

Calladia nipped his lower lip, then sat up straight. She yanked a strand of hair off her head and started wrapping it around her fingers, apparently unwilling to get off him for long enough to grab a sturdier thread from her bag. She tied a few knots, then whispered, "*Condom din convosen.*" A gold foil packet dropped from thin air into her waiting hand.

"That's a neat trick," he said.

"It's amazing what you learn in college." She opened the packet and rolled the condom over his erection. Then she lifted up on her knees, notched his cock at her soaked entrance, and started sinking down.

"Bloody hell," he choked out as he watched her take him to the root in one smooth stroke. Her pussy squeezed him so tightly, he couldn't be sure if he was feeling the throb of his pulse or hers.

Calladia moaned. "Oh, that's good."

Astaroth had a reasonable amount of pride in his penis. It was large without being logistically challenging to accommodate, and he'd received many compliments over the years. But as Calladia shifted on top of him, murmuring about "big" and "thick" and "so full," he felt elevated to the level of a god.

He gripped her hips. "Ride me," he ordered.

Calladia braced her palms against his chest and lifted off him in a long, slow drag. When she sank back down, they groaned in unison.

How could this feel so perfect? Astaroth had had a lot of sex over the centuries, but nothing came close to the first few moments of being inside Calladia. The ground was hard beneath the sleeping bag, his hair was wet and smelled faintly sulfurous, and rain smacked against the tent fabric as a sudden wind threatened to tear the flimsy structure down, but he wouldn't trade any of it for a more luxurious setting. After a lifetime of lies and political games, this moment was raw and real.

Calladia set a steady rhythm, her body arching sensuously with each roll of her hips and her arousal dripping between them. Her strong thighs held him trapped as her arse flexed under his fingertips, and Astaroth deliriously thought that she would make a hell of an equestrian. He mirrored her movements, and soon they were moving in tandem, graceful as dancers. Or as fighters, rather, battling together toward a common goal.

Astaroth moved his thumb to Calladia's clit. She gasped and tilted her head back, exposing the elegant line of her throat, and her short nails dug into his pecs, a slight pain he wanted more of. He wanted her to claw him up, mark him as hers. He wanted to wear her possession on his skin.

Calladia's rhythm stuttered, and he knew she was close. He took control, thrusting up in hard, fast strokes while his thumb pressed and rubbed. "Come on," he told her through gritted teeth. "Come for me."

Her inner muscles clenched, and then she was jerking and crying out, shaking all over as her cunt squeezed him in rhythmic flutters. He watched pleasure seize her, memorizing every detail: her opened mouth and tightly closed eyes, the flush sweeping her cheeks and upper chest.

She was beautiful.

Calladia collapsed against him, hands winding into his hair and stroking over his horns as she mouthed at his neck. "Your turn," she whispered.

Thank Lucifer. The sight of her orgasm had brought him to the edge. He gripped her hips, thrusting up aggressively as tension seized him tighter and tighter. Then it released all at once, an explosion of sensation that left him gasping as he filled the condom.

Limp from pleasure, Astaroth wrapped his arms around Calladia and held her against his chest while his breathing gradually slowed. Her skin was soft and damp from exertion, and he felt the tap of her heartbeat against his chest.

Astaroth's thoughts drifted, hazy and unformed. He wanted to stay in this blissful cocoon forever.

Eventually, Calladia shifted and groaned. "Gonna pee," she said.

Astaroth nodded and released her, though not before an affectionate pat to her bottom. "Sounds good," he slurred. "Prevent those UTIs." He closed his eyes, listening to the rustle as she crawled to the entrance. When she unzipped the door, cold air swept into the tent, but he was too relaxed to care. His restless mind had stilled, the thoughts and feelings coalescing into one undeniable truth.

For the first time in his long existence, Astaroth was in love.

TWENTY-SIX

CALLADIA STAGGERED BACK TOWARD THE TENT AFTER DO-
ing her business. Her knees were wobbly, and her mouth was
stuck in a goofy smile. Three orgasms would do that to a person.

When she ducked under the tent flap, her smile widened at the
sight of Astaroth lying where she'd left him. His arm was flung
over his eyes, and his breathing was slow and even. Asleep?

"Don't suppose you can demanifest a condom," he said, his normally crisp accent turned slow and lazy.

Not asleep. Calladia knelt next to him, eyeing the condom still
attached to his softening cock. "You might want to remove it first,"
she said. "Just in case."

He lifted his arm and squinted at her. "Is my penis in danger?"

Maybe of being excessively fondled. Calladia shook her head.
"Not at present."

He grunted, then tugged off the condom and knotted it. Calladia yanked out another hair from her scalp and tied the knots to
reverse the summoning. She sent the condom to a dumpster they'd
passed near the trailhead.

Astaroth started to sit up, then groaned and collapsed onto the sleeping bag. "Witch, you've killed me."

She lay down next to him, pulling a blanket over them. Later, she'd put on pajamas, but right now skin to skin was nice. She hooked an arm over him and nuzzled her nose into the crook of his neck. "So," she said. "How did the sex rank?"

"What?"

"You're a legendary fuckboy, right?" she teased. "I'm curious how I stack up against Lucrezia Borgia." She was joking, but part of her did wonder. He'd been with so many people; this probably hadn't meant anything to him besides an opportunity to get off.

The idea made her feel ill.

Astaroth sank his fingers into her hair and pulled her head back to look her in the eye. His expression was uncharacteristically solemn. "Calladia, there's no comparison."

"Oh. Right." Lucrezia had been notorious for her hedonism, while Calladia had only had a handful of partners. Of course there was no comparison. Embarrassment heated her cheeks. "Never mind."

"Wait." Astaroth shifted onto his side, pillowing his head on his bicep as he faced her. "I don't think you took that the right way."

She shrugged, even though she was feeling smaller with every moment. Sam had thought her performance was mediocre, too. *You just need to practice*, he'd told her, guiding her head to his crotch. *You'll get better eventually.* "I'm a big girl," she said. "My ego's not that fragile."

Her ego was that fragile, but she'd be damned before she admitted it.

Astaroth pursed his lips and blew a raspberry, startling her. "Calladia, that was the best sex I've ever had."

She blinked. "What? There's no way."

He looked earnest though. "It's true."

"But we only did one position."

"And what a position it was." His sigh sounded blissful. "Having you ride me was practically a religious experience."

She flicked his shoulder. "Shut up."

"I mean it." He tucked a loose strand of hair behind her ear. "That wasn't just a bit of casual fun. Not for me anyway."

There had been a minuscule pause before the last sentence, and although he was smiling, there was something wary about his expression.

Was he also worried she'd seen this as nothing but a quick, meaningless fuck?

It should have been a quick, meaningless fuck. There was no world in which the two of them started a relationship. He had his immortality and position on the demon council to worry about. After he recovered his memories, there would be no reason for him to stay, and Calladia had her own future to focus on.

Her chest felt tight at the thought of leaving him.

Oh, no.

Calladia was officially emotionally compromised.

She cleared her throat. "It wasn't casual for me either." Saying it made her feel vulnerable, so she focused on the dip of his collarbone so she didn't have to see whatever was in his eyes. Calladia didn't do emotional openness, hadn't tried since she'd been burned for it. And now she was trying it with a demon?

Astaroth's fingers brushed her chin, tipping it up. His expression was as soft as she'd ever seen it. "Well," he said, "we've certainly complicated things for ourselves, haven't we?"

Calladia inexplicably teared up. She wiped her eyes, chuckling uneasily. "Please ignore me."

Astaroth's hand moved under the blanket to settle on her hip. "Why are you crying?"

"I'm not crying."

One brow crept up. "Have you sprung a leak, then?"

"I never cry." Another tear slipped out. "Damn it."

"Are you crying because you only had three orgasms? I'll happily give you more."

Ridiculous demon. She rolled her eyes. "Never let it be said you lack ambition."

His fingers flexed on her hip. "Calladia," he said in a cajoling tone. "Why are you crying?"

She wasn't entirely sure. "I don't know. It's just . . . I don't do this, you know?"

"Sex?"

"No. I mean, yes, I haven't done that in a while either." She gestured between them. "I don't do *this*."

His forehead furrowed, and she could see him trying to work through her confusing words. "I need a bit more than that to go on," he said.

"Ugh." She blew out a breath, puffing stray hairs out of her face. "The whole emotional shit." She squirmed, uncomfortable even saying it. "Not that it's . . . yeah. No."

She was making less sense than ever, but Astaroth seemed to catch on, because his brow cleared. "Ah. You don't like feeling vulnerable."

"I'm not vulnerable," she replied instantly.

"I don't like being vulnerable either," he said, ignoring her rebuttal. "It's dashed uncomfortable."

Humor was easier to manage than emotional honesty, so Calladia tried to make light of the situation. "There you go, sounding like a Jane Austen character again. Next I'll find out you have a country estate and a fondness for waltzing."

"When was the last time you were vulnerable?" Astaroth asked.

He cut to the core of the issue as deftly as if he'd sliced through her bullshit with a sword. Calladia thought about making a run for it, but it was cold and wet outside, and she'd have to face him eventually. "If I don't answer, what are the odds you'll let it go?"

"Zero."

She smiled despite herself. "A gentleman wouldn't pry."

His long lashes swept his cheekbones as he smiled at her. "Good thing I'm a villain, then."

Despite herself, Calladia found herself wanting to share the story, as foolish and weak as it made her seem. "I had a boyfriend in college," she blurted out. "Though maybe it's weird to call him that, since he was fifteen years older than me."

"Taylor Swift would call that a problematic age gap," Astaroth said.

"Yeah, well, I would, too. Now, anyway." She took a deep breath, letting herself pick at the scab that barely covered this hurt, even years later. "He was my professor, actually, at Crabtree College a few hours from Glimmer Falls. He taught a general education class I took freshman year."

"Freshman year?" Astaroth asked, brows rising. "You would have been very young."

"Eighteen, yeah. Though he didn't ask me out until the next fall, when I was nineteen." She remembered the shock of it—his earnest declaration that he'd been thinking about her all summer, that she was so mature for her age, that he admired her sharp mind and strident opinions.

"So he would have been thirty-four." Astaroth scowled. "I don't like that. What's his name?"

"Sam," she said. "Sam Templeton." He'd seemed so sophisticated to her back then. Someone had finally seen the worth in troublemaker tomboy Calladia, and it was a handsome, tenured professor who wore suits and had the ear of every person of influence in a hundred miles. The kind of man her mother respected.

He'd asked her to keep their relationship on the down-low on campus, of course. At the time, it had felt like a thrilling secret.

"We dated the entire time I was in college," Calladia continued. "My mother adored him, of course. He came from East Coast money and had a job she respected, and I guess she thought he was a civilizing influence on me."

Astaroth scoffed. "Bloody nonsense."

"Not according to my mother." Calladia picked at a stray thread from the blanket. "She didn't know how bad it got though. She just saw me dressing nicely and spending less time at the gym and figured I was finally growing up. Becoming a proper woman, as she called it." And Calladia, sick with the need for validation, had clung to that shred of approval. She'd gotten her ears pierced, started wearing pearls, even invested in a cream-colored pantsuit that Mariel and Themmie had helped her burn when the whole mess was over.

Astaroth made a low, angry sound. "What did he do, Calladia?"

"He didn't hit me or anything." Maybe if he had she'd have recognized his true nature earlier. "He just wanted me to be someone I wasn't." She bit her lip, despising how thinking about that time still hurt, when she was sure Sam never gave a second thought to the young women left in his wake. "It started small. He said I was too loud, that I swore too much. So I toned it down. Then he thought my fashion sense was childish and wanted me to look more grown-up. For my own good, of course," she said sarcastically. "He said he wanted other people to respect me the way he did, and he didn't like hearing them make fun of me behind my back." Now she doubted those people had existed outside of Sam's manipulative fantasies.

"If he wanted to date someone more grown-up," Astaroth said tightly, "he could have chosen someone his own age."

"Exactly." She smiled crookedly at the demon. "But my youth was the point. He'd dated at least one undergrad before me, I found out, and after we broke up and before I blocked him on social media, I saw his new girlfriend on Pixtagram, and she looked *so* young. Even though I was the one to break up with him, it felt like he'd replaced me with someone younger and prettier."

"I'd like to point out that no one is prettier than you," Astaroth said, running his hand in soothing strokes over her side, "though I acknowledge that's not the point."

She laughed awkwardly. "You may need your eyes checked, but thank you."

He frowned. "I've noticed you don't like compliments."

"I don't get a lot of them." She knew how to react to a challenge or insult—hit back—but she'd never quite known what to do with praise.

"Then clearly I need to compliment you all the time." Astaroth ducked his head and pressed a kiss to her bicep. "Tell me more about this Sam wanker."

Calladia sighed. "He didn't like me working out. He thought it made me look too masculine for his tastes." A sentiment her mother had echoed, so a younger Calladia had let them convince her that was a bad thing. "So I stopped working out, stopped speaking up, stopped swearing. Then he wanted me to lose weight. I made myself small and quiet and biddable, and it was never enough." The critiques had grown crueler, until she'd dreaded the sound of his footsteps outside the apartment in the evening.

"It never would be," Astaroth said. "Some bastards want power but don't know how to get it without tearing other people down. If they can't earn respect on their own merits, they'll create a victim with no choice in the matter."

His eyes held the weight of ages, and Calladia was struck by the vast difference between them. Astaroth looked young, and he could be as funny and petty and ridiculous as any human, but he was very, very old. "If Sam was problematic at fifteen years older than me, then what is this?" she asked, gesturing between them.

"The problematic part is when an older partner specifically chooses someone young and naive to take advantage of or demean," Astaroth said. "I'm interested in you for who you are, exactly as you are. And you're fully capable of . . . what did you threaten me with again? Exploding my testicles if I try any funny business."

Who you are, exactly as you are. Flustered by the praise, Calladia scrambled for a joke. "It helps that you're a very immature six hundred."

"Precisely," Astaroth agreed. "I'm fairly sure I haven't experienced emotional growth since the Thirty Years' War."

That blatantly wasn't true—because what had the last few days been, if not emotional growth?—but Calladia appreciated the attempt at humor. It made it easier for her to finish the story.

"Anyway," she said, "I finally came to my senses, thanks to Mariel." Mariel had staged a few interventions over the years, but Calladia had been too blinded by love to listen—and later, too browbeaten. "She wasn't getting results reasoning with me, so she did something tricky after Sam proposed. She invited me to come hiking with her back in Glimmer Falls." Mariel had never been a fitness nut the way Calladia was, but she loved hiking, and the two of them had spent countless hours wandering the woods together. "We hadn't gone in a while, and Sam had been limiting the time I spent with my friends, but he was out of town one weekend. So I drove up to Glimmer Falls and joined Mariel on a hike to the hot springs."

She could picture it clearly. Calladia hadn't exercised in a long time, and her workout pants and tank top had hung loose. When she'd looked in the mirror, she hadn't recognized the frail woman playing dress-up in the old Calladia's clothes.

"I couldn't keep up," Calladia said. "I used to run half-marathons, but I was winded within minutes of starting a gentle hike. After fifteen minutes, I nearly passed out. It was then I realized Sam hadn't been improving me the way he claimed to be. Instead, he had made me weak."

She'd cried her eyes out at the side of that trail while Mariel had held her and whispered assurances that this wasn't the end, and she would be strong again.

Then Mariel had driven back to Sam's apartment next to Crabtree College, helped Calladia pack her things, and brought her home.

"I dumped him by text," Calladia told Astaroth. "I couldn't bear to look at him again. He blew up my phone for a few weeks, then moved on. His new girlfriend was posted on Pixtagram within the month."

Silence fell as her story concluded. That hadn't been the real end of it, of course. It had taken time to build up her strength and confidence again. It would still take time for all the damage Sam had inflicted to heal. But like building a muscle, the places she had torn had become stronger with time. She would never let anyone make her feel small again.

Rain pattered gently against the tent, and wind soughed through the trees. It was wet and cold outside, but under the blanket with Astaroth, with magic glowing overhead, Calladia felt warm and safe.

Safe with her enemy—who would have thought? But she'd thought Sam an ally once, and look how that had turned out.

Astaroth cupped her cheek. "You're strong."

"Now I am. Back then I wasn't." It was embarrassing how much time she'd spent letting Sam tear her down. She hadn't recognized the bars of her cage until she was too weak to open the cell door and escape.

"Being strong doesn't mean winning every battle. Sometimes it means surviving to fight again."

Her vision blurred with fresh tears. "Wow," she said with a watery laugh. "That's deep. Have you thought about writing advice columns?" Dear Sphinxie from the *Glimmer Falls Gazette* couldn't touch his level of eloquence.

"Most of my advice is much less wholesome." His thumb traced her cheekbone. "I'm sorry that bastard hurt you. Is he still alive?"

That didn't sound enough like a joke for her comfort. "You're not allowed to murder him."

Astaroth pouted. "Why not?"

Ridiculous demon. "Because we're working on your redemption arc."

He sighed dramatically. "Redemption sounds boring."

"Does it?" Calladia shoved him to his back, then clambered on top, the blanket draping from her shoulders like a cape. "Even if only redeemed demons get laid?"

"A compelling argument." He reached up to massage her breasts, then abruptly stopped, expression turning serious. "We only do this if you want to, understand? Not because you think you owe it to me or that I'm not interested in you without the sex."

Oh, Hecate. Had this kindness and consideration been hiding under his ruthless façade all along? Or had losing his memory given Astaroth the chance to reclaim the person he'd been before the centuries had hardened him?

Calladia wasn't sure, but she wasn't going to waste the night debating the issue. Maybe this would all go tits up and Astaroth would turn back into a villain. She'd survive. And not just survive, but thrive. Calladia was done letting other people try to diminish or reshape her. Sam hadn't broken her; if it came down to it, Astaroth wouldn't either.

Calladia covered his hands on her chest with hers. She swallowed, feeling the giddy lure of the cliff edge. This time, she jumped. "I want this," she said. "I want *you*."

The grin that lit up Astaroth's face was a wonder to behold. "Then take whatever you want. It's yours."

And Calladia did.

TWENTY-SEVEN

"IS THAT IT?" ASTAROTH ASKED SKEPTICALLY. A RED DOOR WAS positioned between two trees a short distance away, but no accompanying structure could be seen. "Bit dodgy."

"Probably a concealment spell." Next to him, Calladia was winding yarn around her knuckles, setting a base pattern for whatever defensive or offensive spell she wanted to be ready to use. There were shadows beneath her eyes—a night of marathon sex would do that—but she had been smiling and relaxed all morning, and Astaroth had been staring at her like a besotted swain since she'd woken up.

Since before that, actually. He'd woken early and spent long, drowsy moments admiring her. She'd been curled up facing him, fists balled under her chin and lips parted around soft breaths. An unbearably tender feeling had swelled beneath his rib cage, yet more evidence of what he'd acknowledged the night before.

He had fallen in love with Calladia.

It was a seismic shift in his worldview, and he wondered if he would have been open to the possibility if he hadn't had his brains scrambled and his memory erased. His past was still jumbled, but the present felt so vividly intense that Astaroth couldn't comprehend how he'd hidden his human emotions for so long.

He was starting to wonder *why* he'd hidden them for so long.

There were practical reasons, of course. If he didn't remember joining the demon high council, he at least remembered the bite of unbridled ambition in his youth. Lilith, too, had encouraged him to mask his feelings to avoid being punished for his genetics while he sought power. He'd attained heights few demons dared aspire to, and he'd done all that despite the human tendencies that might make him a less ruthless competitor.

But the memories Astaroth had now, scattered as they were, were largely limited to his time with humans. If ambition had been the sum of his existence, why couldn't he remember serving on the demon council?

Maybe living on Earth had given him an outlet to explore humanity. And Calladia, with all her fire and foibles, was humanity in its most tantalizing form.

"So," she said, squaring her shoulders as she faced the door. "What now?"

"I advise knocking for the initial approach," he said. "Unless you're desperate to kick it in."

She gave him a faux-chiding look. "You're no fun."

"That's not what you said last night."

To his delight, she looked flustered at the reminder. "I suppose you have your moments," she said, eyes flicking to his crotch. Then she marched up to the door and rapped on it.

Astaroth followed, adjusting his grip on a branch he'd picked up during the hike. It was sword-length and fairly straight, and it was better than nothing should the witch prove dangerous.

The door creaked open, revealing . . . darkness. "Who goes there?" a female voice called.

"My name's Calladia, and this here is Astaroth," Calladia said. "We're looking for Isobel."

"I'm Isobel. And did you say Astaroth? As in the demon?" A hand curved around the door, pulling it wider, and a witch stepped into view. She wore a long blue dress belted with a silver chain and had straight black hair, pointed ears that indicated mixed heritage, and dark, fathomless eyes. Her silver necklace held an odd pendant: a filigree cage with something blue inside.

Astaroth felt a strange sense of déjà vu. "One and the same," he said. "Have we met?"

The witch looked him up and down. "You're quite the notorious figure." Her lilting accent was unidentifiable in the way many immortal accents were, heavy with the weight of varied places and times. If what Alzapraz claimed was true, Isobel had mastered life magic to the point of extending her life span indefinitely.

"Alzapraz sent us in your direction," Calladia said. "He says you can help with memory issues and possibly restoring immortality."

"That old warlock is still causing mischief, hmm?" Isobel pulled the door all the way open and beckoned them inside. "Come, have a cup of tea and tell me what you seek."

She waved a hand and whispered something, and torches flared to life, revealing stone walls and a flagstone floor topped with woven rugs. The furniture was heavy and Gothic-looking, herbs hung in bunches from the rafters, and a cauldron bubbled in the fireplace. At the back of the room were several closed doors, and a wrought-iron staircase wound up to the next story. A wall-mounted television was the only modern touch—it was paused on a scene that showed a group of people in yellow, red, and blue shirts pointing odd-looking guns at someone in a poorly constructed dragon costume.

"This place is great," Calladia said, looking around. "My friend Themmie would say it has 'vibes for days.'"

"Please, sit." Isobel gestured toward a red velvet couch with carved lion heads protruding from the armrests. She retrieved two mugs from a shelf above the fireplace that held tableware and occult-looking figurines. Astaroth squinted at one of the figurines, whose head had started bobbling when Isobel's sleeve brushed it. Its base was inscribed with the odd word *Spock*, and the black hair, pointed ears, and blue shirt were vaguely familiar—perhaps an elven deity?

Isobel ladled steaming liquid from the cauldron into the mugs and handed them over.

"Oh," Calladia said. "Thank you. You brew tea in a cauldron?"

"Cauldrons are useful for many things," Isobel said.

Astaroth sniffed his tea suspiciously. His eyebrows shot up at the familiar, delicious scent. "This is proper English breakfast tea."

Calladia sniffed her own mug. "What? It smells like orange and ginger."

Isobel poured her own tea, then settled into a wooden chair that resembled a throne. "The cauldron produces whatever your favorite blend is. It also works for soup."

Astaroth looked at Calladia. "Your favorite tea is orange and ginger?" He'd need to stock up on some. He had a tea cabinet in his flat in London, and he liked the idea of her tea leaves nestled next to his.

"I'm amazed someone as precious as you is happy with plain old breakfast tea," Calladia said. "I expected you to be into oolong seasoned with rose petals and civet poop or something."

"Excuse you," he said. "There is nothing plain about a proper breakfast tea. The flavor profile is quite robust."

Calladia shook her head. "You really leaned into the British thing, didn't you? You probably have a collection of rare tea bags."

The horror! "I would never steep tea from a bag. Loose leaf is superior in every way."

"You probably have a kettle, too." Calladia smirked over the rim of her mug.

"Of course I do." Both an electric kettle and an old-fashioned ceramic teapot. His forehead furrowed. "Wait, do you not?"

Calladia raised her mug in a toast. "Microwave, baby."

"No!" Astaroth was appalled. "That's a crime against gastronomy."

"What can I say? I like to live on the edge." Calladia sipped and made an appreciative noise. "That's delicious."

Isobel had been watching the exchange with interest. "How did the two of you become acquainted?" she asked.

"Oh, he's my nemesis," Calladia said, raising a challenging brow at him.

"Exactly," Astaroth said. "Just two sworn enemies on a quest."

"I see." Isobel did not look like she, in fact, saw. "And this quest led you to me?"

Astaroth quickly explained the situation, from the amnesia to the witch who had apparently stripped away his immortality.

"Well," Isobel said when he was done. "That's a lot."

"Can you help?" he asked.

"Possibly." She set the tea aside. "May I examine you?"

Unsure what that would entail, Astaroth agreed. She stood and moved toward him, the hem of her dress whispering over the floor, then placed her fingers at his temples and closed her eyes.

"Is it possible the witch took away my memories, too?" Astaroth asked.

Isobel shushed him. "Let me look."

Astaroth sat still while she palpated his skull, feeling awkward.

Finally, Isobel opened her eyes and dropped her hands. "Your memory loss is from a blow to the head, not a spell."

"Well, that's good news," Astaroth said. Then he reconsidered. Being mortal meant he didn't heal quickly anymore. "Or is it?"

"Recovering will come down to time and willpower," Isobel said. "I cannot force your mind to produce the memories it has lost. They will return once you've healed and are ready to seize the life you want."

"Cryptic." And unhelpful. "I'm ready to seize that life now though."

She shook her head. "Memories can be planted, altered, erased. They cannot be pulled forth unwillingly, at least not with my powers. The damage is not irreversible though—you gain more with every hour, and a time will come soon when your will, your reality, and your mind reach an accord. When you are ready, all shall be restored as it once was."

"Can we hurry that process up?" Calladia asked. "It's pretty urgent."

"One cannot rush such things."

Why was nothing ever straightforward, especially when it came to witch business? Astaroth eyed Isobel, wondering if that had been a final answer or the beginning of negotiations. "What if we pay you a lot of money?"

Isobel pursed her lips, looking between them. "You don't look rich."

"We've been roughing it," Calladia said. "And I did recently lose most of my worldly possessions, but I can scrounge up some cash."

If Isobel was as old as Astaroth suspected, she wouldn't be inclined to trust fiat currency versus something more tangible. "I have a safe full of gold doubloons," he offered.

"Doubloons?" Calladia asked incredulously. "Who are you, Blackbeard?"

"No, but I did enjoy a brief stint in piracy." Talk about a group that understood the importance of branding. From their flags to their wildly original methods of execution, pirates had nailed the creative brief.

Interest flared in Isobel's eyes. "Where are these coins?"

"London." He was fairly sure they were still there anyway, though if Lilith had been poking around, who knew? "I can write a promissory note."

Isobel pursed her lips. "If you sign a contract in blood, I'll accept it."

She was definitely old. These days, most witches accepted digital signatures in WarlockuSign.

"So you can restore his memories after all?" Calladia asked.

"No, but I can encourage the brain to heal. The moment the memories return will still depend on Astaroth, but a stable foundation will make the rest of the process easier."

"Let's do it," Astaroth said.

Isobel produced a piece of parchment, a quill pen, and a knife, and Astaroth wrote a promise to pay fifty gold doubloons in exchange for her assistance regaining his memories. He signed it, then cut his finger and dabbed blood on the signature.

Isobel inspected it, then folded the contract and set it on the fireplace mantel. "Relax and close your eyes," she said.

A moment later, her fingers touched his temples. She spoke spells under her breath, and as her fingers fluttered and tapped against his skull, a wave of cool, soothing energy spread through his head before dissipating.

"There," she said. "The physical damage will heal more quickly."

He opened his eyes. "That was fast."

Isobel inclined her head with a small smile. "I have been honing my skills for a long time. Brains are complex, so this will need a period of natural healing as well, but I fixed your superficial injuries while I was at it. Consider it a first-time customer bonus."

He'd gotten so used to avoiding touching the scab on his head, he hadn't realized it was gone. When he tentatively prodded his skull, he found unbroken skin, and his black eye felt similarly healed. Even his cut finger was whole again. "Cheers, appreciate it."

"About the other issue," Calladia said. "How many witches can reduce an immortal life span?"

"Several that I'm aware of can manipulate human lives," Isobel said, resuming her seat. "That's the reason a witch was able to turn you mortal," she told Astaroth. "The ones I know can't influence the life spans of other species, but your human half made you an acceptable target." She tapped her chin, looking thoughtful. "Although I suppose someone out there might be capable of influencing a pure demon. Life magic is a rare discipline, but there are enough practitioners I can't say who was responsible." She shrugged. "Alas."

"Let's say there's a purebred demon we want to eliminate," Astaroth said. "You're saying you can't kill him with your magic?"

"With magic? No. With a guillotine? Sure."

Curses. Isobel was a dead end on the "kill Moloch" front, but maybe the witch could still assist them. "Can you restore my immortality?" Astaroth asked, hoping it would be that easy.

"That is more complicated," Isobel said. "It isn't as easy as telling someone to 'live long and prosper.' No one can conjure life from nothing; it must be a trade. That is why Alzapraz looks the way he does. To attain eternal life without harvesting it from others, he had to trade away his physical health." She sighed. "A shame. He was such a virile lover."

"Why don't you look old, then?" Calladia asked.

"I trade the lives of others to extend my own," she said calmly.

"What?" Calladia demanded, sitting up straight. "You kill people?"

Isobel shrugged. "I outsource most of the murder."

Astaroth was getting the sense Isobel wasn't an empathetic sort. He considered his options. "So you're saying if I want to be immortal and not physically decrepit, I need to kill people and harvest their lives?"

"No," Isobel said. "You'll need to bring *me* the people to kill so I can harvest their lives and add them to your life span. Otherwise they'll just be dead." She cocked her head, studying Calladia. "We can start with her, if you like. No charge for the first one, as proof of concept."

Calladia shot to her feet. "What the hell? You are not harvesting my life, you creep." Her hands fisted at her sides like she was thinking about punching the witch.

Astaroth would punch the witch first if she lifted a finger against Calladia. "She's off-limits," he snapped, standing as well.

Calladia shot him a damning look. "So are other people. You do not get to hop off the redemption train just to get on the murder train."

That seemed unfair. "What if I only kill annoying people?"

"No!"

He made a frustrated noise. "It's no different than bargaining. Well, a little different." A lot different, actually, and the more he thought about the concept, the more it nauseated him. For all his flaws, Astaroth didn't kill indiscriminately.

But if it was between that and becoming so physically frail he could barely function . . .

"The people whose souls you harvest consent to that," Calladia said. "Not that I approve of soul bargains either."

"Some people consent to being killed," Isobel said. "You might try Hagslist."

Astaroth wasn't familiar. "Hagslist?"

"It's an online marketplace," Isobel explained. "Most often used to find housing, odd items, and unusual sexual encounters."

"And you can find consensual murder victims on there?" How intriguing. Humans were such a strange species. "I wonder if the platform can be leveraged for soul bargains."

"We are not having this conversation," Calladia said. She pointed sternly at Astaroth. "No Hagslist. No murder!"

Astaroth had a burst of inspiration. He turned to Isobel. "What if I bring you an immortal? Would it be possible to harvest their life, and then we only need to do it once?"

"Only if they're half human."

He could probably rustle up another immortal demon-human hybrid, but the idea of trading their life for his didn't sit well. "Otherwise I've got to bring you a mortal every few decades to top off." That didn't sit well either.

"That's the unfortunate thing about humans," Isobel said. "Like Snickers bars, they're good for brief bursts of energy, but they're not filling."

Calladia looked appalled. "Why do you talk about people like that?" she asked Isobel. "You used to be human—or at least part human."

Isobel fingered the pointed tips of her ears. "After you've lived many life spans, the kinship with other mortals falls away."

"Maybe if you weren't murdering them, you would still feel a kinship." Calladia's voice was growing louder. "Witches aren't supposed to use their powers to prey on other people."

Isobel sipped her tea, looking unbothered. "The youth are always full of moral outrage."

Calladia looked like she was about to start punching, so Astaroth stepped between them. "Excuse us a moment, Isobel."

Astaroth took Calladia's elbow and guided her out of earshot. "She's not going to stop killing people because you're upset with her," he whispered. "And frankly, if she's that murder-happy, we probably shouldn't antagonize her."

Calladia glared at him. "I'm more worried about her convincing you to murder people to regain your stupid immortality."

"What if they consent to be killed? And it isn't stupid," Astaroth said. "I need to regain my position on the high council. I can't do that as a mortal."

"Why not? Who says you have to be a pure-blooded demon or even an immortal to serve on the council?"

He scoffed. "Because that's how it's always been."

"Things can change."

"Not this thing." Council appointments were for life unless someone retired, was removed by group consensus, or was executed. Debates could last for decades. How could a mortal accomplish anything in such a brief span of years?

Calladia thumped his shoulder, brown eyes burning with fury. "How many people will have to die to keep you in power? One every century? Every fifty years? Every twenty? For how long? Indefinitely?"

Astaroth felt sick at the thought. He didn't want to kill mortals for the sake of extending his life span, but if they consented, as Isobel said they sometimes did, would that absolve him of blame?

He knew what Calladia would say.

As much as Astaroth wanted an instant solution to his mortality problem, he wanted Calladia's good opinion more. "It might not come to that," he said, backing down from the argument. "Isobel doesn't know every life witch—there might be one who can restore my immortality without any murder." Calladia still looked pissed, so Astaroth grabbed her hand and kissed it. "This is only one option. We'll find another."

"You're damn right we will," she snapped. She looked toward Isobel, then sighed. "So what do we do now, if she can't kill Moloch and you can't regain your immortality or your memories here?"

It was a setback, but the solution to his amnesia was somewhere inside his head. He just had to figure out how to trigger the return of his memories now that Isobel had healed some of the damage. "She said the memories will return when I'm ready to seize the life I want, right?"

"Not the most helpful instructions," Calladia said.

"Still, my amnesia isn't permanent." It was a massive relief. He'd been afraid he would stay broken forever. "So we'll carry on, and maybe Lilith will have some answers the next time we talk. Or who knows, maybe I can meditate or see a hypnotist or something."

Calladia bit her lip. When she looked back at him, her expression was still wary but slightly softer. "Where do we carry on to?" she asked. "This was the end point of the quest."

What? No. "We'll go back to Glimmer Falls," Astaroth said, fighting a wave of panic at the thought of his time with her ending. "We can consult Alzapraz again. And I'll call Lilith as soon as we're done here to see if she found anything in my den." A brilliant idea came to him, a way to extend the trip even farther. "We can go to London and search my flat! Have you ever been to London?"

"No."

"Oh, you must. You'll love it." He'd take her to see all the sights, walk with her along the Thames, share the wonders of a full English breakfast or a Sunday roast. She'd look lovely in a wool peacoat, and he had to take her to his haberdasher, of course; everyone deserved a favorite hat—

"Astaroth." Calladia interrupted his fantasies. "How long do we keep doing this? What if the ideal moment for your memories to come back is in eighty years or something?"

"Bloody hell, I hope not." Although he suspected they could get up to a great deal of fun in eighty years. And that led to another possibility: maybe he could convince her to seek immortality with him. "Have you ever wanted to live forever?" he asked.

She grimaced. "You sound like an informercial spokesperson. *Interested in eternal life?*" she said in a mockery of his accent. "*Look no further than our range of weaponry you can use to murder innocents and steal their lives!*"

Apparently Astaroth's potential murder spree was still a sensitive subject. "Well, ah, like I said, there may be another way—"

Calladia stiffened and clapped her hand to his mouth. He tried to protest, but she shook her head. "Listen."

He strained his ears, wondering what had gotten her attention. The fire crackled softly; the cauldron bubbled. Through the shuttered windows, he heard wind whipping through the trees.

Leaves crunched, and a man's voice murmured outside. The words were too indistinct to make out, but the tone was familiar.

He met Calladia's wide eyes. *Moloch*, he mouthed.

They moved in unison, preparing for battle. Astaroth rushed to retrieve his branch, while Calladia pulled some yarn from her pocket. Isobel was now standing beside the front door, slipping a cell phone into the pocket of her dress. Firelight flickered across her face, and déjà vu spun Astaroth's head again.

He'd seen the witch before, illuminated by fire as she was now. Her black eyes had stared deep into him, and her mouth had opened around a spell. Astaroth had tried to get away, but something had held him in place . . .

Shock rattled him to his bones. "You!" He pointed a damning finger at Isobel. "You're the witch who cursed me."

"What?" Calladia's head whipped around. "Wait, the one who took your immortality?"

"The very one. I just remembered." He was seething. How could she have lied to their faces?

"Well, this is awkward," Isobel said, stifling a yawn. "It was nothing personal, you understand. Just business."

"Give me my immortality back," Astaroth ordered, advancing on her.

"I can't. It's already been applied to my own life." Her lips curved in a mean smile. "A half-human immortal is a rare find. Thanks to you, I won't need to harvest shorter mortal lives ever again."

Outrage burned through him. The witch had been working with Moloch all along. She'd cursed him with mortality and stolen his eternal life, and now she'd alerted the demon to their location. "How much is he paying you?" he demanded.

"More than fifty gold doubloons," Isobel said coolly. "Which you still owe me, by the way."

"Did you even heal him?" Calladia asked. "Or was that a trick?"

"I do not accept money and then fail to deliver on my promises," Isobel said. "I applied magic to heal his brain. The rest of what I told you about recovering his memories is true as well."

Calladia was practically snarling. "How are we supposed to believe a filthy liar?"

"I didn't lie. I omitted the truth."

Blast, this was a trick Astaroth ought to have seen coming. His instincts were growing dull. "We need to get out of here," he told Calladia. "Now, before Moloch sends some fireballs in and roasts us alive."

Isobel looked startled at that. She whipped out her phone and started typing, presumably a text along the lines of *NO FIRE-BALLS*. "It's been a tepid experience doing business with you," she said, gesturing at the door. "There's the exit."

Calladia looked murderous. She wore bloodthirstiness well, but attacking Isobel would only delay them. "She's not worth it," he told Calladia. "We need to get out of here."

Calladia sneered at Isobel. "I hope you choke on those gold doubloons, bitch."

"Blame capitalism," Isobel said. "Good luck with everything."

Astaroth stood at the front door, ready to burst out with metaphorical guns blazing. And by metaphorical guns he meant a big stick and a pissed-off witch. He could think of worse weapons. "Come on," he told Calladia. "Your arse-kicking skills are needed."

Calladia nodded, then strode past Isobel. Then she pivoted and booted the witch in the chest with a side kick, sending Isobel crashing into her cauldron. Isobel shrieked as boiling tea splashed on her.

"Nice," Astaroth said.

"I would have done worse if we had time." Calladia joined him at the door, thread stretched taut between her fingers. "Let's Butch Cassidy and Sundance Kid this shit."

Astaroth had a vague recollection that perhaps that story

hadn't worked out so well. "Which one are you?" he asked. "And wait, didn't they die?"

Calladia grabbed the knob and ripped the door open. "Yippee-ki-yay, motherfucker!" she yelled as she sprinted outside.

Astaroth followed hot on her heels . . .

Straight into a wall of fire.

TWENTY-EIGHT

HEAT FLARED OVER CALLADIA'S SKIN, AND HER VISION WAS obscured by a brilliant orange glow. She covered her face with a forearm and kept running, and moments later she burst through the flames.

The fire had been set in a ring around Isobel's house—thankfully a narrow ring, because otherwise Calladia's impulsive decision would have been significantly less badass and much crispier.

Three demons faced her, blocking the path down the slope. Moloch was instantly recognizable with his rosy cheeks and dimpled smile. Next to him stood a demoness wielding a flaming whip and a massive demon who looked like a Viking and carried a sword.

Astaroth skidded to a stop next to her. "Baphomet?" he asked incredulously.

The redheaded Viking shot a look at Moloch. "I thought the witch said he'd lost his memory." His horns were ivory-colored and looked alarmingly sharp.

"She did," Moloch said. "I'll resolve that issue with Isobel later."

"I still can't believe Isobel ratted us out," Calladia muttered, running a list of possible spells through her head. "What happened to witch solidarity?"

"Money happened," Astaroth replied succinctly. He hefted the tree branch higher. "I find it interesting, Baphomet," he declared loudly, "that you, famously the centrist of the high council, have joined Moloch on a mission to kill me."

Baphomet scowled. "You earned your punishment."

The demoness with the whip cracked it, sending sparks through the air. She had dirty-blond chin-length hair and marbled gray horns. "Let me snap his head off, Moloch."

"Ah, Tirana," Astaroth said, giving an elaborate bow. "You are as charming as ever."

The name was familiar, and Calladia racked her brain for what she'd learned about high council politics. Baphomet was the oldest demon on the court and its ostensible leader, and Sandranella had mentioned him seeming sympathetic to Moloch's cause. Sympathetic to both Moloch and Tirana, she remembered, Tirana being the anti-hybrid extremist who wanted to claim Astaroth's former position on the council.

Two conservative hard-liners were collaborating with the powerful centrist demon everyone wanted to sway to their side. That Tirana had asked *Moloch* for permission to attack Astaroth, rather than Baphomet, told Calladia the swaying had already happened. "Looks like Baphomet is no longer in charge," she told Astaroth. "I wonder if the rest of the council knows?"

Baphomet glared at her. "Who are you?"

"None of your business." Calladia looped thread over her fingers, whispering as she tied knots faster than she ever had in her life. A defensive shield formed in front of them, invisible to the naked eye.

"She's casting a spell," Tirana said. The whip flashed forward in a bright blur, and Calladia flinched when it ricocheted off the shield.

Astaroth shoved her behind him. "Your quarrel is with me, not her."

Calladia made an irritated sound. "I can fight."

"I know," he replied. "So can I."

"You have a stick."

"Indeed I do." He waved the branch in front of him. "Come on, you cowards. Who wants to face me first?"

Moloch burst out laughing. "Oh, this is too good," he said between chuckles. "What a fearsome stick you wield."

Calladia kept tying knots. "What are you doing?" she whispered hotly.

"It's called a diversion," Astaroth muttered. "So hurry up with whatever diabolical spell you're working on."

Oh! Astaroth knew he couldn't win against three armed demons, so he was distracting them until Calladia could come up with something dramatic enough to get them away safely.

Calladia didn't have a plan, but that hadn't stopped her before. Remembering a spell from her textbook, she focused on the earth at the feet of the three demons. "*Descendren ti talammven*," she said, weaving a pattern like a spiderweb between her fingers.

The ground collapsed beneath the three demons. The pit was only a few feet deep, but it would at least slow them down.

"Run!" Astaroth said.

"Already on it!"

They sprinted into the forest together. Calladia hurdled over logs and wound around trees like escaping demons was an Olympic event. When a vine stretched across the path, Astaroth sliced through it with a swing of his branch, clearing the way.

Behind them came shouts and crashing noises as the demons

pursued. Calladia desperately wanted to weave a new spell, but it was impossible to get the precision she needed while running. Damn it, why couldn't she have an ounce of Mariel's nature gifts? Mariel could have made the forest attack their pursuers with little but a whispered request.

Calladia's throat burned with her heaving breaths. She leaped over a log, then ducked under a branch.

A cracking noise accompanied a sting at the side of her head, and Calladia cried out as pain burst white hot over her skin. When she touched the spot, her fingers came away wet with blood, and the smell of burned hair filled her nostrils. Tirana had cracked her whip, and only Calladia's incidental dodge had prevented it from doing further damage.

Astaroth turned and flung the branch like a javelin, and a cry of pain followed. "Leave her alone," he shouted.

"Just run," Calladia gasped. The pain of the strike numbed out as adrenaline kicked in, and despite the blood, it didn't seem like a devastating injury. Head wounds always bled excessively. It was too bad the whip hadn't contacted her skin long enough to cauterize the cut.

The river glinted through the trees downslope. They were nearing the trailhead and Clifford the Little Red Truck, but the demons were far too close. "Lilith," Calladia wheezed. "She needs to know." Shit had officially hit the fan, and this situation was more than they could take on alone.

Astaroth yanked his phone out of his pocket. "Baphomet, Moloch, Tirana," he panted a moment later. "Working together, very murdery. We're at . . . fuck, no idea where."

A flurry of alarmed female voices followed, but Calladia couldn't make out what was being said. She wanted to laugh hysterically at the futility of it all. Was this how she was going to die? Filleted by a fire whip in the middle of the woods?

Astaroth scooped up a rock and threw it at their pursuers. In response, the whip slashed at him, narrowly missing his face.

At last, the ground leveled out, and the parking lot appeared ahead. A familiar green SUV was parked next to Calladia's truck, and it took a moment to process what she was seeing.

Ben, Mariel, Oz, and Themmie were getting out of Ben's vehicle. Hope swelled in Calladia's breast, followed by terror. "Demons!" she screamed as her feet hit the asphalt. "Watch out!"

A second SUV pulled up. To her shock, Kai, Avram, and three other werewolves jumped out. They were armed with a variety of makeshift weapons, from baseball bats to . . . was that a home-brewed crossbow?

Was this a bounty hunter mission again? Who were they here to hunt?

Mariel faced the forest, a determined look on her face. The curvy witch wore a long-sleeved burgundy dress and her usual hiking boots. She braced her feet, then lifted her hands and spoke a few words.

Behind Calladia, Tirana cried out. When Calladia looked over her shoulder, she saw the demoness's whip had been yanked out of her hands by a dangling vine. Another vine wrapped around Tirana's throat before dragging her into a bush.

Astaroth had fallen a few feet behind after throwing the rock. "Eat shit, wankers," he shouted, scooping up another stone and flinging it at Moloch. It grazed the demon's dun-colored horn, and Moloch grimaced. He raised his hands, and the air around them began to glow orange.

"Astaroth," Calladia shouted, fear beating frantic wings in her chest.

Oz had been running toward Calladia, but he stopped short, staring at the scene like he'd seen a ghost. "Astaroth?" he asked.

"Fight now, ask questions later!" Themmie yelled. The pixie

scooped up an armful of the rocks ringing the parking lot and launched into the air, wings blurring. She began dropping the rocks on the heads of their pursuers.

A crossbow bolt zinged toward Moloch, answering the question of who the wolves were there to hunt. It struck the demon in the shoulder right as he unleashed a fireball. It barely missed Astaroth, hitting a tree instead. The tree went up in flames as splinters shot everywhere like shrapnel. Astaroth grunted and staggered, and Calladia was horrified to see a large fragment of wood jutting from his shoulder.

She turned back without hesitation, ignoring Ben's calls to get in the truck and get out of there. Astaroth was still moving, but his face was tight with pain.

"He did not just do that to a tree," Mariel said. She looked pissed. As the woods thrashed and grabbed at Baphomet and Moloch, she raised her hands to the sky and chanted a spell to summon rain. Soon the fire was smoldering under a localized deluge.

Calladia wrapped her arm around Astaroth to help support his weight. "Come on."

He groaned. "You try running with a skewer in your chest."

"Suck it up, fragile little buttercup."

She didn't mean it, but the taunt worked. Astaroth made an outraged noise and staggered forward with Calladia's support. By the time they reached Clifford, he was sweating and even paler than normal.

"Reconvene in Griffin's Nest," Ben told her. The werewolf was wearing his usual sweater vest, gold-rimmed glasses, and a nervous but determined expression. Next to him, Avram punched his palm, showing off a pair of brass knuckles. Side by side, the two werewolves were clearly related.

Calladia had a lot of questions, but now was not the time. She bundled Astaroth into the passenger side of her truck, then headed for the driver's seat. As she was about to get in, the three demons finally escaped the now-hostile woods and Mariel's magic. They squared off against the werewolves and Calladia's friends.

For a moment no one moved. Tension stretched tight between the two groups as each weighed their next steps.

A portal shimmered to life next to Calladia's truck. She spun, ready to throat-punch whoever came through, only to stop when Lilith emerged.

Astaroth's mother looked furious. Bones were woven into her red braids, and she wore an iron breastplate and greaves over a black catsuit. She was holding a sword with a wickedly barbed end. "Who's ready to bleed?" she called out. "Mama's thirsty."

"Oh, shit." Tirana sketched an oval in the air with her finger, and another portal opened, which the demoness immediately disappeared into.

"Coward," Moloch muttered.

Sandranella stepped through the portal after Lilith. At the sight of her, Baphomet hastily made his own portal exit, but not before Sandranella pointed at him and shouted, "You!"

Moloch looked between the various people facing him and apparently came to the same conclusion as the others. He bared his teeth. "This isn't over." He opened a portal and disappeared.

Silence fell.

Kai was the first to break it. "Aw, bugger," the werewolf said, lowering his crossbow. "I was hoping for a decent fight." The other werewolves grumbled in agreement.

Themmie landed next to Ben's SUV, and Mariel and Oz joined her. Calladia winced as Oz pointedly looked at Astaroth in the passenger seat of her truck.

"So," Mariel said, planting her hands on her hips. "Care to explain what the heck is going on?"

◆   ◆   ◆

THEY AGREED TO MEET IN GRIFFIN'S NEST FOR A DEBRIEF. SINCE
the werewolves showed no signs of leaving—*I sniff good trouble!*
Kai had cheerfully declared—they picked the only restaurant that
wasn't overrun with tourists for the Mariachi Festival. This was,
unfortunately, NecroNomNomNoms, which catered mostly to
creatures of the night and smelled even more strongly of blood
inside. The walls were black, the windows were painted over, and
the only light came from dramatic candelabra. The day shift waitress was a nonmagical human, but she seemed unruffled by the
eclectic mix of supernaturals that had descended on her. She led
them to a back room and left them with menus and water glasses.

The mystery of how the werewolves and Calladia's friends had
teamed up had been solved by the revelation that Ben and Avram
were cousins. After Avram had shared news about the brawl in a
family chat, Ben had decided the Glimmer Falls gang needed to
investigate what Calladia was up to. Bronwyn had given Avram
the same directions she'd given Calladia and Astaroth, and the
combined expedition had reached them just in time.

Calladia was grateful for the intervention, if not particularly
eager to explain what she'd been up to. She squinted at the menu
to avoid looking at Mariel, whose initial confused look had settled
firmly into the "damning gaze" category. The reason for that gaze
sat to Calladia's right, playing nonchalantly with his water goblet.

Or maybe Astaroth wasn't so nonchalant, after all. His expression was relaxed, but his shoulders were tense, and he kept sneaking
glances at Oz.

The waitress returned with a tray. "Chips and salsa," she declared, plunking down a bowl of what looked like dried severed
ears and a ramekin holding a very liquid salsa Calladia suspected
was not made from tomatoes. The waitress handed a steaming
goblet to Astaroth. "Regenerative potion."

"Cheers," he murmured, giving her a smile that made the waitress do a stutter step and nearly walk into a wall. He downed the drink in one go and grimaced. "Whew. I've got to say, I prefer immortality to whatever that was."

Calladia had done what she could to patch Astaroth up, but it had been a relief to find out the restaurant had a wide potion selection. As Calladia watched, the wound left by the splinter she'd pulled out of Astaroth's shoulder closed until all that was visible through the hole in his shirt was smooth skin.

"Feeling better?" Calladia asked him.

"Much." He turned his smile on her, though it was a softer, more genuine version of what he'd given the waitress. Calladia wanted to smile back, but her skin itched under the weight of too many stares.

Time to face the music. She was seated at the head of a long table, and she took a deep breath before confronting the rest of the group. It was like presiding over the weirdest Last Supper ever. On her right were Astaroth, Lilith, Sandranella, Kai, and two random werewolves. On her left were Mariel, Oz, Themmie, Ben, Avram, and the last unnamed werewolf. The wolves were eagerly digging into the "chips and salsa," but the atmosphere on Calladia's end of the table felt more like a standoff. Oz and Mariel in particular were glaring daggers at Astaroth.

"So," Astaroth said. "Who talks first?"

Oz exploded out of his seat and slammed his hands on the table. "What the fuck are you doing here?"

Mariel aimed a similar question at Calladia. "Are you seriously hanging out with Astaroth?"

Calladia squirmed uncomfortably in her seat. "It's complicated."

"You'd better uncomplicate it quickly," Mariel said. "Because I'm honestly really hurt that you're helping the demon who took my soul and wanted to kill Oz."

"I mean, you got the soul back . . ." Calladia said, trailing off when she saw Themmie wince, shake her head, and drag her finger over her throat.

Astaroth did not get the same message, apparently. "And clearly I didn't succeed at killing Ozroth," he said, "so let's let bygones be bygones, shall we?"

Lilith frowned and pressed the back of her hand to his forehead. "You failed to kill someone? Are you feeling all right?"

"Who is that?" Themmie asked, wings twitching. "Who are any of these people, for that matter?"

Calladia sighed and made quick introductions. "To my left, my friend Mariel and her boyfriend Oz, formerly of the soul-bargaining persuasion. Then my friends Themmie and Ben, Avram, Ben's cousin who I met in a brawl, and . . ." She squinted. "Some other werewolves I fought."

The werewolves cheered and raised their ear-chips in a toast.

"Then Kai," she said, continuing her way around the table, "also from the brawl."

"Damn straight," Kai said, thumping his chest. "She skewered me in the chest and stole my heart."

Astaroth bared his teeth at that, so Calladia hurried on. "Next to him is Sandranella of the Nine, member of the demon high council, and Lilith, Astaroth's mother." She cleared her throat. "Everyone knows Astaroth already."

Silence followed the introductions. Then multiple people began talking at once.

"You're brawling with werewolves again?"

"Wait, Lilith the Mother of All Demons?"

"It's been less than a week, and suddenly you're hanging out with—"

"Is he forcing you to be here?"

"—a pack of werewolves and multiple demons?"

"Bro, Lilith is hot."

"Did you make a bargain?"

Calladia raised her voice. "Enough! Let me speak."

"This had better be good," Mariel said.

"Why yes, I am that Lilith," Lilith said, ignoring Calladia's in-struction as she fluffed her hair. "Reports of my offspring are wildly overstated, but reports of my promiscuity are sadly under-stated."

Kai clapped a hand to his chest. "Knock me over. I heard bed-time stories about you. My mum told me you'd dismember me if I wasn't a good pup."

Lilith eyed the buff werewolf. "I prefer my bad pups in one piece." She winked. "Unless you cross me." Then she pulled a knife out of nowhere, leaned across Sandranella, and plunged it into the wooden table a few inches from Kai's hand.

Kai shuddered. "I think I'm in love."

Oz glared at Astaroth. "I ought to sever your head after how you betrayed me."

Calladia tried again. "If you'll all just be quiet—"

"Seems excessive," Astaroth said. "In this state, a decent clob-bering will take me out."

Calladia took a deep breath, then yelled at the top of her lungs. "Shut up!"

Silence fell. Every eye in the room fixed on her.

"So, the short version," Calladia said, taking advantage of the pause. "Astaroth has amnesia, and he's mortal now."

"What?" Oz asked, looking shocked.

"It's true," Calladia said. "He made a bet with Moloch on the demon high council. If Oz succeeded in taking Mariel's soul, Astaroth could do whatever he wanted to Moloch. If Oz failed, the reverse was true."

"That was the dumbest wager I'd ever heard," Sandranella said. "I tried to talk him out of it, but nooooo, he was so sure Oz-roth would succeed."

Oz recoiled. "That was the bet?" he asked Astaroth. "Why didn't you tell me?"

"I don't know." Astaroth's gaze was fixed on his clasped hands, and Calladia could tell he was deeply uncomfortable. "Amnesia and all that. But since you're now dating the mortal you were supposed to target, I suspect learning the terms of the wager wouldn't have altered the outcome."

Oz looked at Mariel, and his gruff features softened. "No," he said. "It wouldn't have."

"Apparently I had far too much faith in you," Astaroth said.

Calladia smacked his thigh under the table. "Not a helpful response. We want to get them on our side."

"Your side?" Mariel looked between Astaroth and Calladia, hurt shining from her hazel eyes. "I thought you were on my side."

"I am," Calladia said. "Like I said, it's complicated."

"Uncomplicate it," Oz said. He put a protective arm around Mariel, and she leaned into him.

Calladia was torn between conflicting impulses. A longing for that kind of casual intimacy, the urge to scoot closer to Astaroth, and the guilt of having let down her friends. How could she have fallen so quickly for him? Seeing her friends' horror was a blunt reminder that the demon she'd been fighting so hard to save had committed crimes against them mere days before.

Haltingly, she gave an overview of events, from finding Astaroth bleeding on the street to Sandranella's concerns about the balance of power on the demon plane. "Moloch wants to eliminate half-demon hybrids," she said, "or at least strip them of rights." She looked at Astaroth, wondering if it was okay to share his secret.

He sighed. "Go on, then."

"Astaroth has always supported hybrid rights," Calladia said. "Among other reasons, he's half human."

That set off a flurry of questions. How and why, why he'd lied, what it meant. Astaroth was growing tenser with every moment, so Calladia did her best to answer succinctly. When she mentioned how Isobel had stolen his immortality to supplement her own life, she reached under the table to grip his hand. Astaroth looked surprised, then squeezed her fingers in return.

"So," Mariel said when the explanation was done. "Where we're at now is that Astaroth doesn't remember the last few hundred years, but he apparently knows something about Moloch that might defeat him."

"He was going to share what it was at the council meeting," Sandranella offered. "Baphomet intervened." She clenched the stem of her water goblet so tightly, Calladia wondered if it would shatter. "He must have been working with Moloch for some time. Why else would he have agreed to such an extreme punishment?"

"Today's murder attempt was a bit suspicious as well," Astaroth said.

"We need to remove him from the council. Him and Moloch both. But how do we do that without leverage?"

Themmie piped up from halfway down the table, where she was sipping on a sickeningly pink milkshake the waitress had sworn contained no blood but lots of sugar. "Make leverage."

"That's why we're trying to recover my memory," Astaroth said. "Were you even listening?"

"Don't be a dick," Calladia said, smacking his arm.

He gave her a half smile. "But I do it so well."

Themmie stuck out her now-bright pink tongue. "You aren't thinking big enough. So maybe Astaroth has some kind of leverage on Moloch. Cool. But he can't remember it, and Moloch's already making moves, so we need to expand our approach."

"Our approach?" Mariel asked, looking askance at the pixie. "Are you suddenly on Astaroth's side, too?"

"No, I'm on the side of justice." Themmie tucked her green-and-pink hair behind her ears, revealing a scattering of piercings.

"However you feel about Astaroth, there are countless other hybrids who might be exiled, oppressed, or killed if Moloch gets his way. That's worth fighting for."

"Oh." Mariel frowned. "Good point."

"Moloch made a speech the other day," Sandranella said. "He went to a public square and declared our species has grown weak because we accommodate impure demons. He wants to close the borders and outlaw breeding with humans or other species."

"Boo," Lilith said around a mouthful of questionable meat, which she'd ordered along with the werewolves—other than Ben, who was picking at a wilted-looking salad. Blood trickled down her chin. "That's no fun."

"He and Tirana have been planting hateful posters around town," Sandranella continued. "There was a counterprotest from a few hybrids, but it went poorly, and most were thrown in the dungeon for inciting violence."

Themmie's dark brown eyes widened. "Whoa, you have a dungeon?"

"What happened to a fair trial?" Mariel asked, looking distressed.

"Being more level-headed, we don't have as many . . . incidents . . . as humans do," Sandranella replied. "If an incident is serious enough to require imprisonment, the high council normally presides over a trial." Sandranella winced. "Moloch wants to skip that though. He's advocating for banishment or execution of all hybrids."

Mariel gasped. "That's awful!"

Themmie slurped noisily on her milkshake. How the pixie could consume so much sugar every day was a mystery, but then again, Calladia didn't have wings to power. "So," Themmie said. "We have a wannabe dictator and his violent stooge spreading propaganda and imprisoning the opposition, with plans to kill them. The small group of demons who rule the plane are split between conservatives and liberals, but without Astaroth, they're leaning conservative, especially since Baphomet is apparently in cahoots with Moloch."

"Correct," Sandranella said.

Themmie waved her milkshake wildly enough to slop some on the table. "Astaroth needs to rejoin the high council, but he'll need to eliminate Moloch first. He theoretically knows how to but has an inconvenient case of amnesia. The plan so far seems to be spinning our wheels while waiting for his memory to return."

"There's been more of a plan than that," Calladia protested. "We went to Isobel to see if she could help."

"Sure," Themmie said, "but the goal was all about Astaroth, right? Restore his immortality, heal his brain, get the memories back, defeat Moloch, everyone's happy. Badda bing, badda boom."

"Well . . . yes."

Themmie shook her head. "Dumb plan."

"With all due indifference," Sandranella said, "you don't know what you're talking about."

Lilith shushed her. "Let the colorful bug speak. I want to hear." She'd swapped seats with Sandranella and now sat next to Kai, who held a forkful of mystery meat to her lips. When Lilith snapped up the meat faster than a cobra, Kai flinched, then beamed, looking besotted.

Themmie practically radiated sunshine with her vibrant hair and frilly yellow dress. She didn't look like a master tactician, but Calladia had witnessed her rise as a social media influencer and knew how competent and whip-smart the pixie was.

"A cause needs a movement," Themmie said. "It isn't enough to swap Moloch out and sub Astaroth in—there's still a fundamental issue to be solved. Namely, hybrid rights. You need to sway the minds of the people, build support from the ground up. Otherwise this issue will keep cropping up."

"I agree," Calladia said. She looked at Astaroth. "Remember

what I told you? Maybe hybrids aren't just victims. Maybe they can be warriors."

Themmie snapped her fingers. "Exactly. So we spread word on social media—wait, do demons have social media?"

"Yes," Oz confirmed. "Or so I hear. I never wasted my time on such puerile activities."

Mariel practically had hearts in her eyes. "That's the curmudgeon I know and love."

Oz returned her adoring look. "As much as I love you, my *velina*."

"So," Themmie continued, "we start a social media campaign." She pulled out her phone, and her fingers danced over the screen. "I'll set up a private server for logistics and start recruiting any hybrids I find. We'll arrange some protests, maybe a march. Ooh, T-shirts!"

"And then what?" Astaroth asked. "Those protestors get thrown in prison, too? I'm sure the matching T-shirts will make up for it."

Calladia elbowed him in the ribs for the sarcasm.

"Not if there are enough of them," Themmie said, undeterred. "And not if we can figure out a decent defensive strategy."

"If that means fighting, count the pack in," Kai said. The other wolves cheered and pounded their fists on the table.

"I can help with magical defense," Mariel said. "I've always wanted to see the demon plane anyway."

Oz's brow furrowed. "It will be dangerous."

She pecked his cheek. "That's why you'll be with me to scare everyone off with your big, frowny face."

"We also need high-profile allies." Themmie looked at the two demonesses across the table. "If you would be willing to denounce Moloch's bigotry and voice support of the hybrid community, it will sway some people."

"Sounds chaotic," Lilith said. "Fun!" She pulled a bone out of her hair and started gnawing on it.

"It will be complicated politically," Sandranella said, drumming her fingers against the table. "The high council has always presented a united front. Publicly feuding with Moloch goes against precedence."

"So because Moloch got his hateful message out first, he gets to be the only one speaking up?" Calladia asked. "If you don't oppose him, you're complicit in what he does."

Sandranella pursed her lips. "True, but tradition . . ."

"Fuck tradition," Astaroth said suddenly. "Calladia's right. The demon plane has grown stagnant. We have a chance to change things."

"If only you hadn't conveniently forgotten your leverage over Moloch," Oz said nastily. "Or is that part of your game? Fake amnesia, stir up unrest, then seize power once other people have taken care of him for you?"

"Hey!" Calladia straightened in her chair. "That's not fair."

"How would you know?" Oz asked. "I was mentored by him for centuries. The Astaroth I know is cold, calculating, and willing to do anything for advancement."

Lilith beamed at Astaroth. "That's my boy."

Rather than looking pleased at his mother's praise, Astaroth flinched.

"He's not like that anymore," Calladia said.

Oz scoffed. "He's manipulating you, Calladia. Why can't you see that?"

"I'm not manipulating her." Astaroth's fists were clenched on the table, and he'd still barely made eye contact with Oz. "And whatever I've done in the past doesn't matter right now."

"It matters to me!" Oz roared, shooting to his feet. "You trained me to suppress any soft emotions. You taught me how to torture, manipulate, and take advantage of humans. Now you claim to have suddenly changed?"

"I don't expect you to understand."

"I don't expect anyone to understand," Oz replied. "Because this amnesia scheme is obviously bullshit."

"Oz," Mariel said softly, touching his arm.

He looked down at her hand. A muscle in his jaw ticked. "It isn't right," he told her. "He can't come back acting like some hero."

"I'm not a hero." Astaroth looked solemn and sad; even his shoulders were drooping. "I don't remember what I did to you," he said, his eyes fixing on Oz at last, "and I don't expect you to forgive me, but if nothing else, think of this as a way to make amends. I could have come out as half human centuries ago, helped codify hybrid rights into law, but I didn't because I was afraid to lose power. Now an entire group of people like me are in danger." His lips twisted bitterly. "Hate me all you want. I'm still going to fight for this."

Calladia's chest ached for him. She squeezed his hand, wishing she could lend him strength.

Oz, Mariel, and Themmie clearly had no idea what to make of that. "He does seem a bit different," Themmie said at last. "I mean, not that I saw much of him before Calladia punched him over a mountain."

Mariel lightly brushed Oz's forearm. "Sweetheart, I'm going to suggest something that you may think is a terrible idea."

Oz looked down at her warily. "What?"

"I think the two of you should talk."

"We are talking," Oz said.

Mariel shook her head. "Not like this. Alone. Go hash some things out while we make plans for Themmie's protest."

"I don't want to talk to him."

"That hasn't stopped you from shouting at me so far, has it?"

Astaroth asked. Calladia lightly kicked him, and Astaroth exhaled and held up his hands. "All right, all right. We can talk."

Oz glowered at Astaroth. "I don't like this." He took another look at Mariel's pleading hazel eyes, then sighed. "Fine. Let's go outside."

TWENTY-NINE

THEY EMERGED FROM NECRONOMNOMNOMS INTO THE SUN-shine. Once Astaroth's eyes had adjusted, he couldn't stop staring at Ozroth. It was like viewing a sculpture or a painting that reminded you of someone you'd once known, but the details were lost to time, leaving only an echo of resemblance.

Ozroth was taller and broader than Astaroth, with craggy features. His skin was tawny gold and his wavy hair was as black as his horns. A tattoo wreathed his left bicep, runes spelling out his duty as a soul bargainer.

Ozroth noticed the direction of his look. "You had this tattoo inked on me when I was a child," he said. "Remember?"

"No."

"I'm going to get it removed."

"All right." When Ozroth kept staring at him, Astaroth fumbled for something more to say. "Do you want recommendations for tattoo artists?"

"No, I don't want recommendations." Ozroth jammed a hand in his hair and tugged in a gesture Astaroth was startled to realize echoed one of his own tics when frustrated. "You're supposed to threaten me for removing it," he said. "Tell me bargaining is my duty, that I'm weak and a failure to my species for quitting. That I've let a mortal poison my mind, and my emotions are embarrassing."

Astaroth winced. Ozroth spoke with the ingrained bitterness of someone who had been told those things many times. "I don't remember saying that, but I'm not going to say it again."

"Oh, please." Ozroth laughed bitterly. "You don't have to pretend to be some new, improved person. Clearly you've fooled Calladia, but you can't fool me."

Astaroth snorted. "Like anyone could fool Calladia. You should give her more credit."

Ozroth's irises were metallic gold, and when he cocked his head, it made Astaroth think of a bird of prey. Déjà vu spun his head, and for a moment he had a vision of a small boy with gold eyes and small black horns looking up at him trustingly.

"Damn," Astaroth said, rubbing his temples. It wasn't that his head hurt—Isobel had taken care of that—but he was becoming increasingly aware of the pressure of memories building up. It was like floating on dark water, unable to see the danger lurking beneath the surface but knowing it was there. He leaned against the wall for support.

Ozroth's face flickered from adult to young and back again. "What is it?" the demon asked, crossing his arms and scowling.

Across the street, a family was out for a walk. The father was a pixie, the mother human. One child had tiny pink wings, the other none, but they looked thrilled to be out together.

Astaroth imagined their lives as they grew older. Would the wingless child envy their sibling? Or would those minuscule wings be one more trait to love, the same as a mop of red hair or a crooked grin? Would the parents try to change or hide those half-breed traits, or would they embrace them?

Embrace them, he decided, considering their bright smiles. And those children would make it to adulthood feeling valuable just as they were, rather than feeling like they fell short of an impossible expectation.

Astaroth had done the opposite. He'd taken in a young child, then shaped that child to reflect the person Astaroth had secretly wished he could be: a pure-blood, ruthless demon, unafflicted by the doubts and fears of humans.

There was no such thing as a demon entirely unafflicted by doubt or fear though, or if there was, it would be someone like Moloch, whose worldview had become an exercise in sadism.

"When did I take you in?" Astaroth asked.

Ozroth's forehead furrowed. "Right after my father died during the French Revolution. I was six years old."

Astaroth winced. That was very young. And yes, bargainers were trained from youth—Lilith herself had trained him in secret on Earth until he'd grown old enough for her to realize he could pass as a full demon—but Astaroth knew his methods of teaching would have been far less cordial than his mother's. "And then?"

Ozroth settled against the wall beside him. His eyes tracked the family across the way, too. "You took me to your palace in the Obsidian Realm, where you raised me to adulthood."

Ozroth's rumbling voice tugged at a stray thread in Astaroth's brain. The Obsidian Realm was a barren, black wasteland below an extinct volcano. Astaroth closed his eyes, focusing on that thread of connection. "Tell me more."

He heard Ozroth's heavy sigh. "It was cold. Stone walls, stone floors. Only the basics required for survival and learning, because you said forming any kind of emotional connection to a person, place, or object would give my enemies a weapon to wield against me."

Astaroth's throat felt like it was being squeezed in a fist. It was similar to what Lilith had taught him. "Be cautious about your emotional connections," she'd said long ago. "They can be wielded against you."

She hadn't told him he wasn't allowed any connections though, had she? She'd taught him to conceal his human tendencies and limit emotional outbursts around others, but she'd never commanded him not to have them at all.

"Go on," he said.

"You trained me in bargainer magic, had me read demon and human histories, taught me swordplay and torture techniques."

At least that was standard for young bargainers, so Astaroth hadn't failed in that sense. An effective bargainer was a knowledgeable, well-rounded one.

"You told me the most important thing a bargainer could be was cold," Ozroth continued. "'Make your heart ice,' you said. 'No one will ever be able to hurt you.'"

Had Astaroth been right in that? In some sense, perhaps. But now he saw an ugly truth. "In doing so, *I* hurt you though. Didn't I?"

Ozroth didn't answer for so long that Astaroth opened his eyes to see if he was still there. Ozroth was staring at him, confusion stamped over his face.

"Well?" Astaroth pressed. "Don't hold back."

Ozroth swallowed. "Yes," he said. "You did."

The words cut into Astaroth's chest, sharp as a sword. He'd known the answer, of course. He'd just needed to hear it spoken from his victim's lips. "I'm sorry." The words scraped his throat raw.

Ozroth sucked in a harsh breath. "Don't lie."

"I mean it," Astaroth said. "I'm sorry. I don't remember doing those things, but I'm sure I did, and it was wrong." The words scraped less this time. He repeated them, marveling at their shape. "*I* was wrong."

A flood of memories surged into his mind all at once. Astaroth dropped to his knees, gripping his head.

A little boy with golden eyes and tiny nubs of horns was curled up on a pillow before a fireplace, weeping.

"He's crying," Astaroth said flatly.

"His father died." The speaker, a demoness with black hair and mahogany horns, looked exhausted. "And he's young. He doesn't understand."

Astaroth felt the web of potential around the boy, as surely as he knew the feel of his own magic or the golden glimmer of a mortal soul. This Ozroth could be a powerful bargainer with the right training. The demon plane needed bargainers more than ever; fewer were born with the talent each century, and occasionally some died in the course of duty. Ozroth's father, Trinitatis the Trickster, had been one of them.

Except Trinitatis hadn't died in the line of duty. He'd died on vacation to Earth, of all things, since he'd apparently failed to research what was happening in France before portaling straight into a revolution. An inconceivable, unforgivable error, since any decent bargainer studied the affairs of humans. Astaroth himself lived more than half-time on Earth in order to stay abreast of developments and learn how best to manipulate mortals.

That's not why, a tiny voice in his head said, but Astaroth shoved it down. Power, ambition, and intent; that was all that mattered.

Astaroth struggled every day to hold himself to the standards of a true demon. If he had been trained properly on the plane, rather than in secret on Earth, maybe he wouldn't have developed an affinity for humans. Maybe his hidden weakness would never have had the chance to burrow into his brain, digging roots so deep he was still trying to get them out centuries later.

Ozroth could be a hero to the species. He could be the perfect demon Astaroth wasn't.

Resolved, Astaroth nodded. "I'll train him myself. Starting today."

Someone was shaking his shoulder. "What's wrong with you?"

Astaroth blinked, and the world returned. A cool November day, a charming small-town street, and a half-pixie, half-human

family now watching him with alarm. Beside him was the grown—
and then some—version of the child Astaroth had taken from his
mother and ruthlessly shaped to become the perfect weapon.

To Astaroth's surprise, his eyes were damp. "I remembered,"
he said. "That first day, when I took you in. I remembered."

Ozroth stiffened. Pain flashed across his expression. "And my
mother?" he asked, voice rough. "You remember her, too?"

Ozroth's mother had handed him over, her grief assuaged by
the knowledge that with Astaroth's mentorship, her son's future
would be bright. Bargainers were always taken young, after all,
and she would have been preparing herself for that separation
ever since she'd decided to have a child with a bargainer. It was an
honor to make such a sacrifice for the species. And if Ozroth had
been a bit too young for training, and if it had been a difficult time
in the boy's development to do so, Astaroth hadn't cared.

Astaroth had never allowed himself to feel grief. If he never
felt it, he didn't have to understand it or empathize with those who
did. "I remember," he said through a tight throat. "Elwenna was
her name."

"Elwenna," Ozroth breathed. "I'd forgotten." His eyes widened
with obvious panic. "Wait, you said it *was* her name. Is she dead?"

Astaroth's brain had filled up with other memories after that
first flashback. He remembered training Ozroth, from logic puz-
zles to emotional denial to physical tests of endurance. He remembered bringing the boy along on his missions, pleased when Ozroth
asked the right questions or suggested subtle shifts in wording to
make a bargain more advantageous. He remembered Ozroth's first
soul bargain, and how proud he'd been to see years of labor bear
fruit.

Astaroth's labor, that was. Because Ozroth had been the answer
to Astaroth's self-doubt, and to see the younger demon succeed
was to know his own success. It had never been about Ozroth at all.

Taken all at once, the memories painted a damning picture.

Astaroth had been a selfish, sometimes cruel mentor so focused on ambition that he'd failed to give his protégé space to be a child, or even his own person. Ozroth had been an extension of Astaroth, like his sword: a weapon to be wielded to ensure the demon plane thrived, and Astaroth's reputation with it.

There was something he didn't remember though, and it wasn't because of the amnesia. This would damn him even more, but it would be cowardly to hide behind evasions or half-truths.

"I don't know if she's dead," he admitted. "Maybe. After you became my ward, I . . ." He broke off, swallowing past the lump in his throat. "I forgot about her. She was no longer relevant to my plans."

Ozroth's nostrils flared, and his fists clenched like he was imagining pummeling Astaroth.

Well, it wasn't the worst olive branch to extend. "You can hit me," Astaroth said, a feeble offer at letting Ozroth get out some frustration, if not undoing the damage Astaroth had wrought. "If you like."

In response, Ozroth gripped Astaroth's hand and pulled, helping him stand upright. Then he punched Astaroth in the face.

"Ow," Astaroth said, cupping his jaw. Did the bloke have bowling balls for fists? At least he'd apparently taught Ozroth well. "Feel better?"

Ozroth scowled. "No."

Well, atonement couldn't be that easy, or therapists would have long ago traded the chaise longue for the boxing ring. He moved his jaw from side to side, then traced his tongue over his teeth, checking for damage. The copper tang of blood met his tongue, and a hot throb had started beneath skin and bone, but otherwise he was intact. "Want to do it again?" he asked.

Ozroth considered the question, then nodded. "Yes."

He punched Astaroth in the gut.

The breath wheezed out of Astaroth as he bent over. "Bloody hell," he gasped, bracing his hands on his knees. "That was a good one." He breathed deeply, then coughed. Lucifer, he hoped Ozroth's anger ran out soon, or he would end up more tenderized than a decent steak. "Where next? Though I should remind you I'm mortal at the moment, and while a beating is fine and justified, I don't consent to being murdered."

"I don't understand you," Ozroth said. When Astaroth looked up, he saw the larger demon glowering at him with his hands on his hips. Some variant of brooding or scowling seemed to be his default expression when he wasn't going starry-eyed over Mariel Spark, but this glare held a substantial amount of confusion. "Even a month ago you would have had my hide for defying you in any way."

"Hopefully not literally," Astaroth said, wincing as he straightened. "If my degeneracy has extended to skinning people, it's worse than I feared."

"No, not literally."

What a relief. "I'm recovered enough to continue," Astaroth said, bracing his feet and squaring his shoulders. "Punch away."

Ozroth's lips parted. "You really are different, aren't you?"

It was a strange notion, that Astaroth could be a wholly different person without his memories. Maybe identity was just a story people told themselves. When Astaroth's past had been stripped away, it had put an abrupt end to the narrative he'd told himself for centuries, and a new story had begun.

Was Astaroth truly different? No and yes, in the way all things were after enough time had passed. When the plank of a ship rotted and was replaced by fresh wood, that ship might bear the same name, but its composition had shifted.

Astaroth's internal composition had shifted drastically over the past few days. He bore the same name, carried the same legacy, but losing his memories had allowed a rotting board to be swapped out for something better. Something stronger.

"Yes," he said. "I've changed."

"Huh." Ozroth ran his hand through his hair again, tugging at the roots of the dark, wavy strands. He shifted from foot to foot. "Well," he said after a long pause. "What now?"

Astaroth had been bracing himself for anything from a punch to fresh accusations of being a manipulative, lying monster. He blinked. "What do you mean, what now?"

Ozroth gestured between them. "The talking. Is it over yet?"

Astaroth resisted the urge to laugh. Whatever Mariel had expected from their conversation, it probably wasn't this. "Do you want it to be over?"

"I don't know."

Astaroth didn't know either. This was deuced awkward, and guilt still churned in his gut over how he'd trained Ozroth, but it also felt good. Like a broken bone had been set back in place.

Your memories will return when you're ready to seize the life you want. The moment he'd apologized to Ozroth, he'd regained that segment of memory.

His course was clear. There would be no going back to who he had been.

"I suspect I'll be apologizing to you for a long time," Astaroth said. "Not that you've got to accept it, or even care. And I promise to help find out about your mother, if you let me." He hesitated, then asked a final question. "Are you happy here?"

Ozroth looked toward the door of the restaurant, and his expression softened. "Yes, I am."

"Even losing your immortality?" Astaroth pressed.

"Especially losing my immortality." Ozroth's mouth curved in a small smile. "My life may be shorter, but it's so much brighter. Why would I want to go back to what I was before?"

Why, indeed? With fresh Earth air in Astaroth's nostrils and laughter echoing from some raucous group nearby, it was tempting to remain. To squeeze as much brightness as he could from this colorful world.

Ozroth had never wanted a career in politics though. He hadn't been born to it the way Astaroth had. The demon plane was already short a bargainer in Ozroth; if Astaroth never returned, they'd be short another bargainer and a powerful voice for change.

No, Astaroth needed to return to power, and he needed his immortality to do it. Just because a new story had started didn't mean his responsibilities had ended.

There wasn't room for loving a mortal in that story.

Human emotions couldn't be reshaped so easily though. Astaroth loved Calladia, and he would keep loving her for as long as he could.

And if his heart ached at the thought of their inevitable separation?

Well, as Elwenna had known when she'd given her child up, sacrifices had to be made for the species.

Time for Astaroth to make one.

THIRTY

CALLADIA EYED THE DOOR NERVOUSLY. WITH LOGISTICS FOR the upcoming Hybrid Rights Campaign hammered out, most of the group had dispersed, but Oz and Astaroth still weren't back.

"Don't worry," Themmie said as she drank her third milkshake. Her wings twitched, and she was practically quivering from sugar intake. "If they'd killed each other, we would have heard screaming by now."

"How comforting."

"Unless the kill was quick. Oz could have gutted him and disposed of the body before anyone noticed."

"Hey," Calladia said, offended on Astaroth's behalf. "Why do you assume Oz would win?"

Mariel, Ben, and Themmie gave her matching skeptical looks.

The werewolves had decamped for a rugby game, and the demonesses had returned to their home plane to set plans in motion, so only the four friends were left at NecroNomNomNoms. It felt nice to be with them, though Calladia still felt awkward about the whole sleeping-with-the-enemy thing. Not that she'd outright admitted to sleeping with the demon, but Mariel had given her a series of knowing and judgmental looks that said she knew what Calladia had been up to.

"Oh, come on," Calladia said, leaning into the argument to cover up her worry. "Astaroth would totally win in a fight. He's more experienced than Oz."

"And at least forty pounds lighter," Ben said.

"He's an accomplished swordsman."

"Yeah?" Themmie asked. "Where's his sword?"

"He's very good with a stick, too."

"Oh, is that what you're calling it?" Mariel asked. "Has he been bludgeoning you with his stick frequently?"

Busted. Calladia's cheeks grew hot. "None of your business."

"That is exactly my business," Mariel said. "I'm your best friend, and the last I knew, you hated Astaroth's guts. Now you're hooking up with him?"

Themmie slurped loudly. "Mmmm," she said. "This is delicious."

Bless Themmie for trying to distract from the awkward conversation. Calladia shot her a grateful look.

"Maybe I'll get one, too," Ben said, looking warily between the three women. The introverted werewolf had been helpful in strategizing an approach for their campaign, but it was clear the emotional undercurrents at the table made him uncomfortable.

"Not the milkshake," Themmie said. "Well, the milkshake is good, too, if a little savory. I mean this role reversal." She brought her fingers to her lips for a chef's kiss gesture. "Delectable."

Curse Themmie for being a drama-mongering agent of chaos. Calladia scowled at her.

"What do you mean a role reversal?" Ben asked.

Calladia braced herself. She should have known she wouldn't get away without, as Astaroth would say, getting the absolute piss taken out of her. Mariel was a forgiving type, but her raised brows and pursed lips told Calladia she was going to make her squirm first.

"Well," Themmie said with gleeful vindictiveness, "Calladia here was adamantly anti-Oz when he first showed up. I seem to recall a late night at the Centaur Cafe when we had a heated discussion about Mariel hooking up with him."

Mariel snapped her fingers. "Now that you mention it, I remember that night, too."

Calladia groaned and thumped her forehead against the table.

"Calladia was appalled," Themmie explained to Ben. "Kissing a demon! Just imagine it!"

"I'd rather not," Ben said.

Themmie was just getting started. "Calladia was practically clutching her pearls. How could Mariel want to bump uglies with someone who wanted to steal her soul?"

"The horror!" Mariel echoed.

"Our dear Calladia would never do such a thing herself, right? And definitely not with the demon who *actually* wanted to steal Mariel's soul. No, sir, she's far too discerning for that."

Calladia glared at her friends. "Are you done mocking me?"

"Let me think," Mariel said, tapping her chin. "No."

Themmie cackled. "You brought this on yourself, Calladia. If you expect us to give you grace for bagging and tagging that jackass, you need to let us roast you first."

"Okay, fine," Calladia grumbled. "But I will have you know I never would have done any bagging, much less tagging, if he wasn't different."

"You really believe that?" Mariel leaned in, expression turning serious. "You honestly believe his amnesia is real and he's a better person now?"

It sounded ludicrous. Astaroth of the Nine, legendary demon bargainer, magically transformed into a better person by amnesia? Calladia ought to scoff at the very thought. She *had* scoffed when

Mariel had claimed Oz was genuine and really cared for her. As experience had taught her, some people were liars who would say and do anything to get power over a partner, then gradually chip away at that partner's independence and self-worth.

Calladia had always been a creature of instinct. After Sam, she'd stopped trusting her heart, but it was still beating, and it insisted that Astaroth truly had changed. Sure, it had been alarming when Isobel had proposed killing mortals to extend Astaroth's life span, but he'd promised they'd find another way.

Was it irrational? Maybe. But she believed him.

"Yes," she said, looking Mariel in the eye. "I do."

Mariel bit her lip. Then she held out her hand, pinkie up. "Pinkie swear?"

"What is this, grade school?" Ben asked, nudging his gold-frame glasses up his nose.

"Shhh," Themmie said, whacking him on the shoulder. "The pinkie swear is a sacred pact."

"If you say so . . ." Ben had the baffled, nervous expression of a man introduced to space aliens and trying to respect their customs.

Growing up, Calladia and Mariel had played pranks, teased, and sometimes lied to each other, as all children did. Coupled with unpredictable mothers, they'd realized they needed to implement a foolproof system of trust with each other whenever absolute honesty was required. Mariel had been skeeved out by the idea of a blood pact, so they'd settled on the tried-and-true method of the pinkie swear. The tradition had lasted to adulthood.

Calladia extended her hand and looped her pinkie finger around Mariel's. "I pinkie swear I believe Astaroth has truly changed after getting amnesia and that he's much nicer and not nearly as ruthless or murdery anymore. I pinkie swear that I think his feelings for me are genuine. I also pinkie swear that if I find out he's been lying to me, I will kick his ass so hard he'll cough it up."

They shook once, then released hands.

"Pinkie swear witnessed!" Themmie crowed.

"Weird women," Ben said.

Mariel set her hands on the table and leaned in. "In that case," she said, eyes gleaming with interest. "I need all the details."

"Well, he really is good with a stick," Calladia said. "Literally. He fought off Kai's pack."

"Avram told me that," Ben said. "I still can't believe you got in a fight with my cousin."

"We got in a fight with each other," Calladia said. "Very consensual. And speaking of consensual, about Astaroth's metaphorical stick . . ."

She broke off as the door swung open, letting afternoon light into the restaurant. Two familiar horned silhouettes appeared.

"Oz!" Mariel shot to her feet and hurried over. "Everything okay?"

Calladia stood, too. After the door closed, it took her eyes a moment to adjust, and then warmth flooded her chest at the sight of Astaroth, whole and seemingly unharmed.

Then she noticed the bruising on his jaw. "What happened?" she asked, jogging over. She turned his face in her hands, inspecting the mark. Thankfully, she still had half a restorative potion left after healing the cut on her head from Tirana's whip.

"Ozroth hit me," he said.

Mariel gasped. "Oz, you were supposed to talk, not beat him up."

"We did talk," Oz said. "After I beat him up."

"I had it coming," Astaroth pointed out. The two demons shared a look, then a nod of acknowledgment.

Reconciled, then, or at least on the way. Calladia felt a massive surge of relief, not just for her friendship with Mariel, but for Astaroth and Oz. Astaroth had basically raised Oz, and when a relationship like that turned toxic, it was almost impossible to correct course.

Her phone seemed to burn a hole in her pocket. After calling multiple times the previous night, her own mother had gone quiet. It wouldn't last though. And Calladia was beginning to accept that, unlike Astaroth and Oz, there might not be a way back for her and her mother.

She forced a smile. "I'm sure he did have it coming," she said, patting Astaroth's cheek. "But I'm glad you didn't permanently maim him."

"Yeah, she needs all his parts in working order," Themmie called out.

Mariel started snickering, and Calladia rolled her eyes. "We're meeting in the demon plane tomorrow, right?"

"Right," Themmie said. "I'm making protest signs tonight."

"Then I'm going to say goodbye for now." Calladia winked at Mariel. "If it's our last night on Earth, I want to take my time appreciating all of Astaroth's parts before Moloch chops them off."

Oz nearly choked. Mariel and Themmie collapsed into hysterical giggles. Ben eyed the door longingly.

And Astaroth? He gave her a wicked smile and palmed her ass. "Then hurry up and start appreciating, my warrior queen."

◆　◆　◆

CALLADIA AND ASTAROTH STAYED IN THE SAME TREEHOUSE from before, this time with Tansy's cawed assurance that the griffin would not allow any visitors. Candles flickered in the windowsills, champagne was chilling in a bucket, and claw-punctured rose petals had been sprinkled over the bed.

"Seems a tad cliché," Astaroth said, eyeing the setup.

Calladia rolled her eyes. "Of course you have a pretentious opinion."

"What's going to happen to those petals? They'll be crushed or end up in my unmentionables. It's impractical."

"If you want me to stuff them up your ass, just say so." Calladia uncorked the champagne and sniffed appreciatively at the vapor wafting out.

"When I ask you to stuff something up my ass," Astaroth said, "it will not be flower petals." He held the flutes out so Calladia could pour.

"I've always wondered what pegging someone would be like," she mused. The guys she'd slept with had *not* been interested in letting her peg them, though they'd had no qualms about asking her for anal.

"We can try it sometime."

She laughed, pleasantly surprised. "You mean it?"

Astaroth lifted his glass and grinned. "Calladia, I am over six hundred years old. I have been there, done that with most carnal activities, and if I haven't done something already, I'd probably like to try it out."

"Fascinating." Calladia would have to make a list of possible carnal activities. She took a gulp of champagne, and the flavor burst on her tongue, crisp, bready, and faintly fruity. She'd sampled enough champagne at political events to recognize it was a quality vintage.

"What, no toast?" Astaroth asked. "Poor form, Calladia."

"Good point." She raised the flute. "What should we toast to? A successful protest tomorrow? The imminent recovery of your memory?" As soon as she said the latter, she regretted it. Yes, he might have some secret piece of information to defeat Moloch hidden away in that devious brain, but she was feeling optimistic about the group's plan. What if, when the old Astaroth merged with this new version, he went straight back to his old ways? Would he decide sacrificing humans on the altar of his immortality was worth it, after all?

Astaroth seemed oblivious to her inner debate. He was relaxed and smiling, looking utterly dashing in a crisp gray button-up and charcoal slacks he'd sourced at a local store. Candlelight flickered off his obsidian-smooth horns and played over the sharp contours of his face. The light loved him, as much as she was beginning to—

"I'd rather toast to you," he said. "A toast to Calladia Cunnington, as fair as she is fierce. Long may she terrorize werewolves."

Calladia laughed, though her heart was racing from that thought she'd almost completed. *The light loved him* . . . "I can hardly toast to myself," she said.

"There's an obvious solution." Astaroth tipped his chin to a haughty angle. "You can toast to my beauty and brilliance."

"More like your vanity." She shook her head, still grinning. She smiled around him an unreasonable amount, truly. "I would like to propose a toast to Astaroth, soon to be of the Nine again, as beautiful as he is brilliant. Long may he fight for hybrid rights."

A lump formed in her throat. Hecate, she was beyond emotionally compromised for this ridiculous, charming, intense demon. If he could just stay mortal . . .

Astaroth's expression had softened. "Long may he fight," he repeated. "I like that."

They clinked glasses, maintaining eye contact as they swallowed. It felt like a ritual, as if the words of the toast were a spell and the champagne a potion, and together they were reshaping reality into a shared vision.

Astaroth set his flute down on an end table. "Calladia," he said softly, stepping toward her.

Calladia's phone started buzzing. "Ugh," she said, putting the glass down and heading for her backpack. "This had better not be Themmie calling to ask about a color scheme for her protest posters."

Her heart sank when she saw the name on the caller ID. She should have known this reckoning would come sooner rather than later. Her mother would never stay silent for long.

Astaroth took one look at her face and intuited the issue. "You don't have to talk to her."

"I have to at some point. She's like a terrier with a rat when she's upset about something. She doesn't let go until she's absolutely brutalized the topic."

This conversation was going to be especially ugly. Calladia butted heads with her mother frequently, but she hadn't missed a mandatory event before.

They'd been building to this for a long time though. Every snide comment about Calladia's career or appearance, every time Calladia had snapped back . . . it had been escalating. When Calladia had opposed her mother at a recent town hall discussing the construction project that would have harmed the forest, it had pushed their relationship troubles into the public eye. *I know you're selfish and don't want to let anyone else enjoy nice things*, Cynthia had said in front of everyone. It had felt like being slapped.

Maybe a better person would de-escalate to salvage the relationship, but Calladia wasn't built like that. And why should she be the one to cede ground?

Calladia Cunnington, as fair as she is fierce. She fixed the words in her mind, took a deep breath, and answered the phone. "Hello."

"Oh, so now you can bother to answer the phone when I call?" Her mother sounded seriously steamed.

"I was busy last night." Busy getting her proverbial socks knocked off by a sexy demon. She checked her smartwatch, wondering how long this talk was going to take. If they were facing Moloch tomorrow, she wanted to have those metaphorical socks completely obliterated by Astaroth.

"I'm sure you'll be pleased to know people have been asking why you didn't show up. Rumors have been swirling ever since your shameful display at the town hall."

"*My* shameful display?" Calladia asked, temper igniting. "You were the one backing corporate greed over the well-being of your constituents."

"Oh, please. Like you know a thing about politics."

Calladia let out a disbelieving laugh. "I've watched you manipulate and threaten your way to power for years. I'm pretty sure I understand politics." She was also sure she never, ever wanted to engage in them herself.

"I'm willing to overlook this misstep," Cynthia said, ignoring the jab, "so long as you modify your behavior going forward. An influential lobbyist is in town this weekend, and we're meeting at that new restaurant on Pine Street for dinner and drinks. His son will be there, and I expect you to be as well."

Calladia's instincts told her this was more than a mere meeting with a lobbyist and her mother had ulterior motives. "How old is this son?"

"Thirty-five," her mother said. "And looking to settle down."

Yep, ulterior motives. "Absolutely not."

Cynthia let out an exasperated sigh. "You haven't even met the man. He'd be perfect for you."

This ought to be rich. "How so?"

"He's wealthy, handsome, and works in finance. He has a house in Seattle and a condo in New York City, and he travels frequently for work."

"That sounds terrible," Calladia said. "Why would I want a husband who travels all the time?"

Next to her, Astaroth stiffened.

"A spouse who travels is the best thing an ambitious witch can have," Cynthia said. "Why do you think Bertrand and I get along so well? He has his life, I have mine."

An old, familiar hurt seized Calladia's heart. Her father had been absent for most of her life, jet-setting around the world as a consulting expert in the dismantling and selling of companies. If a company was in danger of going under, he was there to make sure the circling sharks got their teeth into it. She'd seen him on major holidays as a child, but since she'd come of age, he'd effectively vanished.

He wasn't worth hurting over, so Calladia shoved the pain down and focused on her other shitty parent. "I don't want your marriage," she said. "I want someone who loves me and wants to spend time with me."

Cynthia's laugh was ugly. "You already had that, and you threw it away out of selfishness."

Ice formed in Calladia's veins. "What are you talking about?"

She knew though. There was only one boyfriend Calladia had brought home to meet her family. Only one man she'd talked about marrying, only one her status-obsessed mother had approved of.

"I'm talking about Sam, of course," Cynthia said. "I still don't understand why you sabotaged that relationship. He was perfect."

"Perfectly awful," Calladia said.

"A rich, handsome, tenured professor. Yes, that sounds dreadful." Her mother's tone was beyond condescending. "You were turning your life around, dressing well, meeting important people . . . do you know how high you could have risen in society? But you couldn't bear dating anyone I approved of, could you? Just a spiteful little girl, spitting in my face every chance you get."

The words were meant to flay Calladia to the bone. Make her weep, make her apologize. Make her regret ever abandoning *perfect* Sam and her mother's dreams of a high-class, ambitious, equally *perfect* daughter.

Fuck perfect.

"You don't know a thing about our relationship," Calladia snapped. "Sam verbally and emotionally abused me."

She had hinted at it before but never admitted it outright to her mother. It felt equally good and terrible, like scratching at a scab to expose the tender skin beneath.

Maybe that had been the problem all along. Calladia's wounds from that first, disastrous love had never fully healed. She'd ignored the pain, instead shutting down the parts of her that were capable of love and vulnerability. And what did she have to show for that?

Anger problems, trust issues, and a relationship with her mother that had stagnated in its awfulness. She'd gotten stuck in self-destructive habits, never shaking off the weight of her trauma.

Astaroth's fingers curled around her free hand. The heat of his skin sank into her, melting the ice in her veins. She squeezed his hand hard, using it as an anchor.

His beautiful eyes, blue like the heart of a flame, met hers. In them she saw understanding and support.

Calladia would be strong. She would be fierce. It was long past time.

Her mother didn't respond right away. The gears in her android brain were probably ticking, calculating how to use this revelation to her own advantage. Because that's what it always was with Cynthia Cunnington, wasn't it? *Her* life. *Her* ambitions. *Her* advantage.

"I never heard Sam say a mean word to you," Cynthia finally said.

"You wouldn't, would you?" Calladia replied. "It happened at home."

"Are you sure he wasn't just advising you on how to improve yourself? Loving someone means trying to help them be the best version of themselves." Cynthia sighed. "But you've always mistreated anyone who wants to help you—I know that better than anyone."

The words hit like a lightning strike, illuminating decades of lies before splitting them apart. Calladia stood stock-still, letting the realization burn through her.

Sam had been an abuser. She'd left him.

Her mother was an abuser, too.

Calladia looked to Astaroth, drinking in the sympathy in his gaze. She clutched his fingers, drawing strength from them. She wasn't alone. And even if she was, the toxic relationship with her mother couldn't continue like this.

What she was about to do would hurt for a long time to come, she suspected . . . but it would also be a liberation. The best outcome for Calladia's heart and health. *Her* life, not her mother's. *Her* dreams. *Her* future.

Calladia was a fighter. This time she would fight not to cover up her pain, but to release it.

"Love does mean helping someone be the best version of themselves," she said. "It means supporting and uplifting them. It means even when you argue, you do it from a place of compassion." Her eyes pricked with tears. Rather than knuckle them away, she let them trickle down her cheeks. "That's not what Sam did," she continued, "and it isn't what you've been doing either. Both of you want a Calladia who doesn't exist."

"You could—"

"I'm still talking," Calladia said firmly. "I'm not going to meet that lobbyist's son. In fact, I won't be attending any more political events. I'm done trying to placate you. If you don't love me as I am now, you don't love me at all."

Cynthia made a shocked sound. "That's not fair. You have so much potential—"

"Stop!" Calladia was shouting now. "Loving my potential isn't the same as loving me. I'm done letting you tear me down. I suggest you get therapy to address your anger and your impossible expectations, but I'm not going to wait for that. We're done."

"Done?" Cynthia sounded confused. "What do you mean, done?"

"I'm not going to see or talk to you anymore." Calladia's throat ached, but she forced the words out. It was time. It was *past* time.

"I'm your daughter, not a pet project. And where you see a failure, I see someone fierce and bold. Someone worthy of being loved just as she is."

Astaroth raised her hand to his mouth and kissed it. His eyes were glistening, too, and in them she saw something equally terrifying and amazing.

Possibility.

Her mother was screeching about how cruel and unreasonable she was being, but Calladia was done being the family punching bag. "Don't contact me again unless it's an apology and a sincere promise to do better."

She hung up.

The phone vibrated immediately. Calladia put it on silent and tossed it aside.

She took a deep breath of pine- and cedar-scented air. "Well," she said into the silence. "That's done."

Astaroth's arms wrapped around her, and she squawked as he hauled her into a tight hug. He bent back, lifting her toes off the floor before setting her down again. "You," he said, "are magnificent."

She sniffled and buried her face in his hair, letting the soft strands soak up her tears. Her heart hurt, but she felt light enough to float away. A burden had been lifted from her shoulders, one she'd been carrying for so long, she hadn't realized how heavy it had gotten. "I can't believe I did that."

"I can. You're a warrior, Calladia."

"I am, aren't I?" Not a messy brawler or a reckless disaster or any of the other negative things she and others had said about her. A *warrior*.

An unbearably tender emotion welled in her breast. Calladia cupped Astaroth's cheeks and kissed him.

He tasted like fire and sin and freedom. Like deliverance.

Like hope.

His lips parted under hers, and he kissed her back with matching passion.

In trying to protect her heart, Calladia had instead created a prison for her true self. She let the final walls around her heart fall away and gave herself over wholly to this moment and this man, who, despite his flaws and his troubled history, had helped her find the key to her shackles.

Love wasn't trying to force someone to be who you thought they should be. It was loving them as they were while supporting them on their journey toward becoming their best self. Astaroth liked her temper and attitude. Calladia liked his snark and pretentiousness. And just as he'd supported her in taking this crucial step of cutting off her abusive mother, she would support him as he fought to bring change to the demon plane.

Maybe regaining his memories would turn him into a dick again. But if that happened, Calladia would be there to kick his ass and encourage his better impulses. It might end badly, but she was done being afraid.

She stripped his shirt off urgently, sending buttons flying. In response, he tugged her shirt and sports bra over her head. Then they were pressed chest to chest, hearts pounding in a fervent duet.

Calladia backed Astaroth toward the bed and shoved him down. He grinned as he scooted up the mattress, making room for her. He started undoing his slacks, but Calladia shook her head as she planted a knee on the bed and crawled between his legs. "Mine," she said, batting his hand aside.

"Yes, goddess," he said, reclining on his elbows. The muscles in his abdomen tightened with the curve of his spine, and Calladia's mouth watered. She ripped his pants off, then his underwear, sending them flying. Then she lowered her head to his crotch and wrapped her lips around his dick.

Astaroth shouted, and his hips bucked up, sending his shaft

deeper. Calladia opened wider, letting saliva pool in her mouth as she bobbed up and down. She used her fist on the base of his erection, pumping in time with her movements.

"Not yet," he gasped after a minute, pushing lightly on her forehead. "You're going to make me come."

She popped off his dick with a wicked grin, then licked her lips. "Already? You'd think your endurance would be higher after all these years."

"When it comes to you, all bets are off." He sat upright, abs rippling deliciously, then tossed her to her back and went for the waistband of her leggings. She was nude in seconds, and then he was returning the favor, mouth glued between her legs as he ate her out ravenously. He plunged two fingers into her and crooked them, dragging them over her inner wall in a sensuous rhythm that had her cursing and arching her back.

She gripped his horns, tugging him harder against her, and Astaroth moaned before redoubling his efforts. A third finger worked inside her, stretching her wide. Then he focused on her clit, sucking hard. The sensations were intense, just this side of uncomfortable—exactly how she liked it.

She came quickly, hips jerking as a jolt of pure ecstasy rocketed through her. When she was done twitching and gasping, Astaroth lifted his head and pulled his fingers out. He sucked them clean, then smirked at her. "Whose endurance is lacking now?"

She cackled, high off the feelings and the moment and *him*. "Get up here, you menace."

He crawled up her body, settling his hips between her spread thighs. Then he was kissing her, hard and hungry. "I'll never get enough of you," he said against her lips. "The sun could die and the stars could fall and the earth could rip itself apart, and none of that would matter, so long as you were in my arms."

It was a beautiful and intense sentiment. As Calladia did when faced with an overwhelming influx of feeling, she cracked a joke.

"Pussy good enough to overshadow the apocalypse? High praise, indeed."

"Not just that," he said, cupping her chin in one hand. "All of you. Your mind and heart and ferocious spirit. I've never met anyone like you."

How was that possible? "You've met a lot of people," she said, heart threatening to beat out of her chest.

"I know. That's what makes this so remarkable." He kissed her, soft at first, then with more pressure. She wrapped her arms around him, plunging one hand into his hair and gripping his ass with the other.

"Want you inside me," she whispered.

He hummed and nodded, still kissing her. But when she reached up to yank out a strand of hair to summon a condom, he pulled back. "Use mine," he said.

"What?"

"My hair," he said. "It isn't fair to use yours each time."

She'd never felt this mix of ardor and tenderness before. She nodded, then reached for a hair at the top of his head and plucked it. The strand was only a few inches long, but she could make it work. She briefly let go of his ass to tie a series of knots, then whispered the spell, and a condom plopped to the bed beside them.

"Somewhere, a pharmacist is confused about their dwindling condom supply." Astaroth put the condom on with neat, efficient movements. Another thing she liked about him—he didn't try to convince her not to use one. She had an IUD, too, but Calladia was paranoid about maintaining full bodily autonomy, and getting her exes to agree to condoms had been an ordeal.

How telling that an immortal demon with a deadly reputation valued consent more than the human men she'd been with.

"I take them from an RA's condom bowl at my old college," she said. "They're free for anyone who needs them."

"Ah, I was hoping you'd developed a larcenous streak. But trust you to summon condoms ethically."

She laughed. "Trying to corrupt me?"

"It's only fair I try in exchange for you redeeming me." Joking words, but she heard the serious edge beneath them.

She met his eyes. "We're a good influence on each other." Against all odds, combining their questionable impulses and combative natures had a net positive effect.

On them, at least. A certain werewolf pack might disagree.

"Long may it remain so." Astaroth kissed her lingeringly, then reached down to notch his cock in place. She was incredibly wet, and he slid in slowly but easily. When their hips were flush and he was seated as deep as he could go, Calladia let out a shuddering breath. She was stretched tight around him, full in a way that made her nerves spark.

Like the rest of him, his dick was almost too much to handle. Almost. Calladia had always liked to dance at a cliff's edge, and like every other risk she'd taken with him, this one paid off.

She rocked her hips. "Come on," she whispered. "Fuck me."

He dropped his mouth to her ear. "Make love to you," he corrected.

Before she could question that, he started moving, and all thoughts fled her head. He pumped into her with sure strokes, taking his time. His back flexed under her fingers, and when she trailed them down to his ass, every thrust turned the muscles there to iron.

She grew wetter, her body loosening to accommodate him. Soon she was desperate for more, harder, faster, but even as she sank her nails into his back, Astaroth maintained the same maddeningly moderate tempo. This was where his immortality became evident. His control was preternatural, and that steadiness allowed her to relax even more. This wouldn't be over before she was ready.

Calladia let go and let herself *feel*.

She mouthed at his neck, licking up the sheen of sweat, then bit down. He groaned and returned the favor, kissing down her jawline to her neck. His tongue pressed against her flickering pulse, and then his teeth seized the delicate skin there. The prick of pain mixed with the pleasure, intensifying it.

Calladia rocked her hips, trying to get him to speed up. When he didn't react, she bared her teeth. "Hurry up, damn you."

His laugh ghosted against her cheek. "Still so impatient."

Calladia bucked up hard enough to throw off his rhythm, then took advantage of his distraction to roll him over onto his back. She mounted him like a warrior queen and began riding him in an aggressive rhythm.

"That's how it's going to be?" he asked, voice gone guttural. His fingers dug imprints into her hips. "You want to fight me for it?"

"Mm-hmm." She raised her hands over her head, twining her fingers together as she snapped her hips.

Astaroth's eyes dropped to her breasts. "Gorgeous," he said, reaching up to squeeze them. He toyed with her nipples, then pinched hard enough to make her gasp and lose her rhythm.

Astaroth grabbed her hips and flipped her. "Two can play that game," he said as he drove back into her.

Calladia laughed and clawed at his shoulders. "Cheat."

"That's the secret to winning."

They rolled over and over, kissing and groping as they fought for supremacy. At one point they nearly toppled off the bed, saved only by Astaroth's quick reflexes and powerful arms. He dumped her onto her belly in the middle of the mattress, and before Calladia could turn over, he was on top of her, erection nudging between her thighs.

He bit down on the juncture between her neck and shoulder like a wolf pinning down his mate. "Stay," he growled against her skin, and a shudder raced down Calladia's spine. She nudged her ass up, silently begging.

Astaroth shifted until he was kneeling between her spread legs, then tucked a hand under her torso and lifted her onto hands and knees. The hot, slick head of his erection notched inside her, and then he slammed in hard and fast.

Calladia cried out. "More," she demanded when he stilled. "More!"

Astaroth gave her more. He gripped her hips and pumped into her from behind, striking impossibly deep each time. Every thrust threatened to knock her up the bed, so Calladia braced her hands against the mattress.

Astaroth gripped her hair and tugged her up until she had nothing to hold on to but him. She looped her fingers behind his neck, arching her spine.

"Mine," he said as he thrust up into her. "You're *mine*, Calladia."

"Same," she panted. She was just as possessive and bloody-minded as him, and as far as she was concerned, this demon belonged to her.

They set a rhythm together, hot and hard. The backs of her thighs pressed against the tops of his, and his chest flexed against her back. He kissed the side of her neck, and then his hand slid down her stomach and settled between her legs to strum her clit.

"Oh!" Calladia gasped. Each swirl of his fingers sent lighting strikes of pleasure through her. Her clit was the center of a gathering hurricane, and her inner muscles tightened in preparation for the storm.

Astaroth rubbed and rubbed, thrusting up in a rhythm that was making her see stars. "Are you going to come for me?" he asked against her neck.

"Yes," she panted.

"Good." His fingers pressed harder, and Calladia whimpered. She was so close, just a little more . . .

The orgasm crashed over her, fierce and fiery. She shouted as her pussy clenched in devastating, uncontrollable pulses, and heat raced over her skin. She bucked in his arms, shaking apart.

"That's it," he crooned in her ear. "Let go."

The pleasure swelled, then shivered into her extremities. Her fingers tingled, her toes cramped, and her vision briefly went dark.

When the orgasm ebbed, Calladia slumped back against Astaroth. He banded both arms around her torso and thrust up once, twice, then held, his strong body shaking as he let out a strangled groan.

He held her tightly, chest heaving. Then he toppled slowly to the side, taking her with him. "Lucifer save me," he gasped. "I'm a dead demon."

Calladia giggled. Her head was spinning, and she felt drunk or high or both. Astaroth's dick slipped out of her, but she made no effort to move. His body curved around her, two equal-sized spoons in a very happy drawer.

She closed her eyes and drifted, head blissfully empty. She felt cleansed, despite the sweat sticking them together. It was as if their passion had burned away everything nonessential. The world and its worries still waited, but right now, there was nothing in the universe but the two of them.

"Calladia Cunnington," Astaroth whispered as she drifted off, "you're my miracle."

THIRTY-ONE

WAKING UP WITH CALLADIA IN HIS ARMS WAS ASTAROTH'S new favorite thing. Of course, every moment with her brought a new favorite thing. The soft skin behind her ear, the groan she made when she was convinced she couldn't possibly orgasm again (only to discover she could), the discovery that she was ticklish, but though her ribs would elicit giggles, attacking her feet was risking death. She was a puzzle box, constantly revealing new secrets, and he hoarded them like a greedy dragon.

She was soft and relaxed, her face pressed against his pectoral and an arm and leg slung possessively over him. A wet patch on his skin under her lax mouth suggested she'd been drooling. He'd never found drool so delightful.

Maybe humans were on to something with this nightly sleeping thing. They weren't wasting time; they were optimizing cuddles.

The sun was peering through the gaps in the curtains though, and the day was going to be a busy one. He reluctantly called her name.

She lifted her head, bleary-eyed and adorably tousled. "Wha—?"

He wiped his thumb over her lower lip, collecting a trace of saliva. "Time to wake up, warrior queen."

His queen pouted, then dove back down, ramming her nose into his chest. "No," she told his armpit.

Astaroth jostled her. "Come on," he coaxed. "There are arses to be kicked and demons to defeat. You wouldn't want to miss a fight, would you?"

She was stubbornly silent. Right when he was about to consider extreme measures—feet tickling would certainly get her up, though Lucifer knew if his testicles would survive the endeavor—she let out a gusty sigh. "Fine."

He watched as she got out of bed and stretched, her body a long, elegant line. Her bikini tan lines were still fading from the summer, and it amused him that her bottom and breasts were paler than the rest of her. Giving in to temptation, he leaned over and lightly spanked her.

She yawned. "I'm up, I'm up. You don't have to whip me like a pony."

Now that was an intriguing idea. He wondered if there were any sex toy shops in Glimmer Falls. "Would you be interested in whipping sometime? Giving or receiving?" She would be a menace with a flogger, but he also liked the idea of tying her up and spanking her until her bum was rosy and she was begging him to shag her.

She rolled her eyes. "Let's revisit that after coffee."

She slouched off to the loo like W. B. Yeats's beast in search of Bethlehem. What a grump. Astaroth grinned as he got up and did his own stretching. Then he pulled out his phone and called Tansy for a delivery.

When Calladia emerged from her shower to see coffee and a breakfast sandwich waiting for her, she looked like she might cry. "You angel."

He nearly choked. "Not quite."

"You terrible, wonderful demon," she corrected, rushing for the caffeine.

After eating, Astaroth hit the bath area for his morning preparations. He'd stocked up on a few changes of clothes the previous day, and once he was clean, he laid options on the bed.

"Trouble deciding?" Calladia asked, rubbing her damp hair with a towel. She'd dressed in jeans and a yellow T-shirt that said *Fear My Fists* in a cursive script dotted with flowers.

"I need to send the right message."

"Pretty sure 'fully clothed' is enough of a message."

Astaroth shook his head. "This is my triumphant return from banishment, and I'm facing the high council, so I need to look powerful. But I'm also campaigning for hybrid rights, so I've got to look accessible to the public."

Calladia looked down at her shirt. "Should I have put more thought into this?"

"It's perfect," he said. "Jeans are more protective than leggings during a fight, and the shirt is an overt threat. Plus, the yellow is the exact shade of your house, which will tell Moloch you're out for vengeance."

"Wow." Calladia looked startled. "I didn't do it intentionally or anything."

"You have good instincts." Astaroth decided on black jeans and motorcycle boots and paired them with a long-sleeved red satin shirt that moved like liquid over his muscles. He accessorized with spiky silver rings—a more fashionable version of brass knuckles. He wished he had his cane sword to finish the look, but alas, he'd need to make do.

He turned to Calladia with his arms out. "What do you think?"

Her eyes trailed over him in what could only be termed a leer. "I think I'd like to get you back in bed."

His cock stirred. "An interesting proposition. Do we have time?"

Calladia checked her watch. "Themmie, Oz, and Mariel headed out an hour ago to start putting up signs, and Lilith and Sandranella have been stirring demons up for a protest march since yesterday. They ought to be gathering now, and we have forty minutes before you're supposed to make your appearance and lead the march to the high council chambers."

"I can work with that." Astaroth reached for the fly of his jeans.

A portal opened in the middle of the room, and Themmie tumbled through, wings smoking. "Ambush!" she screeched.

Calladia grabbed her water bottle and dumped it over the pixie, extinguishing the embers that had settled on Themmie's wings. "Are you all right?" Calladia asked.

Themmie shook her wings out, then inspected them over her shoulder. "Yep, superficial damage. They'll heal right up." Her cheek was smudged with soot, and embers had burned holes in her *Pixie Pride* T-shirt.

"What do you mean, an ambush?" Astaroth asked.

Ozroth stuck his head through the portal. "It means get over here," he shouted. "Moloch and his followers ambushed the protestors."

Fuck. If the protestors didn't get a chance to gain public attention or confront the high council, there was only one option. Fight Moloch and his allies. Finish this battle, once and for all.

Astaroth grabbed the fireplace poker and headed for the portal, Calladia by his side. "Ready?" she asked, yarn stretched between her fingers.

He nodded. "Let's do this."

◆　　◆　　◆

ON THE OTHER SIDE OF THE PORTAL, SCREAMS FILLED THE AIR. Smoke roiled over cobblestones and cast a veil over the torches lining the street. The sky ought to be the hazy purple-gray of daylight, but the heavy smoke made it seem like night.

The street was packed with demons, many of whom carried glittery neon signs with various slogans: HORNS OFF MY RIGHTS, HYBRIDS CAN BE HEROES, DIVERSITY = STRENGTH. Someone was screaming a chant. "Two, four, six, eight, Moloch, don't discriminate!" Astaroth saw many familiar faces, both hybrid and full-blood, and among the ones he didn't know, he spotted a variety of horn sizes, ear shapes, and other traits that indicated mixed heritage.

A fireball streaked past, narrowly missing a demon. It crashed into the side of a building, igniting the black-and-red vines climbing the stone wall. A demoness tossed a bucket of water on the flames, extinguishing them, and a new chant went up. "Two, four, six, eight, don't send us to a fiery fate!"

"That's got to be Themmie's doing," Calladia said from beside Astaroth. "She loves chants."

Astaroth took in the scene and recognized exactly what had happened. The protestors had gathered in a public square a block away—chosen because it was centrally located and had multiple access points—and then started the march early. Moloch had clearly been keeping tabs on the activity, because his troops had ambushed them on the narrowest stretch of the route—this cobbled street that connected the square to a major thoroughfare leading to council chambers.

Astaroth skirted the fray, scanning for enemies. Both ends of the street were blocked by a mix of heavily armed demons and stone gargoyles. A movement on a rooftop caught his attention, and he dodged just in time to avoid a boulder that had been flung by a demon's shoulder-mounted trebuchet. It hit a barrel next to him, exploding it in a spray of potent liquid. A splash hit Astaroth's cheek, reeking of alcohol.

A demon wearing a stained apron emerged from a nearby doorway. "My firewine!" he wailed. "Please, stop this fighting."

"Tell that to Moloch of the Nine," Astaroth shouted over the din, keeping an eye on the trebuchet demon. "This was a peaceful protest until he had his supporters attack."

"A protest against what?" The demon flinched when a protestor crashed into another barrel.

"Moloch wants to strip hybrids of rights. He wants to close the demon plane to outsiders and institute a dictatorship, returning us to the fundamentalist values of the Middle Ages."

"Oh. Not great." The demon looked between Astaroth and the rioting crowd. "But my wine . . ."

"Hang the wine," Astaroth snapped. "Your community is in danger."

The demon on the roof was winding up again, but before Astaroth could formulate a plan, Calladia scooped up a hand-sized rock from the curb bordering the street and threw it overhand. It hit the demon square between the eyes, and he toppled off the roof.

"Nice shot," Astaroth said.

"I knew I joined Little League for a reason," Calladia said.

A stocky demoness retrieved the portable trebuchet from the fallen demon and lifted it to her shoulder, and a hybrid with pointy ears and moss-green hair loaded a stone into it. Arming the protestors was a good start, but they couldn't win from a vulnerable position, and Moloch and his supporters were clearly willing to kill.

Moloch himself wasn't anywhere in sight, and the fireballs whizzing past were on the small side, so Astaroth suspected they were being launched by lesser warriors. It made sense. If the attack succeeded, Moloch could claim credit. If it didn't, he could truthfully state he was never there.

A fireball hit a nearby pixie-demon hybrid on the arm, and she screamed as her sleeve caught fire. Her small wings fluttered but couldn't get her off the ground. Thankfully, someone doused her with water, but this had to stop immediately. Demonic fireballs were superheated, and while a direct hit wouldn't kill a full-blooded demon, mortal hybrids might die.

"Can you cast a spell?" Astaroth asked Calladia. "Something to break through the front lines so we can get out of this death trap?"

She held up a string. "On it."

Astaroth positioned himself in front of her as she wove the spell. He spotted Ozroth smashing a demon's face into a wall while Themmie dropped rocks on another's head. Mariel stood in the shadows near Ozroth, lips moving as her hands inscribed elegant arcs in the air. Vines peeled away from a nearby building, shot toward one of the demons blocking the exit, and picked him up before flinging him over the rooftops. The werewolf pack was there, too, howling as they led an assault against the guards.

Calladia recited a spell, and three stone gargoyles were launched into the air, their screams like grinding gravel. With their heavy bodies no longer in the way, protestors sprinted toward the remaining demons blocking the exit. As the crowd surged, the danger of being trampled underfoot grew.

"Can you levitate me?" Astaroth asked Calladia.

More gargoyles at the rear went sailing. Calladia threw that knotted string aside, then pulled out another. "How high?"

"Speech-making high."

The firewine brewer was cowering behind a barrel. At that, he popped his head out. "Who are you anyway?"

Astaroth's smile was grim. "You're about to find out."

The ground shifted under him, and he staggered before an invisible hand righted him. No, not the ground—Calladia's spell. Soon he was floating above the crowd. "I am Astaroth of the Nine," Astaroth shouted, "and I am here to fight for the rights of all demons."

Faces turned toward him, followed by exclamations.

"Didn't that bloke get booted off the council?"

"I thought he was dead."

"Is he *flying*?"

"Moloch of the Nine plans to round up all hybrids," Astaroth continued, flourishing the fireplace poker. "He won't be satisfied with imprisoning them. As you see here, he's willing to kill them."

Another fireball punctuated the sentence, shooting toward Astaroth's face before abruptly veering away. When he looked down, he saw Mariel standing beside Calladia, hands outstretched and a determined look on her face. The witches were on defense.

"He will not keep us down," Astaroth said. "We will not lay down our lives or our cause here. We will take this fight straight to the steps of the high council!"

A cheer went up. At that moment, the front lines of protestors finally broke through the ranks of Moloch's supporters.

Astaroth looked at Calladia. "You can let me down now."

Calladia shook her head. "This is a heck of an aesthetic, Astaroth. We're floating your badass self to council chambers."

Well, if it was an *aesthetic* . . . Astaroth nodded and straightened his posture, extending his arms. "Vocal amplification?" he asked.

"On it," Mariel said. "Almost zero percent chance of accidentally exploding you."

Astaroth wasn't going to think about that too closely. He was risking death already; if Mariel blew him up, at least it would be quick and dramatic, and everyone loved a martyr.

He cleared his throat, twitching when the sound echoed. Explosion avoided, thankfully. "Demons," he called, Mariel's spell amplifying the words as if he were shouting into a megaphone. "Join us! Fight for the rights of every demon, regardless of heritage!"

Calladia was moving him through the air above the surging crowd, keeping him apace of the protestors. Heads popped out from nearby windows, their faces turned to him.

"Moloch wants to destroy hybrids," he continued. "After that, he will come for those with liberal leanings. He won't stop until this is a conservative dictatorship. We can stop him today. We *must* stop him."

"Yeah!" someone shouted.

They reached the main thoroughfare, where more bystanders had begun to gather, gawking at the proceedings.

"I am Astaroth of the Nine," he declared, "and I am here to end Moloch's tyranny."

"Why should we believe you?" someone called out. "You've been on the council as long as him."

Astaroth took a deep breath. There was no going back. "I have hidden the truth for far too long out of fear of losing my position," he said. "I regret that. Now I declare, with pride and a commitment to fight for our rights, that I am a human-demon hybrid."

Bystanders and protestors burst into a frenzy of shouts and cheers. He could see the gossip spreading into the distance, surging through the crowd like a tidal wave.

He looked down at Calladia, who gave him a grin and a thumbs-up. He smiled back before bellowing orders. "To the high council chambers! The fight has only begun."

THIRTY-TWO

EVEN KNOWING HER MAGIC WAS KEEPING ASTAROTH IN THE air, Calladia was awestruck by the sight of him. As the procession made its way down the road toward a temple-like structure in the distance, Astaroth floated above it all, arms spread like a savior or a martyr. His red shirt rippled in the breeze, highlighting his lean, muscular body, and his stunning beauty was even more striking in these dim surroundings. His hair was a pale halo, the dark slash of his horns echoed the roiling smoke, and shadows lurked beneath his stark cheekbones.

"This is wild," Mariel said. The eerie gray-black-purple atmosphere had affected her looks, too; her skin seemed luminous, while her green dress was so vibrant it nearly hurt the eye. "Oz described the plane, but I don't think anything could have prepared me."

Calladia agreed. The stark stone buildings and cobbled streets gave a medieval flavor to the scene, and the air smelled of smoke and spice. Flickering torches lined the road, but most startling of all was the scatter of golden orbs drifting through the air. Human souls, bringing light to this alien realm. They were different sizes and brightnesses, but each contained the emotions and magic of a person.

Mariel could have become one of those orbs. She would have been, had Oz not pulled a clever switcheroo after she'd been forced into a bargain with Astaroth.

Astaroth now reigned over the chaotic procession like Woden leading the Wild Hunt. He'd gone from villain to savior so quickly, it was hard to believe.

Calladia believed though. And she was committed to creating a safer world for him and those like him. She'd fight at his side until they won—and then fight whatever battles came next.

She kept an eye on their surroundings, checking for adversaries. Mariel was intercepting periodic rocks, spears, arrows, and fireballs, and Calladia had looped the levitation spell around her wrist and started a new weaving to cast a defensive shield around Astaroth. Themmie was zooming around, throwing rocks at people.

Mariel inscribed a swirl in the air, and a spear clattered to the ground.

Wait a second. Calladia frowned. "Mariel, raise your hand again."

Mariel did, and as her fingers were silhouetted against the sky, Calladia saw a faint light emanating from her skin. Calladia lifted her own hand and saw the same thing.

"We're glowing," Calladia said.

"Weird." Mariel turned her hand this way and that. "I feel fine."

Calladia noticed small, dark green sprouts pushing up between the cobblestones at their feet. When she turned to look behind them, she saw a trail of greenery that hadn't been there before.

A hunch formed, and Calladia studied a nearby soul. This one was the size of a grapefruit, bobbing along at head height between the road and a stream running parallel to it. The bank of the stream was narrow and steep, dotted with strange flowers. As the soul passed over a patch of dark purple buds, their petals opened, revealing gold centers. The flowers turned their faces to the soul as if it were the sun.

"It's the magic," Calladia said, excitement swelling in her breast. "Look, the plants are growing."

Mariel closed her eyes, and Calladia knew she was consulting her nature magic. Her eyes popped open, and a wondering look suffused her face. "They're feeding on the magic."

"Should we be worried?"

Mariel shook her head. "They're not stealing it from us. It's like being adjacent to the souls, or to us, is enough to make them thrive."

Calladia's heart raced. If that was true, this could have enormous implications for the demon plane and the fraught witch-demon dynamic. "If witches and warlocks were allowed to live here," she said, "bargainers wouldn't need to harvest as many souls. Just the presence of magic users would give the plane energy."

Themmie landed next to them. "Why do you look like you just got the shock of your life?" she asked. Calladia explained what they'd noticed, and Themmie gasped. "Ooh. Am I glowing, too?"

Pixies had minor magical abilities, mostly limited to cleaning magic. It had been a huge source of irritation to Themmie, who tended toward disorganization, that her one magical ability was something she hated doing.

Calladia leaned in, inspecting the pixie's hand. Her rich brown skin didn't seem to be glowing, but when Calladia cupped Themmie's hand in her own, cutting off outside illumination, and put her eye to the gap in their fingers, she saw a faint bluish-green light. It was like looking at a glow-in-the-dark pattern in a darkened room. "You are!" she exclaimed.

Themmie screeched and fluttered off the ground in a show of excitement. "You know what this means, right?"

Calladia nodded, feeling giddy. "It means the demon plane's problem with needing outside magic has a simple solution."

"Immigration!" Themmie crowed. "Throw open the borders and let other species settle here. More magic! More hybrids! More life!"

Astaroth needed to know this information before he confronted Moloch and the high council, and they were quickly approaching the intimidating black building at the end of the road. Along the way, the protestors had been joined by a groundswell of other demons.

"Cover me?" Calladia asked her friends, who nodded. She tied a new spell that mirrored what she'd cast on Astaroth and rose into the air, trying not to panic as the ground fell away. If the thread was severed or she lost concentration, she'd fall.

Astaroth looked startled when she drifted to his side. "Fancy seeing you here," he said. Mariel's loudspeaker spell had been terminated while she was playing defense, so his voice was normal volume. "Are you joining me?"

"Only briefly." She was acutely aware of the demons whispering and pointing at her. It couldn't be often that a fully ensouled witch showed up in this plane. "I just learned something."

She explained the discovery to Astaroth, whose eyes widened. "Fiery Lucifer," he said when she was done. "You're not jesting?"

In response, Calladia held up her hand. The sky had darkened from purple-gray to purple-black, and golden light shone from her fingers, brighter now that they were heading into the demon plane's version of night.

Astaroth seized her hand and held it to his lips for a kiss. "Goddess, you have no idea the weapon you just gave me."

"My hand?"

He shook his head. "Even better. An idea. No, an *ideal*. Moloch's influence relies on fear and oppression. This?" He held her hand to his chest. "This is hope."

They'd reached the steps leading up to a colossal black structure. It was constructed like a Maya step pyramid, and a platform at the top of the first flight of stairs held large stone doors covered in intricate carvings. The doors swung open slowly, revealing nine demons silhouetted by a fiery red background.

"Time for me to head down," Calladia said. "Go get 'em, tiger."

Astaroth's posture shifted. He seemed taller, more rigid, and his expression was hard as iron. His bearing screamed of power and influence, and Calladia felt a twinge of unease. This wasn't Calladia's Astaroth—it was the demon the council had known for centuries.

He was playing a part, she told herself. Committing to the aesthetic.

She expected him to bid her a formal farewell, rather than expose his feelings for her, but as she started to sink back down, he looped an arm around her waist and hauled her in for a fierce kiss.

"Fight well, my warrior queen," he said when he let her go.

She smiled, heart thumping with a mix of adoration, exhilaration, and fear. "Fight well, my warrior king."

Then she dropped to the ground, readying herself for the confrontation to come.

◆　◆　◆

THE NINE DEMONS SPREAD OUT ON THE PLATFORM. MOLOCH and Baphomet were in the center, and Calladia recognized Tirana to Moloch's right. Had Astaroth's position already been claimed by the demoness?

"How dare you return, Astaroth?" Baphomet asked. "You were banished."

The head of the council could certainly project. Calladia

wouldn't have been surprised to learn he had a microphone hidden beneath those layers of fur and leather.

"Yeah, banishment wasn't really my thing," Astaroth said.

Calladia jumped. Mariel had resumed her amplification spell.

"That's not how banishment works," Moloch said. He'd adopted a more archaic form of dress: his brown leather pants were topped with a blue shirt and leather jerkin, and he wore knee-high boots with daggers tucked into them. Leather bands covered his forearms, a blue cape linked with a silver chain draped from his shoulders, and a sword was sheathed at his hip.

Calladia scanned the other high council members. Sandranella was there, looking unflappable in a deep purple gown covered with silver filigree. She hadn't decided to abandon their cause, had she?

The white-haired demoness met Calladia's eyes and winked.

An ally on the inside. It was a smart call; if she had marched, it might have diminished her credibility as a council member. This way she could argue on Astaroth's behalf from a position of authority.

That didn't explain where Lilith was, but from what little Calladia had learned about her, the demoness, like her son, would time her entrance for when it would have the greatest impact.

"I learned some alarming things while on Earth," Astaroth said. "My concern was so great, I chose to return for the sake of our people."

"You are no longer a council member," Moloch said. "You have no influence."

"Is Tirana a council member?" Astaroth gestured to the demoness with the dirty-blond hair and coiled whip.

Moloch's eyelids flickered. "We were just meeting to discuss that matter."

"So that's a no." Astaroth turned until he was half facing the assembled crowd. "For those who are just joining us, we gathered for a peaceful protest on behalf of demon hybrids and were viciously attacked by Moloch's minions."

"Lies," Moloch said. "You caused the conflict yourself to undermine me and regain your council seat."

Astaroth kept speaking. "We were protesting because Moloch, Baphomet, and Tirana, as well as potentially other council members, support the destruction of hybrids. They want to close all entrances to the plane and usher in a totalitarian rule based on violent, outdated ideals."

Murmurs sounded from the restless crowd. Someone threw a rock at the dais.

"Be silent," Baphomet ordered.

Astaroth stroked his chin, looking thoughtful. "No."

"Astaroth is afraid of change," Moloch told the crowd. "He doesn't want to acknowledge that our species has become weak over the centuries."

"How are we weak?" Astaroth asked. "I'd argue our weakness is in refusing to embrace diversity. Hybrids have much to offer our community."

Pride swelled in Calladia's breast. How far he'd come—from despising his human half to embracing it, from playing politics to leading a revolution.

Moloch scoffed. "Half a demon is no demon at all. They lack our intelligence, strength, and sense of honor."

"Boo," Calladia called out, and echoing hisses came from behind her. Someone fired an arrow, which unfortunately missed Moloch.

"See? What coward hides behind a bow?" Moloch gestured to the arrow. "Who attacks an enemy without a fair fight?"

"You do," Astaroth said. "After Moloch vindictively had a witch turn me mortal, I was grievously wounded. He followed me to Earth and tried to kill me outside the view of the high council, which everyone should know is against the council's sacred precepts."

Sandranella gasped loudly and turned to Moloch. "Is this true?" she asked with a convincing display of concern.

"Don't play games, Sandranella," Moloch snapped. "You support Astaroth's unhinged schemes."

"I support keeping all inhabitants of our plane safe," she replied. "And the reason you know I agree with Astaroth is that I saw you, Tirana, and Baphomet try to murder him and his witch companion just yesterday."

The other council members shifted, looking uneasy. "Baphomet, is that so?" one asked. "Assassinations can't proceed without the council's full support."

"Sandranella has succumbed to the same weakness of thought Astaroth has," Baphomet said. "She seeks to undermine our power."

"How is protecting hybrids weak?" The question came from overhead, where Themmie sat cross-legged in midair, smartphone held in front of her. Livestreaming on a demon social media site, presumably. Woe to anyone who underestimated the power of a sunshiny influencer with a cause to champion.

"This is the future progressives want," Moloch said, pointing up at Themmie. "Our sacred realm invaded by interlopers. The strength of our bloodlines polluted by lesser beings."

Calladia gritted her teeth to resist the urge to throw something at Moloch. If Themmie was streaming, it was best to let the demon dig his own grave.

"Do you know why Astaroth supports so-called 'hybrid rights'?" Moloch sneered. "Because he himself is half human."

Astaroth shrugged, looking unbothered. "A bit late on that revelation, Moloch. I already announced it."

Moloch's face twisted with hate. "Astaroth is an abomination and a criminal who lied to the high council. We had to remove him, lest he corrupt the rule of law further."

"I'm not ashamed of being a hybrid," Astaroth said. He met Calladia's eyes. "I've learned my human half is a strength."

Calladia would have clapped and started cheering if she hadn't been holding the yarn—and the knots shielding him—in place. She smiled up at him, hoping he could see the hope and pride shining from her eyes. *Fuck yeah*, she mouthed up at him.

Tirana guffawed, puncturing the moment. "Listen to this fool." She uncoiled her whip and waved a hand, and a tiny fireball danced from her fingers to the leather, setting the length ablaze.

Baphomet puffed up his broad chest. "For defying banishment and lying about your bloodline, I, Baphomet of the Nine, sentence Astaroth, formerly of the Nine, to death."

Calladia's hope abruptly warped into fury and terror. Her horrified gasp was echoed by others. "No!" she shouted, turning a vicious glare on Baphomet. She would gut him before she let him set a finger on Astaroth.

"You can't just decide that," Sandranella said. "It's up to the whole council."

"I am the council," Baphomet replied. "My word will be law."

Moloch's grin was diabolical. "Do let me carry out the sentence."

"What authority do you have anymore, Baphomet?" Astaroth asked. "You lost it when you tried to assassinate me before I could reveal the extent of Moloch's own crimes."

Calladia's heart skipped a beat. Had he remembered something at last? *Please*, she silently begged. If ever there was a moment for him to rediscover his leverage over Moloch, it was now. She didn't fear him becoming the worst version of himself anymore—what mattered was keeping him alive. Keeping him safe.

"What crimes?" Moloch asked derisively.

Astaroth opened his mouth, then closed it again. "I will reveal that when the time is right."

Calladia's stomach sank. Shit. He'd been bluffing.

Moloch laughed. "More lies. Let's end this farce."

"If you recant your accusations against Moloch," Baphomet said, "and cease this useless civil agitating, I may consider life imprisonment instead of death."

"I refuse." Astaroth lifted his chin. "And if you slay me here, know this moment will echo through history. Your legacy will be one of censorship and oppression, and the next uprising, when it comes, will not be nearly so peaceful."

Baphomet gestured, but Calladia couldn't tell who it was aimed at. She looked around, but the crowd pressed in, making it impossible to see far. Fear seized her throat and chest in iron claws, as suffocating as the packed gathering.

"I will give you one more chance," Baphomet said. "If you prove you are committed to the pure-blood cause and denounce your human ties, you may be spared."

Someone seized Calladia from behind. She shrieked and fought, but her assailant was impossibly strong, with rigid gray arms. Her yarn was ripped out of her hands, the levitation bracelet snapped as if it—and the spell—had never been. Next to her, Mariel was also being manhandled by what looked like a stone gargoyle. Oz roared and launched at the gargoyle, but his fists were no match for stone, and soon he'd been corralled, too. Their hands were bound with chains, and they were dragged up the steps to the platform where the high council stood.

Astaroth had fallen when Calladia's concentration—and the spell—had broken. He scrambled to his feet at the base of the steps. Panic washed over his face before he steeled his expression. "What is the meaning of this?" he demanded.

Calladia, Mariel, and Oz were shoved to their knees facing the crowd, and Calladia winced as her kneecaps cracked against the stone. Heavy hands landed on her shoulders, keeping her down. She bared her teeth at the gargoyle, then at Baphomet and Moloch, continuing to struggle even though her fiercest efforts accomplished nothing.

Calladia refused to stop fighting though—for herself, for Astaroth, for Mariel and Oz and Themmie and the demon hybrids and the werewolves who had shown up because it was the right thing to do. For hope and justice.

For love.

Baphomet unsheathed his broadsword. The silver length of it gleamed in the firelight. "I have a proposition, Astaroth," the demon said. "I will spare your life . . . if you take theirs."

THIRTY-THREE

Astaroth wanted to scream as Calladia was shoved to her knees. This wasn't supposed to happen. The people were meant to rise up beside him, spurred by Sandranella and Lilith's support, and together they would storm the high council chambers once Moloch's dastardly plot was revealed. But although the crowd surged and seethed like an angry sea, no one seemed willing to openly defy the council.

Calladia's expression was fierce, though her ponytail was lopsided, and there were red marks on her arms where the gargoyle had gripped her.

Astaroth was going to rip Moloch's throat out with his teeth.

"Well?" Baphomet asked, holding out the broadsword. "Kill them, renounce your radical politics, and I won't just suspend your sentence. I'll allow you to be a special adviser to the high council as we discuss hybrid rights."

As if that conversation would go any way but Moloch's, but the offer let Baphomet save face.

It would also give Astaroth more time to scheme his way back to power.

He looked at Calladia, Mariel, and Ozroth. All mortal, all wearing matching expressions of defiance. Braver than Moloch and Baphomet and all their cronies combined.

Fuck Baphomet's deal. Astaroth had lived a long time, but he'd finally found something worth dying for.

He took a deep breath. "I will surrender to your judgment if you let the mortals go."

"No!" Calladia shouted. She struggled harder, but the gargoyle held her in place.

"You can chop my head off right here in front of everyone," Astaroth continued. A tremor raced through him, and he clenched his fists as he fought the sour twist of fear in his gut. It had only been a matter of time anyway. Whether in seventy years or this instant, Astaroth's death had been written when Isobel had laid her life curse.

"Gladly." Moloch unsheathed his sword. His dimpled cheeks were flushed with bloodlust, and his smile was sharp as a blade.

"Wait." Sandranella rushed forward, hands out. "Don't do this, Moloch. He deserves a trial."

"The council can vote on his fate, if you prefer," Moloch sneered at her. "But your side will lose."

They would. With Baphomet allied with Moloch, and Astaroth out of power, the council was no longer in balance. Sandranella looked at Astaroth, and the grim look in her eyes said she knew how futile a vote would be.

Fight another day, he mouthed, hoping she would read his lips. The demon plane would need her in the dark days to come.

She nodded, then stepped back in line.

Astaroth began climbing the steps toward his doom. "I defy your reign of cruelty," he said. There was no spell amplifying his voice now, so he spoke loudly, willing his words to reach to the back of the crowd and beyond. "I renounce any former alliances. I renounce my power and the cowardly choice I made not to reveal my heritage." As he approached the platform, he met Calladia's terrified eyes. "I choose the hybrids," he announced, still holding her gaze. "And I choose these mortals."

At the top, he knelt before Calladia. "I choose you," he murmured, cupping her cheeks.

Tears shone in her beautiful brown eyes. "Please, no," she said, voice breaking.

He would not be deterred. After a lifetime of manipulation and lies, Astaroth had found something more important than power.

"I choose love," he told her. "I love you."

All at once, his memories came flooding back.

✦　✦　✦

ASTAROTH'S FIRST MEMORY WAS OF HIS MOTHER'S RED HAIR and black horns shining in the sunlight. "You mustn't tell anyone who you are, my sweet," Lilith had said, cuddling him close. "They won't understand. They won't let you seize the power you deserve."

She'd trained him in secret, teaching him about bargaining and how to access the magic within himself. How delighted she'd been to learn he'd inherited it! And even more delighted when, as an adult, Astaroth had ceased to show any signs of aging.

"You can pass as a full demon," she'd crowed, spinning in wild circles. Her eyes had gleamed with a frenzied light, but love burned beneath the madness, and Astaroth had been determined to claw his way to power for her.

He'd enjoyed it, too: the deals, the stratagems, the wars and manipulations and seductions. It had been addictive. Every time a soul floated out of a mortal and into the demon plane thanks to his doing, he'd told himself he was as good as a pure-blooded demon. Better, even, for he rarely left Earth, determined to craft a deadly reputation as quickly as possible. He'd fought, shagged, and charmed his way through witch after warlock, stealing their essence and sending it off, smugly thinking how fortunate it was he took after his demon mother, rather than his human father. He had no mortal soul to worry about, no fragile mortal emotions. He was Lilith's true heir.

Except the mortal emotions had crept in anyway. Moments of doubt. Moments of sorrow. And sometimes, like the first time he'd used particularly brutal methods to force a warlock to fulfill a deal, a deep, gnawing guilt.

Bargainers shouldn't feel guilt. They were perfectly in control, Lilith excepted, but that was due to vast age twisting her sanity. The higher Astaroth rose, the more he encountered demons who embodied everything he wanted to be: cruel, cold, untouchable.

Centuries in, he no longer sought power for his mother's sake. Everything he did was to further his own ambitions. *Act like who you want to be, and you will become it.* He didn't recall which mortal had given him that advice, but it had held true. Astaroth had acted as cold and vicious as any of the preeminent demons, and his tender emotions had withered, or else he'd buried them so deep he'd ceased to acknowledge their existence.

Moloch had been the example Astaroth had measured himself against. Perfectly devious, perfectly cruel, unbothered by regret. The demon was ambition personified, and as Astaroth had honed his own ambition to deadly sharpness, the two had come into frequent conflict. They'd spread rumors, sabotaged each other's plans, and jockeyed for favor with Baphomet. There had been no greater day in Astaroth's existence than when a council member had been beheaded during the Thirty Years' War and he had been selected to fill the position ahead of Moloch.

Astaroth of the Nine at last.

Unfortunately, a second council member had died that same day, and Moloch had been chosen for the other vacant spot. The two had taken their battle to a higher stage. There was one position yet to claim: the center of the high council itself.

Astaroth had done everything to bring that goal closer. Achieving ultimate power would be proof that, despite his embarrassing origins, he had become the perfect demon.

While Moloch led military campaigns against the demon plane's enemies—the immortal fae, a rebel centaur faction, and others who tried to infiltrate the plane for its resources and land—Astaroth had collected souls at a breakneck pace. He'd taken on an apprentice to prove his worthiness as a mentor, and he'd shaped that child into a weapon. Ozroth the Ruthless had become the second-greatest soul bargainer of all time, after Astaroth himself.

When Moloch had veered toward traditional demon values, Astaroth had positioned himself strategically with the progressives on the council, calculating they had the better odds in the long run. And if the progressives argued for the rights of half demons? Astaroth told himself supporting that cause was a clever political move, not a reflection of his heritage.

Still, he had remained in deadlock with Moloch. Baphomet seemed impossible to sway. As the years ticked by and humanity moved into an era of cell phones and internet searches that made them less likely to succumb to demonic trickery, Astaroth had struggled to maintain his pace of soul bargaining. Increasingly, he'd woken from nightmares in a cold sweat, imagining his carefully hoarded power being stripped away. He dreamed of his charade being exposed while demons pointed and laughed at the hybrid who thought he was good enough to rule.

Then Ozroth had made a crucial mistake on a soul bargain. He hadn't listened closely enough to a warlock's final wishes, and when he'd delivered the illness-stricken man a peaceful death, the warlock's soul hadn't gone to the demon plane at all. It had taken up residence in Ozroth's chest instead, cursing him with mortal emotions. When Ozroth had struggled with guilt during his next bargains, the council had discussed what to do about him. Strip him from power? Submit him to brutal reconditioning?

"Kill him," Moloch had said, to Astaroth's fury. "A faulty weapon is worse than no weapon at all."

Wagers were a crucial tool among the council, good for a bit of humiliation or to wrangle political concessions out of an enemy. With Astaroth's own dealmaking dwindling and his protégé failing, his chance of seizing ultimate power was vanishing. So he'd cast aside his carefully crafted schemes, stopped playing the long game, and made a reckless, bold move.

One wager. No limits. If Ozroth succeeded in his next soul bargain within the allotted time, Astaroth would seize whatever concession he wanted from Moloch. If Ozroth failed, Moloch could take his own concession.

Astaroth remembered the hungry gleam in Moloch's eyes as they'd shaken hands. They both knew what this meant. After nearly six centuries of rivalry, one of them would win at last.

The memories flew past faster than he could track. He recalled threatening Ozroth if he failed, lying to him about the demon plane dying, anything to force him to take Mariel's soul after the witch had inadvertently summoned him. He remembered Moloch's taunts and Sandranella's concern about the outcome. And still, he'd been confident he would win. He always won.

Until he lost.

The memory of Calladia attacking him merged with the rest. It had been the final, violent cherry on an utterly shite cake. He'd staggered into council chambers, wounded and panicked. He couldn't fail, not after all this time.

Moloch's taunts. Isobel's curse. Falling through the portal and hitting his head.

Past and present merged. The vicious, desperate demon he'd

been for centuries melded with the softer version Calladia had brought out, two halves melding into a whole.

That vicious, cold self settled into the realm of memory though. Who he'd been the last few days felt immediate and real.

That new, better person couldn't have existed without the amnesia, he realized. He'd been twisted by ambition, and only by forgetting it had he managed to uncover the human half he'd buried so deep.

Your memories will return when you're ready to seize the life you want.

He blinked, and the world returned.

Calladia was crying in front of him. Moloch's sword hovered close to Astaroth's neck. "Say your goodbyes," the demon sneered.

"I remember," Astaroth told Calladia wonderingly. "I remember everything."

"Everything?" she asked, lip trembling.

The torrent of memory settled, like water from a burst dam forming the lake it was meant to be. The final piece came clear.

Astaroth rolled away from Moloch's sword and leaped to his feet, hope swelling in his chest. "I have something to say," he announced. "It's important."

"Seriously?" Moloch asked.

"Let's hear him out," Sandranella said. When Moloch glared at her, she shrugged an elegant shoulder. "You can always behead him after."

Astaroth shot her a grateful look. "Moloch," he said, turning to face the demon. "Just to confirm, you support pure-blood demons only, right? You don't believe any other species have a place here?"

"Other species are weak," Moloch said. "By allowing them access to our plane, we invite that weakness in."

"And fornicating with them is out of the question, of course." He projected his voice to reach as many ears as possible.

"Obviously." Moloch nudged Calladia's leg with the toe of his boot. "But of course you have no qualms about associating with filth."

Astaroth nearly tackled the demon right then and there. He took a deep breath. "Then would you care to explain why you've been skimming from the high council's gold reserves to pay your elven mistress?"

Silence fell. Moloch's eyes widened.

One heartbeat passed, another . . .

Then everyone started talking and shouting at once. Hybrids screamed accusations from the crowd while council members turned on each other, bickering about what was true and who knew what.

"Silence," Baphomet shouted. "Enough of this nonsense. Either kill the mortals or die yourself, Astaroth."

The other council members looked uneasy though. Murmurs passed down the line, and Sandranella stepped forward. "Tell us more, Astaroth."

"Gladly," he said, feeling a burst of spiteful glee. Astaroth had been hiring investigators to tail Moloch since their rivalry had begun, but it wasn't until he'd discovered Moloch had a secret off-plane bank account that he'd thought to engage human hackers to infiltrate the demon's online accounts. Humans were always more resourceful than others gave them credit for. "He's been carrying on an affair with an elven woman for the last fifteen years. He built her a mansion on Earth in a place called Miami, as well as several more on various planes."

"You don't know that," Moloch gritted out between clenched teeth.

"Remember when we were on the brink of creating an alliance with the dwarves?" Astaroth asked the rest of the council. "They were facing a gold shortage, and we had gold to spare, so we proposed financing some urgent infrastructure upgrades in exchange for more favorable tariffs on imports and exports between planes." Demons operated on the barter system for the most part, but they did hoard various currencies to hold their own with capitalist species.

"I remember," Sandranella said. "Baphomet changed his mind on the morning of the vote."

"I concluded the terms weren't beneficial enough for us," Baphomet said, looking uneasy.

Astaroth had believed him at the time. Even knowing Moloch's perfidy, he'd assumed Baphomet had noticed their own gold shortage and covered it up while investigating. He'd never believed the incorruptible Baphomet had finally been corrupted.

"The gold we were going to offer went missing," Astaroth said. "Moloch funneled it away, and Baphomet covered up the loss."

Baphomet's glare was murderous. "These accusations are treason."

"How is it treason?" Sandranella asked.

"I am the head of the council!" Spittle flew from the demon's mouth.

"The high council is more than just you," Sandranella said. "That you believe yourself to speak for all of us, no matter what, and that you see any accusations against you as treason, is proof you are no longer fit for the position."

That sent the other council members into an uproar. They shouted and pointed fingers, each faction accusing the other of corruption and lies.

"This is the problem," Astaroth shouted over the din. "We are no longer a council comprised of multiple viewpoints, and we've been prioritizing our own power ahead of the well-being of the plane. We have effectively adopted a two-party system, which anyone on Earth can tell you is a recipe for disaster."

Moloch's fingers flexed on the hilt of his sword. "You have no proof to back up these spurious accusations."

Except Astaroth did have proof: written journals locked in his den, scans saved to an external hard drive in his London flat. The hackers had more records. And if Moloch stealing from the demon plane to pay his nondemon mistress wasn't enough to sway the council against him, this next piece ought to do it.

"I have proof," Astaroth said. "Including a very interesting signed confession from an assassin."

Moloch's ruddy cheeks darkened further, and a vein stood out on his forehead. He started to say something, but Astaroth talked over him.

"Moloch arranged for the murder of Cassaviel," he said, naming the demon whose position Astaroth had taken on the high council. The confession had been extracted during a booze-heavy night of high-stakes Bingo with a group of retired immortal assassins. "When Moloch wasn't named to that open position, he had the assassin murder Drivanna as well." The council member whose spot Moloch had ended up taking.

The arguments between high council members stopped. Every eye fixed on Moloch.

Moloch scoffed. "Where is this so-called proof?"

"I have evidence in my den. I would be glad to retrieve it for the council to investigate—"

Moloch laughed loudly. "Astaroth, your den burned to the ground the day you were banished. A tragic accident, of course."

Astaroth ought to have known the demon would pull something like that. Luckily, there were merits to having spent so much time among humans. An IT professional he'd shagged a few years ago had taught him the merits of backing up his data.

He'd be sending that human a thank-you card, should this go as hoped. "Good thing I have duplicates," Astaroth said. "There's a marvelous invention you may not have heard of called a scanner."

"And good thing I was able to post the evidence online!"

The familiar voice came from below. The crowd of protestors parted to reveal Lilith, flanked by two burly werewolves: Avram on her left, Kai on her right.

Astaroth's mother was small, but she carried herself like a queen. Her red hair was bound up in a gold hairpiece that matched her suit of armor—gilt over steel plate, he remembered, a gift from Henry VIII. "I like not knowing if a bed partner wants to lop off my head after," Lilith had said at the time. "Lends some extra excitement." The ensemble was completed by a short sword whose hilt was adorned with electrum.

"It's Lilith herself!" someone shouted, and cries of alarm and awe followed.

"You are not on the high council, Lilith," Baphomet said. "Your input is unwelcome."

"Being on the high council sounds boring. I've turned it down so many times." Lilith mounted the steps with her werewolf honor guard. Her smile was vicious, revealing the sharp points of her canines. "I might change my mind though. Your skull would make a lovely chalice to drink rosé from while I purge the council of your sycophants."

"God, that's hot," Kai said.

Lilith patted the werewolf's forearm and snapped her teeth at him. "Good boy."

"Where did you post the evidence?" Themmie called from on high. Astaroth twitched; he'd forgotten she was hovering there, phone angled toward the dais. "I'm streaming everywhere from Pixtagram to GhoulTube, and I'll cross-promote with my socials."

Given Baphomet's and Moloch's blank expressions, they had no idea what that meant. Yet more evidence one shouldn't dismiss humans, since what they lacked in immortality or super strength they made up for in technical ingenuity and a passion for oversharing.

"I summarized everything and posted it on AO3," Lilith declared proudly.

Oh, Lucifer. Astaroth resisted smacking his forehead with his palm. "You mean Archive of Our Own?" he asked. "That fan fiction site where you post your tentacle porn?"

"She writes tentacle porn?" Themmie asked. "Awesome. I'm gonna need that link. For, uh, research."

Lilith looked up at the pixie. "I knew I liked the colorful bug. My next one-shot will be dedicated to you, flappy one."

Themmie pumped her fist. "Yes!"

Calladia cleared her throat. "Are the scans available online, too?" she asked. "Not just a summary?"

Lilith had reached the dais. "Of course they are," she said, moving to stand at Astaroth's side. "They're linked in the author's notes."

"I'm still not sure what fan fiction is," Moloch said, "but everyone knows you're insane. Who would believe you?"

Lilith snapped her fingers, and Kai pulled a smartphone out of his pocket, unlocked it, and handed it to her. Lilith peered at the screen. "There are already sixteen thousand hits, and I haven't even posted the explicit chapter yet."

Astaroth eyed his mother askance. "There's nothing explicit in my evidence."

"Yes, you were very dull about the forbidden demon-elf affair." She shrugged. "I took some creative license."

"Enough!" Moloch shouted. He raised his sword and held his left hand out, summoning a fireball that hovered over his palm. "This has gone too far."

"Wait just a moment," a council member said. "Shouldn't we talk about this?"

More voices chimed in. Sandranella had been edging toward the kneeling mortals; as Astaroth watched, she whispered a dismissal to the gargoyles, then quickly knelt down and did away with the restraints.

"Thank you," Calladia said, rubbing her wrists. She jumped to her feet, yanked out a strand of hair, and started tying knots.

The council was having a vicious argument with Moloch, which was what Astaroth had hoped for, but the people needed to have a say as well. He faced the gathered onlookers, hybrid and pureblood alike. "Your council is flawed," Astaroth announced. He nearly recoiled as his voice boomed. When he looked to the side, Mariel winked.

"They—*we*—are flawed," he continued, the words magically amplified. "Greedy and power-hungry, hiding behind lies, inventing enemies to justify our actions. Moloch claims hybrids as the enemies, but in truth, they will be part of our deliverance."

Something hit his side hard enough to send him staggering. When he looked down, he saw the hilt of Moloch's dagger sticking out.

Calladia shrieked and launched herself at Moloch, taking the demon down. She punched him in the face repeatedly, sending blood spraying, before Ozroth took over the beating. Mariel started murmuring a spell.

Calladia hurried to Astaroth's side. Moloch's blood painted her knuckles and was spattered over one cheek. "We need to get you to a doctor," she said.

Astaroth swayed, feeling light-headed. Not from blood loss—with the dagger still inside, he wasn't worried about that just yet—but because the experience of being stabbed didn't improve over time. "He missed vital organs," he wheezed. "It'll be fine. I need to finish the speech."

Calladia gave him a murderous look. "If you avoid getting treatment just to give a speech, I will twist this knife. Just try me."

"I swear I'm not in danger of dying at the moment." He kissed her before she could clobber him over the head and drag him away. "Let me finish the speech. Then we'll go to a doctor."

Calladia hesitated before holding out her hand, pinkie extended. "Will you pinkie swear?"

Astaroth didn't know what that meant, but he would swear on

anything she liked. He reached out, looping his pinkie around hers. "I pinkie swear."

She shook his hand solemnly. "The pinkie swear is a sacred vow. You can't break it."

"And I won't." He smiled, then winced at a throb of pain in his side. He was relieved to see Moloch being restrained by multiple council members, progressives and conservatives alike. Baphomet, too, was being hotly questioned by two conservative demons.

Finally, the council was taking action. And all it took was a light stabbing.

"Closing our borders to other species isn't the answer," Astaroth said, addressing the crowd again. "Nor is discriminating against hybrids. We've grown stagnant as a species, and while the souls bring life to our plane, we haven't bothered to think of other options."

He reached for Calladia's hand, twined his fingers with hers, then raised it overhead. Her skin glowed in the demon twilight.

"The plants started blooming when the witches and pixie arrived," Astaroth continued. "That means we don't need to rely on soul bargains to keep the plane alive. We've just got to open our borders to others. Allow them to share their light with us." He kissed Calladia's hand. "In return, perhaps we can share some light and love as well."

Moloch was screaming threats and thrashing against the people chaining him. Tirana and Baphomet were similarly bound. Sandranella called for the gargoyles, who started dragging the three demons away.

"Hold on," Astaroth called. He looked to Calladia. "Do you have something you want to say to Moloch?"

Her grin was vicious. "Do I ever!" She walked up to Moloch, then punched him in the face. "That's for my house." Her next hit went to his gut, and he groaned. "That's for Astaroth." Finally, she tied a series of knots with a strand of her hair. "And this is for the whole demon plane." She muttered a spell, then booted Moloch in the groin.

The demon launched over the rooftops as if shot from a catapult, his scream fading as he disappeared into the distance.

"That was cool," Mariel said, "but, uh, do we know where he went?"

"He's in chains," Calladia said. "He won't get far."

Lilith grabbed Kai by the back of the neck and hauled him down into an aggressively tongue-forward kiss. "Werewolves have an excellent sense of smell," she said after she broke away. "Fetch him for me?"

With a hearty howl at the sky, Kai leaped off the dais and started running.

A demon doctor hurried toward Astaroth. She tugged the knife out, then began treating the wound. Astaroth winced at the sharp pain, but he felt much better once his side was packed with medicinal herbs and gauze.

"So," Sandranella said once the doctor was done. "Fancy being a part of the high council again, Astaroth?"

Calladia stiffened. Astaroth looped an arm around her waist, considering.

Being on the high council would give hybrids a voice in the seat of power, but did he want to keep doing this? The endless machinations, the slow march of progress . . . how long would it take Astaroth to fall back into the pit of cynicism and ambition?

His past was part of him. Not a comfortable part—more akin to a splinter under his skin—but still there. He didn't want to be that person again.

And yet . . .

He faced Calladia, pulling her into his arms. "Calladia," he said seriously, "will you be angry if I stay on the high council? Or at least act as a consultant for hybrid rights?"

A consultancy might be better anyway. More freedom to explore the worlds. More time to spend with his love.

Calladia's face fell, but she recovered quickly, giving him a tight smile. "Guess you decided to take Isobel up on her offer, after all."

Wait, Isobel the life witch? Astaroth was briefly confused before realizing Calladia thought he was planning a return to immortality, not just the high council.

After everything that had happened though, Astaroth had come to a conclusion.

The best aspects of himself didn't come from his demon heritage, though he still wanted to make his mother proud. And though Lilith had a demon's love of ambition and ruthlessness, more importantly she loved *him*.

He'd just seen Calladia, Mariel, Ozroth, Themmie, and a pack of random werewolves fight for demon hybrids for no reason other than that it was the right thing to do. Over the years, he'd watched mortals live with such aggressive passion, it boggled the mind. Living on Earth had provided a contact high of sorts, but Astaroth was done letting other people live boldly while he tried to diminish his emotions.

The best aspects of Astaroth were human.

Maybe it was because human lives were brief. They crammed in so much meaning that each day was an adventure. They cared so fiercely that their love stories echoed through time.

He wanted to make his mother proud, but more importantly, he wanted to make himself proud.

Though she was smiling, fear and sorrow shone from Calladia's beautiful eyes. Astaroth cupped her cheeks, vowing to do whatever it took to erase that pain. "Calladia," he said with his entire heart, "I don't want to be immortal again."

Her brow furrowed. "What?"

"I'm not going to contact Isobel again—well, after I pay her those gold doubloons, damn it. I'm staying mortal."

After a moment, hope bloomed over her face like an exquisite flower. "Really?"

"Really," he confirmed. "I can still do good here, and I hope to get more hybrids on the council going forward—and we should probably expand the council anyway—but as for my life . . ." He trailed off, thinking how to word it.

Words could do a lot, but not everything. His truth was a feeling, precious and warm, held safe within his rib cage. His truth was also in his arms, his equal in every way.

"Calladia Cunnington," Astaroth said, "my warrior queen. I love you, and I want to spend a life with you. The good and bad and annoying and sublime. I want you to shout at me and kick my arse. I want to tickle your feet and tempt death. I want to *live* with you, as fully and aggressively as we can."

By the end of that speech, his eyes were damp.

Calladia was crying, too. "Astaroth, pain in my ass and light of my life . . . I love you, too. I can't believe how fast this happened, but I wouldn't trade a moment of it." She considered. "Well, maybe a few moments. But overall . . . yes. Sign me up for all of that and all of you." And because Calladia was never predictable, her heart-stoppingly tender smile was followed by her gripping his horns in both fists and hauling him to her mouth. "Let's do this, warrior king," she said before kissing him soundly.

The plane erupted with cheers, but Astaroth didn't hear them. He was lost in a new world comprised of him and Calladia and all the possibilities that awaited them.

The fight. The laughter.

The love.

ACKNOWLEDGMENTS

There are so many people who have helped shape this book into its final, gloriously horny, and chaotic form. Thank you first and foremost to Cindy Hwang for taking on these books and encouraging me to be as weird as I want. Thank you to the Penguin Random House team: Jessica Mangicaro, Stephanie Felty, Angela Kim, and Stacy Edwards. You're the dream team when it comes to getting this book in readers' hands, and I'm so grateful for your hard work. Thank you to copyeditor Shana Jones for fixing my commas and fielding my incessant questions about how to balance a British protagonist with an American narrative voice, and thank you to artist Jess Miller and art director Katie Anderson for yet another phenomenal cover. The Gollancz team is wonderful, too: Thank you so much to Áine Feeney, Javerya Iqbal, Jenna Petts, Tawanna Sullivan, Jessica Hart, and Dawn Cooper (who illustrated the gorgeous UK cover). And thank you as always to Jessica Watterson, agent extraordinaire, for being the absolute best and fielding all sorts of panicked or strange inquiries from me.

In my personal life, I'm lucky to know many supportive, creative, kind, and talented people. Thank you to everyone who's cheered me on in this journey: Sarah Tarkoff, Blaise Nutter, John Moore, Jon Jandoc, Bronwyn Beck, Amanda Powers, Brittany Hoirup, Dan Duncan, Rachel Kitzmann, Julie Verive, Meredith Berg, Angela Serranzana, Mish Kriz, Alycia Francis, Ryan and Tina Porterhawk (plus Austin and Asami, the corgi who gives no fucks in any universe's dog park), and a million more people. (Sorry if I missed anyone—writing acknowledgments is stressful!) Thank you to the Berkletes, the Wicked Wallflowers Coven, the SDLA Sisters (Ali, Thea, Kirsten, and Katie, who was also my Taylor Swift advisor), and the Words are Hard crew (Celia, Rebecca, Julie, Victoria, Jenna, Kate, and Claire). Thank you to Village Books and Paper Dreams and the Bellingham Barnes & Noble for all the support, Waterstones Liverpool for the delightful TikToks, and every podcast or website that has invited me to come be my odd self and talk about books.

I'm so grateful for my wonderful family: Mom, Dad, Steve, Mahina, Kennebeck, Lynnea, Nana, Bill, Sandy, and everyone else, with a special shout-out to Cory and Laura for their enthusiastic assault on the little free libraries of Victoria, British Columbia. Thank you to Joy for the years of love, laughter, and thoughtful art; the pens I use to sign and annotate books came from you and I think about you when I use them.

On a more serious note: If you are experiencing or have experienced a relationship like the one Calladia had with Sam, I want to tell you (A) you are not alone and (B) you deserve someone who loves you as you are and will lift you up, not cut you down. You aren't weak or unworthy if someone has abused you verbally, emotionally, financially, physically, or sexually. If you are currently in a situation where you feel unsafe or scared or need to get out but aren't sure how, there are resources that can help. I'm American, so I'll share our National Domestic Violence Hotline: 1-800-799-SAFE (7233), thehotline.org, or text START to 88788.

Wherever you are, whoever you are, you deserve better. You deserve the best.

Now back to the gratitude, because if there's any message I want readers to take away, it's that we all deserve joy. This book is one of my joys.

There are many other people and places that have shaped this narrative. Thank you to Dorothy Dunnett for creating Francis Crawford of Lymond, the gold standard of blond, snarky, morally dubious British literary heroes who my heart seized on many years past and has never let go of. Thank you to *True Blood* for introducing me to (blond, snarky, morally dubious if sadly not British) Eric Northman and a delicious amnesia plotline, and thank you to Meredith Duran's *A Lady's Code of Misconduct* for aiding me in crafting my first amnesia romance. (Why did I do this to myself??? Goodness, that was hard, and thank you to every medical professional who reads this book and forgives me for questionable medical accuracy.) I'm also grateful to my local kickboxing studio for teaching me how to punch things. Thanks to everyone I met while attending the University of Sheffield for teaching me British slang and making me feel welcome when I was lonely and out of my element far from home, and here's to the Red Deer as it was when the archaeology folks were hanging out there after class. Cheers to the venues that host my writing sessions on the weekends today—these books wouldn't exist without you.

I would also like to thank my cats, AO3, coffee, the Reylos, every fictional villain who awoke something in me at a formative time, the sound of rain against the window, colorful socks, woodwicked candles, weekend estate sales, bubble baths, and cheese (so much cheese).

And you, of course, dear reader. Thank you for accompanying me on another whimsical journey to Glimmer Falls. ♥

Keep reading for an excerpt from
Sarah Hawley's next novel . . .

A WEREWOLF'S
GUIDE TO SEDUCING
A VAMPIRE

ON WEREWOLF BEN ROSEWOOD'S LIST OF "THINGS TO AVOID if at All Possible," weddings were near the top.

It wasn't that he hated seeing other people happy or that he disliked cake or an open bar or dancing—well, all right, dancing was mortifying unless one was very drunk, which the open bar took care of—it was that he felt like a terrible person every time he went to one.

He raised his champagne, swaying slightly. The post-ceremony dinner was wrapping up and it was speech-making time. Another mortifying activity best practiced by drunk people or those who didn't have an anxiety disorder.

In vino confidence, he thought.

Mariel and Ozroth Spark, the newlyweds in question, looked at him expectantly from the sweetheart's table. One witch, one demon: both people Ben cared about and didn't want to disappoint with a terrible speech.

"Mariel," he said, addressing his longtime friend and employee at his garden shop, Ben's Plant Emporium, "it has been a privilege to work alongside you and watch you thrive like the plants you care for. You've always given your time, love, and support to everyone around you, and you deserve to receive that love back a thousandfold."

Ben was sweating. He nudged his gold-framed glasses up his nose with his free hand, then peered down at the note card on the table that held his talking points.

"Now that you have Oz by your side," he continued, "you shine more brightly than ever, and I'm happy to see it."

It was a clumsy speech, but Mariel didn't seem to mind. The brunette witch was beaming, looking radiant in a white dress with lacy cap sleeves and a full skirt embroidered with vines and flowers. Next to her and wearing a black suit that matched his usual stark aesthetic was Oz—or as he had once been termed, Oz-roth the Ruthless. The soul bargainer had been on Ben's shit list for a long time before he'd realized the demon was actually considerate, thoughtful, and utterly besotted with Mariel under that gruff exterior. The newlyweds' meet-cute had involved an inadvertent summoning and bargain in which Oz had tried to take Mariel's soul, but that issue had been resolved, and the couple had been devoted to each other for nearly two years now.

The normally surly Oz was now grinning widely, with lines of joy stamped beside his eyes. Those marks deepened with every year on Earth now that Oz was mortal, and Ben felt a surge of longing laced with envy. Not because Oz was marrying Mariel in particular—*marrying Mariel*, Ben's tipsy brain repeated, delighting in the alliteration—but because they were happy and in love.

This was why Ben didn't like weddings. He should be unconditionally delighted for his friends rather than sad about his own single status. He shoved down the shameful envy and glanced at the card again.

"Oz," he continued, addressing the black-haired, black-horned demon, "as you know, I wasn't sure about you at first. It isn't every day a demon comes portaling to Earth demanding your friend's soul." The crowd chuckled at that, and Ben felt a surge of relief. Thank Lycaon, progenitor of werewolves, he wasn't messing this up too badly. "But I saw how hard you fought to protect Mariel, and since then your love has grown and deepened. You prove that love with actions, not just words, which is the measure of a good man. It's an honor to know both of you and to be invited to give this speech."

He wasn't sure why they'd asked him to give a speech, but the reception had been speech-heavy so far, with family and friends of the bride and groom spouting impassioned, brilliant toasts that were all far better than Ben's.

"My skills are in gardening, not public speaking," he said, wrapping things up, "so I'm going to sit down before I embarrass myself." Another few chuckles at that. "In lieu of the brilliant oratory you deserve, I present you with a plant." He nodded toward the side of the room where another of his employees, a naiad named Rani, stood holding an orchid. She strode forward, grinning confidently in the way of well-adjusted people who didn't want to shrivel up and disappear in front of a crowd, and presented the plant to Mariel.

Mariel gasped and clapped her hands to her mouth. "Ben, are you serious? You found a January Sunrise?"

The January Sunrise orchid was rare, found only near the top of a magic-laced mountain in France where the ley lines allowed flowers to bloom through the snow. Its petals were snowy white blending into soft pink, the edges lined with orange, and the golden stamen glittered with magic.

"A rare flower for a rare friend," Ben said. He'd had to trade away a substantial selection of aphrodisiac plants from his shop's inventory to get it, but he didn't regret the transaction.

"It's perfect," Mariel said, beaming at him. The orchid leaned forward in its pot, brushing its petals against her cheek. Mariel wrinkled her freckled nose. "Hi, baby," she whispered to the flower. "You're going to love my greenhouse."

Plants always behaved that way around Mariel. She was brimming with so much nature magic the world came alive around her and plants acted downright besotted. Ben was a bit jealous, since werewolves didn't have any magic other than the truly unfortunate monthly transformation into a feral creature, but he couldn't deny it made her a heck of an employee at the garden shop.

Oz looked at Ben with obvious gratitude. "Thank you," the demon mouthed.

Ben nodded in acknowledgment. Then, glad to have the speech over with, he plopped back into his seat.

His sister, Gigi, nudged him with her fork. A fork that unfortunately had residual sauce on it, leaving a greasy smudge on his navy coat sleeve. "Good speech, bro."

He blew out a heavy breath. "I'm just glad it's over."

"You're a great public speaker. I don't know why you hate it so much." Gigi shrugged and tucked back into her pasta.

At thirty-three, his sister was five years younger than Ben, though he claimed she acted ten years younger and she claimed he acted eighty years older. They were both taller and more broad-shouldered than average and had the same thick brown hair and brown eyes, but personality wise, they couldn't have been more different. Gigi was an extrovert who loved parties and public speaking, while Ben preferred time alone with his plants, books, and knitting.

Tonight Gigi was wearing a gold dress with her favorite pink Converse, and glittering piercings marched up her ears. "Thank Lycaon you're not wearing a sweater vest," she'd said when she'd spotted him wearing the navy suit earlier that day. "Someday you'll let me take you shopping."

That was an "absolutely not," and what was so wrong with

sweater vests, Ben would never understand. They were sophisticated yet cozy, wrapping around his torso like a hug.

Or maybe like one of those ThunderShirts worn by quivering dogs,
his judgmental inner voice said.

Ben drained his champagne and signaled the circulating
waiter for another.

Thankfully, the speeches wrapped up soon after. They'd gone
well, all things considered—especially surprising since Mariel had
allowed her mother, Diantha Spark, to speak. The dynamics in
that family were fraught, since Diantha had put intense pressure
on Mariel to perform magic to her impossible expectations, but
apparently Diantha had been on a "narcissist improvement plan"
over the past two years that involved therapy and some hard
boundaries. She wasn't perfect, but she was vastly improved, since
otherwise Mariel had vowed to cut her off. Her speech had been
pre-vetted, Oz had watched her like a hawk throughout, and Diantha had managed not to veer too far off the deep end in any direction.

With speeches and eating done, it was time for dancing—and
an open bar, thank the neurosis gods. The event space had a ceremony room decorated with stained glass, a large dining room, and
an open air courtyard where the rest of the festivities would take
place. Magical light orbs drifted over the stone courtyard, and the
trees enclosing the yard had been draped with rainbow fairy lights
and gauzy swaths of fabric in bright colors. The night sky was
thankfully clear—never a guarantee in the small town of Glimmer
Falls or Western Washington in general—and the mid-August temperature was ideal. If the temperature or weather had been bad
though, one of the attending witches or warlocks would have taken
care of it with a microclimate spell.

Ben smiled as Oz tromped his way through the choreographed
steps of the couple's first dance with the grim concentration of a

general approaching battle. Mariel didn't seem to mind the demon's straightforward but less-than-graceful ballroom style—she laughed and spun in his arms, dress flaring like a blooming lily. After Oz dipped her low and delivered a decidedly PG-13 kiss— veering toward R-rated—the assembled guests cheered.

Then it was time for the father-daughter and mother-son dance. This had been an object of concern during the year leading up to the wedding. Mariel's relationship with her father was still strained from his years supporting Diantha's absurdities, though they'd made progress in family therapy. The more difficult issue was that Oz had been taken away from his demoness mother at a young age in order to be trained as a soul bargainer and hadn't seen her in hundreds of years—he hadn't even known her name or if she was alive or dead. But Oz's childhood mentor, Astaroth, had made it his mission to atone for his part in that tragedy by finding her, and now Elwenna the demoness stood at the edge of the dance floor, hands clasped to her mouth. When the music started up again and Oz held out a hand, eyes glistening with unshed tears, she took it, and more than a few guests started weeping outright.

Ben had always been a crier, and now he wiped away a tear, sniffling. He couldn't imagine being separated from his family for that long.

He also couldn't imagine the day coming when he could spin his wife around the dance floor in front of their families . . . though he could easily conjure a memory of the last time he'd talked with his mother on the phone and she'd hesitantly asked, "So, I know you're busy, but have you given any thought to dating?"

Yes, Mom. Arguably too much thought. And the moment "anxious, workaholic werewolf" appeared on someone's vision board, she'd be first to know.

But tonight wasn't about him, so Ben gave his full attention to the two pairs spinning (or aggressively tromping, as the case might be) across the dance floor, applauding and cheering them on.

Once the formal dances ended, Mariel grabbed a flute of champagne and raised it high. "Let's party!"

Music started blasting from the speakers as people of a variety of species rushed to the dance floor to begin gyrating with an enviable amount of confidence. Ben sidled up to the bar. It was manned by a centaur named Hylo he recognized as the bartender at the dive bar Le Chapeau Magique. They had buzzed hair and a labrum piercing, and their roan coat had been shaved with heart designs to commemorate the occasion.

"What's your poison?" Hylo asked.

"Whiskey," Ben said. He normally wasn't much of a drinker, but if he was going to dance—and Gigi would certainly drag him onto the floor if Mariel didn't first—he needed to drown his self-consciousness.

"How about an old fashioned?" At Ben's nod, Hylo started mixing ingredients, tapping their hooves rhythmically. The nonbinary centaur was a member of an Irish step dance troupe as well as a popular ClipClop influencer (as Gigi had informed him, being far more social media savvy than he was). Hylo presented the drink with a flourish, and Ben thanked them, slipping money into the tip jar.

He downed the old fashioned in under a minute, then held the empty glass out.

Hylo raised their eyebrows. "Dang, are you trying to get wasted?"

Ben gestured to the dance floor. "Social anxiety," he said succinctly.

"Ah." Hylo nodded knowingly. "Well, don't party too hard, all right? I'll have to cut you off if you get rowdy."

Ben wanted to laugh at the idea. The rest of his extended

family was noisy, chaotic, and prone to brawling, as most were-wolves were, but the number of times he'd done something that might be classified as "rowdy" could be numbered on one hand. "Don't worry, I'm a sad drunk," he said.

Hylo rattled the cocktail shaker before pouring him a second drink. "Weddings can be tough," they said. "Especially for single people."

Was he that transparent? Ben grimaced. "They shouldn't be. I just need to be a better person." He slipped another tip in Hylo's jar.

"It's nothing to do with being good or bad. Being sad or lonely or even jealous is normal—the thing that matters is how you treat people, and as far as I've seen, you've been very kind." Hylo patted his hand. "And who knows? Maybe you'll meet your soulmate here."

"Maybe," Ben said with zero sincerity. His life was consumed by running a small business, and what kind of woman wanted to be saddled with a werewolf who didn't even like howling at the moon?

But Hylo was being kind and understanding in that bartender/therapist way that involved emotional labor they didn't need to be doing, so Ben mustered up a smile. "Thank you," he said. "Maybe tonight's the night I find her at last."

◆　◆　◆

DID BEN HATE DANCING?

He didn't remember. All he knew was that the world was tilt-ing, the glow-orbs overhead had doubled, and he was flailing his arms to a pop song he didn't know the name of. Around him, other guests wiggled or stomped or flapped their wings in similarly cha-otic fashion.

"I love this song!" shouted the pixie hovering a few inches off the ground next to him. Themmie—short for Themmaline—Tibayan was a Pixtagram influencer and a good friend. Her normally black hair was bespelled purple and pink, and her iridescent wings shimmered. Along with Gigi, she'd been one of the instigators of the get-Ben-on-the-dance-floor campaign.

"Me, too!" shouted a British demon with pale blond hair and black horns who was gyrating on the opposite side of the small circle they'd formed. That was Astaroth, Oz's former mentor, who had been kind of evil before a bout of amnesia had improved him immensely. The improvement was also due to his partner, Calladia Cunnington, who had reformed the demon during a road trip nearly two years ago. Astaroth's memories had returned, including the knowledge that he was half human, but he'd remained on Team Good and now lived with Calladia on Earth, visiting the demon plane on occasion to help implement progressive societal reforms.

Astaroth was an *incredible* dancer. He'd spun Calladia around the floor in a waltz earlier—only wincing a few times when she stepped on his toes or head-butted him while trying to take the lead—and now he was doing an enviable John Travolta impression. He was also ridiculously handsome and an expert swordsman, and Ben had reflected more than once that the universe needed to spread out its gifts a bit more evenly.

Thankfully, being surrounded by good dancers and internet-famous pixies meant fewer people were looking at Ben. Thus, he was free to flail.

"When are you going to get hitched?" Themmie asked Astaroth, slurring her words. Ben noticed there were little hearts painted on the apples of her brown cheeks.

Astaroth looked toward the bar where Calladia was ordering drinks, and his face softened into an utterly infatuated expression. "Neither of us particularly believe in the institution of human marriage, and we don't need a ceremony to be bound together forever."

"Aww," Themmie said. "But what about the tax benefits?"

Astaroth grimaced. "Right. Sometimes I forget humans are determined to suck the money and joy out of everything." He shrugged. "Maybe someday, then, but I'll let her lead the way. I'm just fortunate to be able to love her for as long as I can."

A sharp ache took up residence in Ben's chest. What he would give to be able to love someone with all his neurotic heart . . . but who could possibly love him back?

Drunk flailing took a sharp turn into drunk moroseness.

Themmie turned to face Ben. "And you? Got your eye on anyone special?"

Ben's eyes were not fixed on anyone special, but they did abruptly grow watery. The ache spread and deepened, and he stopped waving his arms. "No," he said sadly.

Themmie looked alarmed at his sudden shift in mood. She returned to the ground, then wrapped a small hand around his arm. "Come on," she said. "I need a breather."

She didn't even come up to his shoulder, but pixies were stronger than they looked, and Themmie had no problem manhandling him off the dance floor. The world spun, and Ben staggered before face-planting into a tree.

Themmie winced. "Let's sit you down." She guided him to a bench. "Head between your knees."

Ben obeyed, bracing his elbows on his knees and lowering his head. He closed his eyes, trying to suppress the urge to vomit. Damn the whiskey. If he were a normal person, he wouldn't need to get drunk to dance at his friend's wedding.

He'd said that last bit aloud, unfortunately.

Themmie patted his back. "Normal is overrated," she said. "But want to talk about it?"

Ben didn't. He really, really didn't, especially not to an internet-cool pixie some fifteen years younger than him who generally had at least two or three significant others. That was why he opened his mouth and spilled the entire story to her.

"I'm thirty-eight and single and haven't dated in nearly a decade. My business takes up all my time, and I like to knit, and I'm not even a proper werewolf, and who could ever love someone who feels this anxious most of the time? I should like all the howling and biting things, but I just feel out of control, and no one else likes sweater vests even though they're *wrong* about that, and what if nothing about me is attractive and I die alone in a ditch?"

He sat back up in time to see Themmie blink a few times. "Wow," she said. "That was a lot. Uh, let's back up. For starters, what's wrong with knitting?"

"People think it's boring," he said forlornly. "I should have a manly hobby like . . . like woodworking or sword fighting or hunting elk with my bare hands." The best he'd managed in wolf form was a particularly ornery rabbit, and he'd felt guilty afterward.

"Hobbies don't have genders," Themmie said. "And you don't have to be some stereotypical macho woodsman to be attractive. Also, you're not going to die in a ditch, knitting isn't boring, and sweater vests . . . uh, I'm sure they have many merits."

"Many," he said fervently. "Argyle is wonderful." Such a pleasing pattern.

"I'm sure it is," she said soothingly. "So you're lonely and want to date, but you're also anxious and not sure someone will like you just the way you are?"

"That's precisely it." How quickly she cut to the emotional core of the matter, like Hylo had. "Have you thought about being a bartender?"

Themmie cocked her head, looking confused. "Uh, not really."

"You'd be great at it," he said vehemently. "Not the drink bits— or maybe the drink bits, I don't know—but all the listening and shit. Stuff," he clarified. "Shouldn't swear in front of a lady." His mother had drilled that into him growing up, but it was hard to remember sometimes, like when he was drunk or hanging out with his creatively vulgar cousins and friends.

Themmie laughed. "I fucking encourage swearing. And thanks, but let's go back to you. I think you have many lovely qualities and just need to find the right person who will appreciate them."

That was precisely the problem. "Don't know how."

"Well, you could go to some singles' mixers around town—"

He shook his head, instantly regretting it when his brain sloshed around in his skull. "People. Bad."

"You interact with people all the time at the Emporium."

"That's different," he said. "I know what to say and do there." There were specific rules about interaction in a place of business, and he knew the entire shop top to bottom, down to the well-being of individual leaves. In his sphere, he was the expert and authority. If challenged, he could be brave for the sake of his employees and his business, and if he ever felt uncomfortable, his reputation for being serious and levelheaded meant he could hide his inner turmoil with stoic silence.

At a random public event, much less one designed to spark romance, he'd be a disaster.

"Dating apps, then," Themmie said, pulling her phone from a pocket in her yellow dress. "You don't have to meet anyone in person until you've chatted online."

"Don't know what to write." Also, having never downloaded more than a few basic apps on his smartphone, he had a feeling he was too out of touch for that. He even kept handwritten ledgers at the office, preferring to practice his calligraphy rather than attempting Excel. Spreadsheets were undoubtedly helpful but lacked a certain artistry, and whenever he heard the words *pivot table* or *conditional formatting*, he wanted to flee.

"Just give some details about who you are and what you're looking for. Like *I'm a werewolf, six foot four* or whatever, *I like knitting and own my own business. In search of someone who enjoys gardening,* blah-blah-blah. Then upload a nice picture of you. I'll even take it for you!" She raised her phone and snapped a picture of him, then winced as she eyed the screen. "Okay, maybe when you aren't quite so drunk."

"Cake!" someone screeched from across the dance floor. "Time for cake!"

The music cut off and people started moving toward where an enormous four-tiered cake—half pumpkin spice for Oz and half chocolate for Mariel—was being wheeled out.

"Let's put a pin in this," Themmie said, standing up. "But promise you'll at least try to set up an online dating profile." She reached a hand down to help him up.

"I promise," Ben said, staggering to his feet. "Thanks, Themmie."

He watched from the back of the crowd as Mariel and Oz fed each other slices of cake, taking frequent breaks to kiss each other. They were so in love, and Ben teared up again with a mix of sincere joy and longing. He clapped and hollered as loudly as everyone else and accepted a slice of cake from Mariel with a grin.

She slid an arm around him in a side hug. "Thanks for being here," she said. "You're the best."

Ben certainly wasn't the best, but he would never do anything to dim her blissful glow, so he smiled and laughed and congratulated her again. Later, as the newlyweds exited the venue beneath an archway of sparklers and magic fireworks, he cheered until his throat was hoarse.

Then he took a rideshare car home and threw up in a bush in his front yard. Feeling marginally better after vomiting, he grabbed a glass of water, changed into pajamas, and collapsed on his brown leather couch. Bleary-eyed, he grabbed his phone and started searching for dating sites.

Bumbelina, OkEros, PaganMingle, Match.com, FarmersMarketOnly, Howly Ever After . . . none of them felt right. He sighed and switched to browsing something more practical.

The Emporium had done extremely well in recent years thanks to the quality of the plants, Mariel's magic touch, and the rare varietals he was able to get his hands on from international connections. He'd purchased the empty office next door and would soon be opening an adjoining coffee shop and bakery, with a goal of eventually adding a small stage for lectures, music, and stand-up comedy. He wanted Ben's Plant Emporium to become a real community destination.

Most of the construction work on the Annex—as he was calling the café space—was done, and he was now sourcing decorations. The current project was a rock-and-crystal terrarium to display succulents next to the muffins.

He'd had some luck finding bulk quantities of unusual stones on eBay, so he switched to the site, squinting through the alcohol haze. *Blue sexy rock* he typed in, having briefly forgotten the word *crystal*.

The first listing was for an old blues-rock album on vinyl, which was not helpful. The next was for an outrageously expensive sapphire that would supposedly give the wielder an erotic aura. He briefly considered it, wondering if he would have an easier time meeting women if he had an erotic aura, then decided it would be disingenuous to lure a woman in that way even if he could afford it.

The third entry gave him pause . . . and then he started to laugh.

> *Dark Arts Sexy Succbus She-Vampire TALISMAN PARA-NORMAL POSSESSED BLUE CRYSTAL DARK ARTS SEXY CONJURE ROCK*

The image was of a small, faceted blue stone that looked suspiciously like plastic, and the starting bid price was $0.99. No one had bid thus far, and the listing was closing in a few hours.

Ben read the description, growing more entertained with every word. Questionable capitalization aside, the poster didn't even know how to spell *succubus*, and they were trying to position this as a rare, possessed artifact.

> *This is a dark Vampire Succbus named Eleanora. She is 5'8" tall with flaming red hair and emerald eyes. Very sexy, comes with her own Knives. Hisses. French.*

"... Knives?" Ben muttered, eyeing the photo of the tacky blue "crystal." "Hissing?"

> *She is very Angry in nature but at least some threats are Jokes! Good friend, maybe good girlfriend I do not know, will do Anything if you order it—bite vengeance murder Jenga Star Trek etc, Eleanora does All*

"Murder?"

> *Dark Vampire Succbus Eleanora angry sexy French BUY NOW but BEWARE you must be firm, she has Attitude but very worth it if you want Assassin, TV watcher, best Friend, maybe-girlfriend, you will not regret it, please pay at least One Million gold doubloons. DARK VAMPIRE SUCCBUS ELEANORA*

"Dark Vampire Succbus Elcanora," Ben intoned to himself in a dramatic voice. Then he laughed, feeling better than he had since before he'd started crying on the dance floor. What a hilarious scam. He was too cowardly to set up a dating profile, but by Lycaon, he was just drunk and easily amused enough to buy a vampire succubus—or succbus—assassin girlfriend in the shape of a plastic rock for the low, low price of $0.99.

He put in his bid, then promptly passed out on the couch, still smiling.

✦ ✦ ✦

TWO WEEKS AFTER THE WEDDING AND THIRTEEN DAYS AFTER the worst hangover he'd had in a decade, Ben looked down at the knitting project in his lap and groaned. He'd dropped a stitch a few rows back, and now he was going to have to either find a crochet hook to fix it or rip it back at least four rows.

This project was a scarf for his mother, who had mentioned needing some new warm clothes for the winter. Next he'd make a matching one for his father and a hat for Gigi, and that took care of the first part of his holiday gifts.

He was close with his parents, as he was with his extended family in general. Werewolves were inherently pack creatures, and though Ben had long been the introvert of the family, he still had dinner with his parents and sister whenever he could get away from work—rare these days—and he was a frequent visitor at his aunt's Shabbat dinner. His uncle had married into a Jewish family, and as a result, the extended Rosewood-Levine clan was rarely without good food to eat or something to celebrate.

Knitting for the entire array of grandparents, aunts, uncles, cousins, second cousins, and friends so close they'd become honorary Rosewood-Levines was too daunting a task for a man with only two hands and two knitting needles. For the most part he only knitted for his immediate family, but his second cousin had just announced her pregnancy so he had roughly six months to make his traditional "welcome to the family" baby blanket.

Lots of knitting, which normally wouldn't be a problem . . . if he hadn't currently been preparing to expand the Emporium. His business took up the majority of his time, and arranging the permits, construction, decorating, supplies, and staffing for the expansion had resulted in a lot of lost sleep over the preceding months. But failing to produce gifts for his family was unthinkable, so if he had to cut back on sleep even more, he would.

Ben was reaching for his crochet hook when the doorbell rang. He set the knitting aside and stood, brushing sandwich crumbs off his T-shirt and plaid pajama pants. It was a Saturday, and though normally he'd be at work, the builders had requested *no hovering* as they finished installing appliances. So here he was, catching up on projects at home while fretting about everything that could possibly be going wrong at the office.

He padded to the front door on bare feet and opened it to see a griffin with a palm-sized package in her beak and a clipboard held between two claws. A brown company vest announced the griffin's employment at a prominent shipping chain.

The griffin spit out the box into Ben's hand before holding out the clipboard. "SIIIIIGN," she shrieked.

Griffins were highly intelligent but struggled to speak non-avian languages intelligibly, considering their beaks. They also smelled downright terrible to sensitive werewolf noses. Ben smiled politely and took the clipboard, ignoring the stench. He might smell equally bad to the griffin, after all.

"I didn't order anything," he said, looking between the box and the paper. The sender was listed as THE WITCH IN THE WOODS with no return address, and the signature line on the receipt sat beneath text saying "I assume full responsibility for the hellion, no take backs," which struck him as nonstandard language.

"SIIIIIIIIIIIIGN."

Maybe he'd bought something online for the store and forgotten about it. It was definitely his name and address. Ben didn't want to make a fuss, so he nodded and signed. "Thanks," he said, waving awkwardly at the griffin before she launched into the air to continue her route.

Back in his living room, he sat on the couch and opened the box. Beneath layers of glittery tissue paper was a small plastic bag with a blue faceted stone inside, no bigger than his thumbnail. His brow furrowed. This was vaguely familiar, but why?

The stone proved to be plastic when he pulled it out. He studied the overhead light through it. Why had he ordered a fake plastic jewel? He sniffed it a few times, and *whoa*, it smelled great. Sweet in a luscious, spicy, complicated way even his rarest lilies couldn't match.

A piece of paper was nestled in the bottom of the box. The paper was fragile and browned with age. On it was written: *Eleanora*.

A vague memory surfaced—something about eBay? He grabbed his phone and scrolled through his email. Sure enough, there it was—a receipt from two weeks ago informing him he had won the auction for *Dark Arts Sexy Succbus She-Vampire TALISMAN PARA-NORMAL POSSESSED BLUE CRYSTAL DARK ARTS SEXY CON-JURE ROCK*.

He laughed, surprised all over again by the bonkers listing. No one else had bid, and now for the low price of $0.99—well, $4.28, once shipping was included—he owned a plastic rock that supposedly housed the murderous, red-haired lover of his dreams. He could only imagine how the seller must have cackled realizing some poor sap had fallen for the scam.

"Well, Eleanora," he said, "it's a pleasure to meet you."

The plastic jewel, predictably, did not respond.

Feeling silly and rather sleep-deprived, he dramatically lowered his voice. "Show yourself, succubus."

A sudden wind whipped around the room, rustling the papers on his desk and making the curtains flutter. To Ben's shock, the crystal began glowing electric blue. The wind and light swirled into a tiny cyclone in his palm, which grew and grew before spinning to the middle of the room. Then the blue light flared white-hot, making him shield his eyes.

When he lowered his hand, there was a woman in his living room.

And not just any woman.

The most beautiful woman Ben had ever seen.

She had wavy, waist-length red hair, green eyes, and an hourglass figure that defined the term *bombshell*. Her lips were full, her cheekbones high, and her skin a smooth porcelain he felt the urge to brush his knuckles over to see if it was as soft as it looked. Her form-fitting blue shirt was the same shade as the jewel, and she wore black leather pants and thigh holsters containing knives that took Ben back to his formative crush on Lara Croft.

She smelled *incredible*.

She was also glaring at Ben like she wanted to disembowel him.

"Uh . . ." he said, confused, awed, and deeply alarmed.

In response, she opened her mouth to reveal sharp fangs and hissed.

Photo by Mahina Hawley Photography

SARAH HAWLEY lives in the Pacific Northwest, where her hobbies include rambling through the woods and appreciating fictional villains. She has an MA in archaeology and has excavated at an Inca site in Chile, a Bronze Age palace in Turkey, and a medieval abbey in England. When not dreaming up whimsical love stories, she can be found reading, dancing, or cuddling her two cats.

Ready to find
your next great read?

Let us help.

Visit prh.com/nextread

Penguin
Random
House